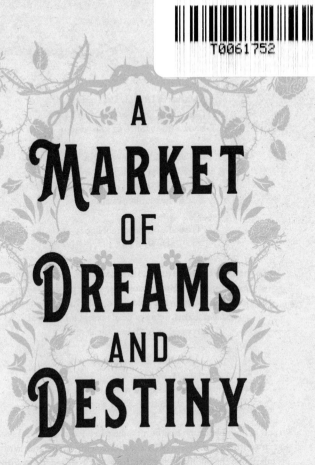

A MARKET OF DREAMS AND DESTINY

TRIP GALEY

TITAN BOOKS

T0061752

A Market of Dreams and Destiny
Print edition ISBN: 9781803363684
E-book edition ISBN: 9781803363691

Published by Titan Books
A division of Titan Publishing Group Ltd
144 Southwark Street, London SE1 0UP
www.titanbooks.com

First edition: September 2023
10 9 8 7 6 5 4 3 2 1

A CIP catalogue record for this title is available from
the British Library.

Printed and bound by CPI Group (UK) Ltd, Croydon, CR0 4YY.

'A book as rich with wonder as the market in its pages. Galey's London is a world where anything – anything – is for sale: a glance, the feeling of moonlight, true love. Careful or you might end up bartering your heart away.'

PATRICK NESS, BESTSELLING AUTHOR OF THE CHAOS WALKING TRILOGY

'Magical and literary, *A Market of Dreams and Destiny* ensnares you in layers and webs of fantasy and alternate history. Galey weaves a fae-touched world where anything can be bought or sold, leaving you to wonder what you would trade to visit it.'

DAVID R. SLAYTON, AUTHOR OF THE ADAM BINDER NOVELS

'You're in for the fantasy thrill of the year with *A Market of Dreams and Destiny*! Deri is our heroic queer navigator through a fascinating, frightening world, like the lead of some eighties dark fantasy film we never got (but always deserved). More, please, Trip Galey!'

ADAM SASS, AWARD–WINNING AUTHOR OF SURRENDER YOUR SONS AND YOUR LONELY NIGHTS ARE OVER

'Intriguing and atmospheric, this compelling tale of drama and danger in the shadows of a goblin market under an alternate Victorian London more than delivers on its promises.'

JULIET E. McKENNA, AUTHOR OF THE CLEAVING AND THE THIEF'S GAMBLE

'An astonishing feat of the imagination, every page bursting with fantastical detail. Trip Galey's debut is striking, and deserves to be celebrated.'

OLIVER K. LANGMEAD, AUTHOR OF
BIRDS OF PARADISE AND GLITTERATI

'I traded a handful of hours for Galey's beautiful epic of an other-London full of magical deals, audacious schemes, outrageous romance and a talking cat. Trip's birthed something really rather extraordinary.'

J.L. WORRAD, AUTHOR OF
PENNYBLADE AND THE KEEP WITHIN

'Intoxicating. A thrilling mix of the magical, the monstrous and the mercantile. Set in an ingenious alternative London with a main character pairing you can't help but love, Galey's cocktail of enchantment, romance and dangerous bargains swept me away.'

TOM POLLOCK, AUTHOR OF
THE SKYSCRAPER THRONE TRILOGY

'I was enthralled by this world, where fairy merchants strike bargains with the precision of contract lawyers. The goblin market shines like enchanted gold, whimsical with dark undercurrents. The tension ratchets up with every trade, and Deri is the loophole-finding rogue we all wish we could be.'

A.J. LANCASTER, AUTHOR OF
THE LORD OF STARIEL

'Galey has created a world you can step inside, full of texture and descriptions so rich you can almost experience the market for yourself... A cracking read all round!'

COURTNEY SMYTH, AUTHOR OF
THE UNDETECTABLES

For Robert, who is worth any price.

Be wary, child, as you go down,
To the place beneath old London town,
Where fey-folk work and goblins frown,
In the market 'neath old London town.

Deri hummed to himself as he dodged through the crowd, an old scrap of rhyme dredged up from a memory so many times bought and sold it was all but worn through. Three more errands left, just three, then he'd be free as the wind-swept sea. Well, as free as possible until he bought himself out of his indenture. Until then, endless errands. Fetch a new vial of ink of night from Merchant Codex. Deliver the parcel he carried to Merchant Blatterbosch. And return with Merchant Maurlocke's lunch before the Market Bell rang the midday hour. Not that there was day, as such, here below London.

The Untermarkt was busier than usual. The lanes that threaded through the market stalls, never terribly wide, were choked with people. Mortals mixed with denizens from Faery and lands even deeper Underhill. A tattooed woman in buckskin and furs traded a small leather pouch to a merchant with the head and paws of a cat for the ability to see in the dark. A pair of young men in evening wear, drunk on a drop of faery wine, nearly crashed into a stall filled with dreams caught in crystal cobwebs. Goblin midwives, big-bellied with the precious charges that they both carried and delivered themselves, waddled past.

Noise crashed and foamed around him. Merchants haggled and hawked their wares, customers haggled back or laughed with their friends, buskers sang songs or brayed on instruments. You could feel the approaching holiday in the air, anticipation and excitement. Threaded through it all were the voices of the bells, ringing out hours and sales, jangling the appearance of customers and, to the rare few like Deri, who could truly hear, sharing gossip and swapping stories.

Did you hear? Did you hear? rang the Bell of Auld St. Cyr. *The Merchant Shade did disappear!*

Pish and tosh! Pish and tosh! rang the bell near Merchant Kosh. *He's simply gone to do his wash!*

The first words Deri could remember hearing had been rang out by the bells. He'd been able to understand them, even then. A gift from having been carried to term by a goblin midwife.

'Memories, sure to please! Sweet memories for modest fees! Come buy! Come buy!'

'How do, Merchant Pryek,' Deri called a greeting to a woman whose fingers were fine white clay and whose face was a porcelain mask. Her stall was a magpie's nest of things that had been shaped: fine china and silver spoons, knots of plaited straw and carefully tatted lace, needles and spindles and rings and chains. Every item held not only its shape but also a memory that could be relived simply by using it.

'Ah! Good morning, Deri,' the merchant replied. 'Come see my latest treasure! Come-come!' She held up a commemorative plate, delicately painted with a distinctive pattern of blue and the profile of a regal young woman. 'Isn't it lovely? Isn't it pristine? Why, it hasn't been eaten from since High Queen Victoria was elected to the throne, nearly forty years ago. And when you look at it, you can hear a memory of the Stone of Destiny singing her confirmation.' She sighed with pleasure. 'It will be a shame to part with it, but should you, or Merchant Maurlocke be interested...' She angled the plate temptingly.

'Not today, Merchant Pryek.' *Not today* was so much safer than *no*. Maurlocke would skin him for shoe leather if he closed down a potential opportunity with a no. 'Have a profitable day!'

Deri slipped behind a trio of young women bearing armfuls of parcels, though he needn't have bothered. Merchant Pryek was already calling out to another.

He wove and darted through the crowd. It was busy, even for the Untermarkt, making running errands even more of a challenge. Deri was looking forward to the Autumnal Equinox as much as any of these punters, but unlike them he still had to work. Didn't get but the bare scrape of holiday allotted by his indenture.

'Good morning, Merchant Creydland!' Deri called, passing a mountain of a man with eyes like coals and hair of fire. One of Merchant Maurlocke's best trading partners; always take the time to pay respect to Merchant Creydland.

Deri received but a grunt of recognition in reply. A smith as much as a merchant, Creydland affected a smith's apron rather than the more elaborate robes many merchants favoured. The majority of his attention was currently bent on hammering the last details of delicate brass filigree into place on a replacement hand for the man standing outside the merchant's stall, who only had one of his own remaining. A soldier, probably, what with the appendage in question being of brass and all.

Creydland's stall commanded an intersection of two market avenues. Left should be quicker, along the Street of Living Flame. Deri turned, but instead of the smell of hot metal and cold coin, his nose filled with a full field of floral bouquets. Fardles, the Market had shifted again.

'Fruit of Knowledge! Fruit of Health! Learn secrets! Never sicken!'

'Seeds! Rich seeds! One grain will sprout a full field of wheat!'

'Flowers of Love, to grow your regard! Flowers of Lust, and passion unbarred! Come buy! Come buy!'

The last exhortation was cast upon the winds by Merchant Peaseblossom. Not good. Their stall, all of living wood that had never known the touch of axe, was so close to the edge of the Untermarkt as to be nearly in London proper.

'Good morning, Deri,' the merchant said, catching sight of him standing near. 'Does Merchant Maurlocke require a fine posey or three?'

'Not today, Merchant Peaseblossom.' Deri flashed an apologetic smile. Peaseblossom was a terrible flirt. He was saved from further conversation by a pair of customers breezing up to the stall.

'Good morning!' Mortals. A pair of them, hand in hand, stepped up to the merchant.

The two young men, for such they were, both wore clothes of excellent cut, with particularly fine waistcoats. One was green and bronze with a chain-like pattern worked across it, while the other was blue and grey and bore repeating circles, like ship's wheels.

It was a far cry from Deri's own garb. He was dressed well enough, to be sure, but as a servant. Simple trousers and waistcoat of grey, with a coat to match. His hat, a nice flat cap which had once been a very fetching maroon, was his sole foray into the more daring side of fashion. As a servant he could only venture so far.

Not like the happy young men in front of him.

'Ah! Messrs Copperfield and Steerforth! You're looking well. I have the boutonnieres for your wedding all ready. Bide but a moment and I will fetch them for you.' Merchant Peaseblossom turned, touched a flower as iridescent and translucent as spun glass, and disappeared.

'Should we get some more rós-a-milis?' Steerforth asked. 'We're here anyway.'

The flowers in question were so named for the enchantment their petals bore, not the specific colour or variety. Plucking a single petal from the bloom and crushing it between the fingers immediately cleansed one of all foul smells and rendered one's clothing as freshly laundered. They were understandably popular amongst the bright young things that partied somewhat excessively but then had to make a presentable appearance at Great-Aunt Augusta's dinner soiree to ensure the inheritance didn't go amiss.

'Depends on the price,' the other, Copperfield, was saying.

'You fret too much. Come now, Daisy! Can't be less than fresh at our own wedding, can we?'

11

'Don't call me Daisy!' Copperfield attempted to look stern but the laugh that burst from his lips spoiled the effect.

Lovers. Easy marks for the right kind of merchant. Nothing opened the purse like devotion or desperation. So much touching, too! Deri hadn't seen many mortals quite so bold in the public display of their affections. He absently ran his fingers down his own arm. Not that he had occasion to flirt with the boundaries of what was or was not proper, himself. His indenture expressly forbade romantic entanglements. Not that he had time, anyway.

Time! He still had three errands to complete and, thanks to the stalls and alleyways shifting, his next stop was halfway across the Untermarkt. Deri briefly considered trying to take a shortcut through the streets *above*. No. Not fast enough. He'd have to do it the other way. At least he had a strong guide to follow to his next destination.

The trick to navigating the Goblin Market was not to ignore temptation. That was an exercise in futility. The trick was choosing which temptations to give in to, just a little, so you could follow them to what you were truly after.

Merchant Codex dealt in books, and parchment, and inks of all kinds. When was the last time he'd had the chance to hear a good story? There were no books or storytellers near, but this was the right place to send messages in the Language of Flowers, and sure enough, the Untermarkt stepped in to tempt him.

'Prose spelt in poseys! In pansies and roseys!'

A single voice leapt out at him, clear above the clamour. Right on cue. The Market couldn't resist an unspoken desire.

Deri followed temptation from the Street of the Flower-Sellers to a niche near an intersection where a bardic initiate sang a ballad of ages past. His feet slowed. He hadn't heard this one before! No! He didn't want to hear it. He wanted to learn it himself. He needed a copy of the ballad. Deri followed that impulse away from the performance, and down a bright and brassy alleyway filled to overflowing with stalls selling all manner of scraps of foolscap printed with dark and determined processions of notes. From music to lyrics and from lyrics to poetry. That brought him at last close enough to Merchant Codex's territory that he was able to spot her stall amongst the many.

Skin pale as paper and ink-dark hair brushed from her face in an inspired scrawl, Merchant Codex was deep in conversation with a young man perhaps six or seven years Deri's senior. A contract of indenture sat on the market stall between them. It was old, judging by the grime darkening the jagged edge marking each of the two halves as belonging to one another.

'Come now, Anwyl, you're being foolish! Why buy out now?' Merchant Codex asked, voice as soft as the rustling of pages in a library. 'You're only a few months from the end of your service. You could work out the time and keep your savings.'

They were negotiating the buy-out of the young man's indenture! Deri angled for a closer vantage point. Wouldn't hurt to listen close, see if he could learn anything that might help him buy free of his own. Fortunately, the two negotiators ignored him.

'I've fallen in love,' Anwyl replied. 'And you know as well as I that I can't fraternise, court, woo, or otherwise pursue marriage while I'm still indentured. I need to be free, now!'

A silly reason to spend one's savings, but if it gave Deri the chance to watch a negotiation like this, well, who was he to stand in the way of love? Deri watched Merchant Codex's response carefully. There had to be a reason the merchant was pushing back on this.

'You've the best eye for quality I've had in a long time. Surely, we can come to an arrangement that keeps you in my employ,' Merchant Codex wheedled. 'I could waive the clause on engagement if you agreed to, say, a three-year extension?'

Anwyl fell silent, considering the offer.

Deri bit back the urge to offer his opinion. Extend the contract? Anwyl would have to be barmy. Even if one clause were waived, there's no way he could trust Codex not to still exert some sort of control over his love life, and he'd be three years further from freedom! Three years of life lived at the mercy and whim of someone else. Sure, the savings would be nice, but in the long term, it was bound to cost more than it was worth. Merchants of the Untermarkt didn't make deals that weren't to their advantage.

What he wouldn't give to have that freedom himself. Well, actually, he knew. There were five years, seven months, and three days left on his indenture. He'd saved up enough that he'd be able to buy his way free in a little over a year, give or take. Of course, that didn't account for how much he'd need to set himself up in business at the Untermarkt. There was no way that would be cheap. Goblin merchants frowned on allowing mortals like him into their ranks.

Sweet Goddess Danu, though, what he wouldn't give for the chance. Others had done it over the years. Not many, but some. Great Gwri, Iden the Spinner, Jack Trades…though Deri had no idea what it had cost them, and finding out would likely set his freedom back three years or more.

'No,' Anwyl said, breaking Deri out of his reverie, 'no deal. I'd like to end the contract.'

'As you wish,' Merchant Codex said. She picked up the two halves of the contract sitting on the stall in front of her and with quick, efficient motions, ripped them to pieces. The contract was ended.

'Ah Deri, there you are. I have the ink of night Merchant Maurlocke requested all ready.' Anwyl was ignored. All potential profit had been wrung from him, so he was no longer worthy of Merchant Codex's time or attention. 'Now, what have you brought me in payment?'

After finishing with Merchant Codex, it didn't take Deri long to locate the next person he had to deal with. The Market's shift had rearranged things in his favour, this time. He wasn't far from the right alley, and the canny old goblin he sought was loud, so if Deri just listened…

'Eyes of every size! Hair so very fair! Come buy! Come buy!'

There. That was Blatterbosch. The old goblin's voice with its strong Black Forest accent was unmistakable. Deri turned toward the sound and shortly found himself standing in front of the stall he sought.

Blatterbosch crouched amidst his wares like a toad in a flowerbed, naked save for a loincloth that only the most discerning of eyes could pick out from the goblin's statuesque form. Ladies' fingers, pale and cold, nestled among jars of grass-green eyes. Twists of hair in all colours of autumn leaves hung like shimmering vines in a fringe across the front of the stall. Things rarer still, iridescent scales and gossamer wings and even a satyr's pride, were scattered about like garden ornaments, calculatingly placed to command attention.

Deri resolutely ignored the satyr's pride. It was never a good idea to be distracted when dealing with a goblin merchant. It was an even worse one to interrupt when said merchant was concluding a deal. So Deri waited, foot tapping, as a young woman with flaming locks of auburn hair traded its luminous beauty for the strength of ten men. She flexed her fingers and Deri prudently took a step to one side. Until she had some practice with her newly bought brawn, there were likely to be broken teacups and broken bones in her future. Deri had no wish to be the first casualty.

Still, as soon as she stepped away from the stall Deri darted in to take her place. Time was precious, not to be wasted. Almost before Blatterbosch could greet him, he had parcel in hand. It was wrapped in snow-white butcher's paper; Deri preferred not to dwell overmuch on the way the somewhat squishy contents regularly pulsed out a beat.

'Ah!' Blatterbosch's eyes – all five of them – glowed. 'You have it! Danu's dugs, how did Maurlocke manage to persuade her to give up her second heart?'

'I'm sure I cannot say, Merchant Blatterbosch.' Manners were important in the Untermarkt. Almost as important as they were to the High Society toffs up top.

'Yes. Well. In any case. Tell your mystrer I am most pleased to have done business with ym. Most pleased.' Blatterbosch held out a hand for the parcel.

'Ah,' Deri said delicately, 'I'm afraid your negotiations with my mystrer only covered my bringing the parcel to your stall. You neglected to settle on a fee for my handing you the parcel.'

It was outright robbery to ask, but Deri had dealt with Blatterbosch often enough to know when he could press his luck.

Still, it was always a risk. His shoulders tensed, but he kept a pleasant-yet-slightly-apologetic look on his face.

The old goblin favoured Deri with a long, measuring look, eyes narrowing. Deri didn't flinch. Didn't dare flinch. Then Blatterbosch laughed, a vast booming sound that set the merchant's mounds of flesh to jiggling – even the display merchandise on his stall.

'And what price do you ask for such a dangerous feat as passing me a parcel, little one?'

Of course the merchant had seen through Deri's polite fiction. He knew Deri was angling for a bit of profit for himself, rather than on behalf of Maurlocke. Deri braced himself, running calculations in his mind. Something minor enough the merchant would part with it, but with enough value that Deri could hope to sell it on for a profit. Ideally, something that would, in the long run, cost the merchant nothing. Deri pointed to the second-finest spill of hair draped across the top of the stall.

'The lustre of those locks for a single evening.'

It was a small thing. The lustre would return, the locks could be sold on with no lessening of value. The question was, would Blatterbosch see it that way?

'Very well.' The merchant laughed again. 'I like your brass, boy. You have a deal.'

'Thank you, Master Merchant.' Deri handed over the parcel and collected his payment, all tied up with a single, intricately knotted hair. 'May your day continue to be a profitable one.'

'Yours as well, young man. Yours as well.' Blatterbosch waved him away absently, four of his five eyes already seeking in the crowd for the next mark.

Deri allowed himself a satisfied grin as he dove back into the crowd, tucking his prize safely away in one of the many hidden pockets sewn throughout his coat. Not bad. It'd taken more time than he'd have liked, but he'd managed a bit of profit, so it all evened out. Now, to sort out Merchant Maurlocke's lunch. He could tell by the bells that he was running out of time.

Deri was two-thirds of the way to collecting Merchant Maurlocke's lunch when a voice hissing down at him caused him to pause.

'Hisst, kit! Slow and hark, and you may find the opportunity for an extra bit of profit.'

Deri followed the sound to a ginger tabby, grooming herself whilst perched atop the pole of a nearby market bell. 'Milady Bess,' he said, 'you're looking well.'

Bess stretched the leg she had been cleaning and shook it. 'Well enough. The first left and third right after and you'll find a nice bit of opportunity. If you are interested, of course.'

Of course he was interested. He was always interested. Even without the bells ringing encouragement in his ears, he would be interested.

He didn't thank Bess, of course. To do so in the Untermarkt would be more than passing dangerous. He did, however, sketch a little bow in her direction and add a bit of fish to his mental list. It paid to keep one's allies happy, even if that meant smelling of cod for a bit.

The first left and the third right sped by quickly, ending on the Street of Sworn Words. Unexpected. What could Bess have been referring to? Deri's eyes raked the crowds. There!

Near the stall of Bruteria Promise-Maker, where vows and oaths and geasa hung in rows, all bound in knots of parchment and chains of silver and pewter and gold, a young man stood with a small bit of paper in his hand and despair in his eyes. About his age, Deri would hazard, with a labourer's arms and a shirt not more than a few days from being disdained by even the rag-pickers. A workhouse boy, judging by the threadbare brown trousers and shirt which might once have aspired to cream but had long since washed away to sullen grey. It was lemon as anything to guess his problem; Promise-Makers were exceptional at finding loopholes, and charging you an arm and a leg on top of your original bargain to hold them to whatever terms were struck.

'You promised Missus Graspar a geas!' the young man was repeating, clearly not for the first, or even seventh, time.

'And she is welcome to have it,' Bruteria countered smugly. 'Why don't you just pop back and tell her to come herself and collect it?'

'But she sent me to fetch it!'

'Does the signature on the receipt say Owain on it?'

'No.'

'Do you have a sealed and witnessed writ conferring Missus Graspar's authority on you?'

'No, but—'

'Then it's not my problem.' Bruteria crossed her arms across her chest.

'Which one is it?' Deri interrupted, stepping up next to the young man apparently named Owain.

'What?' Owain half-turned to Deri.

Bruteria twisted her lips into a lopsided knot of displeasure.

'Deri,' she warned, 'this is none of your concern.'

'Business is business, as they say, Bruteria,' Deri replied. 'Which chain were you sent to collect?' he asked Owain again.

'I – I'm not sure,' came the reply.

'Then hire me to help you. I can promise my price will be much more reasonable than Bruteria's.'

Deri couldn't resist shooting a little smirk at Bruteria. The merchant sneered back. No self-respecting goblin would brag of being reasonable.

It was dangerous. Baiting Bruteria was asking to make enemies. Worse, Maurlocke might take exception to his obviously siding with a fellow human over his adopted market brethren. But Deri didn't like those that penny-and-tuppence'd their customers.

'What's your price?' Owain asked.

Too late to back out now. Bad enough to be seen interfering with another's market business, far worse to back out after offering to make a deal. What was his price? Owain didn't look like he had much to spare. Without quite thinking, Deri blurted out an offer.

'One piece of advice for one night on the town is my going rate.' Deri quirked a smile at Owain. 'It doesn't have to be fancy; it just has to be fun.'

Bruteria made no move to hide her snort of contempt.

'Deal,' Owain said, seizing Deri's hand.

Owain's hand was warm, his grip strong. The touch was like lightning.

Deri pulled his hand away and draped a smile across his face like a veil.

'The receipt gives you enough right to claim your mistress's order. Bruteria never actually said you couldn't take it. She asked you a series of questions that made you think you couldn't, sure. But she isn't going to stop you. She can't. She won't help you, either, unless you pay her, but I suspect she's already made the offer and you will not –' Deri glanced at Owain and corrected himself. '– cannot meet the price for her aid.'

'True enough.' Owain sighed.

'But if you take the right chain, she cannot stop you. So, which one is it?'

Owain looked at the multitude of chains of paper and gold hanging about the market stall.

'I have no idea.'

'Check the receipt,' Deri suggested.

Owain looked down at the slip of paper in his hand.

'…Silver.'

Bruteria's stall was hung predominantly with paper and gold, the former to hold agreements fast, the latter because the truth shines golden, and that metal best holds geasa. There were a few strands of silver and jet amongst the others – modest pieces, for the most part, binding forged for more unusual purposes.

'Finely forged.'

Owain's eyes scanned Bruteria's wares. There were still more choices than one. He looked to Deri, eyes beginning to panic.

'Think about who commissioned the piece. That will always show through. Something of them will have to. It's like a signature on a document. The working is no good without it.'

Owain glanced back at the stall and after a moment, he reached out and picked up a precise length of tightly twisted silver and pewter.

'This one,' he said. 'It has to be.'

'Then take it, and be gone!' Bruteria glared at the two. 'You're keeping honest business from my stall!'

Owain let out an explosive breath of relief. Deri laughed and stuck his arm through Owain's, pulling him away from the stall. The thrill of contact was no less for the presence of cloth between them.

'Best clear the way for other customers,' Deri murmured to Owain.

'Oh, right. Of course.' Owain allowed himself to be steered into the crowd. 'Why does it have to be so complicated? What's wrong with plain money for stuff, no tricks?'

'It's boring,' Deri answered without thinking, 'and what would most of us do with a bunch of dead metal anyway? It's easy enough to get, in Faery. The last blush of innocence, though, that's truly rare. That has lasting value.' Deri bit his tongue before it spilled any more freebies.

'I'd not thought of it that way,' Owain said.

'Most mortals don't need to.' Deri glanced around at the crowded market. 'I suppose you can find your own way. Unless you'd like to hire a guide?'

'I can find my own way.' Owain smiled. 'Thank you, though, for your help.'

Deri recoiled from the words. 'Never thank a merchant,' he said. 'It implies they didn't drive a hard enough bargain. And after all, you paid me for my advice.'

'Right,' Owain agreed. 'A night on the town.'

'Three nights,' Deri corrected.

'What?'

'One for each piece of advice I gave you.' Deri smiled.

'But—' Owain blinked. 'That was the deal, wasn't it?'

'It was indeed, my new friend. It was indeed.'

3

Deri followed a silversmith to Gossips' Row, then trailed a lady's maid to the Street of Sighs. If you had the knack, you could often use other people's temptations to navigate the Market as easily as your own. Some lord or other led him deeper, tempted by the finery of the webwork of market stalls and shops called Spinners' Nook. And if you followed the finer things long enough, sooner or later you would find yourself at Maurlocke's pavilion.

There were mansions less ostentatious, though Deri himself had never seen any. The pavilion commanded a prime position, a small island at the centre of three intersecting market avenues. Great swathes of white samite like ship's sails, threaded with patterns of gold like falling coins, undulated gently in the market air. Censers of gold trailed silver tendrils of incense from each of the three entrances, and delicate chimes of crystal trilled out tempting rills. Anything to tempt the wealthy and unwary.

Deri ignored it all, though he appreciated the way the incense smelled of his favourite meal – fish and chips – and undercut the grasping majesty of Maurlocke's demesne. As he approached the entrance, the fabric writhed of its own accord, warning Deri that Maurlocke was not alone inside the pavilion. Cheeky tent! Assuming Deri would just barge in, possibly upending delicate negotiations. As if he didn't know better by this point. Still, Deri moved with extra care and quiet as he entered.

The entry flaps snapped themselves closed on the heels of his passage. They'd taken an extreme dislike to Deri ever since he'd spilled ink on them. That had been over a dozen years ago! He'd been what? Four, maybe five? Ages ago, anyway, but Maurlocke's tent – like its owner – tended to hold a grudge.

The inside of the pavilion was, if anything, even more lavish than the exterior, and every inch gave Deri a reason to resent it. The rugs were thick and plush, woven with designs like a forest floor, and brushing them clean was about as difficult as brushing the real thing. Light gleamed from mirrors of gold hung about the perimeter, and weren't they a joy to polish. Not to mention the pavilion walls, two-sided and two-faced, as irritable inside as out. Deri entered cautiously, for more reasons than one.

Within the boundaries of the tent, Maurlocke's whim was all but law. Furnishings appeared and disappeared, tapestries shifted and changed, space itself warped and conformed to the merchant's need. At present, the merchant was deep in conversation with a woman dressed all in white. A delicate veil obscured her features, but her voice was a haggard thing clawing its way through that ivory fall. She wore only one shoe, Deri noted, as she paced the confines of the pavilion.

Maurlocke, by contrast, looked all but decked for a funeral. Every thread on the merchant's body was black. And whether or not ys gaze tracked the woman's rovings, Deri could not say. Maurlocke's eyes were of pure flint, and the lack of pupil did present something of a challenge in determining precisely where the merchant was looking at any given moment. Maurlocke clucked in disapproval and raised one shining hand to the elaborate coiffure of silver and gold chains growing in place of hair on ys head. Skin like molten gold glimmered in the light of the pavilion, a bright counterpoint to the costly black gown that dripped from Maurlocke's shoulders, a rippling river of shadows.

'I will require the ring.' Maurlocke's voice was cool and smooth as metal. 'The gold that has seen oaths sworn – and broken – upon it.'

The woman stopped her pacing and began turning, turning, turning a ring of gold upon her finger, not looking at the merchant.

'Come now, this is what you want, is it not?' Maurlocke held out a hand.

The woman did not respond. The ring just kept turning. Silence reigned unbroken in the pavilion for a long moment, and then Maurlocke cast it down.

'He laughed when he bought you that ring,' the merchant said, with all appearance of carelessness. 'The gold remembers.'

The turning stopped. Something inside the woman broke, in that instant, but it was not the kind of breaking that casts a body down, no, it was the kind of breaking that loosed a flood upon the unsuspecting land. Deri involuntarily took a step back. The space inside the tent was suddenly too small, too hot.

'Take it.' She practically snatched the ring from her finger and thrust it at Maurlocke.

The merchant took it deftly, murmuring all the while in the Language of Gold. Deri couldn't understand it himself, but he'd been raised by Maurlocke, and he could recognise the speaking of it in the glints and glimmers of light that shone across Maurlocke's skin.

'Boy, fetch my mirror.' The merchant's attention never left the ring.

Deri obeyed at once, retrieving a small silver hand mirror from its padded case. He took up a position near to the desk and adjusted himself as directed. Then he fixed his eyes at a point just past the merchant's shoulder. Experience had taught him to never get caught looking too closely when magic was performed in his presence.

Maurlocke held the ring so it was reflected in both the mirror and the merchant's cheek, but it was into the reflection shining in Maurlocke's own golden flesh that yse reached, two long, elegant fingers sliding beneath the surface of that golden skin as if it were naught but water. There was resistance, and no small measure of pain involved. The merchant hissed as a mirror reflection of the ring was painstakingly pulled free.

It was of dull grey metal, rather than gold, and where the original held a sparkling diamond, the reflection clutched a dull carnelian. Maurlocke passed it to the woman in white, who took it eagerly.

'Place it on your finger where you wore the other,' the merchant commanded, 'and it will guide you to your revenge, but you must take care to shed no tears while you wear it, or it will melt quite away and be forever lost.'

The woman in white knew better than to thank Maurlocke, so she slowly dropped into a deep curtsey.

'Rise, rise,' yse said, 'our business is not quite yet concluded.'

As the woman rose once again to her full height Maurlocke

drew a single, shining hand across the desk and a bundle appeared. It gurgled happily in the dancing light of the pavilion. A baby. Deri tensed.

'You will take this child and raise her as your own.' The merchant's tone left no room for negotiation. 'You will name her after the Stars and she will grow into a great beauty. The Fog of London will be most desirous to see her destroyed so you must ward her well. Teach her to guard well her heart, and ensure she understands every particular of your story. She is to return to me the day before her twenty-first birthday, without fail, and bring with her a token from every being that has come to her to ask for her hand.'

'I don't understand.' The woman in white held herself rigid.

'It's part of the price we discussed. You agreed to guard something precious for me, did you not? And what is more precious than a child?'

Deri had to bite his tongue particularly hard at that one. Maurlocke ranked several things as more precious than children, though they came through the Market often enough, and were quite a profitable enterprise. But the merchant was laying it on pretty thick. It appeared to be working. The woman in white had gathered the child up stiffly into her arms.

'Do you accept these terms?' Maurlocke's manner was offhand, too casual.

Deri was very familiar with that tone. The woman in white was in for quite the ride, he expected. Not that he would warn her, or that she would listen if he tried.

'I do,' the woman in white said, not bothering to look back to the merchant.

And with that, the contract was set. Deri had heard some merchants describe the feeling, and no two ever described it in quite the same way. Some said it was like a sound only merchants could hear, either a click or a snap or some such. Others described a particular feeling of warmth, or the sweet scent of dew on moss. To Deri's ears it sounded as the ringing of bells, though he only heard it clearly when the deal was one he brokered himself. Maurlocke smiled.

'Deri —' The merchant gestured towards the exit, '— show Mrs — I'm sorry, Miss — Havisham out.'

Miss Havisham paled, but had the sense not to say anything in response. Instead, she whirled to take her leave. Deri rushed to draw back the cloth of gold for her, but all he received for his pains was a look of disdain that would blight an apple orchard.

Before the pavilion had settled itself back into place, Maurlocke was dipping a raven's quill into a pot of gold ink and sketching out the details of the transaction in a ledger whose pages were black as jet. Deri waited in silence. He knew better than to interrupt the scratching of that quill. He had quite some time to wait.

Maurlocke made one final notation in the ledger and closed it. The gown took that as a cue to shimmer back into its true form, a simple merchant's robe. Woven of wise women's insight and young men's dreams, of societal expectations and half-moon's beams, Maurlocke's robe habitually changed its form to match the expectations of the merchant's customers. It had a way of setting them at ease, and making negotiations rather easier.

The merchant, as sexless as gold, had no problem presenting as whichever gender ys customers subconsciously preferred. To ym, the sets of habits and expectations mortals placed on such things were much like clothing: useful, changeable as needed, and occasionally frivolous.

'Deri.' Maurlocke made the name a summons.

'Yes, Mystrer?'

'Fetch me the items on this list, and quickly.' Maurlocke thrust a neat square of paper at him. 'I need them before sunset. And clean yourself up before you return. I will require you to pour wine for an important customer.'

'Yes, Mystrer.' Deri committed the list to memory immediately. The Untermarkt was prone to mischief, and the one time he had lost Maurlocke's list and returned without every appointed item… Deri firmly shoved the memory back into its mental strongbox.

'And keep your ears perked for any who appear to have unwanted mouths to feed,' Maurlocke added. 'My stock of ready labour is running unusually low.'

Deri suddenly found himself under the full weight of the merchant's attention. *Still as stone, still as stone,* he whispered to himself, his face a bland mask. 'Of course, Mystrer. Perhaps from the East End? I heard today there's a strike happening in one of the factories. There's sure to be many as feel the pinch, if not now, soon.' The intensity of Maurlocke's gaze abated.

'Indeed? Useful.' The merchant paged through ys ledger. 'You may tell any prospects you encounter that you heard me offer twenty-one years of prosperity for the last girl child I purchased. That's true enough, though she was an exceptional child. Well worth the expense of the goblin midwife. I only paid your mother seven for you.'

Maurlocke's attention returned, full force. Fortunately, Deri had not allowed himself to drop his guard. He couldn't. He'd been in this situation far too many times. Look unruffled, and the cold-gold monster will lose interest soon enough.

And indeed, after a too-sharp moment of silence, the merchant returned attention to ys desk. Deri took the opportunity to head for the exit. The list was a long one, and if he wanted to be back in time to prepare Maurlocke's dinner, he'd have to move fast.

'And fetch some pears,' the merchant called after his retreating back. 'You know the ones I like.'

Fantastic. One more thing for the list in his head. Deri called out to confirm to the merchant he had heard and would obey, before ducking out of the pavilion.

Just one more year of this, if all went well. Just one more year.

4

Owain clutched the geas-chain so hard it bit into his hand. If he lost it Missus Graspar would take it out on him, and then recoup the cost by adding its value in time to the end of his indenture. Oh Goddess, no, no, no. Not that. The thought of the four-years-and-change he still had to go was almost unbearable as it was. More? Owain shuddered. And he still had to get out of the Goblin Market!

'Find everything you were supposed to, kit?'

Owain looked up to find a ginger tabby looking down at him. 'You again! I mean, yes, th— uh, I did and I am very grateful to everyone who helped me today.' He tried to send a significant look to the cat.

'A fair exchange.' Bess stretched her left hind leg. 'After all, you saved me from the rope that ruffian tangled me in. The least I could do was point you to your Promise-Maker.' She blinked at him. 'Unless you are again in need? To find your way out, perhaps?'

'Th— I mean, as grateful as I would be to anyone who helped me find my way out, I remember the way.' Missus Graspar's words were scorched into his mind: *Escaping the Market is as easy as resisting temptation three times.*

'Well then, off you pop, kit.'

'Have a good day, Mistress Bess.' Owain bobbed his head, finally remembering the cat's name, before turning to make his way out of the Market.

It should be easy, really. The Market offered so many temptations that resisting them shouldn't be hard.

He passed a market stall piled high with fruit, with apples and quinces, lemons and oranges, berries plucked from dreams of high summer and strange, misshapen things that grow wild in the deeps of Underhill and smell of never being cold and hungry again. Owain's stomach growled. He swallowed.

Perhaps harder than he thought. Owain bit the inside of his cheek, hard. No. He needed to get out of here. No time for such delectable, sweet, surely-not-too-expensive… no!

Owain forced himself to stride past quickly. Never mind that he hadn't had a piece of fruit since Yuletide. Never mind that it was more food than he'd ever seen at the workhouse. He mustn't look, mustn't touch. If he did, the temptation would be all too much.

He wouldn't turn into his parents, giving in to the temptations of the market beneath London. He wouldn't trade himself away, piece by piece, for food or drink or silly charms that promised prosperity but never brought more than they cost. And even if he had a child, he wouldn't trade it away too, to be bound in indentured servitude at a workhouse.

Owain realised his eyes were stinging and his stride had carried him quite away from the fruit-seller. However, as if the Market had been listening to his thoughts, he found himself within range of a merchant calling out promises of happiness and home, of family and filial love and security. Ha! Nice try. Owain was well warded against *that* temptation.

He moved on, slipping through a gap in the crowd left by a beast of a man in a blue frock coat and a delicate woman in yellow whose laugh rang out like a bell. The scent of flowers, simple mortal daisies and roses, sweet violets and poseys, told him he neared the place where the Untermarkt exited into Covent Garden Market. Before he won free, however, the Goblin Market tried one last time to ensnare him.

'Owain? Wait up!'

It sounded like Deri's voice. Even though it made no sense the other boy would have followed him here, or be calling out his name, Owain almost turned, an unexpected smile on his face. No. It's another trick. Another reason to turn and walk back into the Market he was almost free of. Owain pushed forward, taking first one step, and then another, away from the Untermarkt, away from that calling voice.

It was harder than he expected.

It had just gone sunset when Owain left Covent Garden Market behind him and headed further east and north. Night came earlier, now the year was beginning to fade. The harvest rolled in, and it was but a few weeks to Samhain. The shouts of the fruit-and-flower-sellers faded as quickly as the light as Owain strode along the cobbled streets and alleys. He passed Drury Lane and the theatre district, a temptation as great as any he'd faced at the Goblin Market. Was it worth a slight detour to walk beneath the lights for a few streets? Best not. Missus Graspar was not a patient woman, and time enough had been lost in dealing with the Promise-Maker.

Lamplighters were busily plying their trade along the Queen's Way, with their satchels and long poles, conjuring spots of bright, alchemical-white light in the evening fog. Owain quickened his step. The fog thickened fast. It would be a dangerous night to be out. Already, vague shapes danced at the corner of his eye, and was that the faint hissing of the alchemical reagents in the lamps or voices from the mist?

He turned off the Queen's Way and onto Gray's Inn Lane, passing the Nag's Head public house as he went. Warm yellow light and drunken laughter spilled out onto the street as the door opened and closed. Owain's pace slowed the nearer he got to the workhouse. He couldn't yet see it but it loomed before him, chilling his heart and turning his feet to granite. The road beneath his feet sloped gently upward, and that hardly helped either.

All too soon, however, the blocky, red-brick form of the workhouse loomed out of the fog. Several storeys high, the façade that faced Gray's Inn Lane was severe. The windows necessary to allow light in were barred with ornamental grates, massive and thickly painted black. Matching gates occupied the centre of the building, framed by smooth grey stone which quickly gave way to the pedestrian brick that composed the majority of the building.

Owain slipped through the gate and crept carefully down the passage through the gatehouse. If he could sneak through without Mister Porthor noticing, the nasty old drunk would catch it but good from Missus Graspar. Fortunately, Mister Porthor was true to form: more concerned with the bottle in his hand, dirty bowler pulled over his eyes, and resting his feet up on the desk in the little gatehouse room. There must have been a delivery expected for the gate to be left open so.

A few tense moments and Owain was through into the forecourt. The bulk of the workhouse enclosed a large square, and the forecourt occupied roughly a third of that space. It was paved with stone, and crates of supplies were often stacked to the left before being carted to storage. Outgoing orders awaited pickup on the right. Missus Graspar and her son Garog ran a very productive workhouse. One might easily be forgiven for thinking the place a traditional factory that ran on paid labour rather than the indentured work of children. One would be wrong, of course, but there it was.

The rest of the quadrangle formed by the outbuildings of the workhouse hid behind the vast bulk of the main factory, which split the square and firmly locked the boys' and girls' exercise yards behind it. Owain would have to go through the factory building, across the floor, and up to Missus Graspar's office to deliver the chain.

There was no guard to slip past, here. Owain pulled the door open and stepped inside the small, protected vestibule that separated the factory floor from the outside. Once there, he paused to take a breath, tensed his shoulders, and stepped through the heavy door onto the factory floor proper.

The sound hit him first. The growl of machinery, fierce as any dragon, fought with raised voices and the thump of shifting crates. Then the smell, acrid and hot, a combination of alchemical concoctions, spent and spending fuel, and sweat. Gangs of children – workers – swarmed across the floor. The youngest carried things: small metal discs, or the etched and filed gears those discs were turned into by the machines; the oldest took on more skilled or dangerous jobs, using quick hands to place and retrieve bits of metal amidst various stamps and shears, or refilling acid reservoirs. Garog Graspar, in his role as 'foreman', lounged over it all from his usual spot on the mezzanine.

Owain's stomach twisted. Back again. He immediately slipped to the right, underneath the overhang from the balcony above, out of Garog's line of sight, and began making his way around the busy floor to the stairs that would take him to Missus Graspar's office. He picked his way past the workbenches that lined this wall, mostly dealing with sorting and checking the finished product from the factory floor for storage and shipping.

'How was it?' The question came from Vimukti, a pretty young woman with warm brown skin and a fiery glint in her brown eyes. A scrap of red ribbon held her night-dark hair in place on her head, safely out of reach of any machines which might grab at it and tear it out of her head. As she spoke, her hands flashed, sorting fine finished gears into batches for special orders. She wore the same style of worn trousers and work shirt as Owain, though in a smaller size, and with more patches.

'Interesting.' The word was out of his mouth before he could think. Vimukti was a friend and he often let slip more than he should to her.

'That sounds like a story I need to hear.' She smiled conspiratorially. 'And you're not the only one with news. Arienh overheard the Graspars talking, and there will be an artificer coming to add some kind of new machinery to the floor. Experimental. She's to have the second storage room as her own personal workshop. Can you believe it?'

A scream tore across the workhouse floor before Owain could reply. A stricken look crossed Vimukti's face and she sprang into action, running toward the sound. It was Nyfain, a boy near Owain's age. He'd been refilling the mister that polished the finished brass gears to a bright sheen with a particularly nasty acid – one of the more dangerous jobs.

Nyfain thrashed on the ground, clutching his wrist. His hand was a fizzing, pitted ruin already. Vimukti dropped to her knees, tears welling up in her eyes. Owain shot a quick look at the crowd gathering around them.

'Hale hands in,' he shouted to them as he stepped up and placed his own hand on Vimukti's shoulder. He felt someone else take his shoulder in turn, and another his free hand. Then he straightened his spine and braced for the pain.

The first of Vimukti's tears fell to splash upon Nyfain's hand and a vicious wave of pain burst within Owain. It was the same for every child on that workhouse floor in physical contact with Vimukti, and the pain did not lessen the further one got along the chain of humanity. In that moment, each child knew the feeling of having their flesh boil away at the touch of that alchemical monstrosity.

It is said that pain shared is pain halved, but with Vimukti acting as catalyst, it was pain healed. Well, mostly healed. Blood seeped from the pores of every child along the chain, and the flesh of Nyfain's hand knitted itself closed. The hand would never be the same, not without magic beyond Vimukti's skill, but Nyfain would live, with no danger that infection would also carry off hand or limb or life.

Vimukti let out an explosive breath and Owain released his grip on her shoulder. She'd take care of Nyfain, but he'd have to see to the rest of them.

'Alright, you lot,' he shouted. 'Bandage up and get back to work!'

The workhouse children grumbled and shuffled but they knew the drill. They'd done it often enough before. Still, they dawdled and took the excuse for a momentary break from the toil and drudgery of the workhouse floor.

At least until Garog appeared, a great hulking brute of a man. His face was craggy and cracked from too much drink and too many fights. Eyes piggish, close-set, and filled with malice dominated the face beneath the green bowler hat and matching waistcoat he thought made him look clever and dashing.

The children scattered before him.

'What's going on here? Owain! Shouldn't you be reporting to the office?'

'I'm on my way, sir. There was an accident.' Owain stated the facts, expecting full well they'd be disregarded.

He was not disappointed on that count.

'Move, boy,' Garog shouted, 'before I kick your worthless arse up there myself!'

Owain ran.

5

Missus Graspar made her den in the old foreman's office. The workhouse had once been a commercial alchemical distillery of some kind. The funk of chemical and reagents permeated every bit of old wood in the place. The workhouse floor, with the heat from the machines, smelled like Balor's armpit. Here though, in Missus Graspar's office, the wood gleamed new and polished.

'Close the door,' Missus Graspar snapped.

Owain hurried to comply, shutting out the noise of the brash and brutal machines that stamped and whirred and hammered and forged a wide variety of cogs and wires and other such things to sate the bottomless appetites of the city's artificers. There, no doubt, the sweat (and no small amount of blood) of Owain and his fellow workers made Missus Graspar a mint. And even then she clearly didn't consider it near enough compensation for the 'charity' of looking after such 'poor unfortunates'. She had designs, had Missus Graspar, and woe betide any who dared stand in her way.

An iron-haired woman with a ramrod back, Missus Graspar

was neat in every particular. She wore a sensible grey dress, with starched white collar and cuffs, pressed very sharply. Her hair was drawn back firm and tight into a businesslike bun. One would never know she lived and worked in a factory. You'd never see grease or dirt on her hands nor under her nails.

Her desk was likewise a model of precision, papers exactingly stacked, inkwells carefully stoppered and labelled. The sole exception to the cleanliness and precision of the office was Bruiser's bed. Bruiser was the one creature Missus Graspar showed the slightest spark of human warmth and kindness for, and there was not a more malicious, rotting sack of old bones anywhere the Crown held sway. As Owain looked at him, the dog attempted to snarl, but instead only managed to leak a bit more out of every orifice.

'You sent for me, Missus?' Manners were no guarantee of protection, but it was the best defence Owain could mount.

'You are rather tardy.' Her voice was as severe as the rest of her. 'And you have made us wait.'

Us? Owain glanced around the room, his eye catching the lanky form of another young man standing by the window. He was thin as a rake and had a face that might have been quite pleasant if time and circumstance hadn't stretched it – and him – so thin and harsh.

He looked to be Owain's age. Another new body for the workhouse? He was older than most that were brought or bought in, though he wore the same worn-but-sensible garb as most of the working poor of London.

'There was an accident—' Owain began to explain.

'No excuses. You've wasted enough of my time. The goods.' She rapped her finger imperiously on the edge of her desk. As Owain began to lay out the small parcels, she carefully set down her fountain pen and opened a locked drawer to retrieve a small bundle of paper slips. 'And the receipts from the market.' It was always merely 'the market' with her. Like she could somehow bludgeon it into something lesser than herself by refusing to call it anything else. 'The receipts, boy!'

Owain started. He'd been distracted by the stack of papers on her desk. His contract of indenture was right there, and the temptation to grab it and run was greater than anything he'd faced down at the Untermarkt.

'Yes, Missus.' His palms sweating, Owain reached into his pocket for the receipts.

Missus Graspar had resumed her notation, ignoring him. There was no way she had made such an error. It was a test. It had to be. And yet. And yet. The temptation was there. So strong. He could grab the papers and run, down the stairs and out to the streets. He was faster than she was. He had to be.

The pen stopped scratching across the page.

He couldn't risk it.

Owain set the last receipt under the parcel holding the chain and turned to leave.

'I don't believe I dismissed you.' Missus Graspar's cool tone froze him in his tracks. 'I have another job. And a lesson, as you seem to need a reminder of the way things are done here.'

'Missus?' Owain turned reluctantly back to face her.

Missus Graspar had placed a contract of indenture upon her desk. It was fresh and new, uncut and unmarked by ink where name and date and signature would go. The broad page was filled with rows of sharp, neat writing outlining two copies of a single agreement, each facing the other almost as if reflected in a mirror. It practically sparkled, fresh and bright, and Owain felt like it sucked all the light out of the room and out of his heart.

'Pierrick,' Missus Graspar's voice lashed like a whip, 'I call you to come and fulfil your bond. As you were caught trying to steal from me, I claim seven years' service from you in return.'

The thin boy – Pierrick – didn't move from his place near the window.

'Now!' The command was cold and blunt and merciless as an avalanche. 'Unless you prefer I return you and that which binds you to Watchman Field?'

Owain caught a flash of fear in the other boy's eyes as Pierrick moved to stand next to the desk. He struggled to imagine someone worse than Missus Graspar or her son, but it was clear from Pierrick's choice that whoever Watchman Field was, he was someone not to be trifled with.

Meanwhile, Missus Graspar deftly snipped the string binding one of the parcels Owain had returned with, revealing two thin rods covered with thorns and a slim silver knife, practically a stiletto. She grasped one of the thin rods, letting the thorns bite deep into her flesh and take her blood for ink as she used it to fill the blank spaces of the contract. The other she thrust at Pierrick once she had finished.

'Sign your name or make your mark if you're illiterate. A simple cross will do.' Her eyes watched both boys with the intensity of a hawk. 'Owain, you will stand as witness.'

It was a formality that was unnecessary both because it was unneeded and because it was cruel. But this was the lesson. Owain stood and nodded.

His eyes caught Pierrick's, passing sympathy to the other boy. Pierrick blinked and quickly looked away before straightening his back and pressing the makeshift pen into his flesh. He made his mark upon the parchment, and as soon as he had, the branch of thorns in his hands snapped and fell to dust.

'Bloody merchants,' Missus Graspar snapped, 'to charge so much for something that is useful but once, when they keep all the best for themselves! Well! They shall not have it all their way! Not if I have anything to say about it.' She sniffed, then took up the stiletto.

Pierrick took a step back. Owain reached out and gently squeezed his arm in support. The other boy looked at him but Owain just flicked his gaze back to the contract.

Missus Graspar took the blade and began slicing the contract in two, carving a unique pattern of jagged looping, curling indentations across the page until it was firmly divided. One half she slid across the desk, waving for Pierrick to take, and the other she placed upon the stack of contracts.

'Owain will show you your duties,' she said to Pierrick, 'and he will begin with a demonstration of what happens should you disobey the one who holds your indenture.'

'Missus—' Owain began to protest but the woman cut him off.

'You were late. I expressly told you to return directly to me once you had the chain.'

'There was an accident—'

'Irrelevant. You disobeyed. And disobedience must be punished.'

That was why she had had his contract of indenture sitting out on his desk. Owain's throat seized up. He couldn't even defend himself. She'd already invoked the punitive clause of his contract. Owain met Pierrick's gaze once more. The other boy's eyes were wide and staring. Then Owain closed his own, braced for what he knew was coming.

'Broken words and broken vows, I claim the due this bond allows.' Missus Graspar's voice slid into his ears like a razor into velvet.

Owain's throat burned as words of fire written in ink as dark as night etched themselves across the inside of his gullet. One by one the words of the contract, words he was sworn to, caught in his throat and scorched his flesh. It would leave not a mark, but was all the more agonising for it.

And he wasn't even allowed to scream.

6

A fortnight passed before Deri had so much as a spare breath to wonder how Owain might fulfil his debt. Maurlocke had heard of Deri's little encounter with Bruteria Promise-Maker and expressed ys displeasure as yse always did: by running Deri ragged. Tonight, though, tonight Deri had finally managed to finish all his errands early enough to steal a bit of much-needed time for himself.

Deri loved wandering the Untermarkt at night. The place came alive in a very different way, with so many mortals feeling daring enough under the so-called cover of dark to revel and make questionable decisions spurred on by too much gin or wine. There was an energy in the air all around that was lacking during the diurnal hours.

'Mistress Bess.' Deri bowed to the cat when he spotted her holding court from the top of a nearby market stall. 'For you.' He pulled a smoked fish from his pocket and gently tossed it up to land at her feet.

Bess nodded regally, but before she could say anything in

response a voice lashed out of the crowd and claimed Deri's attention for its own.

'Boy!'

Deri turned to find a suspiciously average young woman in the severe black dress of a lady's maid. She stared down at him with the bearing of a queen.

It was painfully obvious to Deri that she was in disguise. But then, certain classes rarely came to the Untermarkt openly. The nobility, members of the Artificers' Guild, members of the Society of Magicians, they all had reason to downplay any dealings they may have in faery magics. Particularly the nobility, as it would never do to be seen engaging in something as low as commerce. It would imply they wanted for something.

'Yes, miss?' Deri played along; he smelled profit.

The faux maid stepped close and whispered, casting ridiculously obvious glances to either side and looking positively illicit. Deri counted no less than seven nearby merchants watching them with interest. Someone really should have taught her better than this. The nobility were supposed to revel in intrigue. She was – at best – floundering through it.

'You know the Untermarkt?'

'Like the back of me 'and, miss.' Deri smiled cockily, not least because now he was certain the young woman was nobility in disguise. An artificer would have resorted to the vulgar argot of 'Goblin Market' rather than Untermarkt, and if anyone in the Society of Magicians were capable of lowering themselves to a menial disguise, Deri would eat iron nails.

'Take me to Jack Trades and you'll be well rewarded.' The young woman was holding out a coin to him.

'What would I want with that, miss?' Deri almost laughed in her face. 'Coin buys naught in the Untermarkt.'

It costs you naught to speak her fair, rebuked the Bell of Merchant Eyre.

'But I can take you where you need to go,' Deri added quickly, throwing in his second-most charming smile for good measure.

This chance is rare, set to with will, sang the Bells of Sad St. Sil.

Unlike merchants to the Market born or bound, Deri lacked that odd sixth sense that told him when something of real value was passing nearby. The bells were making it clear that there was something here. The attention of the nearby merchants confirmed it. He needed to be very careful how he proceeded from here.

'All the price I ask is that you tell me, and tell me true, what business it is you have with ol' Jack and I'll take you where you need to go.' Not quite what she was asking for, but close enough for Deri's purposes. 'Who knows, maybe I will even be able to help you in some way – for a fair fee, of course.'

The young woman laughed. 'Of course. I'm to Jack Trades to buy myself a Happily-Ever-After!'

"Lena!' A young man appeared out of the crowd, placing himself between her and Deri. 'There's no need to tell him that!'

'Oh, bother, Lars, there is no harm. It's a small thing he asks, and it's no great secret.'

Deri silently cursed himself for not noticing the young woman's beau. He was handsome, and clearly over-protective. The sort that knew he knew best in spite of never before having set foot in the Untermarkt. Deri had seen his like a hundred times.

What a berk.

'Why are you even bothering with this scrap of nothing?' Lars continued. 'We need a merchant, not a coster boy.'

Deri bristled at the description, though he let nothing of his ire show on his face. Coster boys and costermongers were street sellers, peddling their goods from handcarts. They were far and away from even the sort of merchant you could find topside, let alone a master of the Untermarkt, as Deri aimed one day to be.

'He's kind to animals,' Lena answered, 'and if he's kind, he's trustworthy, which is more than we can expect from most down here. He'll lead us to what we want. I'm sure of it.'

'Happily-Ever-After don't come cheap, miss,' Deri deliberately spoke only to Lena, ignoring Lars, 'unless you mean the kind they sell down Glaze-Eye Alley.'

'I most certainly do not! All I want is a simple life with the man I love.' She looked to Lars. 'Safe from harassment and harm.'

Deri whistled. 'Oh, that's all, is it? Do you know how few people have that kind of life?'

'Simple lives are common as grass,' Lars said, suspicion in his eyes.

'Simple lives full of sorrow are common as grass,' Deri corrected. 'Simple lives of happiness and security, now, those are at a premium. After all, you cannot easily buy what so few have to sell.'

'Surely they can be cobbled or crafted,' Lena protested. 'I've heard faery smiths have such skill.'

'They do, but such things are made of many lives, small pleasures and fortunes that must be collected one by one from countless mortals. It's no simple thing.'

'But it is done.'

'Yes,' Deri conceded, 'but you'll have no easy time of it, getting such from Jack Trades. Particularly if you also must pay him for secrecy.'

'Why would we need to?' Lena was all innocence.

'Now, now, miss.' Deri smiled again. 'Shouldn't lie to someone you want as a guide.'

'How dare you—' Lars began to bluster.

'Because it's true,' Deri cut him off. 'Lie to a guide and they might take you where you say you want, instead of where you really need to be.' He shook his head. 'And it was clear as day the moment you stepped up out of hiding. No need to hide, unless there's something to hide from, which means you'll be wanting secrecy to go with your purchase.'

Lena and Lars were silent. They wanted a Happily-Ever-After and seemed to have no qualms about paying. With what the bells said, Deri was inclined to believe they could easily afford what they wanted, which meant a big score. Bigger than he'd ever been close to before. And if he wanted a reward that size, he must be prepared to take a commensurate risk.

'Follow me. I'll get you to your Happily-Ever-After.'

Deri moved off into the crowd, not looking back, trusting Lena and Lars to follow.

In the Goblin Market, along the Street of Sighs, there is a stretch where the gaiety and noise of commerce thins, where shadow gathers and only the most destitute or desperate of merchants dare set up shop. At the centre of this quiet darkness is the ruin of a market stall, a silent testimony and warning. It is all that remains of the last merchant who dared challenge Maurlocke's position on the Merchant Council.

It was also the safest place Deri knew to engage in behaviours that edged along the boundaries of Market Law. Most merchants shunned the place, not wishing to draw Maurlocke's attention and ire, and without the merchants, there was little to draw mortal attention either. Deri found it an excellent hiding spot for his growing hoard, and now, a good place for some discreet experimentation with dealmaking.

'This way.' Deri motioned Lena and Lars through a rotting curtain after checking carefully to be certain they were unobserved. He couldn't risk even the rumour he was making deals on his own to get back to Maurlocke. A small golden bell hanging hidden at the top of the stall chimed an inquiry, but Deri set it at ease with a quietly whistled note.

'What a dump.' Lars sneered at the surroundings.

'This does not look like Jack Trades' stall,' Lena objected, more diplomatically.

'It's not,' Deri replied, 'but you're better off dealing with me.'

Deri dusted off a chair and sat down. His stomach roiled and blood roared in his ears. He forced himself to maintain a nonchalant air.

'Look, Jack Trades you've heard of, because he's one of the few humans to become a master merchant of the Untermarkt, and everyone thinks that means he's safer to deal with than the goblins.'

Lena opened her mouth to speak.

'He's not.' Deri cut her off. 'He has to be twice as ruthless for half the profit. He'll eat you alive and pick his teeth with your bones.'

'And you are somehow a better option?' Lars' eyes bored into him.

'I am.' Deri laid out his case, watching Lena out of the corner of his eye. She was the one he had to convince. 'You want a Happily-Ever-After, a simple life of safety and health, of non-renown and modest wealth, yes? That, I can provide.'

Before Lars could raise an objection, Deri wordlessly reached into an inner pocket and withdrew a small brass disc on a chain. Holding one end of the chain, he passed the disc to Lena. Her eyes widened as soon as she touched the warm metal, suffused with the sensations of safety and security, redolent with simple pleasures and the faint sharp taste of autumn cider.

'Oh,' she exclaimed softly, and pressed the catch. The lid sprung open.

'A compass to guide your life,' Deri said, before reaching out to close and reclaim it. 'Satisfied?'

'More than,' Lena said firmly, forestalling the protest Lars was clearly about to make.

'You require secrecy,' Deri continued, pressing the advantage, 'I can also provide that, with the added bonus that I am one of the last people anyone would think to question.'

'Because you're nobody special,' Lars said.

'Because I have yet to make a reputation for myself,' Deri countered, 'but what do you care about that? I can give you everything you want, for a fair price. How many people can claim to walk away from the Goblin Market with that? And speaking of price…' Deri prompted.

'The destiny I already have will more than pay for it,' Lena said. 'I won't be needing it, after all.'

'And what makes your destiny so valuable that it is worth the price of a Happily-Ever-After?'

'I should think that being of the blood royal and in line to potentially inherit the throne of the Empire would jolly well be good enough.'

'You have the honour of doing business with Princess Boudicca Helena Victoria of the House of Saxe-Coburg and Gotha.' Lars took an excessive amount of pleasure in that reveal.

That was not the reply Deri was expecting and it hit him like a blow to the solar plexus. That would indeed pay for a Happily-Ever-After. More than, if she were truly destined to one day sit on the Throne. If Deri made this deal, he could be set for three lifetimes.

It was a big 'if'. He first had to untangle and bottle her destiny, no small feat in and of itself, given his inexperience. Then he had to hide it away, or risk Maurlocke exploiting his contract of indenture to simply take it from him. And he could never risk selling such a thing on until he was well and truly bound to the Market and its law could protect him. Terrible things happened to mortals who attempted otherwise. The Market itself moved against them.

'Very well,' Deri acted casual, 'that seems equitable enough.'

'More than equitable,' Lars interjected. 'You will need to offer us something more, if you want to secure this deal.'

'That's not really necessary,' Lena said.

'It is,' Lars said firmly. 'He offered a fair price. If he wants our trust, he can better his offer.'

Deri fought to keep his laissez-faire attitude. He was going to have to offer something more, something he didn't have. He'd have to offer a favour, open-ended and dangerous. Was it worth it? No time to debate. The bells had told him how rare this opportunity was.

'I'll throw in a favour, bound by my word and market magic. At some time in the future, should you ask, I must answer, and do you an equitable service.'

'Swear it?'

'I so swear upon the Market stones, on mother's heart and father's bones. Satisfied?'

Lars sniffed but made no other objections.

'Satisfied, Your Highness?'

'Don't call me that,' Princess Boudicca said, almost automatically. 'And yes, I think I am. How do we do this?'

Deri retrieved a small pot of ink of night and a raven's quill, each painstakingly scavenged from Maurlocke's castoffs. There would be no room for elaborate agreements, scant room for clever loopholes, and little hope of wriggling out of the favour he had just recklessly promised. The destiny it would buy, though – the profit to be had with that merchandise was such that Deri did not need to wring every last drop of advantage. He felt like less of a merchant for it, but beggars and choosers, beggars and choosers.

A few brief lines outlining the agreement, enumerating the merchandise each party was bringing to the deal, the bare necessity of flourishes and the contract was complete. A true merchant of the Market could bind an agreement with naught but words, a handshake, or even a slight nod. Deri had not that skill. Yet.

'Sign here, Highness.' He pointed to the line above the one graced by his signature.

A flourish of ink and it was done. Boudicca, princess for a few minutes more, at least, held out her hand for the compass.

'Not quite yet,' Deri said, shaking his head and pulling out an old comb, all of ivory and horn, worn but still beautiful. 'We need to first part you from your old destiny, or the new will have no hope of taking root. Please, sit and allow me.'

Deri gently unbound the princess' hair and began carefully running the comb through it. Pass after pass he made, drawing the fine teeth through the finer strands of her hair. Destiny tangled golden around the ivory and gleamed bright against the princess's rich chestnut curls. As he did so, Lena sat taller and taller, as if lighter. She giggled, a sharp and weightless sound, too free. With each flick of the comb, stands of gold tangled about the teeth, until it pulled smoothly, nothing left to arrest its passage.

'That should do it.' Deri carefully wrapped the comb with its golden snarl into a silk bag for safe storage. He would have to card and spin it later before it could be of any use. He passed the compass to Lena, princess no longer.

'As agreed.'

Lena ignored him. She was staring at her hands, looking as if she could see right through them. Perhaps she could. Deri had to struggle to see her himself. She kept threatening to slip – out of sight, out of the market stall. It was as if not even the light would touch her.

'Take it,' Deri said sharply.

Lena cocked her head to one side, as if she was hearing someone impossibly far away. Deri reached out and put the compass into her hand, closing her fingers firmly over it. As soon as he did, Lena took on a new weight, a clarity. She blinked, her movements slightly stiff. It was as if the clothes she wore were new, unworn, not yet lived in.

'Thank you,' Lars said, placing his hands on Lena's shoulders.

'Think nothing of it,' Deri replied, his heart beating wildly, 'nothing at all. Now, let's get you on your way before someone comes looking.'

7

Owain jerked back, the wood of the crate in his arms tearing skin and drawing blood as he lost his grip, sending the thing slamming to the workhouse floor, the seam cracking and scattering gears like rain. He and several of the stronger children were busy clearing the southern end of the factory floor. What had once been a mouldering jungle of ageing equipment and things that were no longer of use but might still have value, somehow, was quickly becoming a wide expanse of open space.

Not something one usually saw in the workhouse.

'You alright?' Pierrick asked, setting his own burden down and moving to help Owain gather the spilled gears.

'Little light-headed,' Owain replied, picking splinters out of his hands. 'It's nothing.'

'You missed breakfast,' Vimukti observed as she sailed past, her crate barely weighing her down. 'Not that you missed much.' She grimaced, setting her burden down and joining the other two in gathering gears. 'Bread was even staler than usual, and I think there was more water than gruel in the pot.'

'Garog made me start clearing first thing.' Owain absently rubbed his throat. The Graspars were still making an example of him. And it was hard to be upset about missing breakfast. The food was always thin, and rank enough that even the spice of hunger could barely make it palatable. Sweeter was the opportunity to rest, to sit and steal a few snatches of conversation before returning to the workhouse floor.

Pierrick hesitated, then reached into his pocket and pulled out a hunk of stale bread.

'Here,' he said, offering it to Owain. 'I was saving it for later, but you need it more than I do.'

'Thank you,' Owain said. If there had been a little voice within that said no, Pierrick should keep it for himself, they were all hungry, it had long since been silenced by the brutal practicality fostered by surviving the workhouse.

'I wonder what all this is for,' Pierrick said, making himself look busier than he actually was as the three of them took a moment to catch their breath.

Quick study, that one. Owain felt a grim smile fighting to take shape around the hunk of bread as he gnawed on it. Good. He'd need to be to survive here, and he didn't have the dubious advantage of growing up in this place like Owain and Vimukti.

'New machines, I heard,' Vimukti said. 'The Graspars are bringing in someone from the Artificers' Guild to build something new. We're supposed to clear that lot for a private workshop, even.' Vimukti jerked her chin at the double doors leading to what had been a bit of storage lockup for the less degenerate junk piling up at this end of the building.

'You hear a lot,' Pierrick observed.

'Pays to listen,' Vimukti shot back. 'Might even save your life someday.'

Owain ignored the pair of them. He focused on chewing the stale bread and copied Pierrick, moving just enough to make it *look* like he was working. Garog was nowhere in sight, but you never knew when he would pop up.

Once the bread, crumbs and all, had vanished down his throat, he began working more in earnest. There was still plenty to do, and they'd not be given any slack if it wasn't done on time.

'Have either of you seen her?' Vimukti asked after she'd run through all manner of workhouse gossip, catching Pierrick up on everything he should know, and a great deal he didn't.

'Who?' Owain was only half-listening, his attention on the gears. They were thin and just heavy enough that any that lay flat on the floor were tricky to retrieve. He winced as his fingernail bent back from the pressure.

'High Queen Victoria,' Vimukti snorted. 'The lady artificer that's installing the new machinery. The reason we're doing all this cleaning and moving?'

'What? No. Haven't seen her. I didn't even know it was a her.' Owain tried to use one gear to prise another up from the floor and save his fingertips. It didn't work as well as he'd hoped.

'Sweet Danu, you never listen to a word I say, do you? I just told Pierrick all about it!' Vimukti scowled.

'She has to be evil,' Pierrick said. 'Working with the Graspars? How could you not take one look at that old bat and know you were as good as working with a proper demon?'

'Maybe. Maybe not.' Vimukti tapped her fingernail against the gear in her hand. 'The Graspars can put on a good show. Just watch whenever a customer comes to pick up a shipment or view the premises before making an order. Polite and industrious and nice-as-you-please they are then. Enough to turn your stomach, knowing what they're really like.'

'But we're still stuck doing all this because of her,' Pierrick countered.

'Doesn't make much difference why we're doing this particular bit of work,' Owain said. 'There's always something. Not like the Graspars aren't going to try and wring their money's worth out of each and every one of us.'

'True, but—' Vimukti paused, eyes narrowing. 'Wait. Why're you being so easy about all of this? Normally you're just as happy as I am to – oh!' Vimukti's eyes danced with gleeful fire. 'You're thinking about the lad you met at the Goblin Market, aren't you?'

'What? No.'

'You are!' Vimukti readily traded the new conversation for the old. She had plenty of energy to burn, and the temptation of something brand new was irresistible. 'The one you paid in *nights*.' The word dripped salaciously off her lips.

'What's this?' Pierrick looked from Vimukti to Owain and back again. 'Nights? What?'

'Missus Graspar sent Owain to the Goblin Market on some errands and he came back not only with the goods she wanted, but a little something extra for himself on the side!' Vimukti teased.

'It's nothing at all like that.' Owain coloured. 'Or, it might be, but I don't know. You know how it is, not knowing if it's… or if it's… no, you don't know, do you?' He shook his head. 'Whatever. Three nights on the town. Though how I'm going to sneak out is beyond me. I don't even know how to find him.'

'He'll find you. Goblin boys have all sorts of tricks.' Vimukti looked sage.

Owain snorted and Pierrick laughed. They exchanged a knowing glance. Vimukti glared at them.

'What?' she demanded.

'Nevermind,' Owain replied. 'And he's not a goblin boy. He's as human as you or I.'

'If you say so.' Vimukti's tone made it clear she thought otherwise. 'And don't play innocent. You know as well as I do that if you want out, there are ways. The Graspars don't even try to keep everyone in. Why should they, when they hold our leads?' Vimukti's fingers flexed like talons. 'Goddess, I wish I could burn every single contract of indenture in the Empire.'

'Let me know how that goes.' Owain rose. 'Now come on, if we don't finish this, they'll never let us go to sleep.'

'Yes. Must look fresh for your goblin lover.'

Owain ignored Vimukti's tease. He had enough problems to deal with without trying to out-spark her wit. He heaved up the box of gears he had gathered. The edges of the crate tore at his already bleeding palms.

What was he going to do about his debt to Deri?

'I heard that if you're not careful, goblins will suck out your soul,' Vimukti said, eyes sparkling.

'I heard that's not all they'll—' Pierrick joined in, his grin not yet worn dull by years in the workhouse.

'Yeah? Well, you shouldn't believe everything you hear,' Owain cut him off. 'Rumour has as much power to mislead as it does to warn. Especially when it comes from as dubious a source as that one.' He jerked his chin at Vimukti.

'I beg your pardon?' Vimukti huffed in faux annoyance.

'Beg all you want, sweetie, you're not having any from me!' Owain shouldered the box of gears and turned, cutting off the conversation before anyone else had the chance to steal the last word from him.

8

Deri sat in his borrowed domain after the departure of Lars and Lena, heart slowly winding back down to a normal pace. The enormity of what just happened sat on his lap in a small, silk bag. This was the deal of a lifetime! There was enough here to command a queen's ransom. Possibly literally, if the Stone of Destiny roared out in approval of whomever held this destiny whilst sitting upon it. Why, the number of beings that had killed for less!

That thought stopped him cold. Yes, he had his big chance, but he also had to keep it long enough to find a buyer. One who could afford it. That wouldn't be easy. And if Maurlocke got even the slightest whiff that Deri had something like this, well, that would be the end of it. His contract of indenture had a clause that allowed Maurlocke to claim any of Deri's property or the work of Deri's own hands as ys due. Deri gnawed at his lip. He couldn't let that happen.

He needed Maurlocke preoccupied with looking elsewhere. He needed a way to get the word out to motivated customers that something big was available at the Untermarkt. A slow grin began to spread across his face. He knew just the place to go to find a solution to all his problems.

Whisper Alley was the domain of the gossipmongers. The tents were woven of silken words, and the constant susurration of the wind through the fabric was like a thousand voices all whispering in harmony. Half-heard snatches of conversation spiced the air, teasing at the ears. First-time visitors were constantly glancing over their shoulders, sure they had just heard their name on the breeze.

Of course, they likely were not wrong. What better way to lure the unwary to one's market stall if not by the simple virtue of calling them? Once they were there, it was often immaterial that the merchant in question had nothing touching upon that particular customer. There was a healthy stock in trade with the latest news and scandal, liberally watered down with speculation, conjecture, and outright exaggeration.

There was valuable information to be had here, for sure, but the vast majority of transactions taking place were of an incidental nature. What did the High Queen have for breakfast? For the small, small price of a year's taste of peaches, you could find out. Which gentleman had the most scandalous evening last night? The warmth of your next blush might easily purchase that for you.

It was all highly frivolous and highly profitable. Most gossipmongers made their way thusly. There were a few, however, that specialised. That went further. There were those that worked the high end of the trade, crafting as well as curating. If you knew who to ask for, you could find someone to forge a scandal lethal enough to topple a dynasty, or build a reputation so fearsome none would dare test it.

It was this more specialised service Deri had come in search of. Such things did not come cheap, but recent experience had equipped Deri with a store of rather privileged information, just the sort of thing he could leverage with the gossipmongers to get him some prime merchandise.

Deri passed a merchant with three forked tongues, and one that looked like an old woman with mouths for eyes. He passed by the woman whose pipe smoked tall tales and the youth with a face on the back of his head as well as the front. All called out to him and all he ignored.

The darker silks were quieter; Deri looked for these. One of them would house the merchant he sought. It took a fair bit of searching, but eventually, tucked away in a corner, he found a tent the colour of just-turned-midnight and inside he slipped.

It was dark. Rumour travelled best in the dark, kept best in the dark. Bright light tended to degrade it. Besides, the merchant he had come to see had no need of light. Yse had no eyes to see with. Very fine ears, though, the merchant had aplenty, of all kinds. They flowed down all four arms, not unlike the mane of a horse.

The merchant had six fine fingers on each hand. Each finger had three mouths, each mouth had two tongues. Deri had once seen ym spinning a fresh rumour, whilst attending Maurlocke. The way those tongues moved and wove – it still troubled his dreams, some nights.

'A gift for you, Merchant Clust.' Deri unstoppered the small vial he had been clutching in his hand. As soon as he did, a welter of gossip welled up. He'd spent over a year gathering it all, snatched from the lips of unwitting maids and housewives who shopped at the Market as he ran his errands for Maurlocke, from the laughs and boasts of the sailors and workmen as he made deliveries and collected debts. It was nothing rare, but it was potent, distilled.

'What a thoughtful gift, young Deri.' Clust sounded pleased. 'And so politely presented!'

Listening to Clust was as eerie as looking at ym. Each of Clust's mouths moved and spoke in unison, one voice in a dozen dozen parts, a monotone harmony. It also required quite careful attention. Clust spoke very softly, and was kindest to customers who did the same. It probably had something to do with all those ears.

'What can I do for Merchant Maurlocke today?'

Good. Clust already assumed Deri was here on behalf of Maurlocke. That would make this easier. And Deri would need all the help he could get. Fooling a whispersmith was no easy feat. They could usually hear it when you lied to them.

'I have some truths to trade for rumours, some quite rare and valuable truths.' Deri could barely hear himself talk, he was so quiet in speaking to Clust. Thankfully, he had a very good idea of what he was saying. He'd rehearsed it enough on the way here. 'With your discretion…' Deri offered the standard secrecy agreement.

'Of course,' Clust nodded in agreement, a ripple and a ruffle of twitching ears. 'Do tell.' Clust's fingers moved through the air, almost sieving it, looking for telltale strands to seize upon and draw forth from Deri.

'It touches directly on the royal family, could very well provoke a scandal, and involves what may be the most valuable transaction the Untermarkt has seen in,' Deri paused both for effect and to gauge his words with triple care, 'quite some time.'

Clust made a small sound of pleasure. Small, glimmering strings began to web the merchant's fingers, hanging between them like a cat's cradle. Deri suppressed a shudder and continued on.

'In exchange for these truths, I am to ask you craft three specially woven rumours. One most exacting and particular, which you yourself, as part of the dealings here, disseminate far and wide. One the soft and misty sister to the first, which seems to offer more detail while actually offering less truth. And one rumour all but unwritten, yet full of force and fire, lacking only specificity and direction.'

The first rumour would be that a wandering merchant, passing through the Untermarkt, got the better of an unwary member of the royal family. What the merchandise in question was, well, that would be left vague. It would grow and change as the rumour spread. By tomorrow's dawning there would be talk that the merchant had tricked her into a lifetime of servitude, left her in naught but her chemise, and all manner of other outrageous nonsense. All of which would suit Deri just fine.

The second rumour would have one fragment of truth in it: that there was a pathway to the throne to be had in the Untermarkt. That would motivate buyers and drive up the price. The fact that said pathway was a bit of second-hand destiny was immaterial. That almost no one would think any but a merchant of the Untermarkt would be able to deal in such a thing would provide another level of protection from Maurlocke or other skilled merchants that might come sniffing after Deri's score.

The third and final rumour was Deri's ace in the hole. There was no way to predict what might happen in the coming days, and having a rumour he could start himself, to throw attention away from him (or draw potential customers near) would be invaluable.

Luckily, Clust thought the rumours were for Maurlocke so wouldn't prize them nearly as dearly as yse should.

'Young Deri asks for rumours, fast and fine. Yes, yes, this we can do. Believable, yes? Persuasive, yes?'

'Believable, more than anything. Or at least convincing. I have your agreement and the most exacting of your discretion?'

'As in all my work for Merchant Maurlocke.' Clust's ears twitched in Deri's direction.

Deri bit back a curse. He'd slipped. Almost slipped? It was probably fine. The wording was the same he would use were he truly on Maurlocke's business. But just in case, best to distract Clust.

'A member of the royal family has sold her destiny at the Untermarkt!'

Clust's ears stilled their motion all at once. 'Oh. Oh, what a truth do I hear in your voice! Such a ringing and a singing in the airs!'

'And it's a truth to be yours in exchange for the rumours we discussed,' Deri prompted.

Clust chuckled like the wind over a field of organ pipes. 'I think this arrangement will go very well, young Deri, oh yes indeed. Bide awhile, and watch me work, and I shall have the rumours for you quite soon. Oh yes, quite soon.'

Deri forced a smile. 'It will be a privilege.' Though what exactly Deri thought of said privilege, well, it was better not to say.

When Deri returned to the pavilion, he found Maurlocke finishing a conversation with a creature that wore the face and form of an elderly man, wrapped in much-patched clothes and coat, with fingerless gloves and a stained ivory smile: Fey Ghin. Deri's stomach sank. If Fey Ghin was here, it could only mean that Maurlocke was buying a new child or three to bind into indentured servitude.

Whatever the business was, it was concluded and Fey Ghin was taking his leave. The old goblin with a mortal's face smiled a gap-toothed grin at him. It sent a chill down Deri's spine. Better to play the polite servant, and not react, not speak unless spoken to. Deri found his usual corner and settled into shadow. Maurlocke made a show of ignoring him but Deri could tell the merchant could sense the rumour waiting, buzzing, on Deri's tongue.

'Merchant Maurlocke, always a pleasure,' Fey Ghin was saying.

'A profitable day to you, Fey Ghin,' Maurlocke replied, dismissal glinting off ys skin.

Fey Ghin slipped out the pavilion flap, but Deri knew he'd lurk outside, hoping to overhear some juicy bit of news. It was a futile hope. The pavilion would never allow itself such a dereliction of duty. Though the faster and further the rumour Deri carried spread, the happier he would be.

'You have something for me?' Maurlocke didn't bother to glance at Deri, instead resuming ys seat behind the desk and scratching out something in ys ledger.

'There is a rumour spreading like wildfire through the Untermarkt, Mystrer.' Deri stepped out of the shadows to stand respectfully before the desk. 'They're saying that a royal was here, in the Untermarkt.'

'And?' The quill continued to scratch across the ledger page.

'That he sold his destiny! Gave up a chance at the crown, the throne, and all for love!'

The quill stilled. Deri felt the stony weight of Maurlocke's full attention. He kept his eyes carefully locked to the corner of the desk, not daring to look the merchant in the face. What if yse somehow saw through Deri's act, half-truthful as it was?

'And who amongst the merchants of the Untermarkt has struck such a deal?'

'No one knows, Mystrer,' Deri felt sweat prickle at his temples, 'but, all due respect, many as think it was you, and I thought it best that if that is not truly the case, as no one really knows, that you should be made aware of the situation as soon as possible, so as not to be surprised when others come asking after that particular bit of merchandise.'

'Indeed?' Maurlocke paused, weighing Deri's words. 'Well, your assessment is correct. Well done.'

Deri kept his spine stiff. He didn't dare relax in relief. Not yet.

'Back to your duties now.' Maurlocke dismissed him with a flick of the quill. 'If what you say is true, I shall have to prepare. There will be a great many people coming to the Untermarkt in search of both that destiny and the royal foolish enough to lose it.'

9

Dame Aurelia Steele, Knight of the Verge, and chief bodyguard to the currently missing Princess Boudicca Helena Victoria of the House of Saxe-Coburg and Gotha, stared at the muddy boundary where Thames and shore met in mud. Her leather boots sank halfway to her ankles in the strand and, though the enchantments on her sensible plainclothes kept stray eyes from her and the chill of the breeze from her bones, she felt both stuck and cold. The princess's trail ended here. There was no following it across the moving waters of the river, not by magic or more traditional means.

Aurelia's fist clenched. This wasn't the first time the Hellion had slipped her guards, but it was the first time she'd covered her tracks to the point Aurelia couldn't find her and haul her back home. To make matters worse, she had at least an eight- or ten-hour lead on her bodyguard, and attempts to scry out her location were turning up nothing but darkness.

What had the girl been thinking? She'd endangered her life, the security of the realm, and, by extension, not only Aurelia's career but her life as well. Aurelia had to rescue the princess, and soon, before it was too late. For either of them.

Aurelia's enhanced senses were no longer of use; the princess was out of sight. Magically following her trail was also out, thanks to the shifting waters of the Thames. There would be no easy way out of this.

She was going to have to track the princess down the hard way, with a lot of legwork, investigation, and a bit of luck. If she couldn't follow her quarry to her destination, she'd have to figure out where the princess was headed and meet her there. Not her strongest suit, but fortunately she knew someone who was excellent at assembling disparate pieces of information into a useful whole.

Unfortunately, that meant having breakfast with her sister.

Silvestra was bustling quietly about the kitchen, her hands finding surety in the various devices and rituals of preparing a meal for herself and her sister when Aurelia blew in like a windstorm. Silvestra frowned at her dishevelled appearance. Honestly, you would think someone of her sister's rank would have more care for appearances.

'Sit,' she said, 'the food is nearly ready.' Then, before Aurelia could pull out a chair: 'Wait. The right rear leg of that chair is on the verge of coming loose. Won't be a moment.'

'Enough with the unnecessary fabrefaction!' Aurelia snapped at her. 'Not everything has to be perfect.'

Silvestra ignored both the verbal barb and the needlessly complex idiom. Aurelia waxed sesquipedalian when stressed. The chair was set right with a precise ease, tightening nut to bolt with a small wrench plucked from the chatelain resting in the folds of her gown. She nodded once in satisfaction.

'Better. Now sit.' She turned to the teapot.

'I need—' Aurelia raised her voice. To little avail.

'You can talk just as easily as we eat, and I know you've not had anything since I last fed you, so you might as well sit.' Silvestra settled the teapot firmly in the centre of the table.

Aurelia growled, but caved, reaching over to pour the tea and sweeten it to taste. Silvestra coiled herself smoothly into her chair and opened her napkin with a sharp snap before setting it across her lap.

'You look dreadful,' Silvestra observed. 'Has the Hellion kept you up all night?'

The Hellion was codename for Princess Boudicca. The fiery young royal was forever chafing at the constrictions of court, the insufferable actions of the gang of so-called nursemaids that dogged her every step, and all the other limitations of power that no one who was not royal ever really thought or cared about. Aurelia was designated chief nursemaid, responsible for overseeing the princess' protection, and Silvestra would rust if the little minx didn't make Aurelia's life a misery for it.

'I'm fine,' Aurelia snapped. 'I just need – I'm fine!'

'Fine isn't good,' the two sisters said in unison, Silvestra because she was quoting their father, and Aurelia because she was anticipating Silvestra's response.

'Well, you clearly need something. Any idiot could see that much.' Silvestra took a sip of her tea.

'Don't do that.' Aurelia's eyes narrowed. 'Don't look at me like that.'

'Like what?'

'Like one of your machines.'

Silvestra let the silence stretch out between them. Aurelia would talk when she was ready, and Silvestra estimated she would be ready soon. Time enough for another pot, but not much more. Whatever it was, she could see it was important.

Silvestra rose to add boiling water and tea leaves to the pot before returning to her seat. She pulled out their father's pocket watch and set it on the table, to tick in between moments of companionable silence. It was perhaps not strictly necessary to measure the time the tea steeped, but their father had always taken great delight in the ritual, and after his passing, the sisters continued it.

The watch itself was a thing of beauty, their father's work and his most prized possession. It was driven by an incredibly cunning miniature perpetual motion machine, one that no one else had ever quite managed to replicate perfectly. Silvestra herself had come closest, and her various efforts powered everything from factories to horseless carriages. Many ran for months or even years without needing additional energy, but unlike her father's watch, all were flawed in some way.

That was Silvestra's particular gift, to see the flaws in mechanical works and even sometimes mundane objects as simple as a chair or a teacup. More rarely, like with her sister, she could see the cracks in their relationship. She tried not to look at those too closely. Try though she might, she could never fully eliminate them, the tendency of the universe toward entropy a continual frustration to her striving toward the perfection her father had achieved.

At least mechanical things were easier to fix.

Moderately.

'She's missing,' Aurelia said as Silvestra poured another cup of tea. 'Ran off with a beau, we think.'

'And she's slipped you and your considerable talents, as well as managed to evade young Eghan and his not-inconsiderable talents. My. It is serious this time.'

'Stop that,' Aurelia said again, though this time it was considerably less sharp.

'Just trying to save time. I know you wouldn't be here if any of the obvious avenues were bearing fruit.' Silvestra stared off into the middle distance as she stirred her tea, assembling the pieces she knew and the ones she could guess into some semblance – howsoever flawed – of a whole. 'What else do you have? If you can't follow her, can you figure out where she is going and cut her off? Meet her there?'

'Love letters. One of them might say, but they're enchanted. We can't read them. At least no one at the palace who is allowed to know has figured out how to yet.'

'What else?'

'The inkwell she used to pen them, also enchanted.'

'There. That's your missing piece.' Silvestra took a sip of her tea. 'Figure out where she got it. Whoever sold it to her has to know how the spell works, which will get you the letters, which will tell you where she is going, which will allow you to pick her trail up again.'

'Right. Fine. How do I figure out who sold it to her?' Aurelia crunched a slice of buttered toast aggressively and winced. It was burned. Silvestra left all the cooking to her devices.

'Does she carry money with her, or does she do as every other spoiled noble does and simply have the charges sent to whoever is in charge of her money? That person, I guarantee, will have the receipt you need.'

'Yes. You know, I think you're right.' Aurelia's eyes all but sparked.

'Naturally.'

'You're working for that Graspar woman today?' Aurelia asked, half-absently, her mind knotting together what she had to do next in her pursuit of the princess. It would be good to know where Silvestra was, in case she needed another nudge.

'I'm mapping the space for the generator prototype today, yes.' Silvestra retreated to her chair and raised her teacup like a shield. Aurelia had a tendency to wield her opinions like poniards, and she was possessed of an outright arsenal of them.

'I don't see why you're bothering. It's not like you need the money.'

'It's not about the money,' Silvestra explained, patiently, as she did every time Aurelia pressed her on her artifice work. 'It's the opportunity to see how the design performs under conditions other than the mere theoretical. It's impossible to predict all the flaws or things that could go wrong in a secure laboratory environment.'

'Father doesn't need you to replicate his work.' Aurelia slipped down the path to an old, old argument before she managed to catch herself.

'He might not, but I do,' Silvestra replied, with an air of brittle unconcern polished almost transparent by excessive use. 'And besides, the machine my prototype will run is something even you should appreciate.'

'Oh? What does this one do?' Aurelia took the proffered conversational detour with all the enthusiasm of a man finding sanctuary after a night of running from the wolves.

'It takes old things and makes them new again,' Silvestra said, massively simplifying the concept for ease of dealing with her sister.

'Like my favourite boots?' Aurelia put her feet up on the empty chair to her right.

Silvestra pushed them off with the ease of long – and long-suffering – practice.

'No. Not like your boots. It's not worth it for most things, sadly, but for those few things that are rare and precious—'

'Still sounds like my boots,' Aurelia said.

'How fast do the knights go through camstone?' Silvestra changed tacks. 'It wears away to nothing after, what, two or three uses? Imagine if you could restore it to pristine condition before it wears out, for the price of several truckloads of common river stone.'

'That… that would be useful, yes,' Aurelia admitted. 'And valuable. Only so much camstone comes out of Faery, after all.'

Silvestra sipped her tea, content that she found a scenario her sister could not fault. Though speaking of flaws, she could see the stress lines forming in the porcelain of Aurelia's cup. The strength of ten men was her sister's to command, and Aurelia's fine control sometimes lapsed when she was tired or irritable.

'More tea?' Silvestra drew attention to the cup, thereby forestalling its impending demise.

'Silly question,' Aurelia replied, but her grip eased.

'Yes, of course.'

10

Deri flagged down one of the urchins playing hoop-and-stick and chanting as they ran. So long as they didn't interfere with business, none of the merchants minded them much. The children were too useful.

'I've a message for you,' Deri said, holding up three twists of paper holding penny-sweets. 'For Owain of the Graspars' workhouse.' He rattled off the day he'd be free, when Merchant Maurlocke should be distracted with a good bit of business.

He was looking forward to this, the first of three nights that Owain owed him.

After a thoughtful moment, the child nodded, sweeping the sweets from his hand and dashing over to claim the stick and drive the hoop away. The child began a new chant, rough but rhyming, and the others soon picked it up.

As I was walking by the Thames,
I found a rose with seven stems,
Each blossom bloomed and fell away,
Before the dawning of the day,

What wondrous things, what hidden gems,
Might you find along the Thames?

In moments, that rhyme would spread throughout the city like wildfire, carried by children running and playing all throughout the streets of London, until it came to the ears of one near to the workhouse. They'd make sure the message got to Owain.

It was an old system, and not the swiftest means of communication, nor the clearest, but it was quick and cheap enough, and the rhymes made sure that the messages weren't understood by every man jack that heard them.

Deri was fairly certain the famous rhyme involving fiddles, cattle, and eloping cutlery had started out as a message along this very network, back when High Queen Elizabeth was outmanoeuvring Parliament to ensure the Treaty with Faery came into being.

Then, confident his message would be delivered and he'd be able to meet Owain for the first of their three nights, Deri turned his attention back to the Market. If he was going to have enough time spare, he needed to move quickly.

Maurlocke never wanted for tasks to assign him.

Owain paced along the Thames. Deri was late. Or was he? Owain replayed the last message Deri had sent him via that hackneyed rhyme. It was a cumbersome way to send messages, but they hadn't anything better at present. *No*, Owain thought, *he should be here.* The bells which sounded from the heights of St. Cathbad's Grove rung out thrice past the appointed hour. Another quarter-hour and—

'I'm here! I'm here!'

Deri appeared out of the shadows and out of breath. He leaned rakishly against a lamppost and blew out a great gust.

'Bloody Merchant Maurlocke just would not go out this eve. I had to engineer myself an excuse. But I'm here! The night can now proceed!'

Deri gave a flourish with his arm. Owain laughed, though he wasn't sure if it was nerves or actually finding it funny. Deri grinned at him, and suddenly it didn't matter. Owain was just glad he'd laughed.

'Come on,' he said. 'If we don't hurry, we'll miss our chance.'

'Where are we going?' Deri's eyes were constantly moving, darting from sight to sight.

'You asked what I like to do for fun. Follow me and find out.' Owain smiled, the air of mystery sitting awkwardly about his shoulders. What was he doing? He didn't say things like that! Did he? No. He definitely didn't. This was an act, and Deri was from the Goblin Market! How could he not see right through it?

If Deri noticed, he gave no sign.

'Lead on!'

Owain turned and headed toward a large, thatched building.

Owain had an excellent derrière. Deri glanced at it as often as his eyes darted about the southerly banks of the Thames. Maurlocke had rarely had cause to send him to the theatre district on errands, and when he did time was always tight, so each unhurried sight was a new treasure to add to his hoard of memories. Some he might even keep!

'I hope you can climb,' Owain's voice drifted down to him.

Deri wrenched his gaze away from the lights glimmering through the fog.

'Up here.' Owain waved to get his attention.

Owain was several feet up a length of blackened oak beam. Thick ivy curled around it, providing handholds, though it looked like Owain scarcely needed them.

'Quick, or we'll miss the start.'

'Start of what?' Deri asked, climbing as he did so.

Owain didn't answer. He was focused on scurrying up the pipe. Deri followed, not to be outdone, but one look down was more than enough. He fixed his eyes upwards. *Better view anyway*, he grinned to himself.

There was a small gap at the top of the wall, just under the thatch. Unless Deri missed his guess, some industrious hands had gone a long way toward helping tease out that gap.

'Well, you're just full of surprises, aren't you?'

Owain's head whipped around, finger to his lips. Then he beckoned Deri to follow and started crawling out along one of the short beams supporting the thatched roof. At the other end, he dropped down to a lower beam and sat looking out over a circular courtyard.

Deri followed, more slowly than he would ever admit. He managed to slide into place right next to Owain just as a man in resplendent clothes walked out onto the raised platform on the opposite side of the wooden O from where they sat.

Now, fair Hippolyta, our nuptial hour draws on apace…

Deri was held fast, spellbound by his first experience seeing a show on stage. So enthralled he didn't even notice the glances Owain kept shooting his way. Deri was well and truly caught, a fly in the web of words and wonder spun by the actors on the stage.

When the show was over, it left Deri's mind in a whirl. The play, the lovers, the magic – he'd heard of it, of course, even seen things like it in the declamations of the buskers and musicians that sparkled amidst the rows of stalls in the Untermarkt, but the experience was something else altogether.

'You look like you had fun,' Owain said.

That punctured Deri's mood, slightly.

'The night's not over yet,' he replied, too lightly. His stomach knotted around itself as he glanced at his companion of the evening.

Owain's face was serious. It was a good face, and as much as Deri found himself liking the stone-smooth planes of that grave expression, the bit of mischief in him that made him so very good a goblin apprentice urged a joke or jest to tease forth a smile.

'What shall we do next?' he asked instead. He was already playing with fire, staying away from the Market this long. *If Maurlocke missed him* – Deri ruthlessly crushed that thought. Nothing was going to ruin this night.

'Shall we walk?' Owain asked. 'The Fog isn't too thick, and St. Cathbad's is quite the sight.'

'Is that by way of London Bridge?' Deri's question carefully crouched in that gap between innocence and implication. The stone arches spaced regularly along the bridge's length, ostensibly for the ease and comfort of patrolmen and pedestrians, were notorious even in the Untermarkt for their use by men who enjoyed the company of other men on a truly fundamental level, so to speak.

'It's as easy by London Bridge as it is by Blackfriars,' Owain replied.

'You're the guide.' Deri firmly placed the ball in Owain's court. What better way to see which way he swung?

Was it Deri's imagination or did Owain swallow, slightly, before speaking?

'By way of London Bridge, then,' Owain said. 'It's a bit longer a walk, but the scenery is preferable, I think.'

Hope warred with frustration. He should have bought a few tricks from the Market. A single knowing glance or a pocket square cut from a rather particular bolt of silk would easily solve this quandary he found himself in. Of course, that would have further depleted his reserves, already endangered by the need to engineer some free time so he could meet Owain this evening.

Deri would have to settle for a bit of boldness – though, even then, he couldn't quite bring himself to bluntly ask what he truly wanted to know. So he proffered his arm with a smile that could cut either way, and asked another question instead.

'Shall we?'

Owain took the proffered arm. It was common for young men and young women alike to walk arm-in-arm of an evening. Society still saw it as harmless. Harmless. As if Deri's arm wasn't buzzing with the shock of contact. Harmless indeed.

'You appear to have enjoyed the play,' Owain said.

'Very much.' Deri's reply was bright. 'I could sell that memory for a mint in the Untermarkt.'

Deri did not miss the glance Owain darted his way.

'But I think I'd rather keep it for myself,' Deri continued, more softly.

'It was an excellent performance.' Owain flushed. 'Sorry. I suppose that was obvious.'

'It was my first, so I don't have much of a basis for comparison, but I liked it very much.' Deri pulled Owain a hair closer via their linked arms. 'Very much.'

They discussed the play as the dark waters of the Thames rolled by, the smell of the water salty-sweet and pure. It was a point of pride amongst the druids of London that the city's natural aspects were maintained in holy and healthy condition. Regular lampposts and strings of lights along the bank glimmered through the fog as they went. It was magical.

'This must all seem rather dull to you,' he commented to Deri.

'What must?'

'The lights, the water. The Untermarkt is so full of wonder—'

'And horror.' Deri smiled to take the edge off his words, though. 'But Faery loves beauty and grotesquerie. The eye of a merchant must be able to see both, wherever they may be. And this –' Deri gestured around them but his eyes bored into Owain's '– is one of the most beautiful evenings I have ever seen.'

Owain held that gaze as long as he dared. It seemed an eternity and but a moment all at once. His frantic eyes settled on the nearest landmark, and a shudder clutched him just beneath his belly.

'London Bridge,' he said, too loudly.

They walked arm-in-arm across the bridge in the fog. There was an intimate privacy walking in that soft and otherworldly air. Deri slowly drew himself closer to Owain and was pleased when the other didn't resist. Through the Fog, the glittering heights of St. Cathbad's Grove shone from Ludgate Hill. Deri drew them to a stop near one of the infamous alcoves, though from the sounds of things – or lack thereof – it was unoccupied.

'Have you ever been inside?' Deri pointed across the water to the Grove.

'Me? No. Workhouse boys aren't usually allowed to mix with the quality.'

'I thought the Grove was open to all.'

'It is.' Owain was silent for a moment. 'I'd like to go in someday. Feel the grass beneath my feet.'

'You're not afraid the druids would seize you as a virgin sacrifice?'

'The druids haven't sacrificed anyone in ages,' Owain said.

'That's the joke, mate.' Deri risked the tease and then immediately cursed himself for calling Owain a friend. What if it was his fault Owain wasn't interested? Because he had misspoke. What else had he said wrong? He instinctually rushed back to safer conversational grounds.

'They still talk of it below.'

'At the Untermarkt?' Owain looked interested at that.

'Yes. Sometimes you even hear of a memory of the construction. It's almost always a rumour, of course, but wouldn't that be something to experience?'

'That's not a story I know,' Owain admitted.

'No? But this is London!' Deri actually had a hard time grasping how anyone could not know the story. 'It's right there! All the time! What are people so busy talking about that you haven't heard that story?'

'Marriage and profit margins, mostly.'

'Ah, well, fair dues. In the Market it's the same. Merchandise instead of marriage, though.'

Owain smiled at that. Maybe he almost laughed. Deri didn't know, but he liked to imagine. Next time.

'So, tell me the story,' Owain said after they had stood in silence for awhile, looking at the top of the Grove through the Fog.

Deri's first thought was to ask what Owain would offer him for it. His second was to just name the price as one kiss, willingly given. He went with his third impulse: just tell the bloody story.

But tell it well.

'Once upon a time there was a king who longed, more than anything, for a son,' Deri began. 'Eighth of his name, he married, as so many kings do, not for love but for advantage. But for a time, he and his wife were happy. Their happiness was not to last, however.'

'No?' Owain smiled at Deri's telling of the tale.

'No.' Deri shook his head, all sombre theatricality. 'For the Queen could not give the King the one thing he wanted above all others: a son and heir. And so the gaze of the King strayed, and his heart followed close behind it. The King found love with another.'

Owain feigned shock. Deri took the opportunity to clutch Owain's arm dramatically.

'The passion of the King for his mistress burned white hot, but in the end it would be for naught. The King needed an heir, and in those days, one could not simply purchase Legitimacy at the Untermarkt. No, an heir had to be born firmly within the bounds of marriage, and the King was already married to another.'

The Fog had thickened to a dense shroud. Lights still shone faintly through, but only just. Deri and Owain seemed the only two people in the world.

'The King petitioned the Pope. It was to no avail. But if the Church would not break his marriage for him, the King would break from the Church, a thing unheard of, unthinkable, even, in that time and place. The King's Advisor, you see, had a solution – the return of the Island's hereditary faith.'

'The Druidic Resurgence.'

'Yes. From under the hills of Faery, the Archdruid came to the Court of the King, and advised him that under Druidic Law, divorce was not only possible, but quite a simple thing. Further, should the King restore Druidry to the Land, the Land in its gratitude would yield up seven years of bounty, with richness unseen since before the feet of Rome trammelled across the soil.'

'What did the King do?' Owain asked. Deri couldn't tell if he genuinely didn't know, or was playing along for the fun of it. It didn't really matter: Deri was quite caught up in the tale.

'The King accepted the Archdruid's offer. Druidry was restored to the land and the King set aside the old Queen in favour of a new.'

'But what does that have to do with St. Cathbad's Grove?' Owain pressed.

'In those days, no trees grew upon Ludgate Hill. A grand cathedral stood there, of dead wood and cold stone made. The Archdruid came to the sacred hill, highest of the three ancient hills of London, and pronounced a doom in the Language of the Trees. New life moved within the wood of the cathedral and a grove of trees sprang up, rending the stones and casting down the arrogant spire that had lorded over London.'

The Grove was barely a glimmer through the Fog at this point.

'St. Cathbad's Grove still grows upon Ludgate Hill, changing form and face with the seasons, though it is said to be warm even in winter and cool even in summer, and forever filled with song, if one knows how to hear the Language of the Trees.'

The two stood in silence for a long moment.

'It's a nice story,' Owain finally said.

'It is,' Deri agreed. 'Though I have to say, most of the druids I've met are arrogant pricks.'

Owain gaped for a moment before laughing. The Fog muffled the sound. As if that moment of release had been cue to another, however, the sound of rain hissing along the Thames followed.

'Quick, in here.' Deri pulled Owain by the arm into one of the stone alcoves lining the bridge. Overhead, the rain began to pelt down.

Owain wiped some stray droplets from his face. While the alcove provided some shelter from the deluge, it was far from watertight. The rain was cold – London rain so often was – but Deri was warm and they were huddled close together.

Deri was looking out at the rain, smiling.

'It was a good evening,' he said.

'Is it over, then?' Owain asked. He forced his voice to remain light, in spite of the small pang he felt at the thought.

'Unless you have something else in mind.' Deri gestured out at the rain. 'The weather does put a slight damper on things.'

Something moved in Owain at that, something clenched beneath his stomach and fluttered against his ribs. His breath came shallow and fast and his hand only refrained from shaking through sheerest force of will.

'It doesn't have to.' His voice almost broke under the weight of those words.

The cover of night and rain made him bold. At least that is what he would tell himself later, curled around this memory. He had caught something of Deri's recklessness. Some stray wisp of faery enchantment bound his reticence.

Owain reached over and gently turned Deri's face toward him. Deri's eyes caught what little light there was in the alcove and used it to chain Owain's gaze in place.

'May I kiss you?' Owain's voice was just a slip of silk in the dark.

'I think you'd better.'

The corner of Deri's mouth was crooked in a smile. Owain leaned in, face wet with rain, not caring to wipe it away. Raindrops glistened in Deri's hair and Owain slid his fingers through it, drawing Deri close. They hovered there, all but touching, sharing one breath back and forth between them, before Owain finally closed the distance.

Their lips met and everything else fell away.

II

The trail led Aurelia to the Goblin Market. Never having been before, she was unprepared for the way it called to her. It was in the gleam of light from new-forged blades, in the curve of fine faery bows. Merchant voices surrounded her, yet each was as perfectly audible as the next, none drowned in the cacophony around her. And each clearly heard offer was oddly well-suited to her tastes.

'Yell-hound pups! Fine white pups for sale!'

'Arrows of oak, and ash, and thorn! Obsidian spears!'

'Draughts of love as fine as wine! Many vintages! Filial, fiery, or downright filthy!'

Aurelia coloured. The princess would not have tarried here. None of these things would hold any attraction for her. Why would they? She could have anything and everything she wanted. Aurelia tried to push on, push past, but found herself only more deeply mired in the crowd.

'Whispers from loved ones lost!'

'Aurelia…' Her father's voice teased her ear.

The huntress paused, suddenly quarry in an unexpected noose.

'My darling girl...' Her mother's voice cooed out of nowhere.

Cheap tricks. It had to be. Death was a line inviolate. Still, her feet would not carry her away.

'Beware...' It was her father's voice again. 'Beware the lure of the Market, my girls, the merchant in tatters and patch, beware the baubles and wishes-come-true, the deal and the clause with the catch!'

The words hit her like a pailful of frigid water, shocking her out of her reverie. Aurelia stepped back. This place was dangerous. The princess was in danger.

Back to the scent. The princess's steps still resonated faintly through the stones of the Goblin Market. The charm that allowed Aurelia to hear that echo was strong. She pushed back into the crowd.

It was no simple thing. The stones and streets of the Goblin Market moved and shifted by some unknowable whim or design. More than once, Aurelia found herself backtracking or at a dead end, forced to wander until she again caught a hint of the music of Boudicca's steps.

She tracked the sound past gossipmongers and rumour-smiths, through the labyrinth of stalls selling dreams and memories and surges of emotion caught up in string or rolled up in tobacco or cinnamon. She dodged the temptations of sugar and steel and song. In the end, she found herself in front of an empty and decaying merchant stall, something that stood shadowed and silent in this world of light and colour and cacophonous sound.

Boudicca's steps thrummed in the stones, as loud as she had yet heard them. This was as close as she had been. The sound beckoned her forward, invited her to part the curtain and step inside.

Aurelia eased her way in, quiet and careful. Her eyes darted around, taking in the rot, the decay. A chair was disturbed, and her eagle eyes easily picked out the trace patterns in the dust that indicated two – no, three – people had been here, not so long ago.

The trail ended here. The stones fell silent. That made no sense. Aurelia ranged across the room, criss-crossing, searching. There was no hint of the princess past that last final point, under the chair. Crouching down, she spied a few strands of hair, long and fine, in the dust on the floor. They were lustreless, but otherwise the right colour. The princess had been here.

But where had she gone? What magic had carried her away? She hadn't walked out. But if she had been transported, or turned into a summer's breeze, or cloaked in a swallow's shape, where had she gotten the magic? Not from this stall. There was nothing of that sort here.

Aurelia was so caught up in her search she failed to hear the rustling outside. So it was with great surprise she found herself not alone. A young man had slipped quickly and quietly into the market stall. For his part, he was looking over his shoulder and did not see Aurelia until he was already fully inside.

They caught sight of one another simultaneously. Aurelia's first reaction was to draw. Her reflexes were far superior, so whatever the young man's first response might have been, it was swiftly subsumed by his reaction to three feet of gleaming steel.

He promptly turned and fled.

Aurelia cursed and gave chase.

Deri hummed as he went, remembering the feel of Owain's lips upon his own. The memory welled up in him like a torrent of bubbles and gave an extra spring to his step. Who would have guessed stopping to make a deal with the other lad would have produced such a result!?

Then he frowned. That deal had strangely turned out better than the one he was attempting to strike in exchange for the princess's destiny. Three merchants in a row had flat out refused the opportunity the destiny in his pocket represented. Three! And now he was out of time. There was only so much he could claw back for himself by being incredibly efficient with Merchant Maurlocke's errands. He walked a coin across his fingers and flipped it into the air as he ducked into the abandoned market stall that was his haven.

There was someone already there. A woman in sensible clothes of far too expensive a make for their appearance. Deri barely had time to register that fact before another was screaming for his attention: the sword levelled directly at his throat. Deri was nothing if not attentive to the urgings of the better part of valour.

So he ran. Heart pounding, muscles straining, he ran. His legs carried him far faster than most mortal men could run. Unfortunately, his pursuer was as fast – if not faster. She was right on his heels.

Think, blast it! Always have a plan, even if the cussed thing goes wrong. Can't run much farther without being seen by a merchant of substance. Maurlocke would find out! No. No no no.

Deri stopped abruptly. He had time for one deep, steadying breath before a hand grabbed his shoulder and hauled him around. He found himself face to face with a striking woman with too-sharp eyes. Eagle's sight, unless he missed his guess. Not good. She might even be able to see when he lied.

'Where is she?' The woman's eyes raked his face.

'Who?' Deri didn't have to feign confusion. The question was not the one he was expecting.

'The princess.' The woman leaned in close. 'Where is she?'

She was definitely looking for lies. Bollocks. He couldn't pretend innocence here. She'd know if he lied. Deri screwed a goblin smile into place. He'd just have to lie with the truth, then.

'Which princess is that, ma'am? There are so many. I'm afraid I don't keep tabs on all of them.'

'The one that was in that ruined market stall.' The woman's voice was heavy with threat. 'Don't play your goblin games with me. You were there when no one else was. You know something.'

'Say that I do,' Deri replied. 'What's it worth? Or rather, how much you got? 'Cause it's pretty evident it's worth more'n a pennyworth of pretty.'

'You expect me to pay you?'

There was shock in her voice. She was surprised he asked for payment? What, was this her first time at the Market? He looked at her face. It was. Deri viciously shoved down a laugh.

'That is how the Market works, ma'am.' Deri was all politeness and superficial compliance.

'I don't carry much money with me.'

Why did mortals have such an obsession with money? Deri shook his head.

'What use is money here, ma'am? No, you'll not be able to buy the information you need that way.'

'You're not getting my soul.'

Deri did laugh at that.

'What in Underhill would I want with that? No, your soul is yours to keep. I want your strength.'

'My strength is not mine to barter away.'

'The use of it then, for no more than five minutes, say.'

'You can do that?' Unease flitted across the woman's face.

'Borrowing is much easier than trading.'

She considered.

'And you will tell me everything you know about what went on in that stall.'

'I will truthfully answer three questions about events that have transpired within that stall, to the best of my ability,' Deri countered.

'My strength will not be used to hurt or kill anyone. I won't have that on my conscience.'

She caught on fast, for one so inexperienced in Market matters. No matter. Deri was better at this game than any human other than old Jack Trades.

'Alright. Strength for truth, within these limitations, is agreed, yes?'

The woman stood silent, clearly turning the offer over and over in her mind, looking for loopholes. She should be looking more closely at the terms unmutable, but Deri wasn't going to tell her that.

'Agreed,' she said finally.

Deri offered his hand. She took it, and it was a bargain struck.

'The use of your strength, then. See that merchant, there?'

Deri pointed to a figure of stone with hair like clouds on a mountain peak and a voice like wind through the rocks by the sea. Knots of all kinds hung about the merchant's stall, and bound up in them were stray bits of luck and misfortune, sunny days, and even death. The woman nodded.

'I want you to go over there and punch ym in the face.'

'What?' The woman turned back to him, her face incredulous.

'Punch ym in the face. Use your strength. It won't hurt them.'

'I'm not doing that.'

'We have an agreement. Strength for truth. If you want your truth, you'll have to use your strength as I ask.'

'No.' The woman crossed her arms. 'Never gonna happen.'

There was a crack of displaced air as she vanished from the Untermarkt. Deri considered the spot where she had stood for a moment, a mischievous grin on his face. The Market tolerated many things, but it would brook no assault on its merchants, and it would in no way tolerate the breaking of an agreement under its auspices. That woman wouldn't even be able to set foot in the Market again for at least three phases of the moon.

Deri turned and began to whistle his way back toward the busier areas of the Market. Maurlocke would be wanting dinner soon, and there was no more time to spare on his own concerns. Not if he wanted to keep escaping notice.

Aurelia found herself standing in one of the more noisome sections of Smithfield Market. The ground squelched under her feet and hundreds of cattle shifted and lowed about her. Beside her, one of the cows lifted its tail and, with a bored expression on its face, added a copious deposit to the shifting mess beneath Aurelia's feet.

'I have no idea how he did that,' she told the cow, 'but that little abydocomist is going to regret it.'

The cow was unimpressed by her words.

12

Maurlocke was frowning. It was not an uncommon occurrence but every time it did occur, Deri had to force his muscles not to knot into a quivering ball of tension. Maurlocke was dangerous at all times. The frown shouldn't make a bit of difference, yet it did. So Deri took slow, deep breaths and tried to act nonchalant.

'Have you heard anything more of this so-called destiny in the Market?' yse asked abruptly.

'More, yes,' Deri replied slowly, heart hammering, 'but nothing *new*, if'n you take my meaning, Mystrer.' A bit of respect slipped out. Deri couldn't help it. It was likely as much use as a straw in a shipwreck, but he clung to it nonetheless.

Maurlocke's fingers slowly drummed across the desk before ym. Deri waited quietly. The merchant consulted two ledgers in quick succession before shaking ys head.

'No hints as of yet, and it's far too early to *pay* someone for information. Particularly as I still benefit from the increased amount of custom those ridiculous rumours are bringing me.' The merchant spoke more to ymself than to Deri. Or perhaps yse spoke to the pavilion around them. 'But it is clear from the movements of trade that *something* is here in the Market, something of great value, and it is curious that no one seems willing to claim ownership. Very curious indeed.'

Deri bit his tongue. The last thing he needed right now was for a stray word to rouse Maurlocke's suspicions further. Better to let the merchant ponder. Maurlocke was already far too interested, and that was *dangerous*.

'Now,' Maurlocke said after a long space of silence, 'you are to keep a sharp ear out on this, do you understand? I want to know every new rumour; I want to know when gossip shifts; I certainly want to be told the moment a merchant actually admits to holding this treasure. If they even dare. Her High Majesty must be in high dudgeon over this, after all. Do you understand me, boy?'

'Yes, Mystrer,' Deri answered quickly. 'Clear as crystal, it is.'

'Good. For now, matters are to my benefit. As soon as that destiny comes up for sale they may not be. I have no intention of allowing some upstart to eclipse me on a deal like this.' Maurlocke's skin flushed red-gold and the steel in ys gaze nearly struck sparks. 'When I find the holder of that destiny I'm going to take them for everything they're worth, and more.'

The temperature in the pavilion plummeted. Deri did his best to simply nod along with Maurlocke's words. He bit the inside of his cheek hoping the pain would help him focus. Then, as suddenly as ys ire appeared, it was gone.

'On to other business. You have your list of errands for the day; be about them.' Maurlocke flicked ys fingers dismissively in Deri's direction.

'Yes, Mystrer.' Deri nodded and all but bolted for the exit.

He needed to unload that merchandise, and soon.

✼

Deri was all but out of options. None of the merchants he had approached so far had been willing to buy the destiny from him, though he'd been smart enough to structure his dealings so that if they refused to buy his merchandise, Deri was entitled to walk away with their memories of the negotiation. It was safety, of a sort, but with this many merchants it would be wearing thin. Eventually someone would notice a pattern, someone would remember him arriving and be curious as to why they couldn't remember what he might have come for or what he might have left with.

Now he was down to the last merchant on his list, the last one he dared bring this offer to.

Karusine was a greasy little thing, pale as the underbelly of a fish and about as fragrant. Cold blue fire burned in her eyes and her mouth was overfull of needle-like teeth. One of the scavengers of the Untermarkt, preying on the weakest, the most foolish, snapping up the last threads that tatters came down below to sell: a last spark of hope, a final breath, a horrible death. She was a dealer in misery, but she would deal with anyone, and Deri had had little choice but to hope her hoard would be a match for his wares.

She was almost as filthy as the alleyway they stood in, a little crack of a thing winding its way between the backs of merchant stalls that didn't quite trust one another. The Market was full of dark crevices like this one. Deri had been in far, far too many of them in his quest for a buyer. It was hard enough eking out time outside of Maurlocke's watchful eye, but standing in slop and shadows was making things exponentially less pleasant.

Getting her to agree to sell him all memory of the transaction in the event that their negotiations came to nothing was as easy as it had been with all the other gutter merchants he had approached. They all assumed, quite correctly, that he was afraid of word getting back to Maurlocke. What they didn't bother to think was that he, a human lad, had managed to get his hands on anything as valuable as a royal destiny. Their loss. Literally. It was a grim sort of solace, revelling in the defeat of his opponents when he himself gained nothing from the exchange, but waste not want not.

'Well, little one?' Karusine was standing close enough that Deri was treated to the full effect of her bottom-feeding breath. 'What is it you have to offer?'

Her tone implied it would not be much, if anything. At least the look on her face would be gratifying. Deri tried to breathe as shallowly as possible as he pulled out the bundle of silk yet again and flipped the corner of it open, revealing a smooth stretch of glass and the destiny glimmering within.

Karusine's face did not disappoint. Her eyes, all four of them, bulged and her deathtrap of a mouth gaped, jaw as nearly unhinged as Karusine herself.

'What—? Where—?'

'That information isn't for sale,' Deri said, flipping the silk back over the bottle. 'I take it from your reaction that you are, indeed, interested.' He made it more a statement than a question.

'You've shown this to no one else?' Karusine's fingers twitched toward the silken bundle, a shocking loss of control in a merchant of the Untermarkt, even one so low as she.

'You and I are the only ones who know I have it,' Deri hedged.

Karusine was staring so intently at the bundle of silk she

didn't notice the slight prevarication. Deri struggled to keep his face impassive. It was tempting to take advantage of Karusine's distraction and press his luck, but his luck was running thin today.

'What would you offer me in trade for this piece?' He prodded.

Two of Karusine's eyes flicked up to his face. The other two remained fixated on the bundle of silk in his hands. She ran a purple tongue over her teeth and made a show of considering the matter.

'Mercy,' she said.

'Mercy?' Mercy was valuable but hardly something Karusine dealt in regularly. How she had amassed a store sufficient to – Deri noticed her claws flexing a moment before she attacked.

'Our negotiations are concl—' he shouted, but panicked, choked on the last word.

Deri reached out to *rip* the memories he was owed from Karusine's mind. He'd gotten a good deal of practice at this particular art today, but it was still not something he excelled at, particularly under the stress of facing a set of particularly lethal claws.

'Give me that bottle!' Karusine's voice came as if from underwater and Deri felt the wet touch of her power rising around them. 'Give it to me and I'll give you the mercy of a quick death. Don't make me work for it. I'll take the cost of the effort out in your hide.'

The last word! He'd missed it out. She was still negotiating. Negotiating in bad faith, but negotiating it was. Bloody bollocking loopholes.

'Concluded!' In retrospect, Deri would be less than proud of yelping that out, but in the heat of the moment, he managed to forgive himself. 'Our negotiations are concluded!'

Karusine gave no indication she intended to accept his word on the matter and lunged for the bottle. Deri frantically shot his hand out and grabbed, his fingers tangled about the memories he sought and he yanked. Karusine wailed and spun around, crashing into the back of a nearby stall.

Deri took the opportunity to make a strategic withdrawal. Better to not leave any sign he had been here when Karusine regained her footing. He ran.

Deri stumbled out of the dank little alleyway, the Market bright and chiming around him. He attempted to wriggle through the crowd, but his mind was so heavy it dragged at his feet and his usual nimbleness was quite beyond him. He was buffeted by the bustle of an imposing woman with raven-feather hair and ricocheted off the waistcoat of some minor nobleman with pits where his eyes used to be. Eventually, he managed to claw his way to a small nook formed by an uneven crossroads.

Karusine had been the last contact in the Untermarkt he could safely approach about selling the bottled destiny burning in his pocket. None of the bottom feeders would touch it for some reason, and he didn't dare approach any of the truly successful fey merchants.

He'd had no better chance finding a mortal to sell the destiny to. He'd been thinking only of the value, not of how many customers had the power to make such a purchase. Most that came through the Untermarkt were armed only with petty goods for petty trades. The truly wealthy rarely bestirred themselves to visit the Market, and when they did, they drew far too much attention for Deri to risk being seen approaching one of them.

No. There was only one avenue left for him.

'Jack Trades,' he muttered.

Immediately, the sound of bells filled his ears, a symphony of concern.

Beware, beware, there's danger there! rang out the Bell of Merchant Eyre.

There's danger, true, but hope there too! pealed Balfour's Bell with wild tattoo.

The Language of Bells was a thing of ringing tones, more than words, and though Deri spoke it with quite the accent, speak it he could. And if he wandered through the Market bonging to himself, well, he was still far from the most unusual sight on those cobblestones and drew next to no attention to himself in so doing.

'I don't like it any more than you do,' he told the bells, 'but Jack Trades hates Maurlocke. If anyone will risk partnering with me on this deal, it's him. I might even be able to get him to buy out my contract from Maurlocke if I can't get enough from the deal to buy my freedom outright.'

That thought was a new one. Deri turned it over several times in his mind. It wasn't what he wanted, but as a compromise, it had some potential.

And would you dare to be his heir? the question jangled through the air.

Jack Trades' heir. Now there was a thought. Mortals aged. They died. And then, provided they had anything to pass on, they left an inheritance. The Trades inheritance, now, that would be a thing. Best of all, it would mean Deri could become a merchant of the Untermarkt himself, when the current Jack Trades retired.

The more he thought about it, the more Deri liked the idea.

It would certainly solve his problems. So what if he had to wait a few years? And while Jack Trades might be a tyrant to serve under as an indentured servant, surely being his heir would be better. It was hard to imagine it possibly being worse than the years he had left dancing to Maurlocke's whims if he couldn't buy himself free.

Deri's feet began to move faster, his tread falling with less and less weight as the idea filled him with the buoyancy of possibility. Jack Trades' heir. One of the few humans allowed to be a merchant of the Untermarkt. It could work. Deri would make it work.

He just had to figure out a plan.

13

Deri took several slow, deep breaths as he approached Jack Trades' stall. Aside from Jack's own reputation, there was also the small fact that he and Maurlocke hated one another with a legendary passion. Their enmity fuelled dozens of tales, whispered in hushed tones in between business hours. Deri was sure he'd heard only the barest few fragments. He was too often in Maurlocke's company, and no one quite trusted him enough to believe he wasn't the merchant's eyes and ears in all things. No one wanted word of their gossip to reach back to Maurlocke.

That was one reason he was dressed as he was. A set of worn but respectable clothing, easy enough to acquire from a gladrags merchant. An air of mild prosperity, so popular with those who could not afford real wealth but wanted to save face with their social set. And a brief borrowing of Browderch's face in exchange for some faery wine. The lout was handsome, and he'd be sleeping off the effects of the wine far longer than Deri would be using his appearance. He'd never even miss it.

Jack smiled, leaning on the counter. His was a general-purpose operation, and as such, he had little need to advertise or display his wares. Chances were, if you wanted it, Jack either had it, knew who did, or could – for a very steep price – obtain it for you. He was human, as were the majority of the customers gathered about the stall. They flocked to him, drawn by the (false) belief that a fellow mortal would offer them better rates than the goblins. More than enough reason for his fellow merchants to distrust and dislike him. Jack was doing a brisk business. Deri watched for awhile, telling himself it was to get a sense of the way Jack operated.

He was handsome, and charming, though whether born with those gifts or the result of a canny purchase Deri couldn't quite tell. He was probably born with them. Deri had heard that every heir to the Trades name was chosen, not born. If you were going to pick yourself an heir, you'd pick the best one you could find.

That was the loophole the Trades family exploited to keep themselves in business. Very few humans were permitted to trade as part of the Untermarkt, almost all of them granted their places as part of the initial Treaty negotiations between Queens Elizabeth and Titania. Jack Trades was one of the few remaining. Most had been tricked, cheated, or driven out of their place at the Market. Few goblins were keen to share power or profits with humanity, and even less keen to share their secrets. Jack Trades endured because he had cleverly worded his part of the initial contract. Deri didn't know the particulars, but he knew every Jack Trades eventually grew old, and passed all his knowledge, secrets, and cunning on to a carefully chosen heir, who in turn took up the name of Jack Trades. What happened to the older Trades no one really knew, though it was whispered they had to be kept in a very fine house, with very strong servants, and cared for as babes for the rest of their days because in passing the mantle of Jack Trades along to their heirs, they passed along all their memories with their knowledge, leaving them all but mindless husks.

Deri preferred to think they retained a bit more personality than that, enough to enjoy their retirement, howsoever bizarre. But he'd dawdled long enough. He didn't have an excess of time before Maurlocke would need him again. Best be to it before the old merchant summoned him back. Another deep breath to fortify himself, a quick check to ensure his disguise was still in place, and Deri moved to brace the dragon in its lair.

'Jack Trades?' Deri took the most direct approach possible. 'I've a proposition of some value for you, should you like to step aside to somewheres private and discuss it, professional like.'

Jack Trades looked the disguised Deri up and down. He didn't answer right away. He gave Deri another, more measured look. Deri felt a chill from that regard, bone deep. Jack nodded once and flipped a sign over the counter, signalling to the other customers that he'd be back shortly.

'Through here.' He motioned Deri into the back of his stall. Deri's skin crawled as he passed the threshold. It practically buzzed with magic. It would have to, to keep out all the sinister spellcraft jealous merchants might sling Jack's way.

The back of the stall was not at all what Deri had expected. He had expected something more like Maurlocke's lair: expensive, tasteful, and every element calculated to put the merchant's customers at a disadvantage in negotiations. Maurlocke's chambers spoke of personal power, Jack Trades' were… homey. Or what Deri imagined homey would be like in a human family. He didn't have personal experience to go on.

The furniture was of high quality but chosen for comfort rather than to impress. The room was lit with candles rather than magelights or other ostentatious shows of power. Deri did steal a closer look at one of the candles to confirm it was enchanted, though not by goblin magic. Deri spotted the lines and runes of mortal magic, the kind practised by the magicians of the Uberseide. Sigils. Curious and strange. Most striking, however, were the portraits scattered around the room. They ranged from expert oil paintings to photographs. Deri counted seven different men, at least.

'I'm the eighth,' Jack said, setting a cup of tea near Deri's hand.

'Pardon?'

'The eighth Jack Trades.' He nodded to the portraits. 'I noticed you looking. People often do. And in case you were wondering, that's the man that started it all though, there.'

Jack pointed to the largest – though not by much – of the portraits. It was placed centrally, but not in such a way that it dominated the room or suggested it was any more important than the others. The man in the portrait looked nothing like Jack, though he was handsome in a similar way, and they shared the same dark hair colour, but there was something about the eyes that proclaimed a kinship. It was well, and eerily, done.

In that moment, Deri saw the genius of Jack's parlour – that it was no less dangerous in its way than Maurlocke's. Where Maurlocke went for an overt show of power, Jack was more subtle. As most of his customers were human, the surroundings would put them at ease, persuade them that Jack was one of them, that they were safe. Even the merchant's clothing fed into that illusion: the spotless black wool suit and shining white cravat, the understated touches of gold cuff links and watch chain – precisely what a prosperous man of business would be seen wearing topside.

It was an exquisite trap. Deri suddenly realised just how much danger he was in, dealing with this man.

Fortunately, Deri had been raised by goblins, not humans. He could do this. He had surprises of his own to unbalance Jack Trades.

'If you could remove your disguise, we can get down to business.'

Though perhaps not as many surprises to spring as he had thought. Deri cleared his throat, then kicked himself for showing any sign of nervousness.

'As soon as we agree to a price for your complete discretion in this matter. My concerns are… weighty ones.'

They haggled a bit, but such agreements were standard, so they quickly came to an arrangement that suited Deri. It put Jack on his guard, as Deri closed all the standard loopholes, but that couldn't be helped. If Deri was going to reveal who he was, let alone what he was carrying, he needed a measure of trust that he wouldn't immediately be turned over to Maurlocke.

Deri dropped his disguise. Jack did not look surprised, but Deri grew up in the Untermarkt. He knew how tight a grasp the merchants here kept on their reactions.

'One-time offer.' Deri lunged straight for the negotiating jugular. 'I want to be your heir.'

'And what do you have to offer that would tempt me to risk outright war with Maurlocke in buying out your contract to do so?' Jack didn't laugh at him. He trusted Deri had something that Deri, at least, thought valuable enough to make this offer tempting.

He'd survived seventeen years as Maurlocke's servant: that had to speak well of his abilities.

'The bottled destiny of one of royal blood.' Deri pulled the bottle from inside his jacket and set it on the table.

Whatever Jack had been expecting, that had not been it. Stunned silence reigned in the tent. Deri let it ride. The moments stretched on. Stretched too long. Jack was still staring at the bottled destiny, making no move to touch it.

'It's genuine,' Deri said, somewhat awkwardly.

'Oh, I know.' Jack's fingers twitched. 'I can tell that from here.'

'And?'

'What?' Jack finally turned his eyes to Deri. 'I'm sorry, what did you say?'

'Is the price sufficient?'

'Yes—' Jack spoke and Deri's heart leapt – 'and no.' – and fell a moment later.

'What?' Apparently it was Deri's turn for that particular expletive.

'This –' Jack pointed to the bottle, a mixture of fascination and caution warring across his features '– is too much. You've wildly overreached, my young friend. No one in the Market will buy this from you—'

'Because they're afraid of Maurlocke. But you aren't.'

'No, they won't buy it from you because it touches on the Crown. To have something like this, it endangers the Treaty with Faery itself. No merchant would risk that. Not Maurlocke, not me, no. Even the itinerant merchants that pass through – you'd have to find someone utterly mad or dangerously arrogant to risk Titania's wrath like this.'

'But this is a once-in-a-lifetime opportunity!' Deri's protests came out a bit shrill, even to his ears. 'How could anyone not want to take advantage of it?'

'Oh, many will want to. But you don't become a goblin merchant by being foolish, and dealing in something this hot is titanically foolish.'

'It could put the buyer on the Throne!'

'It could put them in line for the Throne, but they'd have to be incredibly well prepared or, as soon as they announce themselves, they're likely to face the business end of an assassin's blade.'

'I hadn't thought of that.'

'High-profile, black-market items are never worth as much as most people think. They're so dangerous to deal that it depresses the price. I'm surprised Maurlocke hasn't taught you that.'

'He doesn't teach me anything! Everything I know I had to figure out myself!'

Deri was too upset to notice how Jack looked at him then. His fists clenched, he stared down at the floor.

'Everything I've learned I taught myself, from watching and listening. You don't know what it's like, to want something and not get it. To be alone, with no parents, working for someone who cares absolutely nothing for you except as the value your service provides. I'm a person, not merchandise!'

It was all coming loose. The bottle Deri kept, deep within, where he poured all his fear, his rage, all the emotions he couldn't afford to indulge in if he wanted to survive, the cap was coming off and the contents threatened to overwhelm him completely. Deri stood, suddenly, grabbing the bottled destiny and stuffing it back into his jacket.

'I have to go. I need to get out of here.'

'I thought you wanted to be my heir.'

'I want to be free from Maurlocke. I can't wait another five years. You were just the easiest way out.' Deri's vision was blurring. 'But you said you weren't interested in making a deal, so our negotiations have concluded. Hand over the memories of this conversation, as we agreed, and I'll leave you to your business. I'm sure you have a lot of eager customers outside.'

'Just a moment.' Jack Trades held up a restraining hand. 'How about we renegotiate those terms a little bit. I said I don't want that bottle or the trouble it's going to cause, but I might want you as my heir. Perhaps even enough to take on the burden of partnering with you to make sure that bottle is safely – and profitably – dealt with. Perhaps.'

'Only a fool would barter for a maybe.' Anger, hot and white surged in Deri's throat, but he managed to bite back a sharper retort. Much as he hated himself for it, the hope of a way out of his predicament made the offer more attractive than insulting.

'Then allow me to offer you a certainty. If you can procure me three items, I will buy out your contract from Maurlocke and make you my heir. My word as a merchant.'

'What are the items?' Deri asked, a sinking feeling in the pit of his stomach.

'A taste of freedom, enough prosperity to last three lifetimes, and –' Jack Trades paused to look at Deri for a long moment '– a peal of laughter from Merchant Maurlocke.'

There it was. The other shoe had dropped. Maurlocke? Laugh? In seventeen years he'd never heard the like. But still. It was hope.

'Your word as a merchant?' Deri asked, to be sure.

'My word as a merchant,' Jack affirmed.

'I want it in writing, three copies, properly signed and sealed, because I'm taking the memory of this meeting with me when I go,' Deri said firmly. 'I won't risk—'

'Of course, of course.' Jack waved off Deri's demands. 'As you like.'

When Deri left Jack Trades' stall, hope and despair were warring in his breast. Make Maurlocke laugh? He might have more luck offloading the bottled destiny by himself.

14

'**R**eport.'

Dame Aurelia Steele, Knight of the Verge, stood in the presence of her superior, the leader of her order, Dame Eigyr MacNicol. Dame Eigyr sat behind her massive oaken desk, in the spartan office she had occupied for the better part of two decades. It smelled strongly of mint and black pepper, the aroma rising with the steam from a cup of fresh tea to the Dame's left.

'Yes, ma'am.' Aurelia paused to clear her throat. Was it her imagination or was the room around her shrinking? It wasn't terribly large at the best of times. Dame Eigyr did not see much use for voluminous space, particularly one she only occupied when she had little alternative. The stern glares from past commanders of the Knights of the Verge, staring down from portraits and paintings, did Aurelia no favours either.

'Well?' Dame Eigyr prompted.

'I managed to trace the princess's trail to the Untermarkt, where I lost it. Why it ended, I cannot say. There are any number of possibilities, from transformation to translocation.' Aurelia paused, conscious of her tendency toward complex terminology when under pressure. No. That was fine. She hadn't gone too far. 'I am confident, however, that the key to locating her also lies in the Untermarkt.'

'What further investigations do you propose?' Dame Eigyr took a sip of her tea.

'I can offer suggestions, but my recommendation is to have another knight assigned to retrieving the princess.' Aurelia winced internally, anticipating Dame Eigyr's reaction.

'Explain.' The word was cold and clipped as a frost fair penny.

'I had a run-in with one of denizens of the Untermarkt –' No need to specify it was a teenage boy '– and he tricked me. I can't seem to enter the Untermarkt. I've been barred.'

'Have you now.' Dame Eigyr folded her hands over her cup. No doubt the warmth was welcome. It was always chill and dark here in the warrens beneath the palace where the Knights of the Verge had their main headquarters.

Aurelia remained silent as Dame Eigyr stared thoughtfully into the middle distance.

'No,' she said finally, 'I'm not taking you off the case. The princess is your charge and it is your responsibility to see her returned. You have no other duties than this, for the present moment. It is highest priority. I will assign you what assistance I can, and equip you to commandeer more with what royal writs we may muster. No one else has your sharp eyes. You'll see things no one else might.'

Aurelia straightened at the words, and at the reminder of those supernatural enhancements she had been imbued with upon joining the Knights of the Verge. Those were not gifts lightly passed on.

'However, you are to employ the gravest discretion in invoking these writs. Her High Majesty has commanded we keep the flight of the princess as secret as possible, and has ordered the employment of various magics to conceal the absence of her wayward granddaughter. There are political ramifications to consider.' Dame Eigyr looked Aurelia up and down. 'I suggest you find a way back into the Untermarkt. You are our best chance to find and recover the princess without the matter becoming more than rumour.'

'Yes, Commander.' Aurelia didn't quite snap to attention, but she was still glad for the weight of the armour on her limbs. It added steel to her spine. 'I won't let you down.'

'See that you don't.' Dame Eigyr looked over the rim of her cup. 'Your career depends upon it.'

Owain jerked away as a drop of acid flew from the mechanised applicator and sailed over the sagging splash guard. It was rough work, jury-rigged into place by a workhouse child long since gone from the floor. It didn't stop everything, but every little bit helped. The smell when the acid sizzled into the greasy floorboards at his feet stung Owain's nostrils, and the back of his throat swelled with an acidic echo in response to the near miss.

'Pay attention!' Vimukti scolded from the other side of the machine. 'I don't want to have to come over there and suffer secondhand acid burns because you're gathering gossamer for the gentry! Especially with this lot. If either of the Graspars think you're the reason any one of these turns out less than perfect they'll flay you alive from the inside out. You know how they feel about work that gets sent to the Society of Magicians.'

'Sorry,' Owain said, stepped up to the machine and hefting the splash guard up, wedging a new chunk of wood into place to try and keep it there. 'I don't know what I was thinking.'

'More likely a who than a what,' Pierrick observed slyly from where he was standing, carefully plucking the finished etchings from the machine and wrapping each one in a layer of soft paper before stowing them neatly in a small box.

'Are you still mooning over your goblin lover?' Vimukti grinned.

'He is,' Pierrick confirmed. 'You can hear him whispering love poems to the wind at night, hoping the breeze will carry his words to Faeryland.'

'I do no such thing!' Owain's face flamed scarlet. 'And you tell me to pay attention? Look to your own work before one of you gets hurt.'

'I haven't been injured once,' Pierrick protested.

'You've not even been here a season yet,' Vimukti shot back. 'Give it time. It's inevitable.' Then she sighed. 'I wish it wasn't. It's so exhausting.' She snorted. 'Everyone calls it a gift, but I swear sometimes it feels like a curse. I can't do anything to prevent bad things happening. I can only react. It's so…' she ended in a garbled noise of anger and frustration.

Neither Owain nor Pierrick knew what to say to that, so they let the hiss and clang of the machinery all around them fill the silence instead. Several etchings were polished and packed before the mood shifted when Vimukti caught a glimpse of something behind Owain.

'That's her!' she said excitedly.

'Who?' Pierrick craned his neck. 'I don't see anyone.'

'I'm guessing she spotted the lady artificer that's working on the new machinery,' Owain said.

The splash guard slipped again. Owain quickly grabbed the bottom of it and hefted it up, the sound of acid splashing hot and sharp against the enamelled surface pittering in his ears. He jammed another wedge into place. At this rate he was going to run out of kindling before they finished the etchings.

'I can't believe she wears a dress in here.' There was a note of longing in Vimukti's voice. She, like all the workhouse girls, wore trousers. They were simpler and safer around all the machinery, and no doubt it saved the Graspars money to buy the ugly, coarse-woven trousers in bulk and garb all the workhouse children in them.

'I heard it's a special dress,' Pierrick said.

'It is.' Vimukti sighed, though the sound was lost in the nearby hum of machinery. 'I saw it myself! The hem got caught in those big gears that drive the steam polisher. Ripped a hunk of it right away. Tore like it was nothing but wet paper! Strangest thing. Then she did something with a device on her chatelaine—'

'Her what?' Pierrick asked.

'The thing at her belt,' Owain said. 'With all those chains on it. Each chain has something useful on the end, keys or scissors or clockwork things.' He looked away from Pierrick's querying glance. 'My grandmother had one, I think. It was a long time ago.'

Before his parents had sold him into indentured servitude.

Owain shoved the thought aside. It was less use to him than the slag the machines at the workhouse produced. At least that could sometimes be sifted for useful materials to reclaim. His memories of his parents weren't worth even that.

'Yes. Her chatelaine.' Vimukti was indecently enthused. 'She activated some machine and a little mechanical spider crawled out and went down to remove the hem of her skirt. It was good as new in no time.'

'And you said *I* was gathering gossamer,' Owain teased. 'I think you have it worse for the lady artificer than I do for anyone.'

Pierrick laughed and Vimukti sputtered in protest.

'Keep laughing, new boy,' Vimukti almost growled. 'Having to worry about healing one less person will really help open up my social calendar.'

Pierrick stopped laughing abruptly and Owain started. It didn't last long, however. Garog must have heard them and popped out from around a hulking bit of machinery.

'Back to work!' he barked. 'And pay attention! If any one of those etchings is marred, I'll take it out of your hide and add it to the time you owe in service!'

The three went very quiet and turned their full attention back to the machine in front of them.

Though, as soon as Garog disappeared, they dared grin at one another once more. An act of rebellion as much as any show of truly good humour.

15

Deri dodged through the crowds of the Untermarkt, Strá Dvari's laugh still ringing in his ears. The stout merchant (though how anyone could get so stout eating only music was a mystery beyond Deri's ability to solve) had been only too happy to deliver Maurlocke's goods to Deri for delivery.

'It's not easy, working with Maurlocke's gold,' Merchant Dvari had boasted. 'Even for a dwarf of Andvari's line! It's very temperamental metal. Ha! *Temperametal!* That's not bad. Not bad at all.'

Deri had been lucky to get away without either of his ears talked off. Now, for his pains, he had to lug a violin of solid gold the length and breadth of the Untermarkt – though it was curiously light for that much gold. Part of Strá Dvari's art, no doubt. Still, the long walk allowed him time to think on how he might complete the task Jack Trades had set before him and the luxury of a quick detour via his sanctuary.

Come in, come in! What's that you hold? rang Deri's gleaming bell of gold.

It was a charming, cheery little thing. Deri had taken great pains to acquire it in the hopes of learning the Language of Gold from it one day. That was a work in progress. For now, though, it also served as an admirable watchdog for his slowly growing hoard.

'A violin of gold, for the Merchant.' Best not to risk using Maurlocke's name around something crafted from gold. Deri was fairly certain that being a bell was more intrinsic to the little ringer's nature than the material it had been forged from, and thus it would be loyal to him, but there was no use tempting wyld Faery fate any more than he had to.

And learning to speak Maurlocke's native language was certainly worth the risk, if he could manage it.

'A pretty prize, for all it is not a nice, juicy mouse.' Bess trotted out from behind the rotting wardrobe in the corner. 'Which, by the way, you are now out of.' She licked her jowls.

'Your skill is admirable, Mistress Bess.' Deri placed the case carefully on the one good chair. The last thing he needed was to arrive with scuffed or dusty merchandise. Hands free, he began to rummage through his collection of bits and bobs.

What do you seek? Please tell me, tell! chimed Deri's little golden bell.

'Something to impress his young man,' Bess opined slyly.

Deri felt his face warm, just a touch. 'Don't be ridiculous.'

'Tis true! 'Tis true! You blush! You do!

'You need not rely on tricks.' Bess began cleaning an ear, feigning disinterest. 'The boy already likes you.'

'Maybe he does,' Deri said with a bit more heat than he intended, 'but I don't know—'

To win your love you must look dapper! Then in his bell you'll be the clapper!

'Quiet!' Deri barely managed not to yell. The last thing he needed was undue attention drawn to his one safe haven in the whole market. 'I don't even know which way he likes me, if indeed, as you say,' he glared at Bess, 'he does.'

In fact, not knowing was driving Deri more than a bit mad. He found himself thinking of Owain at inconvenient moments, multiple times a day. Remembering him. The way his voice crept shyly to the ear, at times. The way his skin glistened with the rain. The way his lips felt, pressed to Deri's own. It was distracting. He'd very nearly slipped up and delivered Merchant Maurlocke's lunch to Merchant Codex instead of the sheaf of blank contracts of indenture!

That would not have ended well for him.

The golden bell above his head tinkled its laughter. For objects without much in the way of discernible, uh, equipment, the bells took what was, in Deri's view, an unhealthy interest in the courtship of mortals and immortals alike.

'He likes you as you like him.' Bess paused between ears. 'A cat knows these things.'

'If I didn't know better, I'd say you were matchmaking,' Deri muttered.

Focused as he was on the collection of trinkets before him, Deri did not see the way Bess's eyes slitted in amusement, nor did he hear her say in the Language of Cats (which he did not speak in any case), *And wouldn't that be a thing if I were?*

When he did turn around, having found the item he was looking for, Bess was very much involved in grooming her paws.

'Well,' he said, 'as you are so invested in matters, perhaps I can persuade you to engage in a little delivery work for me?' He waved a stub of candle in his hand.

'Ah, clever kit.' Bess sniffed at the stub. 'A thief's candle.'

The little golden bell above their heads chimed a question.

'Thief's candle,' Deri replied, 'it burns in reverse, and traps all light and sound in a room within its wick. Good for concealing activities you don't want anyone to see. Although there is the little problem that burning the candle again releases the light, and the sounds and images captured by the candle the first time.'

'And you plan to use this to send messages back and forth,' Bess said, 'provided you can pay me to act as messenger.' She sniffed. 'I will require a favour, to be named at a future date, commensurate with the number of trips I end up making and how inconvenienced I am. One is not, after all, a mere messenger, and that workhouse is no place for a cat, no matter how much the humans love the smell of prosperity they imagine hangs about it.'

'Provided said favour does not interfere with my duties or otherwise endanger my life, livelihood, or wellbeing,' Deri qualified, almost automatically, though a part of his mind seized on the latter part of what Bess had said. A workhouse like the one Owain was bound to was a veritable font of prosperity, producing enough to support several families for years at a time for every week it operated.

Could he capitalise on that somehow? He did need a great deal of prosperity for his deal with Jack Trades.

He might even be able to do Owain a good turn in the process.

'Very well, provided you also provide one fresh brook trout per week I run messages,' Bess said, curling her tail neatly around her feet. 'And fresh cream on the dark of the moon.'

'Deal. Now, give me a bit of space,' Deri leaned down to light the candle and trap his first missive to Owain within its wick. 'I don't have much time. The good merchant will be wanting ys merchandise, and soon.'

He was not wrong in that estimation. Even as he spoke Deri felt a twinge, as if someone had gripped his spine with a hand of ice. Maurlocke was getting impatient. He'd best hurry.

It was torture, Deri reflected. Here he was, hauling a lifetime's worth of prosperity bound in four strings of twisted gut, but none of it advantaged him. It was yet another errand for Merchant Maurlocke. If Deri didn't know better, he might have suspected that Maurlocke knew of his deal with Jack Trades and was deliberately torturing him. But that was ridiculous. If Maurlocke knew, Deri would be in for tortures far worse than this.

Maurlocke too would be taunting him with a taste of freedom and the promise of ys laughter daily, both things the merchant had easy access to, and both things that were rarer even than the staggering amount of prosperity Jack Trades had requested.

No, Maurlocke didn't suspect. If yse did, Deri would know, and suffer for it.

'Ah, here he is,' Maurlocke said as Deri entered the pavilion. With an imperious gesture, yse directed Deri to place his burden on ys desk next to a familiar case of black leather. Deri did so, stealing glances at the other person standing near it as he did so.

It was a young woman, slim and elegant. Her dress was simple, and well-made, but a few years out of fashion. It had clearly been chosen out of necessity rather than out of desire. Deri had had plenty of practice telling the difference. Enough of both kinds showed up to do business with the merchant.

Maurlocke signalled Deri to open the case. It was a subtle thing, nothing a customer was likely to notice. It gave Maurlocke a greater mystique to have Deri seemingly magically know what to do. Deri remembered night after night of painful bruises, his wages for not picking up on the lessons swiftly enough.

The latches made a crisp sound as they flipped open under Deri's fingers. He raised the lid and spun the case with a bit of a flourish. He probably needn't have bothered: the violin inside was more than breathtaking enough without any embellishment from him. The gold caught the light and cast it back defiantly at all eyes that dared to behold it.

Cocky thing. Deri resisted the urge to shake his head at it and instead stepped back into the shadows. Whatever deal was underway, he knew his place.

'It's beautiful,' the young woman whispered.

'Indeed it is, Mademoiselle Therval,' Maurlocke replied, 'and to conclude our bargain all you need do is play for me.'

'That is all? So simple a thing?'

'As simple as that. You play as I instruct you, and none shall be able to resist your playing, after.'

Deri attempted to glean the niceties of the bargain being discussed. It was a game he sometimes played to sharpen his wits. Mademoiselle Therval was clearly buying some kind of skill – no, she already had skill. She wanted to increase it or control it or… something. He'd need to hear more. What Maurlocke was offering was… well, whatever the young lady wanted. But there would be a cost, and a steep one. Glory, as often as not, was paid for in abject misery.

He wondered briefly what this negotiation might look like at the stall of Jack Trades.

Mademoiselle Therval plucked the violin from the case with delicate fingers. Her hands caressed the cool metal as she did so. 'It's so light,' she marvelled.

'You'll find it has a devilishly good sound to it, as well.' The spectre of a smile played about Maurlocke's lips.

She tucked it up under her chin and walked her fingers across the strings a few times. It fit her grip as if made for her; though, for all Deri knew, it had been. Then the young lady's hands' stilled, one cradling the neck of the violin, the other grasping the bow, and the air in the tent stilled with her, as if the whole world were holding its breath.

'Play,' Maurlocke commanded, 'play until your fingers bleed.'

Mademoiselle Therval looked from Maurlocke to the golden violin in her hands. Deri could see her hesitation and he silently hoped she would surprise him and the merchant both, that she would put the violin back in its case, close it with a snap, and walk out of the pavilion, deal unmade.

But she didn't. Resolve came over her like a storm and she flicked the bow once to get the heft of it. It glittered in the candlelight. Maliciously, Deri thought. How could it glitter any other way, forged as it was from Maurlocke's gold?

Then Mademoiselle Therval touched bow to strings and Deri forgot all thoughts of the wickedness of gold. The music was a flame in the blood that made one glad to burn. Notes swirled through the air like sparks upon the wind and the mademoiselle…

And the mademoiselle, she was fire on the mountain.

She played with passion and it roared within her, consuming her.

Like a fire it cast a beautiful light and brought warmth to those near to it, but Mademoiselle Therval was not herself that flame. No, she was the tinder. Even Deri could see that the music would consume her.

She played fast and she played slow. She played jigs and reels and soaring arias and slow concertos. The music filled the tent, aching in its beauty. Later, Deri would discover that Maurlocke had secretly bottled every single note. But in the moment he just stood there, tears silently sliding down his cheeks, as a lovely young woman played her fingers bloody on that bloody violin.

Even Maurlocke was smiling, pure and uncomplicated. That alone was nearly enough to shock Deri out of the reverie the music placed him in. Could music be the key that unlocked Maurlocke's laughter? If he found the right strain, the right performer? Before he could chase the thought further, however, Mademoiselle Therval's performance ensnared him once again.

When she finally played herself to that stage, to the point where fat, shining beads of blood finally dripped from her fingers to fall upon the strings, the violin – the gold – thirsty as a desert for rain, sucked up each and every ruby drop, leaving not a stain upon the gleaming expanse of it. As soon as it did, Mademoiselle Therval stopped, her playing cut off like wheat before a scythe. She took a deep shuddering breath and Deri almost flinched at the naked pleasure of it.

'I can control it!' she said, delight shining through the exhaustion in her voice.

'And you will do so for the remainder of your life,' Maurlocke said.

Deri heard the unspoken words hovering just beyond: howsoever long – or short – that may be. Maurlocke and the mademoiselle concluded their business, which did not, apparently, include the lady leaving with the violin of gold. That was returned to the case on Maurlocke's desk before Mademoiselle Therval took her leave, still glowing from the experience.

'Close that.' Maurlocke flipped a hand toward the violin case with its golden treasure nestled within. 'It's ready for a specialist client. I'll need you to take it directly to Merchant Strangeways so it reaches the Continent as soon as possible.'

'The Continent?' Deri interest was piqued. It was unusual for Maurlocke to deal so far afield. His curiosity got the better of him. 'Which country?'

Maurlocke must have closed a very fine deal indeed because yse was in a good enough mood to answer. The merchant consulted ys ledger to write out the address for the shipment and replied with a single word.

'Georgia.'

Briefly Deri wondered what it would be like if he were indentured to a merchant operating out of one of the cyclical markets on the Continent, or even elsewhere throughout the Isles. He'd be so cut off from the mortal world, and he'd never have met Owain – no. Deri pressed his lips into a tight line. His contract with Maurlocke was many things, but at least it provided him opportunity.

He just needed to make sure he properly capitalised on it.

16

Vimukti had slipped away from overseeing the girls to watch the lady artificer at work. If the Graspars asked, she'd already planned to say she'd taken Indar's night shift punishment in exchange for her new hair ribbon. That was exactly the sort of idiotic pap the Graspars would buy into. Cleaning this particular bit of machinery was dirty, disgusting, and dangerous, but Vimukti was more than willing to risk a couple of fingers if it meant she learned something useful. And the lady artificer was very, very good at her job.

She had to be, Vimukti thought, moving about all this machinery in those skirts. Her long, elegant fingers were quick, too, and almost caressed the machinery as they worked. She had a way of working that was almost as if she could talk to the machines. She was forever making fine adjustments, coaxing improvements out of minute alterations. Vimukti also noticed, however, that she rarely smiled. No matter how many fixtures she fixed, there was always another, always a further tweak or adjustment. It must be exhausting, to never be satisfied with one's work.

'Miss Steele!' Missus Graspar appeared from nowhere.

Vimukti compressed herself into a handy crevice. The metal was hot on her exposed skin, but not burning, not yet. She could stand it for awhile.

The lady artificer – Miss Steele – carefully finished tightening a bolt, ignoring Missus Graspar until she was finished. That alone was worth the price of a few burns. Vimukti had never seen anyone make Missus Graspar wait before. Politely, no less!

'Yes, Missus Graspar?' The lady artificer barely spared her a glance. 'Do make it quick. Your machinery is in dreadful repair, and I have a good deal more to do to ensure everything is up to standard before I incorporate the new apparatus you've commissioned. But I can see why you have. It's a clever idea and will save you a great deal of money on replacing these ageing components if we can get it to work.'

Vimukti suppressed a giggle as Missus Graspar purpled. Oh, the old bag was angry! She swallowed that fury, however, and forced a pained smile. She must really need the lady artificer.

'Of course. I was simply wondering if there was anything we could do to help you speed up the process.' Missus Graspar glanced hungrily at the machinery.

Vimukti didn't know what the old harpy wanted it for, but she didn't relish finding out. At best, it would be more work, and more injuries. That was just the way of things.

'No. Well…' The lady artificer pursed her lips and looked intently at – almost through – the machinery. 'A dependable assistant would help. The less I have to search and find, the less I have to pause to send out for necessary materials or parts, the faster the work shall proceed. One of the older children, boy or girl, it does not matter. Owain, perhaps, or Vimukti. They both seem dependable sorts.'

Vimukti could see the gears grinding in Graspar's head. Owain would be hard to do without. There wasn't anyone else good at wrangling the boys. Production would suffer, and that meant less profit. If there was anything Missus Graspar despised, it was a lessening of profits. So Vimukti was thrilled when the old bat agreed to lend the lady artificer Vimukti's time.

Though normally even parting with Vimukti, whose healing powers were often needed at a moment's notice, was not something she would have expected Missus Graspar to agree to. What about the new machinery was so important?

A small bell rang. Miss Steele pulled a watch from her chatelaine and consulted it. 'Ah. Please excuse me. If I'm to be working through the night, I need to take an energy restorative.' She swept off without waiting for a response.

Missus Graspar positively sputtered, but, with the lady artificer absent, quickly turned to poking about the work she had been doing.

'How's it going, Mum?' Garog Graspar stepped out of the shadows, far too close to Vimukti's hiding place for comfort.

'Hm,' Missus Graspar grunted. 'She's making preparations. Repairing things as well. She's demanded Owain work as her assistant, though.'

Garog groaned in protest. No doubt because it meant he'd have to do more work. Vimukti felt no pity for that troll. She had to save it all for the boys who would be forced to deal with him more than usual.

'Quiet!' Missus Graspar glared at her son. 'I foisted the girl, Vimukti, off on her instead. And as soon as she's finished, it won't matter anymore. We just need to keep things on an even keel until then. I don't want any trouble, you hear me? We daren't risk anything that might endanger this project. The wealth we stand to gain—'

Missus Graspar suddenly turned and eyed the machinery around her suspiciously. Vimukti froze, heart pounding, as the workhouse tyrant's eyes slowly slid over the place she was hiding.

'We should only discuss this in the office. Come along, Garog.' Missus Graspar strode off, son in tow, bickering about the state of the workhouse floor.

Vimukti waited a long moment before slipping from her hiding place.

The mystery of what the Graspars were up to gnawed at her, but she almost didn't notice. Vimukti was far too busy thinking of all the things she might be able to learn from Mistress Steele.

And dreaming of how those things might win her her freedom.

'Hsst! Kit!'

Owain, not a dozen steps away from Missus Graspar's door, almost jumped out of his skin at the unexpected voice. He did a double take when he traced it to its speaker, the cat he had rescued in the Untermarkt the day he met Deri.

'Follow! Quick quick! Mustn't be seen!'

Bess turned and trotted down the hall, not bothering to look back to see if Owain followed. Bemused, Owain did. It was better than lurking near Missus Graspar's door where he might be discovered talking to a cat.

Though if Bess was going to issue orders, it would be nice if she could dispense some answers as well. How did she even get in here, anyway?

'A cat may go where she pleases,' Bess answered his unspoken question. 'And it is well for you that she might. Follow me. Quietly!'

Bess padded down the hall and around the corner, moving quickly along the western side of the building. Down the hall, up some rickety stairs, and finally to a narrow door. Owain moved quickly and quietly, the virtue of long practice, and eased the door open. The cat, for her part, had already wriggled through a gap in one of the planks of the door. Behind it, Owain found himself in a cramped and dusty attic room, jammed inelegantly amongst several support beams.

He had to be somewhere just under the roof. It was deeply shadowed, hard to see, but Owain could make out bits of old sacking and evidence of several generations of rodents taking refuge in this place. It had clearly once been used for storage, but it looked like those days were long past. Bess scampered up an exposed beam to a small nook formed by a zag of the roofing.

'Here,' Bess said, prodding at a small packet with one paw.

Coarse twine held together scavenged scraps of thick paper, forming a bundle that fit neatly in the palm of his hand. The knot untied itself at the merest touch of his finger and the string began to glow lightly in the dimness. Inside were two things: the stub of a black wax candle and a scrap of paper. Owain held the paper close to the glowing string. He could just make out two simple words.

'Light me,' he whispered.

No sooner had the words escaped his lips than the scrap of paper caught fire. Owain narrowly avoided dropping the thing and setting the room alight. The paper burned fast. It was nearly gone before Owain managed to touch it to the wick, doing so without thinking.

The candle sprang to life, casting ribbons of golden light throughout the space. The shadows it cast were the shadows of the Goblin Market, moving and whispering in tongues wondrous and terrible. It was the heart of the flame that caught Owain's gaze and held it fast, though. Deri smiled, his image flickering just above the wick.

'Hey, boyo,' Deri's voice called out of the candle, unexpectedly loud. Owain shot a nervous glance behind him. It wasn't likely he'd be overheard, but Garog sometimes wandered the workhouse, looking for children who might be shirking, or hiding, or otherwise trying to find a bit of peace or fun.

'Gotta talk fast. Don't have much time. You still owe me—'

'Quiet!' Owain whispered to the image dancing in the candle flame. Either Deri couldn't hear him or didn't care, because the image continued, uninterrupted.

'—two nights. I certainly enjoyed the first!' The image of Deri grinned wickedly and Owain couldn't help but smile. 'Show me your London. Show me what you like to do for fun. And boyo? Make it good. I'd hate to have to sneak out for nothing. Maybe we can manage something for Samhain. They have to give us some freedom for the holiday, after all, and—'

A floorboard creaked outside the door. Owain instinctively reached out and snuffed the candle, heedless of burns or hot wax. The room fell into darkness once more.

For several moments Owain sat in the darkness, hardly daring to breathe. If Garog had heard – Owain bit the inside of his cheek and focused on the pain. No. Garog couldn't have heard. Owain would already be feeling the strap if he had.

He relaxed, just a bit. His hand throbbed where the wax spattered it.

'What in Danu's name?' he wondered aloud.

'A thief's candle,' Bess's voice drifted through the dark. 'Made from thrice-burned wicks and tallow rendered with torn-out tongues. They come as candle stubs. Light one, and it sucks the light out of a room, so that only the one who lit it can see. They melt in reverse, growing taller as they seal up the secret deeds done by their light inside them. But light it again and everything done under cover of darkness is revealed in the flame.' She sniffed. 'I've not seen one used to send messages, before. But then, not many know of them, aside from thieves and the merchants who cater to them. You'll have to light it again to hear the rest of the message.'

'Rest of the message?' Owain fumbled with the idea.

'Keep up, kit,' Bess said. 'You watch all of the message. Figure out what you'd like to say back, then relight the candle by pinching the cold wick and recording your own message. That way you can send a reply.'

Owain turned the potential of it all over in his head. Somewhere in the dark he heard a light thump as Bess jumped down to the floor. When her voice sounded again it was disturbingly close.

'I'll even deliver it myself, for the price of a saucer of milk.'

17

Aurelia hunched within her cloak, small protection against the deepening chill of the year. Samhain was nearing. The year turning and turning, and she was no closer to finding the princess. The cobblestones beneath her feet were damp with the ever-present autumn rain. She squinted against it, a weak, spitting thing almost more mist than rain, as she sought out her destination.

The sign above the door of Rhys ap Arwyn's establishment simply read *PAWNBROKER*, flanked either side by three overlapping rings of gold. The modesty of it all was surprising, if one was acquainted at all with the shop's owner. A small silver bell over the door tinkled as Aurelia pushed her way inside.

The interior of the shop was labyrinthine, composed of many small aisles and a towering forest of shelves bedecked with merchandise of all kinds. Clothes and tools of various low-wage trades predominated, though larger antiques and furniture were scattered throughout. More valuable items rested behind ensorcelled glass and locks of brass. Battered watches and cheap jewellery angled to catch the light next to a set of silver barber's razors.

Small closets or cubicles lined one wall, havens of privacy for those who came to the pawnshop out of desperation and preferred the rest of society not witness their need. They were, for the most part, empty. One was occupied by a young woman and her mother. Another framed a young dandy in his faded-glory finest, a bruise on his cheek hastily covered over with cosmetic paste and a dusting of rouge.

Rhys was behind the counter, wrapping a painting with fine brown paper and twine. The shop was dual-facing. The entry Aurelia had come through opened on a side-alley, the better to provide discretion. Through the door behind Rhys, one could slip into the other half of the shop, the presentable face turned to the high street, where the cream skimmed from these shady transactions could turn an 'honest' profit.

Aurelia donned an air of authority and reached for her service badge. Best to start off with a show of force. Though none had yet to be able to amass sufficient evidence, Rhys was suspected of all manner of black-market dealings, high-end forgery, and confidence games. The constable Aurelia consulted on the way had been most helpful. She glanced around at the sparsely populated shop. The witnesses wouldn't hurt. Her quarry was more likely to comply, and quickly, to limit the damage his business would take when he was seen talking to an authority figure such as herself.

Rhys was escorting his art aficionado to the door, murmuring pleasantries. The pawnbroker gently propelled his customer out the door with a laugh and a light hand in the small of his back. With equal grace, he turned to Aurelia.

'Dame Steele, I've been expecting you.' Rhys smiled, too charming, and motioned for Aurelia to follow him. 'If you would follow me, I have what you require just through here.'

He moved before Aurelia could speak, forcing her to follow him. Her fingers clenched around her badge, then loosened, letting it fall back into its pocket. She stalked after Rhys, ignoring the other customers for now.

The room he led her to was small and spartan, a slightly more elaborate version of the privacy cubicles in the shop proper. There were chairs, but Rhys did not offer her one. Rather, he crossed his arms and offered her a smile just a hair's breadth from insouciant.

'How can I be of assistance, milady?'

'I would have thought you knew,' Aurelia said pointedly. 'You said you had what I required.'

'Ah, that. Well, I couldn't let you barge into my establishment and throw your weight around. How would that look to my clients? That is what you intended, was it not?'

It was, but Aurelia was hardly going to give him the satisfaction of admitting it to him. Her eyes narrowed. 'I don't think you've any right to make assumptions as to my intentions. Not when you're hindering an agent of the Crown on a sanctioned quest. You may think you're clever, that you're impressing someone with this little act, but heed my words: you, or anyone else who gets in my way, will sorely regret crossing me.'

'Threats? That's rather unbecoming to a—'

'I'm no lady,' Aurelia snapped.

'—knight,' Rhys finished. 'Particularly a Knight of the Verge. What would her High Majesty say?'

Aurelia took a breath. This wasn't working. Clearly this was not the first time Rhys had been shaken down by someone in authority. She needed a new tactic.

'Fine. Tell me about the Goblin Market.'

'Why ask me? I'm no goblin merchant, after all.'

'But you're the closest thing to it, up here.'

'Alas, I'm only human.'

'So am I, but that doesn't mean I haven't picked up a trick or two.'

Rhys raised his eyebrows eloquently. To Aurelia's dismay, she felt her cheeks begin to flush. She crumpled the paper and shoved it into a pocket.

'I don't have time to spar with you, Rhys. Please, tell me what you know. The princess may be in danger.'

'More likely threat than threatened, that one,' Rhys replied. Something in Aurelia's manner must have touched him, however. He looked ever so slightly uncertain.

'Please,' Aurelia said simply.

Rhys looked at her for a long moment, two fingers beating a staccato tattoo along his cursedly elegant jawline.

'What do you need to know?'

'I need—' No. That was giving too much away, too quickly. 'One of the knights has been barred from the Market by some means we do not understand. It's interfering with some assigned duties and it's not something I'm prepared to allow to continue.' That should do as an opener. She looked to the pawnbroker expectantly.

'Barred? How do you know?'

'Disappeared from the Untermarkt and reappeared in London. Just like that. Poof. Now, can't find the entrance, even when following someone else headed to market. Sounds like someone who has been barred or banned or otherwise banished from the premises to me.'

'Not just to you,' Rhys laughed and shook his head. 'Did this person violate an agreement whilst in the Market, perhaps?'

'It was an impossible choice,' Aurelia snapped. 'As I understand it.' She forced a cough and cleared her throat.

'I'm sure it was.' Rhys looked at her speculatively. 'So, you –' he held up a hand to forestall Aurelia's protest '– *this person* broke their word and the Untermarkt won't allow them in. And you want me to provide you with a way to – that *said person* – can regain access, yes? Am I understanding correctly what it is you want here?'

'Correct. And I know your weaselly mind either knows, or can come up with, a way to do it.'

'Careful! You might give me an overinflated opinion of myself!'

'Too bloody late for that.' Aurelia didn't bother muttering beneath her breath.

'Say I can help you. Hypothetically.' Rhys smiled. 'What's in it for me?'

'The gratitude of a Knight of the Verge.'

'Not bad, but I prefer something a bit more concrete. What's your budget for matters like this?'

'I could make you tell me.' Aurelia closed her hand around the hilt of her sword.

'Actually, you can't,' Rhys replied mildly. 'You can't force me to help, because if you do, the Market won't let you back in. You got kicked out for not sticking to a deal. Your only way back in, by necessity, has to involve you keeping one. You've got to deal with me, and then you can deal with the Market.'

Aurelia considered that for a long moment. Rhys might be

bluffing, but it sounded too ridiculous to be anything but the truth. It certainly fit with what she'd seen of the Untermarkt so far. Cursed place that it was. No, the pawnbroker might be clever, but Aurelia's instincts were telling her she had to play this game.

'This sounds like it's going to be expensive.' The words were like lemons in her mouth.

'Oh, I assure you, it will be. Nothing this valuable comes cheap.'

'It's just access!' she protested.

'And how much would most of the fawning courtiers pay for access to the High Queen's ear?'

'This isn't the High Queen!'

'No. It's something much more powerful. It's the Untermarkt.'

Aurelia viciously quashed the urge to shove Rhys' head through the door.

'Now that you're listening, shall we do business?'

'What do you want?' The words ground themselves out between Aurelia's teeth.

'I want you to sit for a portrait.'

'You want what?'

'You,' Rhys pointed to Aurelia, 'to sit,' he pointed to a model's stool, 'for a portrait.' He pointed to his easel. 'You can have it afterwards, of course, no strings attached.'

Aurelia considered that for a moment. What was the angle here? Was he just trying to throw her off her game? He'd already done so by anticipating her opening gambit.

'That's an odd thing to ask me.' Aurelia decided to play for time. 'Tell me why you want to paint me.'

'Do I really need a reason?'

'I doubt very sincerely that you are the sort of gentleman that ever does anything without at least three. So I ask you again: why do you want to paint me?'

'Honestly? Because as soon as I have, I can quite nicely and legally say I've been portraitist to the High Queen's household. As a family bodyguard, you do count, you know.'

Well, she hadn't expected that answer. She hadn't expected any answer. Still, maybe she could use it.

'That seems quite the valuable thing,' Aurelia observed, too casually. 'Perhaps you'll come out of this owing me a favour.'

'How quickly did you need access to the Untermarkt, again? Or was there someone else you were planning on asking about the next step in the process? Someone else versed enough in how the Market thinks to guide you to make the right bargain with it?'

'You talk about it like it's alive.'

'Isn't it, in a way? It's got some sort of awareness, certainly. Enough to bargain with directly. *If* –' Rhys drew out the word, '– you know how to speak with it.'

Aurelia rolled the offer over in her mind. It was true the Market seemed to have a mind of its own. And she couldn't see any way in which a painting of her could be used to further some kind of nefarious underworld scheme or shady deal. Was the forger and black marketeer trying to go straight? Did it matter? No. Not if it got her what she needed.

'I pose in my dress uniform or not at all,' she said at last. There were limits.

'Of course.' Rhys inclined his head graciously.

'Now, what is it going to cost me to get back into the Market?'

❋

'Three days of life for three moments of fiendish inventiveness. Final offer.' Deri crossed his arms defiantly across his chest. 'I may be mortal, but I am Merchant Maurlocke's servant and I can make no better – nor worse – deal than that.'

The mention of his mystrer's name did it. Merchant Bright-Sigh huffed resentfully but nodded.

'Done and done,' she said. Her voice echoed prettily from her cowl, but naught could be seen of her face save for two pinpoints of golden light. 'Out of regard for your mystrer, boy.'

Deri didn't call her on that little lie. It cost him nothing, and needling her on it might earn him an enemy he could ill afford. Besides, he had what he needed for the next step in securing the prosperity he owed Jack Trades.

Hopefully.

'Anything else? A spark of genius? Nine sips of sly wit?' She looked Deri up and down. 'Not that you need the latter. Your mystrer has trained you well.'

Wit. His mystrer. The laughter he still needed to coax from those lips of gold somehow.

'How much laughter can the wit elicit?' he asked. 'I might have a use if you can guarantee the one who sips of it can get the laughs they want from their… audience.'

'Ah, a guarantee will cost you!' Merchant Bright-Sigh leaned over the counter, eyes flaring with renewed interest. 'Just what do you have to offer in trade?'

Deri grinned and dove back into negotiations with almost indecent relish.

✽

Owain huddled over the small golden wick of the thief's candle. Deri's voice, though soft, seemed far too loud in the small space, though there was no one else near the tiny attic nook. Owain was reluctant to snuff the flame, however, for the sound of his voice if nothing else.

'...won't be able to slip away for Samhain, I'm afraid. Merchant Maurlocke requires me in attendance at a revel. It'll shave thrice as much time as it takes off of my contract, but I'd still slip out to meet you if I could. Sadly my contract isn't as flexible as yours.'

Owain's body sagged, like a puppet whose strings had been cut. He'd been thinking about Deri constantly. They had so little time together. He rubbed his chest, but the phantom ache in his heart stubbornly refused to leave. The Graspars had been ratcheting up productivity recently, driving the children even more relentlessly than before, and now the holiday date he'd been looking forward to for weeks was also gone? Owain's fingernails cut into his palm. There were few enough moments of rest and respire in the workhouse, nevermind things to look forward to. But this – Owain sighed. It should be expected, really.

The candle continued to burn, and Deri continued to speak. In fact, the longer the candle burned, the clearer and larger the image of him grew, until he might as well have been standing there in person. Owain could see sweat shining on his forehead.

'I don't want to waste too much time. The candle can only catch so much within its wax.' Deri's eyes were sparkling. 'And after that disappointing bit of news, well, boyo, I think we've earned ourselves a bit of relaxation, don't you think?'

Deri undid the ties that held his collar and cuffs and pulled the shirt off over his head. Owain froze on the pile of sacking, not quite believing his eyes. What was happening? Was this really what he thought it was?

The look in Deri's eyes said that yes, it very much was. The candlelight glistened on his skin, the whole scene suffused with a golden hue. Owain swallowed when Deri hooked his thumbs into the top of his trousers.

'Knowing you, you're still standing there, gawping. I suggest you get comfortable, if you haven't already, because this is not the kind of message you take with tea and guests in the parlour.'

Owain began fervently struggling with the ties that held his own clothing in place.

'I hope you lit this candle when you were alone,' Deri's smile was positively rakish, 'but either way I'll be putting on quite the show!'

18

Pierrick slunk through the forest of machinery, which still reeked of hot metal but had gone quiet for the night. Ahead of him two figures moved through the workhouse, lanterns shining brightly and casting a plentitude of shadows to shroud his presence.

The Graspars were arguing. Not loudly, but not so quietly that he couldn't hear them. When Garog had checked on the dormitories, something in Pierrick whispered to him to follow, to see if the foreman might reveal any secret ways in to – or more importantly out of – the workhouse grounds.

'…let me lay into the lazy gits,' Garog was complaining, 'then they'd work harder.'

'We don't need them to work harder right now,' Missus Graspar snapped. 'We need them to work smarter. I don't want any accidents distracting that lady artificer! We need her to complete her work more than we need the piddling little squelch of wealth we could wring out of the brats by terrorising them.'

'And when she's finished, we'll have enough wealth to own this whole city.' Greed dripped from Garog's lips like spittle – though there was plenty of that as well. There always was.

'Provided she completes the work,' Missus Graspar said, voice terse. 'Provided she doesn't realise what we really want the machine for. Provided we can make the necessary alterations ourselves.'

'We can,' her son replied. 'We bought enough bottled genius from the Market to—'

'Cost a pretty penny too, that.' Missus Graspar moved her lantern and peered at a stack of crates in a corner. 'So much profit invested.'

'But it's worth the chance. You said so!'

'Yes. If all goes to plan every wealthy and powerful individual in all of London – all of the Kingdoms – will be lining up to throw money at our feet.'

Pierrick's heart stuttered at the thought of that much wealth. Worse, that much wealth in the hands of these two. What did the machine do that it could produce so much money? Turn lead into gold? He waited to see if the Graspars would drop any more clues, but the two had moved out of earshot.

There was a blank expanse of floor Pierrick would need to dash across if he wished to continue following them. He hesitated, weighing the risk, and felt a cold trickle of sweat inch down the small of his back. The promise of any chance at freedom, howsoever small, lightened his feet, impelling him across the gap.

Pierrick made it safely to the other side without being seen, but not without being heard. Even as the brass pillar supporting the gear-shaft caught his weight and arrested his momentum, a fragment of brass clattered quietly to the floor from the impact.

His blood chilled, freezing him in place.

'What was that?' Missus Graspar turned and squinted into the shadows.

She was looking directly at Pierrick! He froze, hardly daring to breathe as the old woman tried to pierce the darkness with her gaze. The woman and her son both ran their lanterns about the area in front of them, but that had the effect of casting more shadows.

'Who's there?' Garog demanded. 'Come out, you little ratbag. Now. Or I'll string you up with the bedsheets you should be under right now.'

Pierrick fumbled quietly around until he managed to find another fragment of brass. Then he threw it wildly toward the far corner of the workhouse. It clanged off the edge-grinder and the Graspars turned to look in that direction.

Then he ran.

Deri kept his head down as he moved through the streets topside. The cobbles were slick with traces of the Fog but his feet were sure. As he went, one hand stayed deep in his left pocket and clenched around a bundle of nine carefully wrapped metal plates. Each about the size of his palm and each with a different design worked onto it in gold. A sigil, the magician had called it. Deri traced the pattern on the top plate over and over.

As works of mortal magic they were inferior and incomplete. Deri couldn't afford that level of spell work. But with a dash of faery magic from the Market and a dram of ingenuity, he had managed to fill in the gaps and create something that should just about do the trick. He'd named it a prosperity siphon, and it would get him one-third of what he needed to become Jack Trades' heir.

Or at least, it had better. The bloody things had cost so much he was a year further from his freedom than he had been yesterday, judging by his swiftly dwindling hoard of wealth.

He ran his fingertips over the design again. The gold felt more like samite to the touch, and the *zing* he got from the contact tasted like mutton fat with hints of a whole day spent lying in bed. Once in place they would gather up a small portion of any prosperity lost to inefficiency or a broken machine or the like.

And Deri had many such 'likes' to discuss with Owain.

The young man haunted his thoughts. The way he had smiled as they walked along the Thames. The sound of his voice and the easy conversations. The feel of his rain-wet hair between Deri's fingers and the hardnesses pressed between them as they kissed. The way—

Deri shook off the thought. He was getting distracted again! And he was here.

The workhouse loomed above him, dour as anything. And you would think that something so imposing would be, well, somehow vigilant but Deri slipped into the workhouse Owain lived in with surprising ease. Well, perhaps not that surprising. The place was designed to keep people in, not out. For Deri, it was as simple as walking in with a group of deliverymen. Because the workhouse was also a factory, there were always shipments headed in and out, and the guard at the gate was far more interested in talking and drinking that he was in keeping track of a bunch of deliverymen.

'I was told the latest order had arrived?' A tall woman in flowing skirts was talking to the gate guard.

Deri noticed she had a chatelaine dripping with tools. Some kind of artificer, then. Hadn't Owain mentioned something about that? New machinery? Sounded *prosperous* to him. Deri smiled.

'It's not, ma'am, I'm sorry. Girl must have had it wrong.' The gate guard didn't even bother to check his board.

'Vimukti may be young, but she is incredibly conscientious and does not make a habit of being wrong. I suggest you check again.' The lady artificer plucked a lens from her chatelaine and twisted it in the direction of the lazy guard.

'Right away, ma'am!'

Deri looked away before he could get caught. The last thing he needed was to draw more attention to himself. He fell back into his unassuming role.

The key was a purposeful walk. Not slinking, not shady, but a steady pace that ate up the ground and said to anyone watching that Deri had a place to be, a purpose, and he knew what it was. There were enough others about, children and adults, moving in the courtyard that no one gave him a second glance.

Good. Deri picked an ebb in the flow of humanity, then moved quickly to a corner of the courtyard and crouched down. There had to be a loose cobblestone here somewhere – aha! Deri's fingernails protested as he pried the stone up and carefully slipped one of the prosperity siphons beneath it, before replacing the stone and doing his best to cover his tracks. One down, two more to go out here in the outer courtyard.

A part of him cringed to think how much of his wealth he had sunk into creating these things. Wealth he now proposed to leave just lying around for anyone to find. If anything went wrong... but no. That was the risk. Merchants took risks, and if they were smart about it, profits followed. Deri pushed himself up.

Brushing himself off, he moved about the place, working carefully to blend in with the other children. Not that there were many children about, and those that were mostly carried parcels and boxes to and from the large central building that dominated the courtyard. As Deri glanced that way, a bell near the top of that building rang the hour. Aha! Perhaps he had an ally inside the walls, if he could figure out how to get up there.

There didn't seem to be any way to access the other half of the courtyard except through the large building with the clock and bell. It had to be the central workhouse floor. There were certainly enough crates being hauled in and out. Deri slipped in among a handful of children returning to the workhouse from delivering crates to the gate. That earned him a couple glances, but everyone was more tired than curious.

Inside was trickier. Everyone here had a job, knew exactly what they were supposed to be doing. He'd have to be very careful not to draw attention, because if he was caught, he would have no idea what to say. There had to be some stairs around. If he could find those he should be able to make his way up to the bell tower, such as it was.

He didn't see a way to get to the stairs, but he spotted a storage area by the edge of the workhouse proper. Time to see if he could find a loose board to slip the next siphon under. They'd work better exposed, but then they'd be found, and Deri couldn't have that. It was a matter of minutes to find what he needed, and then four of his nine siphons were in place.

Deri picked up a nearby sack and slung it over his shoulder. Hopefully that would help his camouflage. The place was deafening;

hopefully that would cut down on incidental conversation. He hugged the walls as close as he dared and began walking the perimeter of the workhouse floor. Best not to get in anyone's way if he could help it.

The flash of brass and the whirr of the machines kept distracting him. Deri was no full-blown merchant of the Untermarkt, able to assess the value of something with but a glance, but he'd grown up there and watched Maurlocke do it often enough that he could make some educated guesses, and the sheer volume of wealth being produced by these machines was staggering. Even with the costs of the machines, of supporting the children and purchasing the contracts of indenture, the owners of this place must be prosperous indeed. More money than a normal person could spend in at least a hundred lifetimes.

And with a bit of luck, he could swipe more than enough to make Jack Trades happy and get him one step closer to freedom.

Before he could pursue that line of thought further, someone grabbed him by the arm and pulled him through a doorway. It was Owain.

'What are you doing here?' he hissed. 'Are you trying to get yourself killed?'

'Don't be so dramatic,' Deri said, trying to put the throttle on his pounding heart.

'If either of the Graspars find you here—'

'Then let's just make sure they don't, hmm?' Deri grinned wickedly. 'There have to be places around here we can go to have a quiet word or two. Assuming you won't be missed.'

Owain shot a glance around the workhouse floor.

'I'll be missed if I'm gone too long, but come on. There's a storeroom off the kitchen that should be safe for the next hour or so.' Owain gestured for Deri to follow and wouldn't allow him to say anything until the door was safely, quietly, shut behind them.

'What are you doing here?' Owain demanded, a delighted smile painting his words.

'I wanted to see you, since our Samhain plans fell through.' Deri grinned. 'And I may have an angle to work that will help me, and maybe even provide a solution to your Graspar problem at the same time. Well, I can give you a weapon you can use against them, at least.'

'I—' Owain paused. 'You what?'

'Have you ever heard of working to rule?' Deri continued blithely. 'That is, doing exactly what you are told, precisely in the worst way? You should be able to do that, not violate your contract, avoid the punitive clauses, and still hamstring this place.'

'I'm intrigued.' Owain smiled. 'Tell me more.'

'Yeah, tell us more.' Vimukti appeared from behind a crate. 'I want in on this, goblin boy.'

'How do you—' Owain sputtered.

'It's obvious who this is.' Vimukti fluttered her hand in the air as if waving away objections. 'No offence.'

'None taken,' Deri said, bemused. 'Though there will be a price for you to hear what I have to say.'

'I wouldn't expect anything less.' Vimukti smiled, too many teeth. 'What do you want?'

'Help me find good places to install these.' Deri flashed one of the prosperity siphons. 'Out of sight, so no one can see them glow, but near to the bigger – no, the more profitable – machines. I've got two more for the perimeter of this place, then three that need to go in key locations, like the management office or as near to where they store the really valuable stuff as possible.'

'Done,' Vimukti said before Owain could object. 'I can think of a couple places to show you. Now, tell me more about how this is going to gut those greedy—'

'Vimukti! No! You shouldn't risk—' Owain tried to regain some control of events.

'Don't tell me what to risk.' Vimukti levelled a finger in his face. 'I've had enough of the abuse this place heaps on us, enough of being the one to clean up the mess after someone gets hurt. I want to do something. Anything to make those bastards squirm. I want that, and you can't afford to take it away from me.'

'What?'

Owain looked to Deri for support, but he just smiled and shook his head. Owain was on his own in this one. Owain looked back at Vimukti, who stood unmoving and resolute.

For a long moment no one spoke.

'You know,' Deri said casually, not looking directly at either of the two people glaring at one another in front of him, 'desire – knowing what you want – is a good guide. It will rarely steer you wrong in the Untermarkt, for example.'

Owain looked at Vimukti and she raised an eyebrow, refusing to uncross her arms.

'Fine.' Owain sighed. 'Just – be careful?'

'I'm always careful!' Vimukti said, light and pleasant as anything now that she'd won. 'Besides, goblin boy can tell me what I need to know to be safe. Right?'

'Right,' Deri said cheerfully. 'Now then! Let's get these beauties in place! I'll explain everything to you as we work, and then Owain and I can steal an hour or so for ourselves before I have to dash away.' Deri shot the other young man a glance that could have struck sparks from a glacier. 'Don't want my little visit here to end on anything other than a sweet note.'

19

Aurelia worried at the edge of the letter in her hand. Silvestra was going to kill her when she found out. Of course, a voice inside whispered that Silvestra wouldn't have to. Rhys could easily forge a replacement. Her sister need never know.

No. Aurelia straightened. She was already compromising enough making this deal. She wasn't going to add forgery and deception to that list.

'Alright,' she muttered to herself as she stood in the midst of Covent Garden Market, 'let's get this over with.'

She began to walk. She moved past all manner of vegetables and fruits, flowers and herbs both decorative and medicinal. The wild and varied congress of the vegetable kingdom surrounding her in a temple of bounty. The riches of the earth above.

Below. She needed to get below. To get below, she needed to appease the Untermarkt. To appease the Untermarkt, she would have to apologise and strike a bargain.

'Hear me, O cache of wonders undreamed.' Flattery gets one everywhere with things fey in nature, or at least so goes the common wisdom, and all it cost Aurelia was a small measure of her pride. 'I come seeking you to tender my apologies.' Best not call them heartfelt. Lying wouldn't really serve, at this juncture.

'I come to bargain. In return for my restored access to the Untermarkt and all its beauties and terrors, I offer this: a token of love unbroken, promises kept, and trust unbetrayed.'

The air quivered, at that. There was no other way Aurelia could think to describe it. The air quivered and the shadows near her feet grew suddenly darker, as if flooded with something that was more than the mere absence of light. She had the Market's attention.

'My father loved my mother dearly, and she him. At least, so I was told. I don't have very many memories of my mother. She left us before I was terribly old. This is one of the few things we have left of her.'

Aurelia stopped – or found herself stopped – in front of one of the arched passages that arrowed through Covent Garden Market. The air had thickened. The sounds of London were at an unexpected remove. Instead, the wilder, alien chorus of the Untermarkt came softly to her ears.

'…fresh and succulent! Come buy!'

'…to direct me to the stall of Jack Trades! I can offer…'

'…outrageous! Highway robbery, I tell you. Why…'

Aurelia shook off the distraction, focused again on speaking to the Market itself.

'This is the last letter she wrote him during their courtship. The one where—'

All her breath left her at once. How could she give this up? She knew the lines by heart, the elegant loop of her mother's neat script. The careless flick over each 'i' where her mother's love for

157

her father overcame decorum and precision. That single sign of passion, she knew it so well.

Well enough to let it go. Aurelia and Silvestra had their memories. The princess was in danger. Her safety meant more than a folded square of ink and paper. It had to.

Aurelia held out the letter.

'Do we have a deal?'

The letter vanished from her hand.

Deri and Owain managed, somehow, to talk quickly even as their hands roamed all over one another, soaking in every sensation after what seemed like three lifetimes of deprivation. They talked strategies for cutting into the Graspars' bottom line. One might not think that such talk would be erotically invigorating, but one would, in this case, be very wrong.

'Whoever decided that contracts of indenture should bar us from courting needs to be drawn and quartered.' Owain bit off each word after coming up for air.

'Sadistic,' Deri agreed.

'Sweet Danu, but can you imagine what it would be like if we were free?' Owain raised his arms and draped them comfortably around Deri's neck, while feeling the warm circle of his lover's arms around his waist. 'No more small snatches of time, able to take full days together, simple. Easy.'

Deri's mind worried at the problem. Some part of him always did, it seemed: running trades and calculations, looking for loopholes, ways out or around the various strictures that bounded his life. The problem was the contract of indenture. He was working to free himself, and that was no easy feat, but Owain's contract couldn't be as hard to wriggle out of as his own. Could it?

'Still, a taste of freedom is better than none,' Owain said.

'What did you say?' Deri went very still as his mind leapt into action.

'A taste of freedom—'

Deri leapt up from the pile of sacking and began to pace. Was it a coincidence? Or had Jack Trades somehow seen that this moment would happen? He had been the one to sell it to Deri, after all. Was this a trick or a trap? Was it Jack Trades helping him? No. That didn't make any sense. It wouldn't be a proper test if Jack Trades helped him. Besides, it would be too much like giving something away for free. No merchant would do that.

The problem was the contract, not what Jack Trades may or may not have done. The contract was both the problem and the opportunity. A taste of freedom – it depended how much wriggle room there was in Owain's contract. In all the workhouse children's contracts.

'If I could just see it!' Deri punched the air irritably.

'See what?' Owain asked.

'Your contract of indenture.' Deri's voice walked the line between patience and exasperation. 'If I could just get ahold of it, or an exact copy, I'm sure I could ferret out a loophole and free you from it.'

'What if there isn't one?'

'Isn't one what?'

'A loophole.'

'Oh, there is always a loophole. There has to be. When was the last time you saw something truly perfect?'

'Right now, actually,' Owain said, his eyes catching Deri's.

Deri actually blushed.

'Stop it! I'm trying to be serious here.'

'So am I.' Owain stood up and stalked toward Deri, the first hints of a mischievous smile stealing across his face.

Deri swatted half-heartedly at Owain but didn't actually resist as Owain slid his arms around Deri's waist and pulled him in tight. Their faces hovered near to one another's, not quite touching, flushed with one another's breath. Owain leaned in, just a touch, just enough to brush his lips against Deri's, teasing.

'I'm sorry. You were saying?'

Deri heard the smile in Owain's voice, the challenge. Well, far be it for an apprentice of the Untermarkt to leave such a challenge unanswered. He could multitask, keep his mind working whilst his hands were otherwise occupied.

A merchant's hands are as nimble as a craftsman's: Deri's slid skilfully up to catch Owain's face, pulling it close.

'You should be careful when challenging a faery merchant, my lad.'

'Oh really.' There was little light in the cramped attic but Owain's eyes caught and sparkled what there was.

'A kiss is just a kiss, but we know the secret of distilling far more than alcohol. We can twine sunshine and moonbows into our lips, or dust them with the essence of finely wrought ballads. Such kisses are more than mortal, and can quite overwhelm the senses, and leave you transported beyond time's touch for a hundred years.'

'You wouldn't dare do such a thing.'

'Would I not, my lad? I'm warning you, I'm a dangerous fey creature.'

'Oh, that you are.' Owain reached up and grabbed Deri by the cravat. 'But I've tamed you, plumbed your secrets. I know the words writ on the inside of your heart, and I know there is no way you would deprive yourself of my company for a hundred years.'

'What's a century? A hundred years to a steadfast heart are but a day!'

Owain stopped Deri's mouth with a kiss. It was unlikely anything else he might attempt would be similarly effective. When they parted, Deri looked at him.

'Rude,' he said. 'You interrupted me.'

'I could tender my insincere apologies, if you'd like.'

'Now what might I do with those, I wonder?'

'You're the merchant. You tell me. Are they worth anything?'

'To me?' Deri's eyes flicked to Owain's for a split second. 'Everything.'

'But our lives aren't our own to sell or give.' Owain pulled back as reality began to reassert itself.

'They might be. We need to see your contract. Think of it!' Deri pulled Owain close once more. 'If I can break your contract, you would be free. You could walk away from all of this.' It was to Deri's credit that in that moment, he gave not a thought to what that might cost him in terms of his chances at stealing the workhouse's prosperity for his deal with Jack Trades.

'Even if you could find a loophole and end my contract, you'd still be bound by yours.'

'One thing at a time,' Deri smiled mischievously. 'One thing at a time.'

'That's not the only thing.' Owain glanced at the door, rather than look at Deri. 'I'm not sure I can leave, knowing everyone else would have to stay.'

'Then I'll break all the contracts,' Deri promised impulsively.

'What? How?' Owain eyed Deri warily.

'I need to see your contract to be sure, see as many of the workhouse contracts as I can.' Deri paced, his mind running faster than his feet could carry him, particularly in these confines.

'That won't be easy. The Graspars keep them under lock and key.'

'How often have you been in Missus Graspar's office? Have you seen where she keeps the contracts? How they're locked away?'

'I—' Owain blinked through the barrage of questions. 'I'm in her office regularly. Whenever one of the boys does wrong, I'm usually on the hook for it as well. The contracts, I saw her lock mine away, and I've seen some of them sitting out, if she plans on using them to, uh, make a point.' Owain went faintly green at that.

'I need to find something good to trade you for these memories,' Deri mused aloud.

'My memories?'

'Well, I suppose I could scout the place myself, but it's much riskier. Safer to buy your memories and just know the place. They'll not be quite so clear for me as for you, but it'll be better than working from just a description.'

'If you're sure about this,' Owain said reluctantly.

'Trust me.' Deri flashed a smile. 'What could go wrong?'

20

Owain prodded his new memories, sitting so strangely in his head as they did. Deri said the edges would soften soon enough, feel more natural. Owain turned them this way and that, enjoying the sensation of knowing new things. He understood the Untermarkt much better now. He smiled fondly, remembering the time he had slipped pursuit – or rather, the time *Deri* had slipped pursuit. Owain shook his head. It was odd having another's remembrances. He was glad they were Deri's, at least. That made it different, somehow. Made him just a little different. In a way he liked, because it brought him closer to Deri.

And it brought Deri closer to him. He was by no means being as careful as Owain would be, but the tiniest modicum of reserve had tempered Deri's usual cocky approach to things, what with a few shreds of Owain's past dealings with the Graspars now taken up residence in Deri's mind.

They were lurking not far from the door to Missus Graspar's office. Deri had provided the means to see in the dark, for a few hours at least, so they need not betray themselves with light before it was absolutely necessary. Owain had guided them around the squeaky bits of floor. Deri had an enchanted key that would get them past the door. It would turn in any lock, but only once in each case. Once they unlocked the door, the key couldn't be used to relock it. But that was a problem for a bit later.

Satisfied they could make their approach, Owain slipped up to the door, motioning for Deri to handle the lock. The key was a slim silver thing, and the eye slid away from the end of it, could not fix upon any one shape. It turned in the lock with a satisfying click and they were in.

Watch the door, Deri's eyes said to Owain before he moved toward the massive desk hulking in the shadows made slightly less dark to their charmed eyes. The aspiring merchant made short work of the lock protecting the desk and began a quick, efficient search for the lockbox containing the workhouse's cache of contracts of indenture.

'Gotcha!' Deri whispered triumphantly after a few minutes' work.

Owain resisted the urge to add to the noise by shushing him. Telling a cat or a fey lad like Deri what to do was an exercise in futility, and was like as not to produce more of the behaviour one wanted rather less of.

Now things got decidedly more dangerous. While the charm that allowed them to see in the dark was fine for walking corridors and unlocking doors, it was insufficient to make out ink on parchment. Such fine detail required light. Light meant risk. Risks had to be managed.

While Deri had been searching, Owain had been mitigating their future risks. A length of twisted and knotted rags had been untied from about his waist. One length went along the bottom of the door, to block light there. Another small scrap into the keyhole of the door. The rest of the door itself would, hopefully, not betray any light. It was a solid, well-fitted door. The Graspars spared no expense when it came to protecting their gains. No, the corners to be cut were not in security, or their own comforts – Owain had, to his misfortune, seen the small quarters the Graspars maintained for themselves – economies were found and ruthlessly trimmed when it came to the rest of the premises, to the never-seen or easily replaceable bits of the workhouse. Like the children that powered its machinery and produced its goods.

'We good?' Deri looked at Owain, poised to light the candle inside the thief's lantern he held.

'Yes.' Owain was still nervous enough to only risk the barest minimum of syllables.

Deri lit the lamp and quickly narrowed down the shutter, focusing the light. Quickly, but not so quietly as Owain would like, he began rifling through the contracts. He chewed endearingly on his bottom lip as he searched.

'These are all fairly standard,' he said after awhile. 'Boilerplate stuff, it shouldn't be too hard to find a loophole in your – ah! Jackpot!'

Deri drew a single contract from the stack, Owain's. Owain briefly wondered why it had been so deep. Missus Graspar made a habit of threatening him with it on a regular basis. Didn't she?

No, Owain realised. He'd been around Deri long enough to start thinking like him, just a bit. He'd even some of Deri's market memories. He was starting to develop an eye for the finer of details. While Missus Graspar always had what appeared to be a contract handy on her desk, she wouldn't actually risk the real things being exposed like that, and she certainly wouldn't go to the trouble to dig out the contract of each boy or girl summoned to her office. Why bother when just the threat would do? She probably hadn't laid a finger on Owain's contract since the first – and last – time she'd used it to sorcerously torment him. The lesson would last. It had lasted. Owain had the sudden urge to burn the whole place to the ground.

'I can get you out of this,' Deri broke through the red clouding Owain's mind. 'It'll take a little doing, but I can do it.'

Still shaking from anger, Owain was unprepared for the effect a surge of hope would have on him. He'd so rarely felt the real thing. His knees buckled and he had to reach out to the desk to steady himself. As soon as his hand touched the wood of it, he realised his mistake – the place was enspelled against the workhouse children, and the merest touch of his hand was enough to trigger the enchantments warding Missus Graspar's desk.

A great wailing went up and what Owain had always taken as the natural grain of the wood began to writhe and crawl. The long brown strands looped themselves over his hand, binding him fast to the desk, and began to crawl up his arm.

'Deri!' Owain frantically tried to pull himself free.

Deri was swearing, stuffing Owain's contract back into the middle of the pile and returning the lockbox to its place. His lips were moving continuously as he worked, but the wailing was so loud Owain couldn't hear anything else.

'Deri!'

'I've got you! Just hang on.' Deri ran his hands along the wood of the desk. Apparently the spell was so focused on Owain it left Deri quite unmolested. Owain found that incredibly unfair for some reason, his mind seizing on that detail almost to the exclusion of all others. So he was watching quite closely when Deri pulled something from an inner pocket and pressed it into the surface between them.

There was a sudden absence of tension and Owain stumbled backward, no longer tethered to the desk. There was no time for relief, though. The eerie brown whatever-it-was was still crawling slowly up his arm.

'The window. Quickly!' Deri barely managed to leash his voice to a whisper.

Owain made for freedom, struggling with the latched shutters with his off hand, as his dominant one was bound up in a creeping curse. He managed it, biting his tongue to suppress a sob of relief.

'Go, go!' Deri hurried him out the window and closed the shutters behind them, latching them again with a stiff piece of wire.

Together, the two of them made their slow way along the thin ledge circling the higher floor of the workhouse. It was a short distance to the place where an outthrust roof provided a broader highway, to where a nearby wall provided a long step down to the ground, but they made it. Owain's attention focused to a point. That point telescoped wide as soon as his feet touched the ground and too much rushed in.

Deri caught him before he hit the ground.

'No, no, come on, stay with me,' Deri whispered urgently. 'We've got to get that curse off your hand, and quick. That's the sort of thing someone can track, and we can't have them find it on you, can we? Come on, focus.'

Owain nodded. 'Just help me to the wall. I need to sit.'

Deri eased Owain onto the low line of brick and stone and

glanced around. No sign of anyone. Yet. He began to pace wildly, muttering to himself and patting down all his pockets.

'What are you doing?' Owain tried to focus on Deri. The throbbing in his hand made it difficult. He looked at the strange graining staining his hand, but the sight made his head swim threateningly, so he quickly returned full attention – as much as he was capable of, at least – to Deri.

'I don't have anything that can break a curse that strong.' Deri's answer to Owain was as much thinking out loud to himself. 'So, if we can't break it, what can we do? We can't hide you. They'll track you down. We can't run. Same problem. You're in no state to run, anyway.'

Deri grabbed Owain's hand, his eyes raking over the curse mark. Owain had to fight back the urge to vomit. No. No way. He may be cursed but he'd be damned if he was going to throw up in front of – or worse, on – Deri.

There was shouting inside the workhouse. It sounded like Garog Graspar. Owain winced. No, it sounded like Garog Graspar crossed with some kind of bloodhound. The brute was positively howling with rage.

'Fuck. They're coming. I was right, they've got something that lets them sniff out the curse mark. We've only got a couple of minutes. Right. No help for it then.' Deri took Owain's chin and drew his face up so he could look him in the eye. 'We're going to have to make a deal. I'll take that curse, and run with it. That way you can stay here, safe from suspicion, and we don't have to worry about them pulling some kind of shenanigans with your contract. But a deal needs two sides to it, or it won't work. When I take the curse, I'm doing you a great good, or myself a great evil, depending how you look at it. That means you have to do something roughly equivalent for me. I don't have the skill to take this on for a pittance. The closer the trade, the easier for me to work the magic. So, no time to think, just go with the first thing that comes into your head, right?'

'What?' Owain was struggling to follow. Deri talked quickly at the best of times, and now was more like the worst of times.

'Nevermind. Just tell me. Would you rather give me your good luck, or take on my misfortune? I'm not sure how long it will last. With the power of this curse, it'll be at least a moon's turning, maybe a season's.'

'I, uhm, wait, what's the difference?'

'I don't have time to explain, love. Please. Just pick one. We don't have time.'

Deri's eyes burned so intently into his. It was so hard to think. So he didn't. Owain surrendered. He went with his instincts.

'I want to take your misfortunes away, as much as I can. I want to tear down the world and build you a better one.'

Deri's eyes went suspiciously shiny, at that. He lunged in and kissed Owain, hard. The taste of his lips was so sweet at first, but when he pulled away the sweetness took on faint bitter overtones.

'Sorry about that,' Deri said, eyes twinkling, 'easiest way to make the exchange. Transference requires touch, with that particular nasty piece of work.'

Owain looked at his hand. It was clear. Point of fact, his head was rapidly clearing as well.

The sound of boots hitting the stairwell suddenly echoed through the room.

'Quick! Get back to the dormitory! I'll lead them away.'

Before Owain could protest, Deri was gone.

21

Deri ran through the night. He had the advantage of the streets. He'd scrimped and saved and traded and tricked and worked and explored until he knew the city nearly as well as any of the cabbies that plied their trade along the busy thoroughfares. He dodged and weaved, wriggled through tiny alleyways and scampered up and over walls. It wouldn't be enough to lose Garog or the enchanted nose he used to track the curse throbbing in Deri's hand, but it would buy him some time. And with enough time, Deri was sure he could figure out a way to escape.

The howl rose up behind him once again. Garog was closing in. Deri put on a fresh burst of speed, all from his own reserves, for now. He wasn't ready to dip into the stamina he'd bartered and hoarded, not if he didn't have to. His mind darted ahead, scouting potential routes, anything that would confound Junior Graspar's bloodhound nose. The Thames was a vast, glimmering presence to his left. If he could find a boat that would really give him some time to work with.

Deri squirmed through the broken boards of a fence, a gap too small for a full-grown man. He dashed down an alley and came out onto a street busy with nightlife. Deri wove through the people, calling out compliments to the local ladies and gents of the night. He had no idea if the sounds and scents of other people would slow or confuse Junior's nose, but it was worth a shot: if nothing else, the sights would be a distraction. From what he knew of Garog Graspar, the man was hardly a paragon of virtue. Or, you know, any good at remembering what he was doing for any extended period of time.

He was already deep in the Eastside, what the well-to-do oft called 'Darkest London'. Murder and mayhem were easy to find here, safety and solace in short supply. But, faintly, over the noise and the laughter, floating along the water you could just hear the occasional ship's bell ringing from the Docklands beyond.

The Docklands. Deri felt the distinct sensation of a plan beginning to form in the recesses of his mind. He deliberately ignored it and ran on. It was the kind of thing that if he thought about it in advance, he knew it wouldn't work. It would show up – or not – when he most needed it. The rest was up to fortune. He turned his feet to running after the sound of the bells, though. That, at least, sounded like safety to him.

A shout went up, right at his neck. He'd slowed too much, and Garog had almost caught up to him. Deri swore and dipped into his emergency stash. A bit of silk ribbon wrapped around his finger and his form changed from that of a young man to a young woman. That bought him some time, as Garog Graspar stopped dead in confusion, looking around in the crowd for Deri. Typical. Humans relied almost entirely on sight. Even when endowed with magical senses, they'd ignore them as soon as they could rely on their eyes. It was instinctual. Garog would be after him by nose again, soon enough, but until he realised he had to, he'd keep looking, and give Deri time to slip away.

Deri shook as he ran. That had been too close for comfort. Time to lay on some distance. Deri found a straightish street headed in the general direction of the Docklands and sprinted down it. When the howl inevitably went up behind him again, he ducked into an alleyway and began dodging in and out of back streets. Once he nearly tangled himself in someone's washing line. Fortunately, he came away with no more than a rope burn and a rather fetching bonnet tangled about his left hand.

He was almost near enough to hear what the ships' bells were ringing to one another. Garog Graspar was close behind him. The bloody bastard must be using some form of stamina-boosting spell or alchemical draught. Deri's lungs were burning, and his youthful energy was all but spent.

The curse mark had to go, and soon. Garog was too close on his heels for Deri to find and persuade some sailor to take on the curse in exchange for… Deri didn't even know what he might offer. His mind, like his body, was beginning to flag.

Think! What would Jack Trades do? He had no idea. He needed clarity, pure and bright as a belltone.

A belltone. Deri looked up. There had to be a ship nearby, ready to leave soon. He ran along the docks, looking for the telltale signs of onloading cargo. Not that one, not there, no, no, yes! Deri spent several precious moments of his lead waiting for the sailors to clear enough for him to dash up the gangplank. He dodged and danced across the deck, sailors shouting all around him, peals of sound ringing from his lips as he ran for the ship's bell.

Take this curse from me and I shall polish a hundred bells by hand, I swear it, Deri rang out in the Language of Bells.

The bell rang back assent and Deri lunged for it. His fingertips just managed to brush the smooth metal, the wood-like grain that patterned his hand slipping from his flesh as a patina of deep tarnish, before he was grabbed roughly by the collar and dragged bodily away, down the gangplank and off the ship.

'Ere now, we havenae time for stowaways, nor girls aboard this ship!' The sailor shoved Deri roughly away.

Deri for his part, was confused for a long moment, before he remembered the disguise he had donned to dodge Junior Graspar. The sailors would see tresses and a skirt. He yelled something unintelligible at the sailor and shook his fist in mock anger, silently ringing out his thanks to the ship's bell, now holding that pesky curse.

The sailors returned to work as soon as they saw Deri wasn't going to make another break for the ship. Deri turned to leave and came face to face with Garog Graspar. Well, not quite face to face, but too close for comfort. Junior was just a few lengths away and charging fast. Deri could feel the taste of freedom dying on his lips. If he didn't move fast, he was done for.

Taste of freedom. *Danu's dugs!* Deri swore and hurriedly pulled out a small vial. He concentrated on that taste and then spat into the vial, stoppering it just before Garog Graspar's meaty hand closed on his arm.

'Gotcha!'

The taste of freedom evaporated from Deri's mouth. Fortunately he'd already bottled it, though unfortunately at the cost of actually losing his freedom. Now it was up to his wits to get him out of this mess.

This time, Deri remembered he looked like a helpless young woman. He grabbed a deep breath and screamed at the top of his lungs. Garog shook him. Deri screamed again.

Sailors are rough sorts, true, but many hold good hearts within, and, even though the young woman had just tried to jump ship, enough of the nearby dockhands took exception to the sound of a damsel in distress to come to her aid. The look on Garog's face as a handful of angry sailors bore down on him was priceless.

'Help me! Please! He's been trying to assault my virtue all night!' Deri hammered it up a bit, warming to the role. 'Please, help me!'

Garog didn't have to let Deri go. He could have held tight and attempted to run, taking blows from the sailors. Junior Graspar's enhanced strength and stamina might have seen him through.

Garog didn't make that choice though. He let his anger take hold, and as it did, loosed his grip on Deri. And you can bet Deri took full advantage of that slip to slip away into the night, the sounds of brawling swiftly fading behind him as he ran.

22

Merchant Maurlocke was conversing with the tent when a Knight of the Verge swept in like a storm. It was a very polite and constrained storm, but a storm nonetheless. She positively buzzed with tightly controlled energy.

'Merchant Maurlocke,' her words and demeanour bright and dangerous as lightning, 'I had hoped to speak with you regarding a matter that requires both urgency and discretion.'

The fabric of the tent rustled, as if in a wind.

Yes, Maurlocke replied in the Language of Gold, which was a thing of glimmer and gleam, well suited to hidden meanings and veiled comments, like the ore concealed deep in the rock and the darkness of a mine, *she is taking a good deal of care with her words and manners. She's been burned by another merchant already, and quite recently. I can smell it on her.*

'Indeed?' The merchant spoke aloud in response to the knight's unquestioned question. 'I am quite amenable to such a discussion. May I offer you some tea?'

'Thank you, no,' the knight replied. 'The urgency of my business is such that I regret I must decline.'

No, Maurlocke answered the tent, *she doesn't seem all that regretful, does she?*

'Of course. Perhaps you would be so kind as to enlighten me as to the particulars of your specific needs?'

The knight hesitated only a moment, but Maurlocke easily caught the gap in intent. Best put the knight at ease and secure an early advantage while at it.

'You have my word as a master merchant. You can trust my discretion.'

'I have no doubt as to the quality of your trust, Merchant Maurlocke—'

Oh my, there is fire in this one! Polite and deferential on the surface, but the edge on the truth beneath those words! Maurlocke smiled. This was going to be a good deal more fun than expected.

'—but I have had no such assurances from the other entity party to these discussions.'

'I beg your pardon?' A cold line crept down Maurlocke's back like tarnish.

'You've been speaking with someone or something else whilst I've been here. I'm not sure the language, or the entity, but your manner has been that of one speaking.'

The knight glanced around the tent, but not at the tent. Maurlocke relaxed ever so slightly. This woman was observant, nothing more. She was still on goblin territory. In Maurlocke's demesne. Perhaps she should be reminded of that.

'You have very sharp eyes, Dame Steele.'

'You know my name.' She didn't seem ruffled. 'Am I so well-known down here, or were you expecting me?'

'I can assure you, Dame Steele, you are quite unexpected.'

'Might we dispense with the sparring and get down to business, proper? As I mentioned, time is of the essence.'

'Of course. I'm always happy to expedite matters. After all, time is anything but cheap.'

Maurlocke favoured the knight with a sharp, bright smile.

Aurelia had the grace to look nervous.

'What is the price to keep our dealings goblin secret?'

Goblin secrets were bound with magic. They could only be known by a certain number of people, usually one or three. Even were the secret-keeper to blurt the information out in a crowded marketplace, only one person there would hear it – and the information so distributed would entirely vanish from the mind of the speaker, no longer the secret's keeper.

'A secret for a secret, my dear child,' Maurlocke said. 'I'm sure you have a few that would be of interest.'

'I'll only trade you my own,' Aurelia said sharply, 'None touching on the royal family.'

'So conscious of your duty! Commendable.' Maurlocke hid disappointment. Put on a diffident expression. 'Yes, that is acceptable.'

'Then we are agreed.' Aurelia glanced about the tent. 'Do you live alone in this tent?'

'With the exception of my servant, yes.' Maurlocke saw no reason to educate the knight about the awareness of metals or the living nature of certain bolts of faery cloth.

'Your servant?'

'A boy,' Maurlocke said dismissively. Best set her mind at ease. 'You need not worry he might overhear. He is of little value, alas. I keep him about to fetch my meals and tidy my quarters.'

'He's not here?'

'Not at present. A merchant of my stature has many errands to deal with. Allowing my servant to fetch and carry frees up my time for more valuable conversation.'

'Of course, forgive me.' Aurelia picked up Maurlocke's pointed reminder of their business. 'I will not purchase overmuch of your valuable time, particularly as you have already said the information I seek is of so little value to you.'

'I beg your pardon?' Something was wrong, here. A miscalculation had been made.

'Your servant. You said he was of little value. All I require is some information regarding him.'

Maurlocke's mind began to race. What did a Knight of the Verge want with Deri? She had to know the boy would offer no hold over a master merchant, no sneaking insight into the business dealings within this tent. The contract of indenture would see to that.

'My servant? I'm afraid I don't understand.'

Maurlocke played for time. The Master Merchant was unused to being set on the back foot like this. It was neither a pleasant nor welcome feeling. The price for it would be extracted from Dame Steele soon, and from Deri again later. The tent walls rustled.

'I have reason to believe he witnessed a key event pursuant to my current… investigation.' Aurelia said, dancing around some secret.

'You mean the missing princess,' Maurlocke said bluntly, using the secret like a bludgeon, attempting to knock Aurelia off balance. It was time to seize back control of negotiations.

'How do you know about that?' Aurelia all but blazed.

'I'm afraid that answer will cost you rather more than information about my servant.' Maurlocke casually adjusted a gleaming coil of silver and gold hair. 'Shall we add it to the negotiations?'

It was delightful watching the knight think. Her face was as still as the air before a storm, but tension flashed from her like lightning bolts. How far could she be wound before she snapped or recoiled?

'I'm afraid my time is not without limit, Dame Steele. What is it that you want?'

'I want your servant to answer my questions, truthfully.'

'Truthfully?' Maurlocke laughed. 'Truth is rare and expensive. You're more likely to get *honestly*, on your budget, and even then not much of that. Particularly here.'

'Fine. Honestly.' Aurelia's eyes were hard. 'And I don't care how you know about the princess.'

'Oh, come now. Lying like that hardly befits your station, Dame Steele. But we can leave such matters aside from our current negotiations.' Maurlocke feigned thoughtfulness. 'How many answers did you want? I presume those are more valuable to you than questions.'

'Of course there's a difference.' Aurelia pressed her lips into a tight line.

She was really very good at avoiding giving offence. It almost looked like a polite smile, rather than a frustrated grimace.

'Three answers,' she said finally, 'each of them honest and pursuant to my search for the princess.'

'Very well.' That was an easy enough needle to thread. The knight had failed to specify that the answers be of use. After all, an answer of *I don't know* was entirely honest and pursuant to her search. 'Now, to the matter of price.'

'I've enjoyed this encounter very much, Dame Steele, so I'm going to offer you a deal. Three honest answers from my servant in exchange for three dishonest ones from you. A pittance, that.'

'I won't break any oaths or lie to anyone important to me.'

'Of course. I would expect nothing less. Those terms are acceptable.'

'And you must collect them within one turning of the moon, or forfeit any right to them. I won't have an obligation like that hanging over my head indefinitely.'

'That limits the value considerably. I would need a guarantee of merchandise of greater or equivalent value in exchange, should the questions not prove useful in that time.'

'Such as?'

'Well, as you place such stock in honesty, I'm sure you would have no objection to paying, say, a month of dishonesty. I warn you, you would be quite unable to lie directly to anyone for that time.'

Aurelia considered.

'Unless, of course you would prefer to relax the limits on oathsworn and loved ones?' Maurlocke suggested.

'No!' The knight snapped. 'I accept the terms provided I get my answers before I leave this tent.'

Maurlocke hid annoyance behind a satisfied smile. Another loophole closed. Ah well. Small matter.

'Very well. We have a deal. Please,' Maurlocke gestured to a chair, 'make yourself comfortable while I summon my servant. I'm afraid I've sent him to fetch some things and he may take awhile running back.'

'I prefer to stand, thank you.'

'As you wish.' Maurlocke made a show of getting comfortable. Recalling Deri was the work of a moment's thought and a fingertip's contact with the boy's contract of indenture. Naturally, it was always on Maurlocke's person. One didn't leave such valuable things out where highly motivated servants might get their hands on them.

After all, good servants were worth a lot. Particularly ones that drew such interesting flies into the web. And it would certainly prove edifying to hear how his servant had come to witness the flight of a princess and not brought that information immediately to him.

Jack Trades held the small vial containing a taste of freedom up to the light and squinted. 'Very nice,' he said. 'And yours, to boot. Bold move. I like that.'

The merchant slotted the delicate vial into a velvet case to protect it, then locked the whole thing in a drawer. Deri knew he'd likely move it later. No merchant as sharp as Jack Trades let anyone see where he kept his merchandise when it was not on display.

'So,' he said, 'that makes us one-third square. It's taken you awhile, but considering the resources you are working with, I'm impressed. And pleased.'

Had Deri more experience with the mortal world, he might have recognised that look as pride – possibly even filial pride. Alas, he had no such experience and so the detail went entirely unnoted.

'I'm close to halfway, in terms of merchandise gathered,' Deri said, boasting just a touch. He couldn't have Jack Trades getting impatient. He needed to keep the older merchant interested. 'But as you said, I'm working with, ah, somewhat limited means and gathering three lifetimes' worth of prosperity is taking me a bit longer than I'd anticipated.'

'But you do have a line on it,' Jack said shrewdly. 'Quite a lot more than just three lifetimes' worth, from the level of excitement in your voice.'

'Maybe.' Deri was cagey. An interested Jack Trades might be too tempted to look into Deri's doings, and that wouldn't be good for business.

'Any luck on the third item?' Jack moved the conversation on smoothly, though not in any kind of way that was likely to put Deri at ease.

The third item? Merchant Maurlocke's laughter? No. No luck. Deri wasn't certain the gods possessed that much luck among them entire. But he had a plan, and some bottled wit.

'Not as yet, but I'm better positioned than most to look for that particular bit of merchandise.' Yeah. Like the biggest cactus in the desert was in the best position to catch the single drop of rain that falls once a century.

'Well, I'll leave you to your tasks, then, but I am pleased, very pleased, so far.' Jack Trades smiled.

Deri felt simultaneously elated and terrified for his life. A smile from a regular merchant of the Untermarkt was bad enough, but Jack Trades was exponentially more dangerous. Deri couldn't read him as easily as he could the other merchants. He was like Maurlocke in that respect, and any similarities to Deri's mystrer were enough to give anyone pause.

'Thank you,' he said in response. Caution was not out of line, here. 'I know your time is valuable. I appreciate you using some of it to do business with me.'

Jack nodded and Deri took his leave, relaxing slightly as the familiar rush of the Market surrounded him. That relief was rather short-lived, however.

Silvestra flicked the smooth crystalline curve of the double-bell shape before her and listened intently to the ringing sound it produced. The twelve-foot hourglass chased in brass and orichalcum all but sang in a low, thrumming pitch and was more felt than heard. The artificer nodded to her assistant, Vimukti, and the girl pulled carefully on a lever. Arms of brass levered the hourglass up and into the air and slowly began to rotate it end-over-end. Silvestra leaned in and tuned her ear to the pitch, her fingers hovering delicately over the graceful curve of the glass. As it turned the sound shifted, twisting into a subtle self-harmony, scattering notes that seemed to hang just outside time until they could ring together in a flawless chord.

'Good.' Silvestra nodded, before shifting into lecture mode. 'The sound tells me that there are no hidden flaws in the glass. If there were, the danger would be the housing –' she flicked the hourglass again '– exploding when under extreme pressure or extended use. But I don't see that being a concern in the foreseeable future. Particularly given the nature of the glass and the machine of which it is a part.'

'The glass?' Vimukti asked, shooting a glance towards the towering crystalline shape.

'All sand has an innate connection to the concept of time, but the sand that made this glass was gathered from specific beaches around the world, at specific times. It was washed, over and over, with the progression of time in the form of the tides, gathered beneath specific days marked by the sun and moon as horophysical signifiers, and then crafted precisely to schedule.' Silvestra let out a happy sigh. 'Alchemy may be infuriatingly imprecise at times, but occasionally the logic is pleasingly sensical.'

'And what does that have to do with the machine?' Vimukti asked, her eyes tracing over the thing hungrily.

Silvestra nodded approvingly, a slight motion elegant in its efficiency. The child showed curiosity as well as intelligence. Perhaps she would do well as a technician, once her term of indenture at the workhouse was complete. A pity she could not be apprenticed properly. Still, curiosity should be rewarded.

'The point of this machine is to reverse the ravages of time on rare and valuable components. The gears you carefully craft of orichalcum or adamantine? Those metals are rare and valuable, and when they are worn down, used up or broken it is a titanic loss. The machine can restore them, for far less than buying the material once more, by drawing youth and resilience from other, less valuable materials, and transferring it to the worn-out gears or other machine parts. Hence the two chambers.' Silvestra pointed. 'It is a model of efficiency, and Missus Graspar really is to be commended for thinking of such a preservative measure.' The artificer nodded. 'And, of course, it is a highly suitable construct to test in conjunction with my main area of research interest.'

'The perpetual motion engine,' Vimukti offered.

Silvestra allowed herself a moment of glowing satisfaction. The girl really was remarkably intelligent.

'Indeed,' she confirmed. 'With my engine, once this machine is begun it will need no additional fuel or power source. It will be able to run indefinitely, greatly reducing the cost of preserving or replacing valuable materials.' Silvestra was quiet for a moment. 'It was my father's work, you know, that originally perfected perpetual motion. He created such wonders. I've never quite been able to match him. No one has. Not all his secrets were written down.'

Vimukti watched quietly as the normally perfectly composed façade of the lady artificer showed a small crack.

'Someday I will match his work. I'll rediscover every particular of his brilliance and be able to show the world it wasn't just a fluke.'

She paused. Enough of the past. What on earth would the child think of her? She took a deep breath and instead gently prodded her charge toward thinking of the future.

'Have you considered what you might do when your term here is up? I know a good many artificers who would appreciate a skilled assistant, and you are turning into quite a good one. You could even find work as a technician, I imagine, if you applied yourself.'

The girl went suddenly stiff and cold.

'I can't say I think much about that, Mistress,' she said distantly. 'It seems very likely I won't live to see that day.'

Silvestra blinked, but before she could respond, Vimukti continued.

'You don't seem to see people nearly as well as you see machines, ma'am, if you pardon my saying so. Though I suppose we're really not that different from the cogs you're talking about. We wear out a lot, here. Loss of limbs, acid burns, blinding; sometimes one of us even dies. But the thing is, no one is taking the time to build a machine that will restore *us*. I suppose we're too easy to replace.' Vimukti glowered. 'Lives are cheap, Mistress Steele, much easier to get than orichalcum, and there are many who care not as to how many they run through, so long as they are making their profits and stacking their coin.'

It was clear the child was speaking of the Graspars, though she had carefully stepped around naming them specifically. Silvestra felt a familiar alien quiver in the pit of her stomach. The girl was right about one thing, at least. She was much better with machines than with people. She had no idea what to say to that.

Instead, she brushed it off and turned her attention back to the thing she did understand: her work.

'I'm sure you'll make it through your term just fine,' she said. 'And when you do, you need simply to call on me and I shall do whatever I can to help you find your feet.'

That, at least, she could do.

'Thank you, Mistress,' Vimukti said.

Silvestra felt the girl's eyes on her back. There were cracks forming at the edges of her vision. The workhouse was starting to take on a monstrous, mechanistic life all its own, and the cogs – no, children – passing the edges of her workspace began to snap dreadfully into place even as the double-edged sword that was her gift started pointing out all the flaws in the system, the workhouse, around her.

'Well, we'd best crack on,' she said briskly. 'The mechanism is complete, and it can be run briefly off of the general energy sources available in the workhouse, but it will do no long-term good if we cannot power it with my prototype, will it?'

Owain's eyes traced the spots around the workhouse floor where he'd helped Deri install what the merchant apprentice had called 'prosperity siphons'. He could just make them out, though Owain wasn't sure if that was some talent of his own or a lingering effect of some magic Deri had employed at the time. Theoretically, they were soaking up all the wealth that would have been produced if the factory floor was running at capacity, which it should theoretically not be doing now.

Unfortunately, the children of the workhouse could be doing better at being less productive. Doing worse at being productive? In any case, though Owain had carefully explained the idea of working to rule to several of the children, many of them either did not understand or were too afraid of the Graspars to follow through.

'How's it going?' Vimukti popped up out of nowhere.

Owain flinched, staggering back and into one of the nearby machines. It ran hot and the metal nearly seared through his clothes, but Vimukti reached out and pulled him to safety.

'Sorry about that,' she said. 'Didn't mean to nearly cause you a misfortune.'

'It's all right.' Owain grimaced. 'It would have been a distraction from banging my head against this whole working-to-rule thing. I'm talking, but the others aren't understanding. Or aren't believing.'

'Mmm.' Vimukti watched the floor for a minute. 'You're not wrong. They lack a certain motivating fire, I think.'

'Got any ideas that might help?' Owain asked ruefully.

'One or two.' Vimukti refused to say anything more than that. 'I should go. Mistress Steele needs me to make a trip to the Goblin Market for some more materials.'

'Lucky.'

'Don't worry. I'll give your regards to your goblin lover for you.' Vimukti winked as she walked away.

'I—' Owain almost shouted before he caught himself. 'Yes. Fine. *Thank you.*'

Peals of laughter were all that answered him.

Vimukti was not laughing as she slunk down one of the darker alleys of the Untermarkt. Her business for Mistress Steele completed, she'd nabbed a bit of extra time for herself. She had to take this chance now. The Graspars rarely sent her to the Untermarkt, and they never did so without expressly forbidding her to do anything other than go, complete their errands, and return directly after.

Whispers rose around her, and snippets of song danced upon the air. She passed whispersmiths and rumourmongers, following the voice she could almost hear urging her along. She'd listened closely when Deri had described the various ways of navigating the Untermarkt to Owain, and she did her best to follow that advice now.

It was frighteningly easy to be drawn along the path of her desire. One voice promised her freedom. Another voice promised her revenge. Vimukti put them out of her mind. She could get both, and on her own terms. She followed the voice promising her words of fire.

'Hello, child.'

Vimukti was not expecting the voice to be attached to a being like the one before her, however. The merchant was tall and painfully thin. Though she otherwise looked mortal, her hair danced in the air like an ember on the breeze, all light and life and flowing threads of gold and red. She had two arms, but her shoulders were ringed with a mantle of tentacles, which coiled and writhed of their own volition around her.

'You have come to make a deal with Merchant Alys-Ra, yes? I can hear it in your voice.'

'I haven't said anything yet,' Vimukti protested.

'Not that voice, little one. The one that speaks through your eyes. Oh, such a voice of the hearth as I have not heard in a long time. Though it is weak and speaks as if from very very far away.' The merchant's eyes went hard for a moment. 'Your weak blood can barely carry such a burden.' Then she was all smiles. 'Allow me to help lift it from you.'

'If you mean the healing power of my tears, you're going to have to offer me something very, very powerful in exchange,' Vimukti said, aiming for a bold beginning. 'I have little enough, and what I do have that can save lives? That's worth a great deal.'

'Words of fire, yes? I can see it in your eyes. You wish for a voice that can ignite sparks within those who hear. Sparks of understanding, sparks of inspiration, sparks of… revolution? I can give you such a thing, if you wish. The price will be high, however.'

The merchant was talking about her healing power. Vimukti knew that and she felt a twinge of unease. What would it be like to give up her power? To give up the ability to heal and save so many lives on the workhouse floor?

What would it be like to be able to help the others save themselves? To gain their freedom at least, possibly years sooner than they would otherwise? That was saving them in a way as well, wasn't it? In the long run, she'd save more lives with a voice of fire than she would with tears of healing, especially ones that didn't do anything but staunch the blood.

No. This was the right decision. She had to do it now, before she lost her nerve.

'I knew it would be expensive coming down here,' Vimukti snapped. 'Spare me the merchant jumbo-jumbo and vague warnings. Let's talk business.'

She got right down to it. There was little time, and she needed to return to the workhouse with the tools to make sure their rebellion against the Graspars worked.

No matter the cost.

'It's very simple,' Vimukti said, eyes as hypnotic as twin flames, 'you like jokes, right? Think of this as the best of practical jokes. You're doing exactly what you are told, but you get to twist and turn every which way you can to make sure that *how* you do what you're told is *the worst version* of that thing. Think about it. What could you do if Garog asked you to pick up gears and put them away?'

'Pick them up one at a time, real slow like. Then put each one away one at a time before picking up another.' The boy began to glow. 'That wouldn't break any rules, would it, but he'd *hate* it. He likes us to go fast and be scared.'

'Exactly. You've got it.' Vimukti smiled. This new power of hers was going to work out just fine. 'Now, get out there and have some fun! And if you have any more good ideas, be sure to share them with the others.'

The boy, practically smoking with excitement, scurried off to slowly haul gears across the workhouse floor.

''Lo, Vimukti,' Owain said absently as he walked past, head turning to take in the controlled chaos that had overtaken the workhouse floor since Vimukti's return. 'Have you seen Pierrick?'

'No, but one of the younger girls said she saw Garog hauling him up to the Missus's office.' Vimukti shrugged. 'Might be some special job they wanted him for.'

'Mmm.' Owain nodded. 'Looks like they've finally gotten it.' He jutted his chin out at the workhouse floor and the children studiously working to rule across the width and breadth of the workhouse.

'Yes,' she said smugly. 'Yes, they have. I think your goblin lover is going to be very pleased with our progress here indeed. Very pleased. With us on the job, I'll bet he's never had it so easy.'

24

The bells rang out a warning a split second before Deri felt the pull of Maurlocke's summons. Around him, several merchants of Covent Garden Market looked around, confused, as bells that usually sounded the hour rang out with no apparent provocation. But then, this was London, and strange things happened as often as not. Many chalked it up to the vagaries of Faery and returned to the more important business of fleecing customers.

The knight returns, chimed a spray of bluebells. Fortunately the girl selling the flowers didn't notice.

Deri's feet were already walking him toward the nearest entry to the Untermarkt. The knight had returned? And the bells were warning him of it as Maurlocke was summoning him back? Not good. Not good at all.

Think fast. Excuses. Explanations.

Three honest answers must you give, a solemn batch of bellflowers groaned. This time, the flower-seller heard the sound. The palavering poseys were summarily loudly proclaimed 'For the Fair Folk' and cast to the breeze.

No outright lies, then. But Deri lived and breathed the Goblin Market. He knew well enough how to lie with the truth. Aurelia was the least of his problems, however. Whatever she was after, Deri was sure he could wriggle out of that trouble. But she'd brought something far worse in her wake.

She'd brought Maurlocke's attention down on him.

A thousand thoughts burned through Deri as he made his way back beneath the streets of London. Maurlocke's summons thrummed through his bones, drawing him on as fast as it could. Fortunately, Deri was strong enough to dig in his heels, just a bit, just enough to buy him some time to think.

Little enough, though. His bad luck to be so close to Covent Garden when the summons came. Three questions, three questions, what would they be? They'd have something to do with the princess. Where she was, or what Deri knew about her. The Knight of the Verge might be cautious in what she asked in front of Maurlocke, but it would undoubtedly be in that vein.

Deri passed from London into the Untermarkt. There was a different tang to the air, a hint of magic. That and the world around him erupted into sight and sound, smell and activity. The Market surged around him, and the summons pulled him onwards, to Maurlocke's tent.

Maurlocke was the bigger problem. As soon as the knight left, Deri would have to answer to the merchant. That would be far more dangerous. He couldn't risk having a royal destiny on him when he walked into that tent. If he did, Maurlocke would have it, would find out its existence somehow. No, who was he kidding?

Deri'd heard the gossip. Maurlocke knew the destiny was out there. Deri was certain of that. But the merchant had no reason to think Deri had it in his possession, and, if Deri wanted to survive this afternoon, the bottle needed to not be on his person.

But where could he stash it that was safe? The knight knew of his old haven. It wasn't safe anymore. And he couldn't trust any of the goblin merchants to safeguard it for him, not even Jack Trades.

Your time is short! You must make haste! the clangour all around him raced.

The bells. He could trust the bells. Deri mentally traced a path that would lead him past one of the larger market bells before he reached Maurlocke's tent. Fortunately, the Untermarkt was in a favourable configuration for his needs, today. Deri thanked Danu for that tiny bit of luck. He turned down a side alley. The summons in his bones let him. It would get him to Maurlocke's tent faster, this path, after all. But it also took him out of sight.

Deri used the opportunity to pull out a small vial and began spooling out his memories as he walked. He couldn't spill secrets he couldn't remember. It was a dangerous course of action, if he made a mistake, but the alternative was almost certainly worse.

It was painful. He had to stop a couple times to catch his breath, and to make sure he wasn't pulling too much out. He needed to keep bits, enough to back up the story he was creating (the only way to really lie to Maurlocke and the Knight of the Verge was to lie with the truth as much as possible). It only got more and more difficult as he went; as bit and pieces of memories disappeared it was harder and harder to see the edges of what he was trying to do, the story he was trying to shape by the absence of recollection.

There was no denying that he'd seen the princess. The Knight of the Verge had caught him in his sanctuary, so he couldn't deny knowing of it – and would he ever pay for it once Maurlocke found out – if asked. Deri still somewhat hoped the knight wouldn't waste a question on anything touching on that place, but it was unlikely.

Deri pulled too hard at a memory tied to his last night out with Owain and the surge of emotion that was loosed was almost more than he could take. He nearly slammed into the support pole of a merchant's tent, and it was only a lifetime of conditioning that enabled him to swerve at the last moment. It cost him a twinge in the muscle of his left leg, and a fresh blaze of agony as the summons punished him for veering away from Maurlocke's pavilion, but better that than arousing the ire of a strange merchant.

He had to move faster, but also be more careful. Deri laughed, a bit desperately. It was almost enough to make a body regret making the deal of a lifetime. Almost, but not quite. There was no way he was letting this opportunity slip. No way Maurlocke or a Knight of the Verge would take it away from him. Not if he could help it.

And he had a plan. A solid one, if not a good one. Maurlocke was expecting to catch him in some wrongdoing, and there was little Deri could do to change that. What he could change, however, was which misdeeds Maurlocke uncovered. Neither Maurlocke nor the knight would be expecting it, Deri hoped. They'd each get something of what they expected, just not everything they wanted. And Deri, well, he'd suffer enough to sell it, and accept that as fair value for escaping without worse coming down on his head.

The last memory was the trickiest, and by the time Deri had bottled it firmly, he was beginning to suffer from the worst headache he'd ever experienced. He was running up quite the tab of misery, today.

Stepping out from the alleyway and into the throng of the Market only made things worse. Deri tried to thread his way through the crowd, but things were busy. Contact with others was inevitable. Deri gritted his teeth through every small bump and brush, each touch adding fresh agony to the pain in his head and bones.

The closest market bell was mounted atop a tall pole, gaily painted and bedecked with ribbons. Deri scampered up it easily enough without drawing attention to himself. It was common practice for all manner of beings to ascend the pole in a vain attempt to find some path through the ever-shifting flow of the Untermarkt toward their hearts' desires. The various urchins in the employ of merchants were the most frequent.

It was a good cover, and Deri was often enough seen polishing various bells across the Market (in payment for any number of favours, of course) that no one would give him a second look. With a whispered word, Deri secured the bell's assistance in hiding his most precious possession. Belatedly, he realised he'd have to stash his ink of night someplace else. That was also something he didn't dare let Maurlocke catch him with. It would be damning evidence he was experimenting with brokering his own deals, and that was not something the merchant would tolerate.

Once he had stashed everything of vital importance, and retrieved some of his other hidden wealth, Deri pulled out one more memory, wrapped it in a scrap of paper with a scribbled note, and called down a pigeon to carry the message to Owain. If all went well, he'd retrieve that memory later.

The pain in his bones was all but unbearable. He had stretched his time to the breaking point and there was no more resisting the summons. Deri stumbled into a run, each step sending fresh waves of agony through his system, though that was counterbalanced by a lessening of the pain as he neared his destination.

Sooner than he wished, he was standing outside Maurlocke's pavilion. It had been watching for him, he could tell. There was an insouciant drape to the cloth that implied it was smugly pleased that Deri found himself in trouble. The bloody thing was so fucking childish. Deri allowed himself several seconds of fantasising about setting the blazing thing aflame. The tent sent an inviting ripple along the edges of the entryway.

It was sorely tempting to sneak a drop of faery wine to steady his nerves, but Deri needed all his wits about him to survive this encounter. His head throbbed, aching and raw around the new-plucked gap in his memory. It was made worse by the constant impulse to probe at it, like wiggling your tongue into the gap left by a recently lost tooth.

The tent rippled at him. It didn't approve of anyone keeping Maurlocke waiting. 'I'm going, I'm going,' Deri muttered at it, and stepped inside.

It took his eyes a moment to adjust. Deri bit back a grimace. It shouldn't have. Maurlocke had been playing with the lighting to upset his equilibrium. When they cleared, Deri saw Maurlocke sitting behind ys desk, the Knight of the Verge standing in front of it, both looking at him expectantly.

The knight was in full ceremonial armour. That wasn't good. It smacked of an official visit. But then, what about this was good? How did she even manage to get back into the Untermarkt anyway? Deri draped a casual expression across his face and dove in. Might as well get this over with.

'You called?'

'Yes, Deri.' Maurlocke's voice was a caress of golden samite in the night. 'Come here. My guest has some questions for you. Three, to be nice and exact about things.'

Maurlocke smiled and the Knight of the Verge scowled. Well, that was something, at least. Not everyone was going to be getting everything they wanted. Deri tried to take some solace in that thought.

'What is your first question, Dame Steele?'

Deri had time for a flash of surprise at the name – why did it sound so familiar? – before the knight cocked her head and began the interrogation, such as it was.

Before allowing Dame Steele to question Deri, Maurlocke carefully explained the deal the two had struck: Deri would answer three questions, honestly and to the best of his ability (Deri appreciated the subtlety there; he doubted the knight would), and that would be the extent of it.

Deri knew better. Neither Maurlocke nor Dame Steele were likely to be satisfied with what they learned from him this afternoon, so, in some way or another, Deri's troubles would continue. Still, naught for it but to dive right in and come out swinging.

'Pleased to meet you, Dame Steele.' Deri sketched a respectful bow. '*Diwedd y gân yw'r geiniog.*'

'What?' Dame Steele looked blank.

'One pays the piper after he plays,' Deri translated, roughly. 'What were your next two questions?'

Maurlocke smiled as Dame Steele purpled. 'Nicely played,

my boy,' the merchant said, 'but I'm afraid you've already been outmanoeuvred. Dame Steele specified that she receive three answers pursuant to her search for the missing princess. I assume you are familiar with the rumours?'

'Yes, Merchant Maurlocke,' Deri said, inwardly cursing. Still three answers to give. Well, it had been worth a shot, and clearly Maurlocke was amused. That wasn't nothing. Unfortunately, Maurlocke's amusement bought Dame Steele's anger.

'This is a serious matter! The princess is missing. Do you have any idea how much danger she could be in?'

'Yes,' Deri said immediately. Dangerous as it was, at least Dame Steele's anger had prompted her to misstep. 'Now you have two questions remaining.'

Out of the corner of his eye, Deri saw Maurlocke's smile widen, just a fraction. Deri was so relieved that he was pleasing Maurlocke, he almost didn't notice that Maurlocke deliberately allowed Deri to catch ym smiling. Clearly, the less value Deri provided to the knight, the more profit the merchant gleaned from the exchange. Nevermind that it was at Deri's expense, or that the gain under consideration – for Maurlocke, at least – was minimal. It was about winning as much as it was about profit. Wealth was just a way to keep score.

Dame Steele didn't bother appealing to Maurlocke. She already knew the response. It was impressive the way she leashed her anger actually, though Deri was suddenly haunted by the thought of what it might look like were she to loosen those bonds.

'Do you—' Dame Steele stopped herself. 'Where is—' Her fingers flexed like claws before she vented the frustration out her nose with a deep breath. Then, her eyes narrowed and she asked her second question. 'What would you do, if you needed to find Princess Boudicca Helena Victoria of the House of Saxe-Coburg and Gotha, knowing what you do of her current whereabouts and what she did whilst at this market, and presuming you were constrained to working only with the resources at my disposal – that you know to be at my disposal – and what you know to be available for reasonable cost at the Gobli— the Untermarkt?'

It was a good question. She was thinking now. This would be dangerous. Deri ran his tongue over his upper lip as he thought. Fortunately, neither Maurlocke nor Aurelia rushed him (though each for very different reasons). He was almost tempted to just tell her that the princess would have sought out Jack Trades. It was true enough, and directed attention away from him, which was good, but it would also draw Maurlocke's attention to Jack, and Deri did not want the merchant watching Jack Trades carefully right now, not for any reason. So, what was the next logical solution?

Well,' Deri began, 'knowing that the princess came here and traded away her destiny…' That much, at least, was safe to say, as the gossipmongers had been minting coin with that little tidbit. '…I would presume she'd purchased something of roughly equivalent value.' Deri was very glad he did not know, at this moment, precisely what she had traded her destiny for. 'She clearly knew she would be pursued, else why are you here? She'd have purchased some way to hide her trail – no, she wouldn't need to. She traded her destiny away.'

'I don't follow,' Dame Steele said.

'Destiny is part of the self. New destiny, new self,' Deri explained before he thought better of it. Dame Steele nodded and Maurlocke's smile lost a bit of its shine.

'The person that the old strands of hair would lead to no longer exists. Nothing to track. I understand. Go on.' Dame Steele waved magnanimously.

'Right,' Deri continued, beginning to feel hot in the stuffy confines of the pavilion. 'Well, that's the thing. If she bought a new destiny, she had to get it from one of the merchants here. Something like that takes a lot of work, weaving a new destiny out of all manner of days and bits of good and bad fortune and the like. I'd figure out which merchants were capable of producing that kind of merchandise and start there.'

Deri was walking a fine line. It wasn't only merchants capable of this particular bit of work, but Dame Steele had asked what he would do in her position, and, logically, it made the most sense to start with the merchants, as it was known the princess had traded away her destiny. That, at least, was something that supposedly required a merchant.

'That is likely to be a long and difficult list to assemble,' the knight observed.

'Shorter than the list of all merchants in the Untermarkt,' Deri countered. 'Easier than flailing about with no purpose.'

Dame Steele was clearly kicking herself about something. Deri puzzled at it for a moment before realising. The princess – right now her disappearance was still rumour. Querying that many merchants? Rumour would become fact. Not to mention assembling a list like that would strain the knight's resources, possibly past what they could endure. But she had failed to specify that Deri's suggested course of action take secrecy into account. Deri grinned.

'Even if the merchant included a discretionary clause, locking away most of the knowledge, there are ways to work around it. If you can figure out what kind of destiny she would have wanted to purchase, you can isolate those elements that would go into the making of it, and follow those lines of supply to further shorten your list.'

Maurlocke outright frowned at this. Deri immediately clammed up. He was letting his glee at catching Dame Steele out loosen his tongue and edge too close to spilling Market secrets.

'That's what I would do, in your position, anyway,' Deri concluded abruptly. 'You have one question remaining.'

Dame Steele pursed her lips, looking at him through narrowed eyes. Deri met her gaze full on, so he was in a position to note when her gaze flicked to Maurlocke and back to him. He couldn't guess at what the knight was thinking, but even his best estimate would not have prepared him for her next question.

'Do you think the princess is safe, wherever – whoever – she is now?' Dame Steele's voice was anything but reminiscent of her moniker.

Deri gawped at her. The question was entirely unexpected. It threw him. Fortunately, he managed to get ahold of his wits before responding. This question was actually more dangerous than any of the others. He had to calibrate what he said very carefully against what he knew. Too much to one side or the other and Maurlocke or Dame Steele would realise just how much he knew – and wasn't saying.

'She'd almost have to be, with what she was selling and what she could get for it. Even if she was dealing with a less savoury merchant and wasn't negotiating sharply, it'd be hard to come away from that in serious danger. Market Law, what rumour says about the princess—'

'What, precisely, does rumour say about the princess?' Dame Steele interrupted sharply.

'I believe that is beyond the scope of our negotiations,' Maurlocke slid smoothly into the conversation. 'You have answers to your questions, precisely as we negotiated.'

'Yes, precisely as I expected.' Dame Steele bared her teeth. 'I came to the Goblin Market and got cheated, as humans always do.'

'Oh, my, looks like the honesty is settling in already.' Maurlocke tutted. 'Do have a care, dear. It can be quite brutal, a moon's worth of honesty.'

Deri's ears perked up at this. So that's what Maurlocke extracted from the knight in exchange for his three answers. He filed away the fact that Dame Steele would be unable to lie directly for the next month. The way his luck was going, he suspected he had not seen the last of the Knight of the Verge.

Dame Steele clamped her lips shut, inclined her head politely to Maurlocke, ignored Deri, and swept out of the tent. The fabric fluttered with more than the wind of her passing.

Maurlocke said something in the Language of Gold. Deri wished, not for the first time, there was some affordable way of learning it. It would save him so much trouble if he could eavesdrop on what the merchant and tent said to one another.

'Now,' Maurlocke turned to Deri, 'I have some questions of my own for you.'

Deri had known it was coming, but even with that his blood went cold in his veins. At least he wouldn't be able to betray himself with the precautions he'd taken. Hopefully. Well, nothing to do about it but trust and play the part.

'Yes, Merchant Maurlocke.'

❁

Aurelia stormed into the flat she shared with her sister. If Silvestra weren't so prone to reinforcing and perfecting *everything* in the place, Aurelia might well have broken the door, the cloak-rack, and the small table whereupon they dined, in that order.

And if her body weren't reinforced by enchantments provided by her knighthood, she definitely would have broken at least a toe, if not her whole foot.

'Something wrong?' Silvestra's voice drifted drily in from the parlour.

Aurelia wanted to say no. She tried to say no. Her lips formed the word, even, but what came out instead was something quite different: the truth.

'Yes.'

The echoes of that simple syllable were like a northern wind cutting through to her bones and Maurlocke's words echoed mockingly in her inner ear, *one month of honesty.*

It was already happening, Aurelia winced. The timing was less than ideal. But she could get away with written updates to Dame Eigyr, at least for a few weeks, and she didn't spend so much time socialising that her few connections there would be in any danger. She was, after all, a fundamentally honest person to begin with. If she thought something, she often said it, no two ways about it.

But there were a few things she had kept from her sister, recently. One in particular could cause quite the tempest in their teacups. It was a minor thing she had done, really, wasn't it? And in a good cause! And so long as her sister didn't have any reason to bring up their parents—

'Have you been reading mother and father's letters? There seems to be one missing.' Silvestra had a slight frown on her face as she moved to the kitchen to begin preparing tea.

'Do you think I would be so daverdy as to lose something like that?' Aurelia asked quickly.

It was something like a goblin merchant would say, dodging her sister's question with one of her own. A trick that boy might pull. Aurelia felt her guts twist at the thought. She should just be completely honest, tell her sister what had happened to the letter. But if she did... Aurelia shook off the thought. When Silvestra was angry, things tended to break in dangerous and unpredictable ways, things like windows, machines, relationships. And Aurelia didn't have time right now to try and repair whatever it was that might end up broken. She had a princess to find, a royal command to carry out.

'I never said you were careless,' Silvestra replied, adding water to one of her devices. 'I asked if you had been reading the letters. When was the last time you went through them?'

Aurelia's heart sank. Her sister was persistent. And she was no goblin merchant. There was no way to avoid this conversation.

No way to avoid paying in honesty for the answers she had received at the Goblin Market.

'Very recently,' she began, moving to sit across from her sister. 'Here, let me tell you about my day...'

25

The weeks following Maurlocke's interrogation were particularly difficult. The merchant ran Deri ragged, loading him with masses of chores and endless chains of fetch-and-carry, polish-and-shine. Maurlocke would watch and wait, and when Deri was exhausted, wrung out, and least likely to be able to think clearly, would ambush him with all manner of questions. The merchant was not quite as convinced of Deri's lack of involvement with the missing destiny as the Knight of the Verge had been.

Deri dared not even retrieve his hidden memories. Though the bells regularly assured him they were safe, still he fretted. It was a dreadful risk, leaving them outside his head like this. The constant prick of Maurlocke's attention was really wearing down his natural resilience.

But in the end, even the will of gold falters. As Yule approached, Maurlocke became more and more engrossed in ys work. Yuletide was a time of giving, and generosity, and, more to the point, dangerously expensive shows of wealth and love in equal measure. Deri's role in the matter of the missing destiny was, if not forgotten, at least somewhat out of mind. It helped that although rumour still ran rampant about the missing princess, nothing had been seen nor heard of the alleged destiny she had sold to effect her escape. This took a bit more heat off Deri, though it did nothing to bring about his freedom any faster.

Even better than the lessening of Maurlocke's attention, however, was the upcoming holiday. Deri and Owain were both guaranteed days of rest for Yule, and they were finally going to have their long-delayed second outing. Owain had included directions on where and when to meet in his last missive-by-candlelight.

Deri grinned. He was going to have to purchase another new thief's candle. They were wearing through them at a terrible rate. Even with a steady supply of wax, each time the candles were used a little more of the wick burned away to ash, forever. Certainly not the intended use, but fuck the intended use! This was better, and definitely worth the expense. It'd be different if Deri and Owain could meet in person more regularly, but as that was impossible until they were both free of their contracts, well, beggars, choosers, and all that.

In fact, with a bit of bravado, Deri made his way to Jack Trades' stall. He would get the wax there. He could show off his skills at bartering directly to his prospective mentor.

A foolish risk, but the thought of seeing Owain made Deri feel daring.

'One thief's candle please. I'll give you a bully-boy's bluster for it.'

Jack Trades looked at him, his eyes flicking briefly to the surging crowd around them before whispering a word of privacy that shrouded them from sight.

'I expect my heir to take better care,' the merchant said, a slight edge of warning seasoning his tone with an unseasonable tartness.

'You also expect your heir to be bold,' Deri countered. 'And this candle will help me secure one of the items specified in our agreement.'

'Very well,' Jack said. 'You shall have it, for the price of one honest and truthful answer.'

A prickle of warning tried to clamp Deri's mouth shut, but his lightness at the thought of seeing Owain quite overcame it.

'Done!' he said.

'How close are you to securing the laughter we discussed?'

Jack's pointed words temporarily burst the bubble of Deri's euphoria.

'No closer,' he admitted. 'I purchased some very good wit, but it seems what sense of humour is locked within that heart of gold is very different from what flesh might find funny.'

'But you have learned something,' Jack said with unexpected warmth. 'And you are, at least, keeping your eye on the prize. I was worried. The light-o-love in your step made me wonder if you perhaps found something else you wanted more than the name of Trades?'

'I've got my gaze firmly fixed on what I need *and* what I want,' Deri replied. 'Have no fear.' A few more pleasantries and the business concluded.

Deri left the Market smarting slightly at Jack Trades' words, but carrying his prize. He wandered the streets of London, dressed in his scrabble-scrounged best, looking up at the sky and wondering if the Untermarkt would ensure there was snow for Yuletide this year, or if the expense would be considered too great. As it was, the afternoon was clear and cold and pale, pale blue. The air was crisp and was not yet weighed down with the dank chill that could seep into the bones of the unwary and freeze them from the inside out. Not a bad day for a walk.

Up ahead, Deri's destination came into view. He paused a moment at the corner and just stared. The building was massive, with coldly elegant grey pillars standing at attention at the front. He'd never before been to the British Museum.

The pillars of granite that held up the roof of the museum were nothing next to the pillars that held up Owain's frame. Deri spotted him standing near the edge of the street directly in front of the entrance. Now that he'd had a chance or two to climb those workhouse stairs, Deri could see where Owain had gotten them. And that derrière. Deri smiled as he walked slowly toward Owain.

Owain turned before Deri could reach him. A smile broke across his face like dawn across the East. 'Finally,' he said.

'You know the merchant,' Deri said, by way of explanation, avoiding invoking ys name just in case.

'Come on.' Owain snagged Deri's arm and looped it through his own, leading them up the stairs and into the marble-clad entryway. The sound of their footsteps mingled pleasantly with the murmuration of opinionated voices and swishing skirts. Near the top Owain's foot slipped on the slick stone, but Deri caught and steadied him with a smile.

'Careful! That would have been a nasty fall,' he said.

'Good thing you were here to catch me then,' Owain replied, the corners of his mouth teasing up into a grin.

'And where might you be taking me?' Deri asked, furiously craning his neck to take it all in. The ceiling was so very, very high!

And all that chiselled stone, those fine lines, and – a cadre of laughing young men tumbled past – other works of art. 'I can see why you like it here.'

'I thought we'd begin with the Greco-Roman gallery for the statues, and then perhaps see if we can sneak into the Secretum.' Owain shot Deri a glance.

'The Secretum? You mean the – what did The London Eye call it? An abominable monument to human licentiousness?'

'So you're not completely without culture after all,' Owain teased. 'Good. I was beginning to worry.'

'Well, any good merchant keeps his ears open. You never know what might be an opportunity.'

'You're incorrigible,' Owain laughed.

'Ooh, big word. Someone's been reading the dictionary.'

'Not much else to read at the workhouse,' Owain shot back. The sharp humour dulled a bit on the sad truth of the statement. Owain quickly shook it off. 'Come on, the statues are through here.'

They passed through an arch into a long gallery lined with statues of alabaster and limestone and marble. Some were all but intact, others had lost legs or arms of fingers or hands, but in spite of that all were beautiful. Many were the lissome figure of athletes, heroes, and gods. Most of them were perfectly, gloriously, naked.

'Oh,' Deri breathed, 'I think I'm going to enjoy being cultured.'

Owain suppressed a half-laugh.

They began strolling along the gallery, admiring the forms and talking, just enjoying one another's company without the ever-present threat of either Maurlocke or the Graspars looming over them. Not that they weren't still looming, but it was a more distant, removed looming, like thunderclouds on the horizon.

They were far from the only young men enjoying the gallery. A brawny, red-headed lad sporting a green ribbon around his wrist walked past, catching and holding Deri's eye as he passed. Deri cast a glance over his shoulder and caught the redhead staring back. He winked and headed toward the men's lavatory.

'I see I'm not the only one here who really appreciates the culture,' Deri said to Owain.

'It's a very popular gallery,' Owain replied with a straight face. 'Oh, look. Here's my favourite!'

Owain pointed to a white marble figure on a chunky granite plinth. It was a young man, though whereas most of the other statues in the gallery had the motion and bearing of warriors or athletes, this one was more reserved, dignified. There was a gravitas in the grace of his limbs.

'Long, long ago a mighty king fell in love with the beautiful son of two lowly peasants. He raised him up, elevated him to the court, and made him his confidant. They hunted and wrote poetry and fucked until it was all cut tragically short.' Owain stared up at the cold form of the statue, eyes shining. 'Because he died. Antinous died. They were boating on the Nile and he fell in, or was thrown in and drowned, or was drowned. We don't know.

'What we do know is that the king loved him so much that after his passing, he declared Antinous a god, an honour theretofore reserved only for members of the blood royal. And the people worshipped him. Even in death, they were able to look upon his beauty and see something of the divine there, to feel a whisper of a love so powerful it defied death and the gods themselves to raise itself up among their number.'

Owain was staring up at the statue as he spoke, so he didn't notice that the entire time Deri was staring at him. At his face. At the feeling in his eyes. It was only when Owain turned from Antinous to look at Deri that Deri transferred his gaze to the statue.

There was something about it, something in those cold, marble eyes. There was something in the ripple of curls that fell across its forehead, as if they had only just been ruffled by a passing zephyr. Something in the smooth lines left by the chisel, guided by a hand that had long ago gone to dust, but left this monument to love in its wake. And his name was Antinous? How had he never heard of him? Well, he knew how. It wasn't a tale that would echo through the pecuniary hearts of the Untermarkt. At least not near Maurlocke's tent.

Deri leaned in to read the plaque attached to the base of the statue. *The Tivolean Antinous, ca. 130–140* CE. Over a thousand years old? Was even Maurlocke that ancient? Deri sighed. Probably.

But it was humbling. Awe-inspiring, even. There was a gravity about the stone, a surreal sense of vastness. And the resonant sense of lost love, the sheer depth of it reverberated through the stone, reaching out to Deri across more than a millennium, an echo of shared humanity knifing into Deri's core.

Basking in the glory of a long-lost man elevated to godhood by his grieving lover, Deri couldn't resist offering up a small oblation. His hand slid over, all innocuous, and lightly squeezed Owain's arse. Owain jumped.

'Stop it,' he said, voice half an octave higher than its usual register. 'You'll get us thrown out!'

'Have a little faith,' Deri said, voice low and, admittedly, a bit unnecessarily sultry. 'We're in the presence of the divine. I'm sure Antinous will look out for us.' Deri scanned the crowd around the statue. So far as he could see, everyone in the vicinity was an acolyte of the violet-haired demigod.

'How did you find out about this place again?' Deri asked, watching another set of young men trade glances, fall in step, and head toward the lavatory facilities.

'Well, the schoolmaster at the workhouse has mentioned several of the exhibitions as part of our lessons—'

'But that's not the only time it's come up in conversation, is it?' Deri stalked through the conversation like a terrier after a rat. He could see Owain getting a touch flustered and it was adorable.

'Well, no,' he admitted, 'some of the older boys have mentioned the statues and how, ah, beautiful, they are, and—'

'And?' Deri prodded.

'And they may have also mentioned that it's also a place where a lot of young men go to, ah, to…' Owain trailed off and his cheeks went ever-so-slightly pink.

'Spend a penny to take a pounding?' Deri flashed a wicked grin.

Owain flushed full crimson and Deri laughed, the sound lapping at the pulchritudinous marbles. Sweet Danu, but he loved the way Owain blushed. Almost as much as he loved the figure he cut in those tight trousers.

He loved the way Owain moved, and the way he laughed. He loved the way he took everything just a bit too seriously and the way he cared, so deeply, about the people around him, when the world had given him absolutely no fucking reason to. He loved the way there was always a lick of hair trying to escape the shackles of whatever they made Owain use as pomade, and he loved that shot through all the sweetness, kindness, and care was a delightfully wicked spark, when it could be coaxed out.

He loved… Owain.

Well, that settled that question, then. Of course, it spawned a whole new nest of feelings and worries and what-ifs, but Deri could deal with those another day. He nabbed each one firmly by the scruff of the neck and locked them away in the dark. They'd get out, of course, but for now they were safely boxed. Who knew being forced to school his mind around Merchant Maurlocke would come in handy for other things?

It was definitely time to take things to a new level.

'Come on. I have something I want to show you.'

Pierrick padded softly across the workhouse floor, trying to tread as lightly as the snowflakes he liked to imagine would fall any time now. It was Yule, after all. There should be snow. And a frost fair. And something hot to drink that warmed your belly even as your nose and ears turned red from cold.

But there wasn't. Instead, there was this horrible place. And he was trapped here. Trapped with good people, to be sure, like Vimukti and Owain. He smiled at the thought of the other boy. Having a friend inside helped.

The smile faltered. But it didn't stop the torment. Or the pain. Or the fear.

No, if Pierrick was going to stop those things he would have to do it himself. And the key was this new machine. Vimukti had said it was valuable, that it would save the Graspars a lot of money and make them more. And now everyone was out, enjoying their hard-earned holiday, he had the perfect chance to investigate – and possibly break – the thing.

It was eerie, hearing the workhouse so quiet, without the hum and buzz and heat of the machinery, threatening to chew him up and spit him out. But there was still light, here and there, and a bit of residual heat from the steamworks below. It was too expensive to shut them down entirely. They took forever to stoke.

Pierrick found himself drawn to the large hourglass at the centre of the machine. It was raised off the ground just enough that he could see the metal iris that formed the bottom of it. Some kind of hatch to load materials into, as Vimukti had described it.

He had to crouch down and carefully hop forward, ducking his head under the rim to get a good look inside. There had to be some way to sabotage it that wouldn't violate his contract. If he could just get a good enough look—

'Now, Junior!'

Pierrick felt rough hands at his back shove him bodily into the glass enclosure and the metal iris snapped closed, narrowly missing his feet. He spiralled his arms wildly, but it seemed as if the earth had lost all claim to him. He floated, nauseatingly weightless, in the middle of the small chamber.

Through the glass he could see Garog's face leering at him, and Missus Graspar approaching slowly, the monster of a mutt dragging itself panting and wheezing behind her.

'I told you I saw him, mum,' Garog preened. 'Didn't I tell you? You questioned him and everything, but you let him go. I was right though. He came back.'

'You were right indeed, my sweet. And how fortunate for us that you were. Here we are with a volunteer, when I thought we'd have to chase down some of the rats in the attic for our little experiment.'

Experiment? Pierrick began to swing wildly at the glass, but he could get no purchase. He was weightless, and the crystalline walls seemed always just beyond his reach.

'Let me out of here,' he screamed. 'You can't keep me in here! My contract—'

'Your contract gives us the rights to your time, boy,' Missus Graspar's voice was a lash of braided steel. 'You have my word, you will not be harmed. We will keep precisely to the contract, never you fear. Junior, here. Drink this, my sweet.'

Missus Graspar passed her son a glittering vial. Garog unstoppered it and drank the contents down greedily. Pierrick watched in horrid fascination as the dull malice in Garog's eyes was subsumed by sparks of frenzied inspiration.

'You know what to do,' Missus Graspar said. 'Make the adjustments, just as we discussed. You're clever enough to do so. For now, at least.'

Missus Graspar moved over to the levers and began to operate the machine. Pierrick started as the hourglass began to rotate, moving him up and further from the floor, though still he floated weightless in the centre of the chamber.

'In you get, there's mummy's best boy,' Missus Graspar crooned to Bruiser.

The dog, with some prompting, waddled into the other hourglass chamber. With a long, wheezing fart, he began to float as the iris closed behind him. Small droplets of drool fell from his tongue and began circling him in a lazy orbit.

'Let me out of here!' Pierrick shouted again.

'Oh, we will, we will,' Missus Graspar called. 'Just as soon as we collect our due.'

'I don't owe you anything, you withered old crone!'

'Ah, but you do.' The old woman's eyes flashed. 'Your contract of indenture entitled us to almost every moment of your time between now and the time you reach your majority. It belongs to us. So, we're going to collect. Quite frankly, we're doing you a favour, boy. Think of it as getting out of your contract years before you would have otherwise.'

Missus Graspar cackled and moved several levers in quick succession.

'Garog! Are the adjustments made?'

'Yes, Mother.'

Pierrick recoiled. It sounded like Garog but at the same time it didn't. And the malice that oiled every urbane syllable made his hair stand on end.

'Now, this might hurt a bit,' Missus Graspar called. 'Do let us know, won't you? We'll need to know for our future clients. Oh, and remember, even once your contract of indenture is technically complete – which it will be very soon – you're still bound by a geas of secrecy! We made sure to pay extra for a very good one. I do not suggest you test it.'

She threw the lever and Pierrick screamed.

Every fibre of his being felt as though it was being dragged forcibly through a desert of burning hot sands. Worst were his eyes. Shooting stars of pain burst through them, as if to slag the sand they had become to molten glass. Images flashed before him – scenes of things that never happened, things that might have been, reached out to twist his heart with joy and pain and sorrow. Mostly sorrow.

Pierrick saw himself running a hand along Vimukti's bare shoulder. He saw Owain and Vimukti and another girl he did not recognise singing to him around a small cake. He glimpsed himself in mirror-bright brass, tall and broad and brawny from years of lifting and working the shop floor.

His body twisted and stretched, grew old and grew thin, as years of his life were stripped away, turned to sand, and funnelled down through the hourglass to the waiting mutt who yipped happily and lapped up the shining motes of light.

Pierrick tried to scream again, but choked on the sound, sand turning to ashes in his mouth.

26

A little golden bell rang out as Deri ushered Owain into the ruins of the market stall that was his haven, hoard and hideaway. Owain looked around, with no small measure of trepidation but twice that in curiosity.

'What is this place?' he asked.

'It's my secret,' Deri replied. 'I wanted to,' he paused almost imperceptibly, 'share it with you.'

Owain turned to look at him. This was unexpected. Owain felt a warm glow kindle in the pit of his stomach. 'Oh? Did you bring me here to show me your collection of antique bronzes?' he teased.

'Something like that.' Deri stepped close.

The heat in Owain's stomach intensified and his heart sped up. 'Oh?'

Deri pressed his face close, arm sliding around Owain's waist. 'Yes.' He reached past Owain, pulling lightly at a section of fabric. 'Look.' Deri placed his hands on Owain's shoulders and spun him around.

Owain gaped. A small collection of treasures nestled together in a bed of shifting shadows. Most were commonplace items: buttons and knotted string, bits of ribbon and clipped coins and cones of twisted paper, stoppered reeds and fresh cut flowers that had yet to fade. A few finer items held court amidst the commonry, however: a beautiful antique ivory comb, missing but three teeth; an elegant signet ring with a crack running down the centre; a small hourglass with a tiny bit of gilding still clinging to the wood.

'My life's savings,' Deri said. 'Not quite enough to buy us free of our contracts, but it's a start.'

'I can't believe you're showing this to me!' Of all the things Owain might have imagined today might bring, this would have been the last. For Deri to do this, to show him his hoard? It was unbelievable. Owain knew merchants well enough by now, knew Deri well enough now to know what this meant. He spun around and kissed Deri fiercely.

'Thank you,' he said, after they had to break for air.

'No,' Deri replied, 'thank you. Now, if you don't mind, I think I've something else you'd rather like to see.' Deri smiled wickedly and began unlacing his cuffs.

Owain returned the smile, with interest, and went straight for Deri's trousers. 'Here, let me help you with that.'

'Very kind of you, I'm sure, but I insist you make yourself as comfortable as I. I'd be a poor host, otherwise.'

Owain laughed. 'I bet you say that to all the boys you bring here.'

'I do!' Deri crowed, before executing a sharp turn and saying in another, more velvet tone, 'but only because you're the first, so also only and all.'

Owain felt the fire beneath his stomach surge. 'Then why is there a pallet on the floor behind you?'

'Because a merchant is always, always prepared to close the

deal.' Deri flung off his smallclothes as Owain stepped free of his, caught Owain by the forearms, and fell backward, pulling them both down onto the thin mattress.

Above them, the little golden bell blushed rose.

Later – maybe even three times as later – as they were stewing in the – really rather stuffy at this point – ruins of that market stall, Owain asked about that golden bell. He'd had ample time to notice it whilst on his back, after all.

'It took me forever to save for that,' Deri replied. 'I wanted someone to watch over this place, and to teach me the Language of Gold. I figured since I speak Bell and it's made of gold, between the two of us I could learn that way.' Deri grimaced. 'It hasn't been nearly that easy, though. I can just about recognise a few dozen – well, they aren't really words, but I call them that anyway. And I'm absolutely terrible at speaking it. I can't rightly shine – so much of the Language of Gold is glimmering or shooting light off in one direction or another.'

'You don't do too bad,' Owain teased. 'I think you shoot rather prettily.'

Deri almost choked on the laugh he stifled. 'Don't do that! The other merchants avoid this place, but if you set me to pealing like that someone's curiosity might overcome their good sense.'

'What do you mean?' Owain stretched, only half-listening for the answer. 'Yikes. I'm a mess. I'm going to have to find a way to sneak in a bath before I get back to the workhouse.' He sniffed dramatically. 'Though a dip in the Thames might not be enough to freshen this daisy.'

'The merchant that had this stall offended Maurlocke,' Deri had risen and was carefully looking through his hoard for something.

'I don't remember all the details, but it was big. Maurlocke's revenge was, well, extreme. No one's dared come near this place since. Ah! There you are.'

Deri turned back to Owain, a dry and desiccated boutonnière in his hand. It had once been a vibrant rose, but it was much the worse for wear. Half its petals were missing. Carefully, Deri pulled a single petal free and blew it at Owain.

Owain felt a warm breeze whirl around him, fresh and cool and crisp and oh-so-faintly redolent of roses and champagne. When it passed, he felt clean. A life at the warehouse had not given him many opportunities to feel this clean. He felt fit to stand before Her High Majesty herself!

'What was that?'

'The well-to-do up topside, well, lots of them like to enjoy themselves a bit of amorous congress, but society demands certain standards when entering a home, particularly a noble one. Most of the gentlemen wear one of these. The flower-merchants of the Untermarkt grow them or enchant them or something. Between smoking and drinking and the Fog of London, not many survive the night they are purchased.'

Deri crumbled another petal atop his head. Owain watched with a bit of a smirk as the breeze caressed Deri's body and ruffled his hair; after all it had been his hands caressing those selfsame parts not so long ago. When the breeze settled, Deri looked positively regal.

His eyes snapped open and there was a deep spark of unease within them. He began rummaging through their clothes, separating out his to don, and tossing Owain's to him for similar purpose.

'We have to go.'

Owain sat up. 'What is it? What's wrong?'

'Maurlocke's going to call me soon. I can tell.'

Owain dressed quickly as Deri concealed his hoard from sight once more. As the collection of items vanished from sight, Owain felt an echo of warmth once again. For Deri to show him that, well, it must have taken a lot. It was a supreme expression of trust, and Owain would make sure he was worthy of it.

'Got everything?' Deri asked when all was back as it had been: to all appearances a long-abandoned market stall that no one ever dared visit.

'Not quite. Just looking for one more thing.'

'What?' Deri glanced around the floor.

Owain reached out and pulled Deri to him by the ascot. He pressed his lips to his and kissed him deeply, once more, before the day was done.

'That,' he said simply, after.

'Glad you found it.' Deri shot him a grin, then gently guided him out of the tent, his hand on the small of his back.

No one saw them leave. They said their farewells and turned to go their separate ways. Owain sighed as he bent his feet back toward the workhouse. Today had been a wonderful dream, but it was time to once more face reality.

27

The roar of the machinery around him rattled Owain down to the bones. Brass flashed, gears whirled, steam hissed, and Owain spat back at it as he leaned on the control lever for the drive shaft. The thicker metal of the catch had scraped and worn the niche it was supposed to fit into to a nub and the thing kept slipping.

'Hold the blamed thing steady,' Garog Graspar roared at Owain from outside the tangle of stubborn controls and hungry metal. 'You're slowing down production! Put your back into it or I'll kick your backside all the way to the Danu-damned Thames!'

Owain gritted his teeth and leaned into the metal lever with all his weight. This would be much easier with two. Where was Pierrick when you needed him anyway? He threw his weight against the thing once more.

The gears caught and the machine kicked into gear, going from a growling rumble to a smooth roar. The lever in his hands vibrated and kicked, trying to escape the ravenous draw of the drive shaft. Owain shoved it in place, imagining it was Garog's face.

The contrast between his present circumstances and his recent excursion to the British Museum hit him then, and he felt a wild laugh bubble up in his throat. The memory of the cool marble and shadowed galleries was a sharp contrast to the current steamy hell he occupied. Owain quickly rubbed sweat away from his forehead before returning his hands to the lever. It did not want to stay caught in place.

'It's worn away too much,' he shouted to Junior Graspar. 'Get Mistress Steele. This needs to be fixed. I can't let it go without it falling out of gear.'

'What?' Garog roared back.

Owain repeated himself, but louder. The workhouse ate away voices as much as it did will and sanity and hope. It was an insatiable beast like that.

'Hold the blasted thing in place then! If we lose productivity today I'm taking it out of your hide! I'll go get Steele,' Garog roared before stomping off.

Owain stood in place, sweating and vibrating with the force of the rebellious lever. There were much more pleasant sweaty activities with a hard rod that he could think of. Danu willing, he'd get to do them again soon. His face flushed as soon as he thought the thought. Hopefully there would be a candle waiting for him when he returned to his room at the end of the day.

But in that moment, the misfortune that had been hanging over his head since the night he and Deri had snuck into Missus Graspar's office saw its opportunity and struck. The control lever, straining against its confinement, sprang free, recoiling out of its place with the force of every engine and gear in the whole contraption boiled down to a single point. It caught Owain in the midriff and flung him backward, toward the still-churning gears opposite.

Owain's feet twisted about themselves, placed unluckily in one another's way. He spun about; his hand flew wide as he windmilled to keep his balance and went straight into the waiting teeth of the spinning gears. The gears bit through flesh and bone, chewing off three of his fingers. Owain stared dumbly at the three strangely delicate arcs of blood spraying from the stumps. They were so thin!

Then the pain hit and a scream burst from his throat. Owain clutched wildly at his wrist and howled, though the roar of the machinery around him tried to swallow down the sound. Then Garog returned, bellowing over the grumbling jangle of the gears.

'I warned you, boy – shit.' Garog took in the blood. 'Better get the healer girl.' He couldn't quite keep the vindictive smile out of his eyes when he said, 'I warned you.'

'Mister Graspar!' Silvestra snapped. 'The boy is in dire straits! Quickly!' She quickstepped forward and went to her knees next to Owain, blood swiftly seeping into the fibres of her dress. 'Here, pressure here.'

'Healer? Blast it, where are you girl?' Garog roared out across the floor.

Vimukti appeared, with body clenched and a stammer on her lips. Garog grabbed her by the arm and all but threw her at Owain. He pointed with a fat finger.

'I can't,' Vimukti sobbed. 'I can't, I can't, I can't!'

'Fix. Him.' Garog screamed at her. 'What's the matter, you stupid girl? Do your job!'

'I can't!' she screamed back, 'It's gone. I can't heal anyone anymore.'

'What!?' Garog went purple. 'Where did it go? What did you do?'

'What does it matter? It's my power that's gone! Mine! You don't own it, you don't own me, you—' Vimukti choked on the emotion.

Owain continued to scream. Silvestra, ever practical, saw the flaw in the current situation, and the best remaining solution. She plucked a small device from her chatelaine, twisted it awkwardly with one hand, and applied the resultant cherry-red coils of metal to the stumps of Owain's fingers with ruthless efficiency.

The scent of burning meat and the sizzle of crisping flesh filled the air. Garog swore and brought his hand up to cover his nose. Vimukti gagged and collapsed to her knees. Owain, mercifully, passed out.

'Right,' Silvestra said, 'that's cauterised the wound and stopped the bleeding. He'll need further medical attention, and quickly. Mister Graspar, if you would carry him to his bed? I will follow and care for him until appropriate medical attention can be found.' She caught Vimukti's eye and bore into it with her own. 'I'm afraid that we won't be able to save his fingers without magic or some nonsense from the Goblin Market.'

Vimukti blinked. She looked from Silvestra to Owain's severed fingers, bloody and stuck with metal filings on the floor. She looked back and Silvestra nodded, ever so slightly.

'Quickly, Mister Graspar! Quickly!' Silvestra's tone brooked no opposition.

Garog, bemusement on his face, gathered up Owain's limp form in his arms and began to stomp off. As soon as his back was to her, Vimukti's hand snaked out and gathered up Owain's fingers, one, two, three. Her flesh recoiled from the still-warm things, so she wrapped them in her handkerchief. She almost slid them into her pocket, but they bent, slightly, when she tried, so she forced herself just to carry them. Turning, she dashed off the factory floor, slowing only to be sure she wasn't seen.

Vimukti ran through the streets, the cobbles and stones beneath her feet constantly trying to trip her up. She sobbed as she ran, but her tears were just tears. There was no longer any healing virtue in them. She'd sold it all away.

Stupid! Stupid, stupid, stupid. She'd known that there would be a price beyond what she paid. She'd known she'd no longer be able to heal the wounds of the factory floor; as poor as her healing had been, it had still been something! Now, now she had words of fire burning in her breast, but nothing to spend them on, and the fingers of her friend wrapped up in a slip of linen in her hand.

They were going cold. There had been heat, before. Vimukti knew heat. But now there was just sticky blood and chilling flesh.

Vimukti pushed herself to run faster. There. Covent Garden Market. Owain always said – Owain always said it was easiest to get to the Untermarkt from there. Just listen for the stranger voices, listen for offers of flowers fantastical and strange. She burst in amidst the foliage and staggered up and down the aisles, drawing shouts of anger and more than a few blows.

The rich scent of the flowers was thick, cloying and sweet. Vimukti almost choked on it. It was as if these still-beautiful corpses propped up upon the merchants' stands knew she carried dying flesh upon her and they struck out at her as in vengeance for the reminder that they too, for all their beauty, were dead and dying things.

'Kit!' a voice hissed at her. 'This way! Quickly now! Follow me.'

Vimukti caught sight of Bess, the cat, wound tight beneath a nearby flower cart. Her tail was lashing and her eyes flashing. Vimukti stumbled towards her.

'Follow! Follow! This way to market.'

The cat sprang out into the aisle and dashed around a corner. Vimukti followed. She kept her eyes always on the flashing ginger fur of Mistress Bess. She didn't see the transition when it happened but she felt it. The mortal world faded away and her surroundings twitched into hyper-reality.

'Pretty primroses, to get 'em out their hoses! Come buy! Come buy!'

'Poseys of forgetting! Sweet dreams, no regretting!'

'Violents! Sweet violents! Make the other toughs cry! Come buy! Come buy!'

It was even more crowded here than it had been in Covent Garden Market, above. Bess yowled her displeasure at the stomping, stamping feet all around her and swiftly climbed up Vimukti to perch on her shoulder. Her claws were sharp and Vimukti's skin itched where they pricked her.

Panic nearly overtook Vimukti right there. So many people! So many market stalls! How would she ever find Deri in all this, even with help? She didn't have time. Owain's fingers were going cold and stiff in her hand. She started as a nearby market bell rang out. Bess cocked her head and whispered in Vimukti's ear. Her whiskers tickled.

'To Deri, quickly now. Follow as I say. The bells will lead the way. Have heart, little kit, we will find him, soonest.'

Vimukti gulped and nodded. She pushed into the crowd, using her elbows to carve a path. She followed the bells and the directions of Mistress Bess. It was very urgent that she get the fingers to Deri before they went completely cold. For some reason she had to get them to Deri while they still retained a bit of heat, a last final spark of Owain's life inside them. She didn't know why she felt that way, she just did, and the urgency of the cooling fingers in her hand pressed her onwards.

Twisting and turning, voices ringing out all around her. Her blood shivered in her veins at those merchants that seemed to know, instinctively, that she carried the dying flesh of another with her. Promises of healing, of memory, of immortality, of the power of blood magic at her command all assailed her ears. She pushed them all away and listened only to Bess, to the bells.

She nearly cried with relief when she finally caught sight of Deri, standing cocky in the crowd. There was a tall man with him, indecently handsome with an arrogant snit dripping from his nose. Someone important? It didn't matter. Nothing mattered but getting the fingers to Deri.

Vimukti strode forward.

28

Deri sneezed, the musty smell of his hidden cache teasing his nostrils. It didn't seem like the right amount, looking at the wealth he had assembled. It seemed far too little. But then he was still missing some of his memories after that debacle with Dame Aurelia. In front of Maurlocke, no less.

Frustratingly his hoard did not include the two items he most wanted. Or most needed. There was no bottle of prosperity, and no skein of laughter carded from Maurlocke's lips.

The laughter bothered him more than the prosperity. There had to be something that would make the merchant laugh. But what? Perhaps—

A mortal's near! There's danger nigh! his golden bell rang from on high.

Deri paused, the warning only slowly sinking in. A mortal? Here? But who would know – ah. The princess. Or her beau. Probably the beau. The princess already had everything she wanted. Deri quickly stowed and secured the last of his treasures and slipped out of the stall before the great lunk could barge in.

Sure enough, as soon as Deri stepped back into the flow of commerce, there he was: Lars. For a commoner, he sure put on airs like the nobility. There was an arrogant twist to his lips and his nose was stuck so high in the air Deri was surprised he didn't take flight like a kite.

'You!' Lars levelled a finger at Deri when he spotted him. 'We have business.'

'If you say so,' Deri said nonchalantly, walking over. Once close he drew a bored smile across his face and hissed sharply through his teeth. 'What are you doing, idiot? You don't make a spectacle at the Untermarkt! You'll draw too much attention from too many meddling merchants. You want something, you ask quietly. Otherwise, you're in danger of paying far too much for whatever it is you want.'

If Lars appreciated the warning in Deri's words, he gave no sign. 'You owe me a favour, little man, and I have come to collect.'

'Indeed?' Deri's mind raced. 'As I recall I owed someone else a favour, not you. Has something occurred that said favour has changed hands?'

'All you need to know is that the favour is mine now.' Lars was turning a most unflattering shade of red. 'I'm here to collect for everything it's worth.'

'What it's worth depends in part on what I have.' And on how well Lars could bargain. Perhaps it was a good thing the princess traded away the favour. He should have a much easier time getting a good deal off Lars. 'Did you have anything specific in mind?' The sooner he could be done and dusted with this parasite, the better. And it would be one less problem hanging over Deri's head.

'Wealth,' Lars answered immediately. 'Wealth and power would be better, but I've no doubt you'll do your best to cheat me, so I'll settle for a lifetime of wealth.'

'Are you having a laugh?' Deri stared at him. 'What makes you think I have that kind of thing?'

'You've got—'

'That,' Deri said, cutting off any potential mention of a certain bottle of destiny, 'is immaterial to the question at hand.' The last thing he needed was that echoing around all of the perked ears dropping under his eaves. 'I could maybe get you a lifetime of prosperity, but nothing more than you might get as a moderately successful merchant.' Or workhouse owner. 'It would take awhile, though. I don't have that kind of money kept on hand.'

'I suppose I can wait a few days, if you can keep me in food, wine, and restful comfort for the duration.'

Deri blinked. Someone had clearly given Lars some pointers. Unexpected, but nothing he couldn't handle.

'Do I look like an innkeeper? I could maybe, maybe see my way to supplying you with a drop of faery wine, but that's as far as I can go.'

'I—'

'Deri!' Vimukti burst on the scene, cutting off whatever it was Lars was going to say next. 'Emergency! Help!' She breathed in great heaving gasps.

'What is this?' Lars looked affronted.

Deri's instincts were screaming at him, and the bells were ringing warning in his ears. He could barely make out the words they were so agitated. And Bess? What was Bess doing on Vimukti's shoulder?

'What is it?' he asked.

'Owain,' Vimukti gulped. Instead of saying anything more she just held out a small bundle. Her handkerchief. Her rust-red-stained handkerchief.

Deri's world vanished to a pinprick in an instant. He reached out, too fast and too slow all at once, and took the bundle. He unwrapped it and stared at the contents.

'What—' Lars asked again.

'We're done here,' Deri said to him, reaching into a pocket. He shoved a capped reed at the man. 'Here's enough faery wine to last you a fortnight, at least. Don't drink it too fast. You're on your own for food and lodging. Find me in a fortnight and I'll have something for you. Don't come looking for me before then, and keep your mouth shut about anything and everything between us or the deal is off, and Danu damn the consequences. Savvy?'

Lars took one look at Deri's face, grabbed the reed, and ran.

'What happened?' Deri began striding through the Untermarkt, Vimukti following with the story spilling from her lips.

He stopped. He'd need funds. This was going to – never mind. He needed funds for this. No time, no time.

'Wait here.' Deri shot Vimukti and Bess a glance. He snuck back to his hidey-hole, moving far faster than was wise. He risked drawing attention to himself, but in that moment he couldn't bring himself to care. He returned after he had secured the requisite funds for bartering.

'This way.' This was going to be expensive. Deri already knew what he was going to barter for, however. There was no way to have them regrown, not without the proper permissions, and Owain was denied those via his contract of indenture. His body was, in a frustratingly real sense, not fully his own. The Graspars would have to agree, and their agreement would come with a hefty cost, likely in added years to Owain's contract.

Deri led Vimukti and Bess through the twisting alleyways of the Untermarkt, following the scent of fire, hot metal, and sacred oils. They passed workers of bronze and brass, hammerers of copper and tin. He paused briefly at a fork in the way, one branch leading towards those who worked mostly with gold, the other towards those who worked mainly in silver.

'Right or left hand?' Deri asked without looking directly at Vimukti.

'Left,' she said softly.

'Right,' Deri said, and walked down the left branch, towards those who worked in silver. He stopped after three steps. 'Bess, take Vimukti and wait for me under the market bell near old Blatterbosch's stall. It's not far. I'll be there as soon as I can with something for – for Owain.'

'Come, kit,' Bess prodded Vimukti. 'Let us go and I shall tell you stories of the time I bested the Queen of Spain in a game of—'

Deri strode away, trusting Bess and Vimukti would do as he asked. He couldn't afford to have them near while he was negotiating. He'd need every advantage he could muster here.

He stopped outside of the stall of Crednesson. His stall was a combination of showroom and forge, and powerful charms transformed the blasting heat from the forge into cool sea breezes. The air ruffled Deri's hair and the smell, so fresh and wild compared to the more usual enclosed air of the Untermarkt, threw him for a moment, as it was intended to.

Crednesson himself was no less arresting. The smith was willowy and graceful, with the tight musculature of a dancer rather than the massive frame of one who forges metal for a living. But then, Deri knew his arms contained the strength of at least a hundred, if not a thousand, men. And Crednesson's control, that dancer's grace, was legendary. His work was of the highest quality (and priced to match).

The smith drew a strand of fiery hair across his forehead to tuck it behind one of the fine fox ears standing upright on his head. When he smiled, fox fangs glinted in the light. Deri's stomach clenched. Crednesson was nearly as dangerous as Maurlocke, in his dealings.

'Young Master Deri,' the smith said jovially, opening with flattery, always flattery, 'what can I do for Merchant Maurlocke this fine day?'

Deri quickly weighted the pros and cons of attempting to finesse the truth here. He'd have to risk it, he decided. He'd need every advantage he could get his hands on to walk out of here with what Owain needed.

'I'm here to request a hand of ensorcelled silver,' he said, careful to tell the truth without disrupting the idea that he was here on Maurlocke's behalf. It wouldn't be his fault if Crednesson made an incorrect assumption. Though the payment would prove tricky, as none of it would be in the silver or gold Maurlocke customarily paid Crednesson for his services.

'Ah!' Crednesson's eyes lit up. 'The family specialty. Who is the lucky, or perhaps unlucky, personage?'

'He has not given permission to use his name, but I do have this.' Deri held up the bloodstained handkerchief and flipped up the edge, revealing the tip of a finger.

Crednesson inspected the unfortunate digit. He leaned in close and took a deep, huffing breath. He slid his tongue across the points of his fangs and smiled.

'I see! And so fresh. Why, there's still a hint of the original body's warmth, deep within the bone.'

'I trust that will make the working easier, and the price will reflect that.' Deri covered the finger up once more with the handkerchief. The sight of Owain's flesh, without Owain attached to it, was making it harder for him to think.

'You're always so eager, Deri. So sharp and hungry for the deal.' Crednesson laughed. 'You do your mystrer credit.'

Deri bowed. 'I strive to please.' And why wouldn't he, when pleasing someone opened their purses much more easily than antagonising them? 'As you can tell from the state of the, ah, digits in question, this is a matter of some urgency.'

'And you can trust that the price will reflect that.' Crednesson laughed, throwing Deri's words back at him.

Deri had expected that, and set to haggling with a will. Crednesson inflated the price, Deri piqued the merchant's interest by bringing out a variety of unusual items to use as payment. Crednesson, distracted by Deri's wares, let the price slip, but attempted to schedule delivery of the finished product for a later date. Deri countered by revising the order from a full hand down to three fingers.

'Only three fingers? Tch. Disappointing.' Crednesson growled. ''Tis hardly a fit employment of a skill such as mine.'

'On the other hand,' Deri countered, employing the pun because he knew how much Crednesson loved them, 'it has not been done before. It's a refinement of your hereditary art. Think how well regarded you will be if you can produce three perfect fingers and enchant them as to life. Such work will rightly be regarded as more intricate a working than a hand entire.'

The reason Crednesson always opened with flattery is because the merchant himself was so very vulnerable to it. Deri could see the merchant considering his words. A vulpine smile crept across Crednesson's face.

'If nothing else, it would drive my sister mad with jealousy,' he admitted.

'How much of a discount is that worth?' Deri asked, keeping his voice as light as possible.

'Ha! You are bold today, young one. Bold as brass.' Crednesson showed his teeth. 'But you'll have to do better than that.'

They launched once more into negotiations. Deri drove hard, but in the end the price he paid, while within his budget, was far higher than he could truly afford. More than a year of the time he had saved up to end his contract early vanished into Crednesson's coffers. But he would have three fingers of ensorcelled silver to take to Vimukti, to return to Owain.

'A pleasure doing business with you, Master Crednesson,' Deri bowed as he collected his prize.

'Yes, yes. Be off with you, child. I have much to do, and your unexpected arrival has set me behind schedule. My regards to Merchant Maurlocke.' Crednesson waved him off.

It wasn't until after Vimukti had disappeared, precious package in tow, that Deri realised he'd forgotten to invoke discretion with Merchant Crednesson.

29

Vimukti slipped back into the workhouse with some effort. Fortunately, Bess decided to accompany her back and was able to steer her away from watchful eyes. The hour was late, the sky was dark, but Vimukti was surprised to find a delivery at the front gate. Mistress Steele was present, looking grim at a box of rough-cut wood tied up with what looked like frayed rope. A red glow leaked from between the gaps in the box.

'No,' the artificer said to the twisted figure delivering the box. 'I need to inspect it. There is no reason to let this thing onto the grounds if it is not perfectly suited to my needs. It's accursed enough as it is.'

Silvestra opened the box and Vimukti froze, fascination warring with the urgency of her mission. The artificer drew out a large gear that looked to be made of red glass. The thing pulsed with a regular rhythm and Vimukti felt her heart seize in her chest when it happened to beat in conjunction with that dread glow.

'Hsst! Kit! Quickly now, while they are distracted!' Bess called to her.

Vimukti ducked into the workhouse, casting repeated glances over her shoulder at the unsettling scene she left behind. It was swiftly out of sight, but the image of that pulsing light lingered on in her mind, even as she made her way towards the boys' wing.

She moved as quietly as she could down the hallway. Owain would be in his bed, in the dormitory with the boys under his charge. She didn't dare get caught. At least not until after she had delivered the package from Deri.

Vimukti briefly considered finding Pierrick and asking him to carry out the rest of her errand. It was grim business and the thought of – no. She straightened. She would do this. It was the least she could do for Owain since she had been unable to heal him.

The silver weighed heavy in her pocket, wrapped in that self-same handkerchief that had carried the severed fingers, now miraculously clean of blood. Even so, her flesh curled to touch the thing. She knew she'd never use it again.

Here. The door she was seeking. Vimukti glanced carefully up and down the hallway before quietly turning the handle and slipping into the darkness beyond. Fuzzy yellow light, foggy and faint, drifted in from the windows, her sole source of illumination. Owain would be all the way across the room.

She opted for speed over stealth. Several boards squeaked under her feet, provoking a few rustles around her as the boys shifted in their sleep. The Graspars were stingy with bedclothes and space both, so one boy shifting tended to have a knock-on effect.

There. She could see Owain. He had several blankets laid atop him, likely courtesy of the other boys, and he slept as if dead. Certainly he slept the sleep of the drugged.

'I'm so sorry,' Vimukti whispered.

She stood for a moment, struggling to find more words, some way to encapsulate and expunge the guilt she felt for trading away her power. The cost was far higher than she'd thought she'd paid. She should have known. It always was when mortals made deals at the Untermarkt. She had known, she had been warned—

A board creaked outside the dormitory.

Vimukti froze. No. No time for her to get lost in herself now. When the door did not open to reveal Junior Graspar or one of his thugs, she quickly unwrapped Owain's bandaged hand. She bit her tongue to fight back the bile that rose in her throat. The stumps of his fingers were puffy and charred. To it quickly then.

She pulled the silver fingers free from her pocket. Deri had said they were already ensorcelled, and each would know its place as if born to it. That was the virtue of them having been forged from Owain's original fingers, still clinging to a fading bit of life in each.

The silver gleamed in the foggy light, which caught and pooled in the elaborate filigree pattern, engravings that coiled around each finger like ivy. Owain's thumb and smallest finger had survived, so she just needed to place the three middle fingers.

The ring finger was first. As soon as she held it near enough to the stump it all but leapt from her grasp. Sharp silver prongs at the end of the finger bit deep into bone and flesh, and the two embraced like long lost lovers. Before Vimukti's eyes, coils of silver rooted themselves in and around the stump. The finger twitched and the coiling silver stopped.

Vimukti quickly attached both the middle and pointer fingers after that. Each one behaved exactly as had the first, leaping and coiling into place. When the last finger had settled in, Owain seemed to breathe easier in his drugged sleep. It was hard to see in the faint light, but Vimukti thought the flesh around his hand looked healthier too. She'd have to check again in the morning.

From her other pocket, she pulled a stub of candle Deri had given her and placed it under Owain's pillow as instructed. Then, all duties discharged, she made her way back across the room. She froze as she turned. Several boys were sitting up awake, looking at her. None had made so much as a peep as she'd worked, however, so she raised a finger to her lips and fluttered her hands at them. Go back to sleep.

Slowly, they settled back down to prone. Vimukti let out a slow breath and crossed the floor again, treacherous board creaking underfoot. No help for it. Better to get out quickly.

Unfortunately, none of the speed in the world could help her when she opened the door to find Garog Graspar standing in the hallway, arms crossed.

'Huh. Didn't expect to catch you here.' A cruel smile cut across his face. 'Glad I did, though. Mum's been looking for you all afternoon. She wants to have a few words about what might have happened to your little talent.'

The bottom dropped out of Vimukti's stomach. The price of her trade just kept going up. She didn't even struggle when Garog grabbed her by the arm and began hauling her away.

You pay for what you get, after all.

Missus Graspar drummed her fingers across the massive oak desk in front of her. Each rap of the tap-tap-tap-tap sent a needle of dread into Vimukti's eye. The light from a single kerosene lamp cast the workhouse mistress's face into cadaverous relief.

'Let me see if I have this correct,' she said, voice like the sheen of oil across a razor's blade, 'you used workhouse time to go to the Untermarkt and trade away that one quality you possessed that gave you any value at all—'

'No, Missus,' Vimukti blurted out, 'as I said, that was on my own time. Holiday time. As stipulated in my indenture.'

Missus Graspar stilled. Fear warred with anger and resentment in Vimukti's gut. Her teeth felt like they were sparking.

'Very well.' Missus Graspar conceded the point.

Vimukti nearly fell over in shock. She didn't have any time to savour the small victory, however, as the workhouse mistress continued, voice twice as sweet and thrice as venomous.

'The fact remains, however, that you traded away your most valuable ability and have thus done immeasurable harm to the workings here. Why, one of your own friends lost three fingers in an accident earlier, did he not?'

The words cooled Vimukti's fire slightly.

'Why, were it not for the swift action of Mistress Steele, he might have lost even more than he did!' Her voice hardened. 'You have cost us, girl, no mistake about that.'

'It was my gift, and mine to sell by right!' Vimukti flared. 'It's allowed in my indenture! I know my rights.'

'That's true, but do you know mine?' Missus Graspar leaned forward. 'It's possible you do, but just to make them clear I will enumerate the relative ones here. I have the right to extend your contract for any action you take that directly and negatively impacts the functionality or profitability of this workhouse. This most assuredly counts.'

Vimukti opened her mouth to protest but nothing came out.

The old hag wasn't entirely wrong. She couldn't argue that she was without also denying that Owain might have died because she had given up her gift. If Mistress Steele hadn't been there, Garog might have just let Owain bleed out on the floor.

'Furthermore,' Missus Graspar's smile danced spider-like across her lips, 'I have the right to assess the total value lost in calculating the additional years addended to your term. And I fully intend to do so taking into account any and all productivity lost by each and every worker you might have healed in your remaining time here.' She leaned back into her chair. 'I believe the average number of injuries and the average severity taken from the records I've kept since you arrived and began to employ your gift is more than fair.'

Vimukti's heart sank in her chest and the fire in her belly guttered. The workhouse was all but a deathtrap. She herself had lost count of how many children she had healed and sent back to work far earlier than nature would have allowed.

'Let us use Owain's injury, as an example, as it is so fresh in all of our minds.' Missus Graspar's eyes glinted in the dancing flame. 'The loss of three fingers on his dominant hand would leave Owain quite unable to work many of the machines here for his remaining period of five years, three months, and six days. That would decrease productivity accordingly and, further, have quite a negative impact on the resale value of his indenture. Poor boy, who would agree to take him on in those conditions? Possibly an alchemist or an artificer in need of test subjects? I could perhaps ask Mistress Steele. In any case, I'm sure you understand the magnitude of your actions when you consider that loss across hundreds, possibly thousands of injuries over the remaining years of your indenture. In light of that,' she paused, as if to consider, 'I think thirteen additional years is more than fair.'

Vimukti felt the flare of the contract's magic in the taste of blood at the back of her throat. The words expanded, choking her, and almost choking out all of her hope at the same time. The yawning length of time spooled out before her, and she could not see the end. She felt, for a moment, that she would die here before she ever saw true freedom. And then Missus Graspar twisted the knife.

'And an additional three days for the time you did steal today from the workhouse during your little excursion. Your friend now has three brand new fingers of silver, I am told. I presume that was your effort, and your time was spent at the Untermarkt. I do hope you haven't traded away anything else I should know about?'

Stars of rage and hate went nova behind Vimukti's eyes. 'No, Missus Graspar,' she ground out.

'Good. Now go. I have wasted far too much time on you, and this workhouse has desperate need of my attentions elsewhere.' Missus Graspar looked at her suspiciously, as if suspecting Vimukti might be behind all her problems.

Vimukti swore to herself that if she wasn't, she soon would be. She exited Missus Graspar's office in the company of Junior. Yet another punishment.

'I'll just escort you to your bed. Make sure that nothing else goes astray tonight.'

Vimukti stomped off down the hall. She no longer needed to move quietly, and she was in no mood to make herself any less than she was right now. There had been a glimmer of frustration, a spark of worry in Missus Graspar's eyes when she said the workhouse had desperate need of her attentions. Vimukti was willing to bet another thirteen years on the end of her contract that at least part of that came from the slowdown.

She was going to make sure that things slowed even further. That shipments got delivered precisely as they were directed, and not a jot more. She would make sure the storage rooms were crammed inefficiently, that any lock she was not expressly ordered to lock was left unlocked, anything she could get away with within the letter of her contract.

And she'd teach each and every other child in this workhouse how to do it too. The Graspars would burn in inefficiency and hang with the self-same contract whose loopholes they so greedily exploited.

And it looked like she would have plenty of time in which to do it, too.

30

Deri wrinkled his nose. The smell of the Thames was sharp, today. He was walking along the cobbles in his costerboy guise. No one bothered him. Owain's workhouse was a long hike up the hill that loomed in front of him. He'd have to be quick as wit to get there, steal a few moments, and dash back in time to complete his daily tasks, but he hadn't seen nor heard from Owain in the three days since Vimukti had appeared in the Market with his severed fingers.

That place! Deri cracked his knuckles. He would bankrupt it. Drain every iota of profit from within its walls and make sure it was sold on for scrap. And he had an inkling how he might be able to do just that.

Words ran through his mind. Contracts of indenture, and the looping, curling language the merchants of the Untermarkt wrote them in to wring the most profit from the exchange. Somewhere in there were loopholes he could use, and when he found them he'd free up Owain and Vimukti and the other children to engage in a full-on strike. The whole place would shudder to a halt and start haemorrhaging profits. Profits, which the sigils he had planted on the premises would siphon off and turn into prosperity, fuelling his freedom, then Owain's, and then maybe a pretty piece of revenge, if they wanted. Wouldn't that be fine? Using money stolen from the Graspars to bring about their downfall?

Approaching the gate, he could have slipped in easy as pie, but he spotted Owain walking down the road, away from the workhouse. Just who he came to see! He tamed a smile.

Maybe this was his lucky night!

Owain tapped one of his new fingers against the crate he carried. It felt cold. Everything he touched with his new fingers felt cold, except in the moonlight. He took a deep breath. It was a blessing to be out here, outside the workhouse, even if it was just carrying crates down the road to the waiting wagon. At least he was away from the machinery.

His fingers ached at the thought. He would have to get back onto the workhouse floor soon. If he didn't, Garog would come looking for him, just as he had the last two days. And, just as he had the last two days, he would threaten to tear off the rest of Owain's fingers if he didn't get to work.

He hated how well the threat worked. He hated the power the workhouse held over him now. It was so much worse than it had ever been before. His fingers… he did not know how he felt about his new fingers.

He was glad to have them, certainly. It was a vast improvement over not having fingers, and he knew there was no way the Graspars would have paid to get him new ones. He'd have been sold off for tuppence, like as not, if he didn't have them. Brothels, underground experiments: Owain shuddered at the thought of what happened to those whose contracts of indenture sold so cheaply.

Owain flexed his hand. The fingers moved like his old ones had. He could even feel with them, though the sensations were often strange, and never felt quite as he expected them to. Sometimes it was a very pleasant feeling, but those instances were rare. Most things in the workhouse felt – well, horrible.

'Pssst!'

An urgent hiss ensnared his attention and a hand shot out of the shadows, catching his arm in a vice-like grip.

'Owain! You have to help me!'

The hand and the voice belonged to a strangely tall young man, lanky and lean, as if he'd been stretched too quickly on a rack to reach his height. He was waif-thin but his grip on Owain was deathly tight.

Owain had no idea who it was.

'Let go of me!' he said sharply. 'I have to—'

'It's me! Owain, please, you—'

'What's the hold-up?' The sound of Garog's voice suddenly snapped from the shadows. 'Keep it moving. We haven't got all night.'

'No. Not him. Not again.' The thin man's face turned to a rictus of horror, and he fled into the night, his hand falling from Owain's arm like water from an oil-slick canvas.

Owain started. The voice was familiar. The *terror* in that voice was familiar. Why?

He turned to face the foreman, an excuse already on his lips, but the figure that stepped out of the shadows belonged to someone else entirely.

Deri grinned at him, stepping close and grasping the crate so it hung between the two of them. They carried it together, fingertips brushing forearms, and moved through the night as if nothing had happened.

Owain almost jerked his new fingers away in shock. Deri didn't feel cold! Rather, he felt indescribably good.

'Are you alright?' Deri asked eventually.

'I – no.' Owain hesitantly raised his new fingers to trail them down Deri's cheek. The feeling through the metal was like singing. 'No. But I'm alive, and well enough, and I will eventually be okay. I think.' He didn't know whether or not he was lying. He could barely focus on what he was saying for what he was feeling. 'Are you okay? How did you afford—'

'Nevermind that,' Deri said, 'I'll take it out of the Graspars' hides. Did you get my message? Can you get away tonight?' He paused, then asked, more softly. 'Are you alright with… those?'

'I don't know how I feel about them,' Owain admitted.

'I'm so, so sorry, Owain,' Deri said.

This was the most serious Owain had ever seen him. It was a bit unsettling, actually. The sensation in his silver fingertips began to change, to buzz and grow chill and heavy.

The crate hung heavily between them and Owain was glad when they were able to unload it into the wagon and turn back toward the workhouse, though it meant a break in their conversation.

'You're sorry? Why? It was just an accident, a—' Owain asked when they were safely away from the wagon.

'A misfortune?' Deri cut in. 'You don't think this was simple bad luck, do you? There's no way. No, this was my ill fortune. The same measure you took from me the night we broke into that office. I'd stake my future reputation as a merchant on it. So, I'm sorry.'

Owain blinked. He'd forgotten that bargain. Well, not forgotten, but the consequences had been so nebulous a thought and his daily misery so real, the fear had long since faded from his mind. Oddly, it made him feel better. There was a reason this had happened. There was a reason, and it was payment for Deri escaping that night, and passing that curse on, and keeping the both of them safe. It made Owain feel almost in control. Almost. He ran his fingers along Deri's cheek once more.

'You've nothing to be sorry for. I made the bargain, and moreover I'm glad I did.' Owain surprised himself with the fierceness in his tone. 'And yes, this will take some getting used to, but feeling you with them? Yes, I think I am going to be more than alright with them.' He smiled as he felt the tension go out of Deri, and the sensation under his fingers changed again.

'So, we should definitely take a quick detour to the alley and explore that in much greater detail, then.' Deri quirked an eyebrow and smiled.

'Rake!' Owain laughed. The weight of the world didn't shimmy off his shoulders, but it lessened, somewhat. 'We will. But not tonight. I have to get to work or Garog will find me. He's been haunting me like a ghost ever since I woke up with these.' Owain waggled his fingers.

'I shall hold you to that promise. But first…' Deri pulled him in for a tight kiss. 'Just to tide us over.'

'Begone with you!' Owain said, not moving. 'Before it's too late.'

Deri waited just a minute longer than he should before tearing himself away and scampering off with a sly wink, and Owain loved him all the more for it.

Maurlocke paused in his mercantile peregrinations as his ears rang. One of his fellow merchants had called out to ym. Jack Trades? What did that arrogant snot want now? He'd been suspiciously light of heart in Maurlocke's presence recently. It made the merchant suspicious. Maurlocke turned, eyes of flint seeking through the crowd until they found their target. Not Jack Trades, however. It was Merchant Crednesson.

Better, though perhaps not by much. Crednesson could be a bit of a blowhard, and getting away from a conversation once it had begun could be expensive. Not as expensive as the time lost, but still.

'Merchant Maurlocke! I do hope my latest effort was to your satisfaction.'

Maurlocke mentally reviewed ys ledger. Yse had not ordered anything from Crednesson recently. Curious.

'The rush order your servant brought the other day. Three silver fingers, in the grand style of my family.' Crednesson was speaking a trifle more loudly than required.

He always was prone to boasting. And Maurlocke was certain yse had made no such order, through Deri or otherwise. Yet Crednesson was not so foolish as to lie. No, the likelier probability was that Deri was up to something of his own accord, and Crednesson hadn't been sharp enough to catch the boy at it.

'Your work is never less than entirely satisfactory,' the merchant temporised. Three ensorcelled silver fingers? Deri had not lost any that the merchant had noticed. And such a thing would be far from cheap. Who would Deri be working on behalf of? More importantly, if he was doing so, where was Maurlocke's rightful cut of the proceeds as Deri's mystrer?

'Do call upon me again for any such needs,' Merchant Crednesson said eagerly. 'It was a pleasure to work with such a challenge, and on such a short deadline as well.'

The man's boastful nature was going to beggar him if he wasn't careful.

'I assure you, the matter will rest foremost upon my mind. If such a need arises, you will be the first upon whom I shall call.' An easy enough promise, with an easy enough escape clause.

Merchant Crednesson didn't care. He simply accepted Maurlocke's word and swept off. To brag to someone else, no doubt, and to drop Maurlocke's name in a few business negotiations in the hopes of a better deal. Utterly transparent.

Unlike his servant. Maurlocke pursed ys lips of gold. What was the boy up to?

31

Deri sent a message to that wanker, Lars. He wanted a one-way ticket to a life where his every need was accounted for? Well, Deri would see as he got it. Last he checked prisoners were afforded food, clothing, beds, and a roof over their heads. That was needs, sorted, and Deri hadn't promised wants, or comforts, or anything like. And if Dame Aurelia didn't clap the man in irons, well, at least he'd been offered the chance. No skin off Deri's nose if Lars turned it down.

He just needed to get Dame Aurelia to agree. He needed to meet her on neutral ground, and, ideally, get paid for delivering Lars to her. Clear one debt, make one profit, two birds, one stone. Which brought him to his destination.

'How do, Rhys?' Deri doffed his cap to the dangerously handsome pawnbroker. That was one double-edged sword of a saining gift if he'd ever seen one.

'Deri.' Rhys' greeting was cordial, one professional to another, but not stuffy about it.

Deri appreciated that.

'Let's continue this in my office.' The pawnbroker led the way into the back of the shop and up a narrow flight of stairs.

Deri paused in the doorway and elected to cross his arms and lean against it rakishly. This was Rhys' space. He already had the advantage of knowing the terrain. Deri wanted to offset that a bit.

The room itself was small. Too small for that long and twisting hallway. Deri would bet a year's worth of time off his indenture that there was at least one secret passageway that could be accessed from this room.

Rhys stood behind a massive desk. The monster dwarfed the space around it and somehow made the pawnbroker loom larger rather than look smaller by comparison. The walls were hung with exquisite artwork. Oil paintings, several of them in styles from centuries previous. Deri's merchant instincts said that these walls held – as well as hid – a fortune.

'You sent the message as I asked?' Deri opened the discussion.

'I did,' Rhys replied, 'exactly as you paid me to. I should warn you, however, that you won't win any points tricking her like this.'

'I'm sure Dame Aurelia will be so happy with the deal we're going to strike that she'll forgive me.'

'Have you met Dame Aurelia?' Rhys quirked one elegant eyebrow.

'We may have run into – or from – one another once or twice.' Deri flashed a cheeky wink. 'That said, I'm going to need you to warm her up a bit. If she charges in here—'

'Ah, you have met her then.'

'—if she charges in here and sees me, she's more likely to try and arrest me than listen to me, and she needs to save her cuffs for someone else.'

'The third party you told me to expect,' Rhys filled in.

'Exactly.'

Further conversation was cut short by a voice bellowing up from below.

'Ap Arwyn! Where are you?'

Deri blanched, recognising the voice of the Knight of the Verge. Before his mind could grapple with his strange surroundings enough to decide where to hide, Rhys had opened a secret panel behind the desk and shoved him through.

Stay quiet, his look said as he carefully closed the door.

'Up here, Milady Steele!' Deri heard Rhys clearly despite the door between them.

Secret passage. Deri had been right on the money. Dark as the inside of Maurlocke's vault, too.

He had yet to scrounge enough scraps of wealth to buy himself eyes that could see in the dark, but Deri did have a few tricks up his sleeve squirrelled away for just such an occasion. He raised his hands to his mouth and gave each a few good licks with his tongue, then drew the back of his hands across his eyes, much in the same way a cat would groom itself. The bargain sparked to life, his pupils split like a cat's, and the small corridor he found himself in suddenly seemed much brighter.

He'd need to put out a lot of milk and fish throughout the alleys of London to renew the charm, but that was a concern for later. The corridor stretched out beyond his view behind him, and Deri had to firmly quash the surge of curiosity that demanded he investigate, now! Not yet. First there was curiosity to satisfy by listening at this door.

Fortunately, he hadn't missed anything. Dame Aurelia had had to ascend the stair and navigate the twisting upper hallway above the pawnshop to locate Rhys' office.

'Your message said you'd found a way to track someone who isn't themself anymore.' Aurelia more than dispensed with pleasantries. She eradicated them and brushed their shadows off her shoulders. 'I need it now. Do not tell me I have to go back to that bloody place again because you only "sourced" it for me. I know you. You'd keep something this valuable close. So dig through that vault or hidey-hole or magical pocket and pull out a solution for me, no questions asked, and I will pay you and be on my way.'

'Good afternoon to you as well, Dame Steele. Are you quite all right? You seem out of sorts.'

Deri grinned at the amusement in Rhys' voice. It would drive Aurelia quite mad. Good. She deserved to squirm a bit.

'I was unable to have breakfast,' the knight answered brusquely. 'My sister —never mind. Suffice to say that there was nothing for me to eat this morning.' Dame Aurelia looked sad for a moment. 'And I expect there won't be for at least another month.' Then she shook herself. 'What have you got for me?'

'What I've got is for customers who show a little bit of respect and decorum. You're not looking for something easy to find, you know. Even in your solution.'

'If it were easy, I wouldn't need to ask at all.'

'I am not your enemy, Dame Steele. Remember that.'

Deri's smile widened at that. The heat in Rhys' words was subtle, but it promised far more interesting developments in this conversation, should Aurelia not temper her tone. And in Deri's experience, Aurelia was anything but temperate.

'Now,' Rhys continued, 'scrying—'

'Won't work.'

'Precisely.' Rhys was polite enough to act as if she had not just rudely interrupted him. 'So my stock of mirrors and basins and the like will not suit. We could perhaps try cards, bones, or the sticks—'

'Too general. I don't have time to puzzle omens and riddle out fuzzy portunings. I need something simple and strong that I can use to track her.'

'Have you tried the old-fashioned way?' Rhys didn't snap, though he did everything but.

Deri didn't bother to hide his grin. Rhys was really giving him his money's worth. If Aurelia wasn't ready to snap up the solution Deri had for her, he'd eat his hat!

'If I could find her myself, I would! She's changed. No one recognises her, and tracking one person through the maelstrom that is the Goblin Market is beyond even my skill.'

'What if we increased your skill?'

'Do you have something? Because I asked at the Market, and I certainly can't afford what it would take to improve on what I've already got.'

'Ah. No. I don't make a habit of keeping merchandise of that legendary quality around.'

Deri suddenly felt the weight of Rhys' regard through the door. Was that his hint to exit? He likely couldn't draw this out too much further without Aurelia becoming impatient and taking her leave.

'So find me something I can use. Seriously, anything. No questions asked.' Aurelia's voice went suddenly quiet. 'I've got to find her.'

That was it. That was his entrance line. Smoothly, Deri stepped out of his hidey-hole.

'Well,' he drawled, 'no questions asked, you say? I think I can work with that.'

Aurelia's head snapped up. Deri's heart, already pounding, felt like it began to hum in his chest. He covered it with his coolest mask.

'Shall we talk business, then?'

'You.' The knight's eyes were hot.

'Me,' Deri replied, making sure to keep Rhys' very large desk between the two of them. 'And I assure you, Dame Steele, I only asked Rhys to set up this meeting because I knew, beyond any shadow of a doubt, that I have the solution to your missing princess problem. Well. A solution.'

'He's legit,' Rhys put in, voice mild.

'That's like the fox telling me the weasel is safe to watch the chickens,' Aurelia snapped. But she made no move towards Deri.

He held up both hands, fingers spread.

'Fine,' the knight said, 'I'm listening. But watch how you speak. Out of either side of that mouth of yours.'

'You remember that Princess Boudicca left the palace grounds in the company of a certain young gentleman?' Deri asked. 'One who, at this very moment, both knows the current location of the former princess and is prevailing – rather piggishly, I might add – on my own hospitality?'

Dame Aurelia froze, saying nothing.

'I think we're in a position to help one another, Dame Aurelia,' Deri wheedled. 'Surely you can see that.'

'I can see a jumped-up costerboy getting ready to cheat me, again,' the knight snapped.

'It's an honest deal,' Deri protested. 'Or is this not the lead you've been looking for? The resolution to the quest or mission or whatever has been set before you?'

Aurelia growled. Deri knew he had her, then, when she didn't launch herself across the desk and try to throttle him. He was – as he had paid Rhys to carefully and explicitly remind her – her only good option right now.

'And what, pray tell, is this going to cost me?'

'I'm a reasonable person, milady,' Deri said, ignoring the way Rhys rolled his eyes. 'If you take Lars off my hands, and see to it that all of his basic needs are met – I'm sure Newgate would more than cover them, honestly – and perhaps throw in your word that I will no longer be a person of interest in the disappearance of Princess Boudicca, well, I'd say we'd have a deal.'

Aurelia stared at him, clearly trying to find the trap in his words. Deri bit back an exasperated sigh. If she was going to be like this, then he clearly should have asked for something outrageous to top it all off. Then she could have felt pleased to sidestep the obvious trap and save him the time and headache of her trying to find something that wasn't there.

'What's the catch?' the knight asked.

There it was. She was definitely trying to find the trap. Deri had misplayed his hand.

'The catch,' Rhys spoke up unexpectedly, 'is that this is a time-sensitive deal. The longer you wait, the more likely the former princess will move to someplace else, if she hasn't already. The longer Deri waits, the more his freeloading "guest" will cost him. It's in both your interests to move quickly. Though I can't say which will be hurt more by inaction.' He glanced at the knight. 'Though I suspect it will be Deri. You're a Knight of the Verge. You don't have to work so hard just to survive.'

Aurelia clearly didn't like that. She pursed her lips and glared, first at Rhys, then at Deri. She paced the room back and forth a few times, muttering to herself. Finally, she slammed a fist down on the desk.

'I don't like it, but I suppose that wasn't part of the deal.' The knight glared down at her fist, not meeting anyone's eye.

'Do we have a deal then?' Deri's heart sped up. This could still go either way, and he couldn't afford to lose any more time or hoarded wealth to this nonsense. He had his own freedom to purchase, as well as Owain's, and a workhouse to bring down.

Aurelia reached out and took his hand. Her face looked like she'd bitten a Clemens' lemon.

'We have a deal.'

Deri felt a sharp spike of triumph. It lasted all of a moment before Aurelia used their clasped hands to jerk him forward. She glared at him, eye to eye, faces almost touching.

'But if you screw me over, I promise you – for free – that you will regret it.'

Deri blinked. He should have expected that.

32

Merchant Maurlocke listened to the glitter and gleam of ys pavilion as yse paced back and forth across its rich carpeting. Deri was a clever boy. He'd hidden several small things around his small sleeping quarters. Maurlocke knew the location of each and every one. How could yse not? The pavilion walls around were threaded with gold, and the pavilion took such a childish delight on spying upon Deri and bringing all of his secrets to Maurlocke's waiting ears.

The three silver fingers poked at Maurlocke's mind. Where had the boy gotten enough wealth to afford such a thing? And where had he hidden it? Certainly not within the boundaries of this pavilion. Yse dismissed the thought of searching the Untermarkt for likely places. Might as well search for a single thread in a pile of spun gold. As to the amount, the boy couldn't have stolen it, and after reviewing ys ledgers Maurlocke was certain he hadn't lied his way into Maurlocke's purse to fund his purchase. That meant only one thing.

Deri was a good deal cleverer than Maurlocke had given him credit for. He clearly had enough time to run his own schemes and dealings in addition to the work Maurlocke assigned him. That was all well and good. Expected, even, from one indentured to a merchant of the Untermarkt. Though Deri did, in all fairness, owe Maurlocke a percentage, far more than the merchant had thus far received from Deri's efforts.

Maurlocke summoned the contract and read through the terms once again. It was an unnecessary indulgence, yet one that freed more of ys mind to concentrate on the matter at hand. There was no stipulation when such a percentage need be paid, save that it must be paid before the culmination of Deri's term of service, barring early termination of the contract, of course. So, yse had no way of knowing just how much Deri had hoarded. The boy clearly had designs on buying out his contract early.

No easy strings to pull here. Maurlocke dismissed the contract, sending it once more into storage. What yse needed was more information. The better the information the better the deal that could be wrung. And thanks to Merchant Crednesson's inveterate need to boast, yse had one. A small sliver of silver appeared in Maurlocke's hand.

It had cost ym a bit of time, a bit of flattery, but Maurlocke's instincts told ym the profit that this little snippet of silver would bring ym would more than make up for it. It was a bit of metal from the same ingot Crednesson had used to forge those fingers. It wasn't any silver of Maurlocke's own, more's the pity, but even so the merchant spoke the language of the metal almost as well as yse did that of gold. Yse could follow the resonance between the two bits of metal like a bloodhound on a trail.

Of course, that meant a trip topside. A trip topside meant yse'd need a disguise, and perhaps a form better suited to quick and inconspicuous travel. Maurlocke smiled, running a finger along a length of silver chain and twisting it into place along the coronet of hair. Glamour settled into place and, instead of the Merchant Councillor, a kindly-faced old woman with apple cheeks and cornflower blue eyes stared out of the mirror. As mortal as dust.

'Alright, dearies, what have you got for Auld Hazel today?' Maurlocke cackled and the pavilion around ym rustled, an echo of golden mirth.

Then the tenor of the light in the space changed. The gold glittered and gleamed warningly. Maurlocke smiled and nodded.

'Yes, yes, my friend. I have not forgotten. I've just the thing.' The merchant raised one hand and plucked a feather forged of fine, fine gold as if from nowhere. Certain ornithologists at the universities and museums of London would not hesitate to tell you it was the spitting image of a raven's feather, in all save colour and composition. In an instant the form of Auld Hazel changed for that of a golden raven, then switched back again. Yse nodded, satisfied.

Now, time to see where ys nose might lead ym. Perhaps there was some voice topside that could be made to sing for the small price of a sliver of silver or a gram of gold.

There almost always was.

Maurlocke, in the form of a golden raven, perched on a windowsill and watched. There were many things that ys eye picked out of interest. There was the young man on the floor of the workhouse who had three fingers that glimmered silver. There was a young woman whose words glimmered almost as bright as fire and gold as she went from child to child. There was the old woman and her brute of a son that loomed over them all. But most interesting of all was a single item amongst all that greasy brass and accursed machinery: a gallowsglass gear, glinting red.

It took fey magic to create such a thing, though Maurlocke ymself was not familiar with gallowsglass in the form of gears. It was valuable, however, very valuable, and to see it beating like a heart at the centre of a strange machine intrigued ym. That machine was the only one whose purpose yse could not easily glean simply by watching the industry below.

The boy with the silver fingers – Owain, was it not? – was intriguing, and his connection to Deri could prove to Maurlocke's profit. The canny old merchant could see that. More than that, though, it was that gallowsglass gear and the strange machine that had caused ym to tarry here. Yse could smell profit, and that machine reeked of it. Reeked so strongly it overpowered everything else in the vicinity and yse was surprised yse had not scented it from his pavilion. Yse needed to know more.

Maurlocke fluttered ys wings. The old woman was moving toward her office. If yse was fortunate, she and her fool of a son would speak of matters of import regarding that mysterious machine. If not, perhaps there was another, better way for Maurlocke to acquire that which yse sought.

The glass of Missus Graspar's office window was dusty. Even so, Maurlocke crouched close to the sill. Ys feathers were all of gold and yse dared not risk moving overmuch and catching the light. It was afternoon, and the rays were fading, such as there were, but clouds were treacherous allies at the best of times and Maurlocke would not rely upon them.

'Lazy brats, all of 'em,' the young lump of muscle was grunting.

'They serve for now. As soon as Mistress Steele finishes her work, we'll have a use even for the lazy ones,' Missus Graspar said as she sorted through the papers at her desk.

Maurlocke perked up, hearing this, but unfortunately nothing more was said regarding the machinery. There was a great deal of complaining about the brats and how much less productive they had been recently. Tiresome, though Maurlocke could understand the frustration of one's investments not returning as expected.

The two were certainly up to something. Maurlocke could pick that much out of the way they spoke and the things they danced around. They had clearly been so circumspect for so long that it had ingrained the avoidance of certain words and subjects in them, even when they were alone. Whatever that machine was for, it was likely as dangerous as it was profitable. Maurlocke's beak cracked a wide smile. What an utter delight. Yse'd come looking for answers as to ys servant's activities and stumbled across something that might further fuel ys rise to the richest merchant in all the Untermarkt.

Though yse had not the time to constantly be spying and waiting for secrets to uncover themselves. Maurlocke was a merchant of the Untermarkt. Ys time was valuable. Yse had meetings to attend, contracts to write, and deals that must be negotiated in person. Fortunately, he could see an alternative solution to ys little predicament from here.

There was a ring of gold upon her finger and a chain of gold draped in an arc across his waistcoat. Neither were perfectly shining and polished. How could they be, in such a place as this? There was too much dirt, too much oil. That would be ys opening, a commiseration on how difficult it was to maintain a proper shine in such conditions. Maurlocke knew gold. Yse knew how to flatter and how to tease answers from the unwary.

Yse had no need to lurk and wait for secrets to spill from these mortals' lips. All yse need do was ask the gold they bore with them almost everywhere. Maurlocke smiled, and in ys glinting beak of gold was a greeting.

33

The silvered glass was cool beneath Deri's fingertips. Cool, and cracked. His fingertip caught on an exposed edge and a crimson line sank into the mirror. Cool, cracked, and cutting.

Deri stared at the small mirror. Acquiring it had set him back weeks. That is, had cost him weeks of the wealth he had accumulated to buy his freedom. He could have purchased it for a matter of days, but doing so would have also saddled him with the seven years of bad luck that came with the breaking-making of the enchanted mirror. It wasn't worth that price, not for something whose magic would fade, and fade fast.

Not that he had many options. He needed to talk to Owain and Vimukti, but Maurlocke was keeping him too busy to sneak off and speak with them. If things went according to his plan, however, both he and Owain would have the rest of their lives free.

And he would have the prosperity he needed for his deal with Jack Trades. The merchant had been hinting that it was past time Deri deliver it. What if the merchant changed his mind? What if Deri wasn't up to actually *being* his heir? No. Deri shook himself.

Everything would work out. He just had to convince the workhouse pair to go along with his plan.

Deri's conscience gave an uncharacteristic twinge. Was this course of action really in the best interests of them all? It certainly served Deri's purposes. If he could pull this off, his prosperity siphons would soak up years, maybe even decades, of the wealth lost to the strike. Enough to buy his freedom? Almost certainly. To buy Owain and Vimukti free? Less so. Though the strike itself should give them the leverage to improve their conditions. Possibly he could negotiate their freedom. The Graspars would certainly be keen to rid themselves of the troublemakers.

The thought gave him pause. Another thing to worry about. Deri gnawed at his lower lip. All this worry. It was unlike him. He made a mental effort to shove it all aside. Focus! Come on. There was work to be done and vanishingly little time to do it in. Freedom. *That's the goal.* For as many as he could manage.

The ruins of the merchant stall around him – his haven, his secret – were filled with shifting shadow. He'd lit only a single candle of simple, unenchanted tallow for once. The bells had but recently rang out the hour. Owain and Vimukti should have had time to hide themselves away with a simple basin of water. Easy enough to acquire in the workhouse. Far easier than privacy, to be sure.

Well, the mirror was paid in blood already, so Deri whispered to it and felt the magic within it spark to life. At first, nothing happened. He tried again to the same result. Perhaps Owain and Vimukti were not yet ready? He stood and paced the confines of the ruined market stall until he heard the bells ring out the quarter hour. Then and only then he allowed himself to try again.

'Deri?' Owain's voice swam through the mirror, moments before his visage followed. Vimukti was standing next to him.

'It's me,' he replied quietly. No sense risking drawing attention by speaking overly loudly, here. 'Can you hear me? See me?'

'Yes. Can you see and hear us?'

'Of course.' Inwardly, Deri relaxed. This had been far from a guaranteed solution.

'What is so important?' Vimukti asked, shoulder bumping into Owain's. 'Why don't you just sneak in again? I'm sure Owain would appreciate it.' She smirked.

Owain coloured. Deri smiled. Sadly, now was not the time.

'I haven't much time, and I suspect neither do you,' Deri said, forcing the smile away. 'I've come up with a way that you can strike, properly, though it won't be easy and both of you will have to do quite a lot of heavy lifting. You, Vimukti, possibly more than either of us.'

'Me?'

'Yes, you. You've that voice for a reason. Now's the time to use it if you want to do this. If both of you want to do this. It must be unanimous action. You'll need to convince every single child in that workhouse to follow your lead.' Deri watched Vimukti's reaction closely. He needed her to do this, and do it well. 'You know as well as I do that that new machine is going to make things much worse for all of you, and soon. We need to act now.'

'I can do that,' she said after a moment, shoulders straightening.

Or perhaps he was wrong and she was more than equal to the task.

'Sorry,' Owain interrupted, 'what exactly is going to stop them from using the punitive clauses in our contracts to force us back to work?'

'I am,' Deri replied. 'Each and every person involved in the strike will trade me a bit of luck, or time, or hope, or whatever we can manage, and in exchange I will agree to add three days of their contract term onto mine. The exact three days of the strike. I'll take all the pain, because I've got a way to bottle it for later so it won't all hit at once. I'd offer to do more, but three days is all I can manage.' Nevermind that bottling the pain to suffer later would also increase the agony three-fold.

'You can do that?' Vimukti looked excited.

'I'm not sure I like this idea.' Owain looked decidedly unenthused.

'It doesn't matter. It will work.' Deri attempted to cut off further objections. 'That takes care of the magical dangers. We also need to get you all out of the workhouse so they can't physically make you work. Or otherwise convince you to stop the strike.'

There was a moment of silence as everyone considered just how much force Garog Graspar's fists could apply. And how much glee he'd take in the action.

'Do you have an easy way to sneak everyone out?' Deri asked.

'Easy, no, but there might be a way,' Owain said reluctantly. When Vimukti looked at him curiously, he sighed. 'We could get everyone out via the sewers. Pierrick managed to find his way out through there once. He told me about it. Of course, that was before he disappeared. Maybe it was why he disappeared. How. Whatever.'

'Running wouldn't get him free from his contract,' Vimukti objected.

'Well, there's no way the Graspars actually sold his contract on, like they said,' Owain snapped. 'The workhouse is short-handed as it is. There's no way Pierrick would bring enough profit to justify that.'

It sounded like an old argument. Deri didn't have time for old arguments. Or new ones. He certainly didn't have time for arguments that would end up with him having to make clear the connection Owain was still missing: that his friend had clearly been used by the Graspars to test their machine – which obviously was capable of draining youth and resilience from flesh as easily as it did from wood and metal – and the mysterious man that had accosted him in the alleyway was what was left of Pierrick. He quashed the guilt and forced the conversation to shift.

'In the end, it doesn't matter. He showed you a way out. Can you use it? Actually, no, you have to. That's perfect!' An idea bloomed in Deri's mind. 'I can secure you a safe place to hide for three days, maybe even a bit of food. I'll have to negotiate with the mudlarks but – yes, yes. This will work!'

'Okay,' Owain said, trusting Deri, 'so we have a place to hide, a way to handle the punitive clauses, what else do we need? What else should we do?'

'Vimukti needs to practise using her new gift. It'll be key in negotiating with the Graspars as well as securing universal agreement from the other children in the workhouse.' Deri tapped his chin. 'And we've got to figure out the best way to make this hurt. The Graspars have to lose, and lose both big and fast. None of us can afford a prolonged strike.'

'Destroying the machines would hurt, if we could.' There was a voracious eagerness in Vimukti's words.

'Big if. The contracts won't allow that. And trying might be enough to kill Deri outright. No way that's viable.' Owain's voice was heated.

It kindled an answering warmth in Deri's chest. Always nice to know one's life held value. Well, to people other than oneself, that is.

'Owain's right,' he said. 'However, if you could trick the Graspars into doing the damage themselves, they couldn't hold you accountable, morally or magically. Well, technically or magically, at least.' Deri smiled. 'And there is one thing in that workhouse worth more than all the others, and it is the one thing that you just might be able to trick the Graspars into breaking themselves.'

Both Owain and Vimukti were silent, thinking. Deri waited to see who would catch on first. To his surprise and his pleasure, it was Owain. He must have been rubbing off on him even more than he realised!

'The gallowsglass gear,' Owain said. 'Mistress Steele says it's the biggest expense the Graspars have ever added to their ledger.'

'Exactly. And those things are rare. So not only is it expensive, but unless the Graspars are close, personal friends with a powerful merchant of the Untermarkt or a grandmagister of both alchemy and artificing, it will take a great deal of time to replace.' Deri grinned.

'But Mistress Steele told me almost nothing can break a gallowsglass gear,' Vimukti said. 'It's valuable partly because it's so hard to break.'

'Three things, and three things only, can shatter a gallowsglass gear, and all of them relate back to the criminal whose death gave it birth. The first is the touch of the rope that hanged them. The second is speaking aloud the last words they spoke. And the third is a measure of forgiveness matching the heinousness of the crime.'

'Where are we supposed to get any of that?' Vimukti demanded.

'Well, lucky for you I got a nice, long look at the receipt for that particular gear when I was last in Missus Graspar's office, and my memory,' Deri tapped his temple, 'is practically flawless. I know the name of the criminal whose blood was used to forge that gear, and if you know who to ask, all records of public executions – of which this was one – are available free of charge at the Office of Public Records. I've got the words right here.' He held up a scrap of paper.

'What's the catch?' Owain asked. Deri wasn't nearly triumphant enough for there not to be one.

'Neither of you can say the words. No one who is indentured to the Graspars can. It would be a gross violation of your contract.' Deri grimaced. 'There's no wriggle room around that. Indentures take severe damage to business and property very seriously. You're going to have to trick one of the Graspars into saying these words when you meet them. Thankfully, most criminals aren't terribly inspired speakers, especially at the end, and this one is no exception.' He held the paper up so Vimukti could see.

'Yeah,' she said after a glance, 'I can get Junior to say this.' She ran her tongue over her lips in thought. 'It'll be tricky, but I should be able to do it with my new gift.'

'And the lady artificer won't get in the way?' Deri asked, carefully avoiding speaking her name. It was too close a reminder of the knight he kept running into.

'No,' Vimukti said, shooting a glance at Owain. 'She's gone. The machinery is finished. All up and running. She didn't have any other reason to stay.'

Deri didn't miss the fact that she studiously ignored Owain's new fingers as she spoke. She and Owain were going to need to work that out, soonest. They couldn't afford a weak point like that if they were going to go up against the Graspars. He said as much.

'But,' he held up a hand, 'that assumes that we are going to do this. If either of you have any reservations, now is the time. I—'

'Oh, we're doing this,' Owain interrupted him. 'We've got to do something, and this is the closest we've ever come to having a fair shot. And you can stop looking so blank.' He turned to Deri. 'You haven't tricked us into this, or talked us into it, for all you think you've Oghma's own tongue.'

'I didn't—' Deri began.

'You did. You know you did. Drop the guilt. We're making our own decision here, and you holding back because you're worried we didn't won't help any of us. We're doing this. Right?' Owain looked to Vimukti.

'Right.'

'All right.' Deri blinked. 'Then let's get to it.'

34

Aurelia took a deep breath of the clear country air and nearly choked on the smell of manure. Somehow that aroma never really made it into the pastoral ballads, however popular they were. Perhaps because the inane things glossed over all the drawbacks of living in the country. Aurelia had certainly had more than her fair share of experience at this point: mud, rain, surly people who were suspicious of outsiders, not to mention the sharp decrease in the availability of anything that wasn't described as 'hearty' in terms of food or drink.

She stood in the drizzle, looking at the charming home tucked in a small copse of trees. 'Lena's place', the villager had called it. A low wall of hand-assembled stones bordered the farm – for such it was – and gave the whole place an air of rustic charm, a simple beauty. Mud squelched beneath her boots as she followed the well-worn track to the front door.

The door opened before she could bring herself to rap at it. The young woman she'd known as Princess Boudicca stared back at her, though her eyes were those of a stranger. Aurelia stood, at a loss for words. She'd been looking so long.

'Come in, Dame Aurelia. I've been expecting you.'

'You have?' She stepped across the threshold into as cosy a home as she'd ever seen. Clean and bright, with enough space for one to feel comfortable but not so much that you felt like you're rattling around in a great box.

'You were always going to track me down, somehow. Tea?' Lena had already boiled the water.

'Uh, yes. Thank you.' Aurelia stared at the former princess like she was a serpent, one the knight was unsure would strike. Why was she already thinking of her as Lena? Why did it seem so… fitting?

'I'm still me,' the woman said calmly. She smiled. 'Though I will admit I'm probably much more even-keeled these days. I'm sorry about that, actually. I put you though such trouble!'

'Not – not at all.' Aurelia struggled. She hadn't even used the proper form of address. It just seemed so… inappropriate. Whatever she had expected, this was not it.

'Please, sit.' Lena gestured to a wooden stool tucked under the small table. 'No need to stand on ceremony. Especially now.' She laughed.

'My apologies, but you are so…' Aurelia sat as she searched for the word.

'Different? Lars complained of that a great deal.'

'How?' The knight couldn't stop staring. It was the same face, the same voice, but the core of the young woman before her was so different. It was unsettling.

'I traded away my destiny.' Lena shrugged. 'I think it made slightly more of a difference to who I am than I would care to admit. Not that I am complaining, of course! I have never been happier. I can't imagine being any different and I wouldn't want to be even if I were offered the opportunity again.' She laughed. 'Believe me, I know how good I have it now.'

'You really aren't a princess. You don't sound like a princess. You don't carry yourself as a princess. I've known you for years and… it's eerie.' Aurelia fiddled with the handle of her teacup. 'You do seem happy though. Happier than I've ever seen you. Well, happier than I've seen you in the last fifteen years or so, anyway.'

'You'd remember those days far better than I, I'm afraid.' Lena straightened the cuffs of her sleeves. Her dress was a simple, country affair, but well-made and comfortable. Though the material was humble, there was still a bit of wonder in her as Lena touched the fabric.

Aurelia could see it, the way her fingertips lingered just a bit on the cloth, as if the sensation was still new. She'd done the same thing when she was first granted her squire's tunic. The fabric had felt so strong, so clean. Different from the clothing she had worn before. She'd touched it then like Lena was touching her dress now, like someone trying to reassure themselves they wouldn't wake up to find it had all been a dream.

'And there's no way you'd let me take you back, I suppose.'

'I don't think you could even if you tried.' Lena smiled, not unkindly. 'I was sold a new destiny. I don't belong there anymore, and I don't think you've got the power to bend fate to your will. No offence.'

'No, none taken. Though funny you should mention fate.' Aurelia frowned. 'We've had prophecies and divination and soothsaying of all kinds. You can imagine why.'

'Yes. I can imagine. Gran – Her High Majesty – is nothing if not insistent.' Lena blinked. 'It feels so strange to say that.'

'Her High Majesty? Or Granny?'

'Both, I suppose. But you said there was a prophecy?'

'Or a foretelling, or some such nonsense.' Aurelia tried suddenly very hard to downplay the words that her superior had weighted her down with. 'I was supposed to bring you back. Dame Eigyr said—'

'What were the exact words? Did they call me by name? Because if they didn't, you may have been making assumptions.'

'What? Of course she—' Aurelia blinked. Her orders were burned into her memory, and they did not include any names at all. 'No, no she only commanded I return "the princess" and "Her High Majesty's grandchild".'

'There you are then,' Lena said. 'You don't need me. I'm not the princess any longer.'

'Of course! Danu's dugs, but I've been given the runaround by twisting words enough these past several weeks I should have thought of that! But – if not you…?' Aurelia trailed off thoughtfully.

'Look,' Lena said, 'I'm here, but those parts of me – well, probably the most important part anyway – that made me a princess are not. I'm not what – who – you're looking for.'

'Back to square one.' Aurelia's shoulders fell. 'After all that. After he tricked me into dealing with that idiot Lars – no offence.'

'Oh, none taken. Lars did turn out to be quite the idiot. He certainly didn't appreciate the new me.' Lena tapped her finger on the table in front of Aurelia. 'But you're not entirely back to square one. You know exactly where to go next. And I should think it won't take much to fix your predicament.'

'Oh?'

'Just get that boy to trade you a new princess. He should have everything he needs to make you one if he has to. And if he doesn't, I'd wager he's smart enough to get what he's missing.'

'A good merchant has a care to never outsmart themselves,' Jack Trades said, looking Deri square in the eye. 'This is especially true of anyone I might consider as my heir.'

Deri winced at the implied rebuke. He opened his mouth to say something, but closed it again as Jack Trades reached out a hand. The merchant gently brushed a few grains of sand from Deri's shoulder.

'You've invested quite a lot in spare moments, it seems. I expect you're using them well.'

'Yes, Merchant Trades,' Deri replied. 'I expect I'll have all the prosperity you requested, and more, in just a few days' time.'

He'd better. Deri's wealth had shrunk an alarming amount. He'd be lucky to buy himself a fortnight or two of holiday from Maurlocke with all that remained of his once-flush hoard. A bit of extra prosperity on top of what he owed Jack Trades would go a long way towards putting him back in command of the funds he would need to see this all through.

'Very well then!' Jack Trades smiled and it was like the sun breaking through the fog on an early spring morning. 'I look forward to seeing what you bring me with great interest.'

Deri took it as the dismissal it was and made his way covertly back to the thrum and flow of the Untermarkt. The last thing he needed was someone with a wagging tongue to spot him doing business with Jack Trades when he was so close to finally getting his hands on just what he needed.

Well, except for the laughter. How he could trick that out of Maurlocke, he still didn't know. And he needed the spare funds from the excess prosperity before he could try any more ideas. His mystrer was a difficult riddle to solve.

Deri returned to the pavilion, but it was empty. Even if he had wanted to, he wouldn't have been able to make another attempt at teasing the laughter from those cold gold lips.

Now what business could Maurlocke be about this time?

Maurlocke looked through the cornflower blue eyes of ys Auld Hazel guise, though it was a very different sense that had led ym here. The golden wedding band of Missus Graspar has given ym a name, a name that resonated with opportunity, and yse had followed the sound until it dissolved into tears. Now the merchant stood, wearing the face of a kindly old woman, looking down at a man weeping like a boy in the filth of a London alley.

The scent of urine was rank and sharp, the man's face streaked with dirt. His clothes were all far too small for him and he was curled in a nest of faded and fading newsprint. He looked to be in his mid-twenties, but not long ago he would have looked a fresh-faced sixteen.

'Now, now,' Maurlocke crooned in a voice that mimicked kindness, 'what's wrong, my duck?'

The man, Pierrick, who had so recently been a boy in the Graspars' workhouse, flinched back from the sound. It took a great deal of calm and careful coaxing to draw him out of his nest, howsoever little protection the rotting paper offered. Maurlocke, however, was a merchant of the Untermarkt. What patience yse did not naturally possess was easily bought. Yse had more than enough for the task at hand.

'Who are you? What do you want?'

'There, there, my duck. It's just Auld Hazel, innit? I's heard ye cry, and though I haven't much, I might have a bit o' comfort to offer, yes? Come now, let me sit down. I have a small bit o' bread. Why don't ye take half and tell me yer story?'

Pierrick looked at the bit of bread in Maurlocke's extended hand and burst into tears. That these tears might be for the small kindness offered, rather than the prospect of a bit of food after so long, was completely lost on the merchant. Maurlocke had never faced deprivation, had never faced a world that seemed determined to grind ym down and rip every ray of light and hope from ys eyes. No, Maurlocke saw only hunger, and a weakness to exploit.

Pierrick gratefully took the bit of bread and tore into it, almost oblivious to Auld Hazel levering herself down next to him. If he had looked, he would have seen the kind blue of her eyes flicker to hardest flint grey and back. But he did not look. The bread in that moment was his whole existence.

'Better?' Maurlocke asked, voice once again dripping kindness, when Pierrick had finished.

'Yes, thank you.' Pierrick's eyes welled up with tears once again. 'Thank you.'

'Tell Auld Hazel what's wrong, ducks.'

'I – I can't.' The young man's face screwed up in pain and trembling. 'I – contract. It won't let me. I can't even tell anyone what they did.'

The words were followed by more tears. Maurlocke marvelled that the idiot hadn't yet cried out all the tears he had. Usually they were a numb and aching void by this point. Auld Hazel made vaguely comforting sounds and patted the young man gently as he wept. Maurlocke's mind was turning the problem over and over, examining it from all angles. The story yse needed was locked behind the privacy strictures of a contract of indenture.

Many were the secrets that powerful individuals – those that routinely held contracts of indenture on others – wanted kept safe and secure after the contract's term expired. What use was it to have an apprentice to do your work if in the process they learned all your secrets and went away with them at the first opportunity? No. Such secrets were locked behind chains of fey sorcery. Though that didn't mean someone clever couldn't slip them from those chains with a bit of effort.

'Ah, I've heard this tale many a time before, ducks. There's a trick to it. If'n ye listen to Auld Hazel, ye can speak yer woes and then they won't weigh on ye so heavily.'

'Really?'

'Aye. A bit o' hair, a bit o' mud, and a prayer to the Lady of Still Pools and Deep Wells, and ye can tell yer story to someone else as easily as ye tell it to herself in yer memory.' Maurlocke took out a bit of Thames mud and plucked a hair from Pierrick's head. Then ys fingers worked it into a tiny, humanoid form as the voice of Auld Hazel called out a rhyme to one of Maurlocke's old allies. 'There. Speak, ducks, before this dries completely, and ye'll not feel the lash o' that nasty binding.'

'The – the Graspars stole my life,' Pierrick said hesitantly. His eyes widened when he realised he could speak. 'They put me in their new machine, the one with the gallowsglass gear that Mistress Steele built for them. They turned it on and—' He choked on remembered agony. 'They ripped years off my life. They put me in that big hourglass and it felt like I was being scoured away, and they had that ugly old dog in the other chamber-thing and the bloody beast got younger as I got older. My life was stolen away and given to a *dog*.' The words, temporarily freed, spilled from his lips. All the particulars of the story, washing over Maurlocke.

And the merchant understood, then, how Pierrick was still able to cry. The boy had had seven years ripped away from him. His youth, vigour, and opportunity to learn had all been taken, but he had been left with his tears. Seven years' worth of sorrow, all packed into a well overflowing.

It would be a long, long time until Pierrick's weeping would come to an end.

35

Owain tapped his new fingers on the machine he was working on. Over the past weeks it had become something of a habit. The strange sensations that came through the silver were endlessly fascinating. He was sure that eventually he would be able to interpret them. For now, though, they were a welcome distraction from his nerves. Nerves that had only grown more jangled as week after week passed while they made preparations for the strike.

Vimukti walked past, carrying a large sack of processed brass gears. She flicked a glance at Owain and let him see a flicker of a triumphant smile. That was it then. She'd persuaded the last holdouts.

He should send a candle to Deri. Owain had mapped out enough of the sewers underneath the workhouse to provide the basis for their escape route. Deri had paid to access the plans in the Office of Public Records to get the rest of what he needed. As long as the aspiring merchant had also managed to successfully negotiate with the mudlarks, then everything needed for the strike was pretty much in place. And what wasn't would be once they successfully escaped.

Steam hissed from the pressure valve above him. Owain jerked back, instincts flaring. He had been wound tight as clockwork ever since his accident. It served him well now, saving him a scalding. And a scolding, if Missus Graspar were anywhere near. Garog didn't bother with words. The brute just went straight for the beating.

The thought, and the memories it pulled to the surface, stiffened Owain's resolve. The strike was worth the risk. They couldn't go on like this. Conditions were unacceptable, and – Owain sighed – they were all far too disposable. Just like Pierrick.

He knew what had happened. He wasn't an idiot. He just didn't want to say it out loud. That would make it far too real. He needed a bit of a lie, a bit of hope, howsoever false, to get him through this next trial. Who knew? If they managed to secure their freedom, maybe he could seek Pierrick out, and – no. Too much. A little hope sustained. Too much was a danger.

Owain felt a jagged laugh burbling in his throat. Like he could tell where that line was! Though recently it seemed he was edging closer and closer to crossing it, in the direction of more and more hope. Ever since he met Deri.

Deri. Owain smiled faintly, before the roil of conflicting emotions bubbled up in his stomach again. He began tap-tap-tapping on the machinery with his new fingers. The fingers Deri had purchased for him. The fingers that he himself – in a very real way – had sacrificed to ensure Deri's escape from Garog the night they broke into Missus Graspar's office. It had been a reckless purchase, these new fingers.

Owain wasn't sure precisely how he knew that, but he did. Maybe more of Deri rubbing off on him. They were too expensive, too high in quality. They must have cost a great deal, or Deri had

had to make an unwise bargain to secure them. The thought left him uneasy. They were about to embark on another gamble, and so much of their freedom rested on Deri's ability to make a deal.

Not that he had any doubts as to Deri's ability. But these were powerful people they were going up against, whilst hiding from Deri's own mystrer. If anyone could catch Deri in a slip-up, it would be a true merchant of the Untermarkt.

Steam vented above his head once more. Owain hurriedly adjusted the pressure, hauling on a nearby lever and cross-checking with the dancing needle of a nearby gauge. The machine bucked beneath his hand and his grip almost slipped.

His new fingers caught and held, however. The silver bent around the brass with implacable force. They would not bow before a lesser metal! Owain felt the spike of fear flicker and fade. He could do this. He could do all of this.

He had to trust himself. He supposed he had to trust Deri as well. He'd not been given any reason not to, so far. In fact, it was far easier to trust Deri than it was to trust himself.

And there it was. The supplanting core at the centre of that mass of bubbling nerves and feelings in his stomach. He was worried he wouldn't be able to keep up with Deri. Not that he wasn't good enough, no. That had been a worry, but even now it was fading away, replaced instead with the strength of silver. He'd survived losing pieces of himself. He was plenty strong, plenty good enough.

But Deri was like the wind, and you couldn't catch and hold the wind. Not even with fingers of fine, fine silver. Not that Owain had been able to manage, at least.

Of course, you don't catch the wind. He didn't even want to.

He wanted to run with it. To keep pace with it as it made its way across the world.

Steam whistled past his ear and this time Owain didn't even flinch. He was too caught up in his thoughts. Deri didn't have to carry him. Owain was already quick, and getting quicker. A slow smile crept across his face. And if he needed a bit of a boost, well, there was always the Untermarkt. A part of the strike was his to manage, and the gains from that, well, that might indeed move more than enough to make sure he could keep pace with Deri. With his goblin lover.

Owain smiled a little sadly at that, remembering how Pierrick and Vimukti used to tease him.

Though keeping pace didn't mean charging ahead with quite so little forethought as Deri was wont to. Owain's smile quirked itself into a rakish grin. No, he could be the gentle nudge that shifted the breeze, that kept them both on track. So long as they survived this next bit.

He just had to hope Deri was careful enough to survive until they did.

'I'll get you luck, all of you. Luck for days,' Deri blurted recklessly to the group of youths surrounding him.

Thomasina Saunders, leader of the band of mudlarks Deri was currently negotiating with, laughed. The sound rang across the muddy estuary, clear as a bell. It was the only clear thing about Deri's current experience.

The estuary was muddy. The water of the Thames was silty and brown and brackish with the interplay of river and sea. Even the air around was thick and biting, filled with the Fog of London. Half-seen shapes and malevolent motes of phosphorescence like the eyes of vengeful ghosts drifted all around.

'We're supposed to give ye aid on credit?' Thomasina looked at him sceptically. 'Mudlarks don't give credit. We live by our wits, and what we win is hard-won. Why should we give it ye for free?'

Deri almost bit his tongue in frustration. If the young woman would just listen to reason! He'd have luck to spare once he collected payment from the workhouse children in exchange for taking on their pain and obligation for three days; amongst a thousand children, he could garner enough luck to outfit each of the mudlarks in Thomasina's wing for several days, and still turn a profit. But he didn't have the luck now.

He was running dangerously low on any kind of operating funds at this point. Between acquiring the prosperity siphons, securing Owain's replacement fingers (and that deal was nearly bungled by his missing memories), and the endless sands of spare time he'd scrimped and saved now pouring through his fingers as he struggled to complete all the work Maurlocke required and his own schemes, Deri was very nearly spent.

It almost seemed like a dream, having had enough wealth saved up to buy years off his contract. But that hoard had dwindled, spent to fuel his plan, his gamble. And all of it would be gone if he failed. He'd be unable to buy his freedom before his term was up. Unless.

Unless he saved himself some funds by convincing Thomasina's mudlarks to help. Unless the strike went off. Unless he managed to steal years upon years of prosperity from that workhouse over the course of mere days. He needed this deal. He needed it far more than they did.

And they knew it. Mudlarks were sharp as merchants, in their way. They had to have keen senses, or they went hungry. They had to smell opportunity when it presented itself because it did so rarely. And Deri was a big, fat, stinking opportunity.

'Well, if ye don't want luck,' never mind that's not at all what Thomasina had said, 'what else do ye want? There has to be something. Proper scrappers like you lot? Strength to spare for when ye need to haul something up out the water sharpish?'

Deri's eyes darted from mudlark to mudlark. Muddy faces and muddy clothing. Young men and women, children, a few robust elders, all struggling to pry a living – no, bare survival – from the muddy grasp of the Thames. Broken and bloody fingernails and bruises were common, and there were more black eyes than apples among them. Each shrugged and averted their gaze in turn.

Bruises. Black eyes. Deri bit the inside of his cheek. The mudlarks weren't just scavengers in the mud. Sometimes, they were as good as pirates, when a fat barge slipped too close to shore when the Thames ran low. He shot a glance at Thomasina, how she held herself. Sure, a crew might take a bit of a battering when scrapping over a find, but what Deri saw? Those were the badges of a larger battle.

The Fog of London was a glittering haze all around. A bell sounded, muffled and morose, off the end of a nearby pier. Perfect weather for an ambush. And what group living on the edge of the law didn't occasionally need a bit of cover from unwelcome eyes?

'You know,' Deri said slowly, 'if I was in a position such as this, I might want to be able to, on very rare occasion, call upon an ally that could keep prying eyes off my back.' He smiled. 'Treasure hunting being what it is, of course.'

'An' what could ye offer in that department?' There was still scorn in Thomasina's voice, still a bit of posturing for her crew, but there was a spark of interest there as well.

Hooked her! Deri took a breath. Time to calm down. Time to take back control of this negotiation.

'Me? Nothing.' He let the rumble of discontent rise just a shade before he cut it off. 'But I can help you set up your own deal.'

'Yeah? With who?'

He gestured expansively around him. The Fog swirled at his fingertips. It burned, chill and clammy, down his back. Deri tried not to panic. It seemed the Fog had already cottoned on to his intent and it was interested. That… was not a complication he had predicted. He had just planned on asking the bells to deal with the Fog, as intermediaries.

The mudlarks were whispering amongst themselves now. Anyone working along the Thames had to have respect for the Fog. If you didn't you were liable to run afoul of its temper at some time or other. And with the amount of alchemical residue that swam through it, it was wiser not to anger it.

'We would maybe as be interested in something like that,' Thomasina said, struggling to maintain her air of nonchalance.

There it was. He had the deal. Everything else was just details, at this point. Deri relaxed, ever so slightly. Details he could sort. He was just happy he managed to find something he could use to secure the mudlarks' aid now, without dipping further into his hoard. That was a bit of good fortune, there. Deri stopped just short of thanking his lucky stars.

The Fog of London would not like it if he did, and Deri needed all the allies he could muster.

✿

'Merchant Maurlocke!'

A voice rang out of the symphony of the Untermarkt as the merchant concluded a bit of business for seven bolts of cloth, woven of swans' wings and silent tears. Maurlocke blinked eyes of flint as Jack Trades sprang from the crowd. What dread business was in the offing here?

The mortal merchant – a blight that should have been rooted out of the Untermarkt long ago – had the audacity to not only grin at ym but also to clap ym on the shoulder.

The familiarity was almost more than Maurlocke would deign to bear, but bear it yse did. Too many other merchants were watching, and yse would smelt himself to slag before yse would show weakness or discomfort in this place.

'Merchant Trades,' yse said instead, 'you have caught me at an unfortunate time. I have a pressing engagement elsewhere.'

Anywhere else.

'Of course, of course,' Jack Trades said. 'Time is money, and you are richer than most, so much poorer in the time department, I imagine.'

Maurlocke nearly turned to lead on the spot, so base was the anger that kindled in ym at that audacious suggestion. That yse might be poor in anything! The very idea!

'I have a customer in dire need of something only you can provide, and I was hoping I might ask a few questions.' Jack Trades was still talking. 'To ascertain if you are, indeed, fully capable of providing what is required.'

'I'm sure we can come to some form of arrangement,' Maurlocke said, mollified slightly by the suggestion of profit. 'Call on me in three days' time, and perhaps we can reach an accommodation.'

The very least yse could do was make the mortal cool his heels for the indignity of suggesting yse was poor in anything. As if yse were not rich enough to buy a thousand lifetimes!

'I look forward to it, Merchant,' Jack Trades said. Then suddenly he smiled. 'It'll be a laugh!'

The insouciance of his words alone was aggravating. Maurlocke had the distinct feeling yse was being laughed at, and flushed the rose-gold of fury, but yse knew better than to say anything as the human merchant strode off. There were too many eyes watching.

One day that man would pay. With bloody-minded interest.

36

Owain rose quickly as soon as the creaking floorboards told him Garog had left their room behind in his nightly patrol. He had slept (or not) in his clothes, as had the rest of the boys in his charge. Moving quickly he gathered them up and shuffled them out in an orderly file. Something of his gravity hung heavily on all of them for they moved far more quietly than any assemblage of children had a right to.

'Everyone make sure your pockets are full,' Owain whispered. There would be pinched and hungry stomachs before this was all over, and he wanted to make sure everyone carried as many hoarded scraps as they could. He had directed the boys to pocket as much food as they could over the past week.

After carefully checking the hall, Owain slipped out of the room and began leading groups of boys to the tunnel beneath the workhouse garderobe. Several times he met with Vimukti and her parade of girls. A few of the oldest children were sent down first, to gather and organise the younger ones below, until Owain and Vimukti had gotten everyone else out. Then they would follow and lead them through the sewers.

It was exactly as easy as it sounded, and more than once Owain was sure they would be caught, but they were not challenged once. Owain suspected Deri might have employed a bit of luck on their behalf. Though he could have used just a dash more.

Things became more difficult in the sewers. Owain started up small games and songs to distract the other children while Vimukti followed a flickering will o' the wisp, leading them to the bolthole the mudlarks had prepared for them. Owain's nose wrinkled at the stench, but he marshalled his charges and soldiered on. After a long and winding trek, the tunnel opened up into a vast, cavernous space where several other sewer mains met up. It would be unpleasant, but there would be room for them to spread out a bit, and no rain, at least. Maybe it was for flood overflow, or had been built to house a secret ship's dock. Whatever it was, it was massive. It was hard to believe such a space existed beneath the streets of London; though, that said, so did the Untermarkt and that was far vaster than this place. The size did nothing to lessen the smell, however.

'It stinks,' Little Bob complained.

'So do you, when you haven't had a bath,' Owain said back, forcing a lightness into his voice, 'and you still run from the water and the sponge.'

That was rewarded with a scattered chuckle. The less fastidious girls and boys seemed to take heart at this, and began ranging a bit further ahead.

'Stay close,' Vimukti stepped out of the shadows to say. The wisp Deri had given her glowed with a pale phosphorescence and provided a bit of light. Almost their only light. Candles had been expressly forbidden.

Throughout the sewers of London were small chambers, places for workmen to store tools and building or repair materials and the like. Some were still in use, others had been claimed by the various denizens that made a living from (or simply lived in) the sewers. Vimukti ranged down the tunnels that joined to the large cavern and carefully sought out the ones with a mark that flared beneath the light she bore. They were, inevitably, stained and crusted with brackish water, residual salt carried up the Thames by the sea's tides. Between it and the flowing water all around, scrying out their hiding place would be difficult, and, hopefully, far more expensive than the Graspars were willing to countenance.

In small groups they concealed the children, each with a trusted lieutenant. They'd contingency plans in place, but Owain couldn't help worrying. The Graspars were vicious. If this plan failed… He quashed the thought. There wasn't time for that today.

When the last of the children were safely stowed away, Vimukti turned to him. 'Are you ready?' she asked.

'As ready as I'll ever be,' he replied. 'Let's go take our demands to the Graspars.' Several hours had passed over the course of concealing and organising the children. It was well past dawn and the Graspars were likely beside themselves at the sudden disappearance of their workforce.

That, at least, was something Owain was ready to see.

Missus Graspar's quill scratched across the paper. The noise was almost deafening to her ears. Why? She pursed her withered lips into their accustomed frown. Something wasn't right. But what? Everything was quiet. Unease sank into her bowels. Too quiet. Where was the hum of machinery? The shouts of those little brats?

'Junior?' She called. 'Junior! Where are you?'

There was no reply. Missus Graspar growled and capped the inkwell. Her quill went into its sterling silver stand. She rose and locked her desk. Never again would she leave it unattended. Not after that ridiculous attempted theft.

'Come, Bruiser. Up. Come with Mummy,' she called to the dog in the basket by her feet.

Bruiser hauled himself to his feet. He still was no spry young pup, but he could walk again. He padded after his mistress, leaving a trail of drool as he went.

Missus Graspar stepped onto the balcony that overlooked the workhouse floor. The place was silent and still. No steam hissed. No children shouted. Not a gear moved. The place was as empty and still as High Queen Victoria's tomb. Where was everyone?

'Junior!' She yelled again. Again she received no response.

Muttering to herself, she stomped down the stairs to the kitchen. Maybe the great lunk was stuffing his face. Her eyes narrowed as she went. All the doors were closed. Where were those children? How could Garog let them all lie abed? Or that useless tutor, the one she had hired because he was cheap and lacked even the morals of a common alley cat? Why had no one done anything?

She found her son, the cook, and the tutor all passed out in the kitchen. Somehow they'd found her reserve barrel of sherry and drunk the whole thing, the fools! She sniffed. The sweet scent of the booze still hung heady in the air. She'd never smelt anything near this potent before.

'Up! Up! All of you!' She shrieked at them and began laying about with her cane. It took three smacks before she managed to rouse Junior. Before she could get a response from any of the three layabouts, however, the gate guard, Porthor, came running in. The fat fool was gasping for air.

'Missus! Missus! Your office – they—' he wheezed.

'What? What is it?'

'Two children, in your office,' he panted. 'They say they want to talk to you about the strike.'

'Strike? What strike?' Missus Graspar's eyes narrowed and her heart began to rail against her ribcage. 'They wouldn't. They couldn't.'

'I think you had best see for yourself, Missus,' the guard wheezed.

'Junior! Come with me.' Missus Graspar stalked back toward her office.

Owain and Vimukti were waiting for her in her office. As soon as he stepped in, Junior growled and lunged at them. The girl – always so insolent! – intercepted him and, with a quiet deliberateness that was unsettling to see, broke the three middle fingers on his left hand. Unnatural strength. Missus Graspar narrowed her eyes. Should have asked the brat what she had sold her healing for.

'Stop crying, Junior!' she snapped as she stalked over to her desk. She unlocked it and quickly rummaged through her papers until she could pull out a hefty bundle. She waved them in the children's faces. 'You will retrieve the others and return to work at once, do you hear me?' She waved their contracts of indenture. 'At once.'

'No,' Vimukti said calmly.

Missus Graspar snapped out a command invoking the punitive clauses on both their contracts. Nothing happened. Her heart stuttered. What? What was this? The boy, Owain, nonchalantly examined those repulsive silver fingers of his.

'What? What have you done?' Missus Graspar was not often at a loss for words. Here, she found them quite stolen away from her. By those hateful children. She couldn't even find her tongue when Vimukti began laying out the children's demands for improved working conditions. Improved working conditions? What nonsense!

'We'll be back in three days for your answer,' Vimukti said.

Missus Graspar worked her jaw. It felt like she'd swallowed a live toad. Her throat kept bulging and the only sound that escaped her lips was the occasional croak. What had these children done? Why were the contracts not working? She would have the head of each and every merchant who had penned the damnable things! How dare they fail here, now, of all times!

'Maybe by then you'll have regained your composure,' Owain added.

The two turned and walked out of her office. Walked out of her office! She had not dismissed them yet.

'You!' she managed to shout. 'Stop!'

Junior stalked out after them, Missus Graspar herself close behind. Somehow, the two brats had already made it down to the workhouse floor. They turned to look up at the two Graspars looming over the balcony.

'Was there something else?' Owain looked up at them.

'Perhaps you've decided to give into our demands already?' Vimukti's voice was a caress of gold. 'That would be the wise decision.'

It would be, wouldn't it? She should just give in to their demands. How much could it cost? Certainly less than the whole workhouse standing idle for who knows how – wait. Missus Graspar shook her head. The girl had nearly bewitched her! How much had she managed to charm out of those useless idiots at the Goblin Market?

'Watch your words, witch,' Missus Graspar hissed. 'I'm not some weak-minded fool to be so easily manipulated. Why, I could have you up on charges for that, I could!'

She could, couldn't she? While Missus Graspar had a very exacting knowledge of the law when it came to workhouses, child welfare (such as it was), and contracts of indenture, her knowledge in other legal arenas was far more nebulous.

'For what?' Vimukti made a face of faux concern. 'I only have your best interests at heart.'

'Don't you dare toy with me, girl! Do you know who I am?' Missus Graspar could feel the heat blazing from her face at this point. 'Trifle with me and you will regret it, mark my words.'

'Yeah! You'll regret it!' Junior added, undercutting her point in his idiocy. It left him wide open for retort.

'What? You think you'll beat us? Strangle us with those big hands of yours?' Vimukti snorted.

'We're still here. Still standing. Still alive.' Owain shared a glance with Vimukti. They both laughed. Laughed as if they hadn't a care in the world. Laughed as if they had already bested their betters. Their owners.

Missus Graspar was nearly apoplectic with fury. Her son, next to her, was worse. He was doing his best imitation of a high-pressure boiler about to burst.

'You can't touch us.' Owain shrugged. 'There's some crimes as can't be ignored.'

'And certainly won't be ignored by the press, even if they are elsewhere.' Vimukti smiled up brightly. 'So shout all you want, little man. What else are you going to do?'

'I will kill you all!' Garog all but howled.

At his words, there came a sharp crack. The gallowsglass gear, well within range of Garog's bellowing voice, had resonated with the words and blown itself to splinters. Owain and Vimukti stood on the workhouse floor, unharmed, protected by the machine casing that had housed the gear. Missus Graspar understood immediately what had happened.

'Junior!' she shrieked. 'You idiot!'

'Sounds like you two have several things to sort out,' Owain said.

'We'll leave you to consider our terms,' Vimukti added.

'And your position.' Owain glanced at the shattered, useless remains of the most valuable piece of machinery in the whole workhouse.

37

Maurlocke paused, the quill in ys hand freezing in place, as words in the Language of Gold came to ys ears in glimmering whispers. The words were carried to ym via a small, golden feather, wedged in a cranny of Missus Graspar's office window. It seemed the poor woman was cursing what the loss of the workforce meant to her newest enterprise. Ah, and that piece of wickedness was something that not even Maurlocke in all ys centuries had witnessed. Yse was impressed – no easy feat. And the profits from it promised to be similarly impressive. And now yse had the perfect opportunity to secure a piece of it for ymself.

'Boy,' Maurlocke commanded, 'I set you several errands not a glass agone. Why are you still here? Be about them.'

Deri paused in carefully polishing the ornate chair Maurlocke kept for customers of a certain stature. It amused the merchant to watch ys servant bite back an exasperated response. Doubly so as the boy seemed far too rested lately, for all the work he had been assigned. A mystery to delve into when yse had more leisure, perhaps.

'Yes, Mystrer,' Deri said, rising to stow his polishing implements and make his way out of the pavilion.

He trailed fine specks of sand as he went. Maurlocke's eyes narrowed. If the merchant didn't know better... but no. Yse had other matters to attend to. Hopefully very profitable ones, in the streets above.

It was a small matter to transport ymself to the workhouse, post-haste. Gold spent a great deal of time locked in the darkness below the earth, and Maurlocke knew well how to walk those roads of shadow. In no time at all, yse was cooling ys heels outside Missus Graspar's office whilst the old woman and her mental minimus of a son quarrelled.

They had obviously decided to keep ym waiting. It was neither a wise nor an uncommon strategy, and it occurred to neither Missus Graspar nor her son that Maurlocke might have invested in senses more than the mortal. The merchant, of course, had, and the unflattering conversation that was clearly audible despite a firmly closed door was heard, duly catalogued, and added piece by piece to Maurlocke's mental tally of the price of ys information.

Maurlocke had the patience of gold, which was like unto the patience of stone, and there were many corridors in the palace of ys mind down which to wander and do work even as ys body stood, rock-still, in the hallway outside Missus Graspar's office.

'Alright, Junior,' Maurlocke heard the Missus say, 'send him in.'

The merchant logged the error as another potential arrow in ys negotiatory quiver even as the junior Graspar wrenched the door open and grunted at ym to enter. Maurlocke swept in, sleeve of gold billowing. Missus Graspar did not rise. Merchant Maurlocke glanced about ymself, quite obviously, and sniffed once, as if in disdain, and kept ys face immobile as Missus Graspar's fingers clenched around the arms of her chair. The opening engagement was a draw, then.

'Junior, get our guest a chair.' Missus Graspar knew the niceties well enough to just shade her disrespect into something that looked like slight error.

'That would be most welcome.' Maurlocke waited until the brute brought ym a chair to settle into before speaking further. 'I expect you are a very busy woman, so let us get right down to the point. Your business is in danger.'

'What?' Whatever Missus Graspar had been expecting, that was not it.

'Yes.' Maurlocke stored the smile that should have crossed ys lips in a room in ys mind palace. 'It's quite serious, I should think. Your charges have figured out a way to sidestep their contracts to the point of taking, what do they call it? Ah yes, industrial action.'

'How do you know all that?' Junior Graspar narrowed his piggish eyes.

'It's my business to know,' Maurlocke explained.

'Well then,' Missus Graspar snapped. 'You should also know that I won't allow it to continue for long.'

'The thing is, dear lady, you're in no position to stop it. As I said, they've found a way to sidestep the punitive clauses embedded in their contracts. You won't be able to touch them that way.'

'I'll do it the other way then,' Junior said, cracking his massive knuckles.

Maurlocke didn't bother to hide the wince that particular course of action prompted. 'You do realise that would place you in violation of the contract terms? All you'd accomplish is setting them free entirely. If you can even find them. I expect they've taken great care to make sure it's far too expensive for you to do so easily.'

'They'd still bleed though.' Junior smiled.

'Don't be a fool,' Missus Graspar snapped. 'You know how much replacing all these children would cost us!'

'So we pay for day labourers!' Junior said. 'How long can a bunch of children hold out?'

'We haven't the liquidity for that,' Missus Graspar shot back. 'We've committed too much to the new machinery.'

Missus Graspar and her son fell to wrangling, all but forgetting Maurlocke's presence. The thought that they might be quite ruined by the children's plot unsettled them greatly. Maurlocke let that distress play out a bit. It would make his offer all the more appealing.

'Well, what are we supposed to do?' Junior demanded.

'I have a suggestion,' Maurlocke slid smoothly back into the conversation.

'For a price, no doubt,' Missus Graspar said sourly.

'For a price far less than you stand to lose if these children enact their little scheme unopposed,' Maurlocke countered.

The merchant leaned forward, running one golden finger along the edge of Missus Graspar's desk. It was a solid piece of furniture, functional and worn smooth by the years.

'It has not escaped the notice of certain elements at the Untermarkt what, precisely, it is you are attempting here.' Maurlocke rubbed imaginary dust between ys fingers. 'And I can't say that I, for one, begrudge you the attempt. It's not something we're permitted to deal in, after all, so it isn't as if there need be any competition between us. It strikes me, however, that you would be very well served by a friend, well connected, and well placed at the Market. For a reasonable percentage of the profits, you might even do double or triple the business you might have hoped.'

'How very kind of this person,' Missus Graspar said warily. 'Though it seems a very small price for us to pay, if it is a reasonable percentage.'

'The exact percentage is up for negotiation of course,' Maurlocke said with a smile, 'and the more exclusive the arrangement, the more reasonable the percentage.'

Junior grinned, but Missus Graspar held up a cautioning hand.

'I think I would like to know a bit more about the potential solutions you can offer to us,' she said, eyeing Maurlocke.

'There are several we can discuss,' the merchant replied, unruffled. 'But before we discuss that, I think we should establish the price of secrecy. After all, it would hardly suit you to have me sell the information on, and I certainly don't want it bandied about that I might be at all connected to the activities going on in the dark of this workhouse.'

Missus Graspar was a shrewd bargainer, for a Londoner from topside. When Maurlocke pressed for higher percentages, she countered with an offer of machinery access. Maurlocke switched tack and began to itemise additional services, one for each danger the Graspars faced in running their all-but-illegal machinery.

That it was not illegal was a virtue only of the fact that no one had before conceived of a way that mere machinery could accomplish this process. What was simplicity itself for merchants of the Untermarkt was fiendishly difficult to accomplish with brass and steam. Still, the Graspars had found a way, found someone who could find a loophole.

Trading in years, in youth, in immortality, was strictly and explicitly forbidden by the Treaty that allowed Faery continual access to the London market. If anyone had imagined that the Artificers' Guild could find a way to replicate that process, well, Faery might have been able to contest that restriction. As it was, they did not, and now could not. But the potential for profit remained, and if Maurlocke could ensure exclusive access to the process, well, the wealth that would be generated could be incalculable. Yse could think of any number of ageing mortals that would trade all they had for a return to youth. Far more than the labour of a few workhouse urchins was worth. And it was so easy to acquire new indentured servants to replace those that aged – or were forcibly aged – out.

First, however, Maurlocke needed to sink ys claws firmly into the Graspars' souls. There would be time after to wind them in agreements that slowly increased ys share and reduced theirs. Steps would also need to be taken to ensure secrecy. If simply anyone could replicate this process the value would plummet. Maurlocke would need to acquire through means foul or fair the genius behind this creation.

Thoughts of Deri pushed in at the merchant's mind. How had ys servant known? Was it linked to the whiff of destiny that clung to the rapscallion's garments? Or the way he trailed specks of sand? Where had he gathered so much spare time, anyway? The merchant pushed them into a spare room of ys mind palace and firmly closed the door. There would be time enough to deal with Deri later. Right now, yse could not afford the distraction.

The negotiations dragged on all afternoon. Twice Junior disappeared, ostensibly to see about other workhouse business in the

Missus's stead. Maurlocke judged that to be an unlikely occurrence. Garog Graspar, in the merchant's expert opinion, was overburdened with neither brains nor initiative.

The sun was setting when they reached an accord on percentages and the kinds of custom Maurlocke could and would bring to the Graspars. Included therein was the price for the services he would render in aid of the Graspars should the children have concealed further attempts to sabotage the factory. Also itemised were the kinds of sabotage Maurlocke would be responsible for countering, and (by extension) the kinds the merchant would be held blameless for not anticipating. Repairs were not ys purview.

'Now that's settled, tell me how you plan to counter this little plot the children have concocted,' Missus Graspar demanded.

'The contracts of indenture have built into them a certain flexibility. They have to, or they'd eventually run into unforeseen circumstances and vastly limit their usefulness and profitability.'

'Yes yes, it'd be quite useless for us to buy a contract dedicated to shepherding when we need workers of machinery. I understand the concept. What does that have to do with the children's plans?'

'Included in that flexibility are a few clauses that allow for the transfer of labour. Normally, this would be used by the contract holder to farm out the indentured for an additional profit, or to start new ventures. The phrasing is a bit imprecise, however, and it appears that someone has figured out how one of the indentured can, of their own recognisance, invoke these clauses in a kind of informal trade. It's a rather complex bit of work, but it boils down to the fact that they have an ally with a bit of magic purchased at the Untermarkt that will enable them to trade their hours with someone else, for a time. That's why the punitive clauses aren't working. The magic isn't connected to the right names at the right time, so when you invoke the clauses…' Maurlocke raised ys closed fist and flicked it open.

'Who orchestrated this?' Missus Graspar's eyes were hard as agates. 'None of my children know enough to do it on their own.'

'Clearly, someone is helping them for some reason. Perhaps a rival, someone who knows your secrets?' Maurlocke probed.

'That should be impossible, but so should their knowing how to pull off a strike like this. Now. Tell me what we're going to do to stop it.'

Maurlocke smiled. 'Oh, it would be my pleasure, dear woman.'

38

Three days later, the workhouse floor remained motionless and silent. The air was still playing host to the ghosts of hot metal and machine oil, but they were far fainter than Owain or Vimukti were accustomed to. The quiet was oppressive, as well. No machines hummed. No children shouted. It was eerie.

Missus Graspar and Garog were in the office. Of course they were. They would not cede even the slightest of advantages. They would not lower themselves to the workhouse floor, not in this conflict. Not unless Owain and Vimukti could force them to.

Owain and Vimukti paused at the threshold out of habit more than anything else. Missus Graspar took no time in taking advantage of that slip.

'Enter,' she commanded, not looking up from the pen scratching its way across her ledger.

Vimukti inhaled sharply and would have snapped back had Owain not stopped her with a slight nudge.

'Well, what is it? I haven't all day.' Missus Graspar's voice remained cool and detached.

Owain and Vimukti shared an uneasy glance. They had expected more spitting fury and roaring threats. This was a world of difference from the last time they had occupied this exact spot, three days ago. Vimukti cleared her throat.

'We're here on behalf of the children, Missus,' she began.

'Yes, yes.' Missus Graspar still didn't look up. 'Spit it out, girl.' There it was. An edge. That word – *girl* – had lashed out, sharp as a whip.

Vimukti, rather than quailing under that lash, stiffened under it. 'We've had quite enough of your abuse, old woman,' she said crisply. 'You've abused our contracts long enough, and we're here to tell you that unless conditions improve, that factory out there will remain as it is right now: empty, stopped, and unprofitable. We've given you three days to think. Our demands are more than reasonable.'

The pen stopped its scratching at that, and Missus Graspar finally looked up. Owain felt Vimukti stiffen and his own heart seized a moment at the sight of the naked hatred and loathing in Missus Graspar's eyes. No dragon full of fire could have been more terrible. Still, Vimukti and Owain armoured themselves in duty, in the thought of the younger children they were there to protect and to fight for.

'Demands? Reasonable? You ungrateful brats.' The words were drawn from between Missus Graspar's lips like razorwire over a whetstone. 'How dare you accuse me of such things? I have raised you up out of the gutter, fed and clothed you, put a roof over your heads, given your useless lives some shred of worth, and this is how you repay me?'

Garog loomed behind his mother, brutish and threatening, but even he knew better than to add his tuppence at this point. There was an animalistic glee in his eyes and he twitched, often. He clearly longed to join in the anticipated bloodbath.

'We're not here to pay or repay you,' Vimukti replied. 'We are contracted to you for a span of service, but a contract cuts both ways. You've been shorting what you owe us. How dare you accuse us of ingratitude? You sit up here, fat and easy, on the work of our hands, on the breaking of our backs, and give us scraps. No. We are not the ungrateful ones.'

'You will return to work at once.' Missus Graspar's tone was dangerously even. 'Get that floor busy and bustling within the hour and I will forget that this little demonstration ever happened. If you do not...' The sentence trailed off, but the threat in the room spiked.

'No,' Vimukti said, 'I don't think so. We think you need us more than we need you.'

'I own you!' The quill snapped between Missus Graspar's fingers.

'No, we work for you. There's a difference. You can't just do whatever you want. We're people.'

'You're gutter trash, swept up and given a second chance to be useful. You should be down on your knees thanking me for giving your worthless lives some meaning, some use.' Missus Graspar's voice rose steadily in volume as she grew redder and redder in the face. 'You are nothing! We, we are the drivers of industry in this empire! We provide jobs and livelihoods and meaning and purpose where otherwise there would be chaos and poverty. We—'

'Are responsible for keeping children in poverty and bondage!' Vimukti shouted over her. 'You think you're so bloody holy? So wonderful? Why don't you try eating the slop you serve? Sleeping in the beds you provide? I hope you like puke-flavoured gruel and lice, you warty old hag, because that's what your kindness and generosity provides. You'd think if you were so powerful, so kind, you could do a damn sight better than that.' Vimukti punctuated her words by spitting on the floor.

Missus Graspar regained her composure with a titanic effort. Every iota of it was visible on her face. 'I think we have exhausted the possibilities of this conversation. Return to work. Final warning.'

'Not until we have your word, bound with ink and parchment, that things will get better around here.' Vimukti's eyes were hard.

'You've got what you've got an' you ain't gettin' better,' Garog Graspar said, piggish face screwed up in a smile. 'We ain't need you. We gots better.'

Owain resisted the urge to look at Vimukti. This wasn't how things were supposed to go. Missus Graspar hadn't tried to invoke the contracts to harm them. And while there had been some shouting, there hadn't been nearly as much anger as there should have been. Something was wrong. Better workers? How could they afford them?

Garog Graspar was grinning wide. Missus Graspar's smile was small, but vicious.

'Come on in, Mystrer Maurlocke,' her voice rang out, deathly sweet, a poisoned candied apple.

There was a sound like the clatter of gold coins being poured into a treasure chest and two figures appeared out of nowhere. The taller positively gleamed, with twists of gold and silver locked about one another above a curiously androgynous face. Vimukti took a step back, startled, but Owain didn't move. Every fibre of his being was locked into place and he nearly bit through his tongue keeping himself from crying out at the sight of the smaller of the two figures.

It was Deri.

39

'Ready yourself,' Maurlocke commanded Deri. 'You will accompany me today.'

That was unusual. Not unheard of, but unusual, and that the merchant was asking it of Deri today, of all days, sent a chill through his blood. His heart sank even lower when the merchant led them up and out of the Untermarkt and onto the streets above, through alleyways and turnings, along paths of shadow that Deri had never even suspected existed, to the workhouse where Owain lived.

The siphons! They had to be all but bursting with prosperity. Something any merchant worth their salt should be able to sniff out. What if – no, it would be fine. The whole place reeked of profit. It had to be fine.

He kept his face smoothly diffident, a study in dutiful servitude and complacency. More than once he felt those eyes of flint upon him. He didn't dare let even a whisper of reaction through. Owain's safety – as well as his own – depended on it.

They went through the front gate, a novel experience for Deri, some dark corner of his mind noted with hysterical glee. Up the stairs Deri devoutly wished he were not so familiar with, and were not so familiar with his own tread, and into Missus Graspar's office. Fortunately, the Graspars were greedy enough that no hint of gold gilded or flecked any surface in the office, no gleam of silver to tattle on him to Maurlocke.

Whether or not Garog Graspar recognised him, though, that was a different matter. Deri's heart clenched when he saw the big man standing next to Missus Graspar's desk. There had been times the younger Graspar had come very near to catching him. It was possible the brute might remember Deri's face.

'Merchant Maurlocke.' Missus Graspar actually rose in greeting.

Garog Graspar gave no sign of recognising Deri. His eyes slid right over him, concerned as they were with the being of luminous gold and silver in the room. Deri's shoulders relaxed, just a fraction.

'Missus Graspar.' Maurlocke's voice was warmed more than usual.

Deri's ears perked up at that. Maurlocke's voice only warmed to that degree at the prospect of a vast profit. What was going on here? Something more than countering a workers' action, that was certain. But what did the Graspars have that was valuable enough to—

The new machine. The one that siphoned off life. If Maurlocke had negotiated some kind of access to it, exclusive or demi-exclusive, that would be worth–even Deri's mind couldn't process sums of that magnitude with any ease. Fortunes aside, the power and influence the promise of even somewhat eternal youth could bring in from the rich and powerful! But what could Maurlocke offer the Graspars in exchange for access to even a sliver of that pie?

'Shall we see to putting down this little rebellion of yours?' Maurlocke's voice was amused. Missus Graspar's face was not. Deri had his answer, and he didn't like it one jot.

'They should be here presently,' Missus Graspar said. 'If their missive is to be believed.'

'Then allow myself and my servant to conceal ourselves until the proper moment.' Maurlocke made a show of looking about the room. 'There should serve.' The merchant pointed to a section of floor unlikely to be crossed by any of the parties, but that would still serve for a dramatic reveal. Deri knew his mystrer too well.

Maurlocke beckoned Deri over to stand by him and shrouded them with a complex charm that hid them from sight and sound but allowed them to still see events as they progressed in the office. It was not lost on Deri that this particular enchantment would render any warning he might have considered shouting to Owain and Vimukti utterly ineffectual. It's hard to yell a warning to someone who cannot hear you.

Owain and Vimukti arrived shortly after, and Deri spent a great deal of energy keeping his face propped up in a neutral expression as his stomach sank lower and lower. He watched as they traded barbs with Missus Graspar, watched Owain's face and saw all the signs of confusion and wariness as things did not go to plan. Whether or not Maurlocke also saw how the unexpected turns troubled Owain and Vimukti, Deri couldn't say. The merchant was perceptive but didn't know the two to the same extent Deri did.

Things were not going well. What Owain and Vimukti didn't know was that things were about to get much, much worse. Deri could only imagine how much worse. Maurlocke's flair for inventive cruelty was not something he would ever plumb the depths of.

'Come on in, Mystrer Maurlocke,' Missus Graspar's voice rang out.

Maurlocke broke the concealment charm with a sound like cascading coins and Deri froze his features, but his attention was all for Owain. Owain and Vimukti looked shocked, but not even Deri could tell if Owain had reacted to him or to Maurlocke or simply to their unorthodox appearance.

'Missus Graspar,' Maurlocke said, in a voice as smooth as polished silver, 'what can I do for you today?'

'It seems my factory has gone idle. I don't suppose you have an affordable solution for that problem, do you?'

'Why yes, Missus Graspar, as a matter of fact, I do.' Maurlocke smiled.

It was an artful performance, poisonously sweet malice dripping off every word. Deri could imagine Missus Graspar practising in front of a mirror which held the image of Maurlocke. The merchant wouldn't have required such practice, though Deri had noticed Maurlocke took almost as much pleasure in anticipating an experience as in living it.

Deri stole glances at Owain's face whenever he could, searching for any sign of betrayal, or hatred. It would be oh-so-easy for the other boy to take Deri's presence here as a sign of something far more sinister than it was. Owain, however, after that first wave of shock, maintained a steadfastly neutral visage.

Maurlocke had retrieved a small metal case from within ys robes and, setting it upon Missus Graspar's desk, unlatched it. From within, the merchant's nimble fingers retrieved several small humanoid shapes, not unlike toy soldiers. First of lead, then of tin, then of silver, and finally one of gold. Normally, Deri would have watched, fascinated, at this new piece of faery magic, but his eyes kept flicking to Owain.

There was the sound again like the falling of coins but this time there was an eerily martial regularity to it, like the drum and fife calling soldiers to battle. There was a calling to that sound, Deri felt it in his bones. The figures felt it as well. They twitched and jumped upon the desk and began to move. One by one the figures moved to the edge of the desk and leapt off, growing to child-sized mannikins as they fell, first the lead, then the tin, then the silver, and finally, the single gold commander.

They moved in eerie unison, and their footsteps echoed up as they trooped down the stairs. Then, a thunderous roar shook the workhouse as the machinery leapt to life. Deri didn't have to look and see to know that the figures were running the machines, doing the work normally done by the children of the workhouse.

'That should do it,' Maurlocke said to Missus Graspar, ignoring the stricken Vimukti and Owain, though Deri could almost see laughter dancing in ys eyes of flint.

Deri longed to whisper to Owain that it was a bluff. The automatons would consume far more wealth than they could generate, in the long term. Their competence was linked to the Graspars' knowledge of the machinery and that flaw would as likely damage the machinery as run it properly.

But he couldn't. He dared not. Not with Maurlocke right there. So he said nothing.

'Yes,' Missus Graspar said smugly, 'that should do it indeed.' She looked to Vimukti and Owain. 'You may go, for now. We have no need of you. Though remember, we still hold your contracts and you will still need to answer them. Unless we choose to sell them on, that is.' Missus Graspar looked thoughtful. 'Do you, perchance, Merchant Maurlocke, know of any in the Market for some spare workers? I seem to have several more than I need, at present.'

'I suppose I could find a buyer somewhere.' Maurlocke sounded suitably dubious. 'Some mining concern, perhaps, needing children down in the less stable tunnels.'

Vimukti's lips tightened at that, and Owain looked a bit green around the gills.

'Of course,' Missus Graspar said thoughtfully, 'I do so like doing good and helping the less fortunate, so I suppose if all the children have returned by nightfall and are prepared to resume their duties tomorrow morning, I'd be inclined to make sure they all still have a place here, at this wonderful, generous home.'

Missus Graspar's eyes were anything but wonderful and generous. They were as flinty as Maurlocke's, which was no mean feat.

'Now, if you would excuse me, Mystrer Merchant, I'm afraid I have a great deal of business to see to, and this little matter has already taken up a good deal of both our valuable time.'

'It was my pleasure, Missus Graspar.' Maurlocke bowed, then gestured for Deri to follow. 'Come, Deri. We're done here.'

Deri had no choice but to follow the merchant out of the office, past Owain's stony face and unreadable gaze.

It was the worst ten steps of Deri's life (and the ones that came after weren't much better).

40

Step by step, Deri followed in Maurlocke's wake. The merchant moved quickly, flowing like molten gold through the sooty streets of London. Deri kept his eyes fixed on the hem of Maurlocke's robe. He didn't dare look back. There was no way he'd give the merchant the satisfaction.

He followed the merchant thusly through streets and alleyways, the cobblestones ringing with Maurlocke's steps. He followed the merchant through the riot of colour and perfume that was Covent Garden Market, where Maurlocke paused only long enough to purchase the pears yse so loved. Deri was made to carry them, of course. He followed the merchant away from London, into the twisting, vibrant chaos of the Untermarkt.

Finally, they arrived at Maurlocke's pavilion. The merchant swept in, the canvas pulling wide and gleaming with pride. As Deri entered, the canvas yanked itself closed as soon as he stepped over the threshold, snapping at his heels.

Maurlocke was already ensconced behind the massive desk, quill scratching across parchment with a sound not unlike the night breeze through a stand of beech. That alone told Deri that the merchant was working on a new contract. Some things – some magics – were very particular. Deri arranged the pears as artfully as he could manage in the golden bowl on the sideboard.

The quill stilled. 'I have to thank your little friends,' Maurlocke said.

'Mystrer?' Deri made it a question, kept his plausible deniability close as he dared.

'Do you think me a fool, boy?' Maurlocke's voice was suddenly as cool and smooth as gold. 'Do you think me so wrapped up in my own affairs that I don't notice what my servant is up to?'

Deri's pulse began to scream in his veins. He held perfectly still, a mouse before the serpent. Slowly he bit down on his tongue. The pain helped focus his mind, and it was an extra layer of precaution against being tricked into spilling his secrets. If he had any left.

'Silver fingers. Really, such an extravagance. And to afford them? Clearly I have not been keeping you busy enough.' Maurlocke's eyes of flint focused, pupil-less, on Deri's quiet form. 'You must have worked very hard indeed to amass such wealth from your own poor efforts. I presume you were merely waiting to pay me the full percentage I was owed? Technically, you are well within your rights to do so.'

Deri began to tremble. Maurlocke sounded reasonable, which meant yse was about to be anything but. The merchant smiled.

'Of course, I am well within my rights to deal with your little lovers' indiscretion with the workhouse boy. That is certainly outside the bounds of your contract.' Maurlocke tsked. 'I think extending your contract of indenture by another three years, three months, and three days is more than adequate payment for your misstep.'

Deri gasped. He longed to scream out that the merchant couldn't do that, that it wasn't fair, that he had been so close to his freedom that it shouldn't matter. He bit down on his tongue until he tasted blood and said nothing. Nothing was safest.

'No objection? Very well then.' Maurlocke smiled and pulled out Deri's contract, amending it with a flourish.

Deri knew his own copy would now have an identical change made to it, and there was nothing he could do about it. Punishment properly meted out, Maurlocke returned to ys work. The quill resumed its whispering progress.

'That little demonstration your friends staged,' Maurlocke said after several long, agonisingly quiet minutes, 'is going to make me an even wealthier merchant. Not the least because, even now, the Graspars are telling all of their confederates, allies, and enemies just how close they came to losing out on productivity, because their contracts of indenture were, shall we say, too lenient. So, there will very shortly be a massive surge in demand for tighter, better crafted contracts of indenture. New wording for old. New ties to bind the same old servants.'

The quill paused again. Maurlocke snapped golden fingers and a small flame danced above them. The merchant held it close to the ink of night, forcing it to dry faster.

'It will of course be expensive to amend so many contracts.' Maurlocke smiled predatorily. 'Fortunately, all boilerplate contracts include an amendments clause that can be exploited for this purpose.'

Exploited was definitely the word. Deri kept his features carefully neutral. Thankfully he'd had years of practice.

Maurlocke opened a locked drawer of the desk and rummaged

around for a few moments, before finally surfacing with a copy of the cheapest boilerplate contract of indenture one could purchase from the Untermarkt. The merchant set it across the desk from the parchment yse had been working on.

Deri watched, fascinated in spite of himself. It was rare that Maurlocke allowed him to watch ym work. Usually Deri was hustled off on some errand or another, the better to keep the secrets of the Untermarkt, presumably. This time, maybe malice was outweighing sense.

Maurlocke opened ys mouth and strange, eldritch syllables clawed their way past those gleaming lips. Tendrils of shadow coiled through the air, miasma from a gleaming cave, snaking down toward the ink of night upon the parchment and sinking into the words written there.

Ice jittered down Deri's spine as the night-dark loops and angles twitched, spasmed, and began to lever themselves up from the page, slithering and twining about themselves into strange, bestial forms. They paced the borders of the parchment for a few, uneasy moments before skittering and scrabbling across the desk in a scurrilous horde, making a beeline toward the boilerplate contract Maurlocke had set out. Upon reaching it, they buzzed and burrowed into the paper, sliding into it with a sound like the feel of a paper-cut.

The text rippled, like ink in a pool, and went faintly indistinct in a few places, before rearranging itself into new, more complex configurations. The transmuted text was sharper, darker. Maurlocke raised the paper diffidently and inspected ys handiwork.

'Adequate. For a first effort.' Maurlocke's lips pursed. 'Good enough as proof of concept, I suppose, but unfortunately of no value as a contract. Now what – ah.'

One of the ink-creatures was still struggling on the original parchment, its leg caught by some ornamental sealing wax. Served Maurlocke right for experimenting with reused materials. Deri locked his smile in a dark corner of the mind, where no glimmer of it risked coming to light in his eyes. As Deri watched, the little thing broke free (leaving a small segment of its leg behind) and scuttled madly across the desk. It bounced off a letterbox before careening right into the ornate inkwell from which Maurlocke dipped ys ink of night.

Deri lunged, but it was too late. The inkwell tipped, spilling a prince's ransom across Maurlocke's favourite rug. The little beastie that caused the mess hit the puddle a split second later, struggling briefly before dissolving and wicking into the expensive fibres along with the rest of the ink.

'Unfortunate,' was all Maurlocke had to say. The merchant must have been in a supremely good mood, however, as Deri wasn't even threatened with a hint of blame. Merely given a stack of errands. 'Have that cleaned. I want it back here, spotless, by nightfall. I'll also need more ink of night, a stack of high-quality parchment, and an orphan's weight of gold dust.' Maurlocke smiled, toothily. 'I find myself rather peckish.'

Deri was busy carefully rolling up the rug, trying very hard not to stain anything else in the pavilion with ink of night. Maurlocke crumpled the flawed contract into a ball and threw it at him. Fortunately, Deri was expecting some kind of test and managed to nab and pocket the thing while keeping one hand gripped onto the rug.

'I really must thank your little friends,' Maurlocke needled. 'This new process will make me a mint, in addition to all the revenue amending the standard boilerplate contracts will bring in. A most profitable day's work, indeed.'

The pavilion spat gleams of golden light into Deri's eyes as he worked. Spiteful thing was trying to get him to drop the rug. Deri bit his tongue, tempted almost beyond reason to threaten it with a bit of ink on its golden threads. He didn't. That would not end well.

'Do hurry with that,' Maurlocke said, gliding about the pavilion, idly inspecting ys nails. 'I'll need you back here quickly. As soon as I complete the new wording and perfect the dissemination process, you're to deliver both to Merchant Atrementress. On the Street of Binding Words. You will know her by the ink-dark fall of her hair.'

Maurlocke must be slipping if yse thought Deri hadn't already ran several errands to said merchant for Maurlocke in the past. That or his mystrer was insulting Deri's intelligence, again. In any case, the insult lacked the merchant's usual sting. The thought of truly grotesque levels of profit must be mellowing ym. Who knew?

'I said *quickly*.' Maurlocke spoke a single word, invoking the punishment clause of the contract of indenture, and Deri's veins were suddenly on fire.

Deri hissed in pain but otherwise managed not to cry out, stumbling toward the pavilion's exit. The cloth of gold panels drew wide about him. The pain faded as soon as he quickened his steps, and the faster he went the faster it left his body. Deri broke into an awkward jog for several paces, then, when the last of the pain was gone, slowed back down to a walk.

He was halfway to Merchant Elanie – the one Maurlocke usually sent him to when the rare item needed cleaning or restoration – when Deri realised Maurlocke had not, in fact, specified how Deri should have the rug cleaned. There was a small fortune in ink of night in those fibres, if even a small portion could be reclaimed, and it wouldn't cost Deri anything personally. He could merely split the reclaimed ink of night with the one who could coax it from the rug.

The things he could do with that much ink of night. Even accounting for what might be lost or ruined, and the portion he'd have to surrender to pay for the extraction, he'd easily have enough to write two or three full contracts.

His veins throbbed, again, burning with remembered pain. Maurlocke must be thinking about the errands yse would send Deri on next. Delivering the new contracts that would doom his friends. Of course Maurlocke would send Deri, even if it would be smarter to deliver the things ymself. The thought of Deri delivering the doom to his friends must have been just too tempting.

Deri briefly considered misdelivering the contracts, but all that would do is delay the inevitable. He'd be caught, punished, and Maurlocke would still win. Likewise, he couldn't ruin them or obviously mar them – Deri stopped, dead in his tracks. The surge of customers around him hissed and split, crashing around the unexpected rock of his stone-still form.

He couldn't obviously mar them, but he had a store of ink of night at his disposal, enough for one or two contracts. Maurlocke was going to amend the contracts anyway, then pass the amendments to Deri for delivery. If he worked quickly enough, Deri would have the chance to make a slight alteration to that contract, maybe just enough to work in a small loophole, one that could be exploited to all manner of advantage.

The seeds of a plan began to germinate in the back of Deri's mind. Maybe there was a way he could secure his own freedom, as well as righting the wrongs of the past day or so. But first, he had to complete his errands, quickly enough to both satisfy Maurlocke and to afford him some freedom to move on his own.

Deri dove once more into the seething sea of customers, wriggling through, looking for his most reliable shortcuts. There wasn't a lot of time, and he had a great deal to do.

41

Owain stood once more in Missus Graspar's office, veiled in the ruin of his hopes. Vimukti stood next to him, eyes still defiant, but the fire within Owain was barely an ember. Whatever was coming, it would be bad.

'I'm so pleased you have finally come to your senses,' Missus Graspar was saying. The old woman was sat behind her massive desk, stroking the head of her horrible dog, Bruiser, who had the indecency to be looking positively spry. 'And now that everyone is back where they rightfully belong –' her eyes glittered with malice '– we can discuss appropriate disciplinary measures for you as the ringleaders of this little insurrection.'

'We—' Vimukti began hotly.

'No, that's quite enough of that.' Missus Graspar silenced her with a gesture.

Vimukti's jaw worked silently. A glowing mote of light drifted out her open mouth and slowly floated toward Missus Graspar, as if it were struggling against an inexorable current the whole way. When it was near enough, the old woman snapped a dull pewter locket around it, hiding the light from view.

'You've abused your voice quite enough, for now. Perhaps a few days without it will teach you to use it better. I think nine will do as a start.' Missus Graspar smiled and would have made a shark blush in the doing.

Vimukti shouted silently. Her fury was so intense that the locket in Missus Graspar's hand jumped. She hurriedly stuffed it in a drawer in her desk and locked it.

Owain watched, face pale and hand trembling. He curled his fingers into his hand, running his thumb along the smooth silver to calm himself. This was just the beginning. If he lived to see the end of his contract it would be a miracle.

'Now,' Missus Graspar continued, 'as to more general punishments, as each and every child in this workhouse has stolen three days of productivity from us—'

Owain's mind flashed to the prosperity siphons, still hidden around the workhouse, no doubt full to bursting with stolen productivity and prosperity. He had heard nothing from Deri. Would he need to somehow collect them and get them to the other young man before the Graspars discovered them? What if Merchant Maurlocke returned?

'—it is only right that each and every child in this workhouse repay it. However, rather than extend every contract by three times the number of days lost, I have decided to be merciful.'

Like the bloody leech knew the meaning of the word.

'Instead, the days will be taken from the holiday time usually afforded all workers.' Missus Graspar smiled, no doubt thinking of the extra profits that could be culled from working when other factories were forced to close. 'Nine days shall be required from each child. There will be no holiday rest given, starting next fortnight with Imbolc.'

There it was. Owain's heart sank. Not even a day of respite from this hellish place. And nine days! They were given precious few of them over the course of the year as it was. With nine days gone, it would be nearly a year of nonstop work, not counting the one half-day a week they were given to rest. He suspected not even Missus Graspar's anger would allow her to take that away. It would reduce productivity too much, and any further aid from Merchant Maurlocke would likely be far more expensive than the efforts of the workhouse children. What Deri had told him about the cost of those automatons that had briefly run the workhouse! Owain shuddered. Using them again would beggar more than belief.

It also meant he had no way to see Deri. Not without sneaking out, a prospect that was vanishingly small now. Even Bess would find it a challenge getting in and out without being seen. Garog had mounted a watch on all the dormitories. Several of his drinking buddies had been given cushy jobs, but each and every door was both locked and watched every night now. The children no longer had access to the garderobe and each room had one disgusting chamber pot they all had to share. The oldest in each room was in charge of emptying it, nominally to show responsibility, but Owain knew it was to punish himself and Vimukti as much as anything else. The Graspars wanted them demeaned, ground down.

'We will also be working with Merchant Maurlocke to review each and every contract of indenture currently in effect for anyone in this workhouse. We will be exercising our right to add amendments as we see fit. Of course, all who work here will have right of refusal in the renegotiation; however, should any do so, they should know that we fully intend to sell their contract on.' Missus Graspar's voice was honeyed poison.

The other shoes just kept dropping. Owain wasn't certain just how extreme the changes to his indenture could be, but he was sure that Maurlocke would do the utmost worst with every inch of wriggle room in the language. And those that refused the changes? They'd find themselves sold off to mining concerns, or deckhands bound for Australia, or whatever the most dangerous, filthy, and menial work the Graspars could find was. Whichever outcome, a lot of lives were about to get a whole lot worse.

'You, girl, nod to show me you understand,' Missus Graspar ordered.

Vimukti nodded slowly, hate vibrating in every fibre of her being.

'And you, boy, tell me you understand. I want to hear the words from your own lips.'

'I understand,' Owain said. The ember of his defiance began to flare with the draughts of injustice Missus Graspar was wafting their way. She would not be punishing them so harshly if they had not hurt the workhouse so badly. The gallowsglass gear was still broken, and without a replacement that machine could not run. The Graspars couldn't steal more lives to keep themselves and their rich patrons forever young.

At least for now. No doubt Merchant Maurlocke was already searching for materials for a replacement. Though the larger stumbling block might be convincing Mistress Steele to repair the machine. If she even knew what it was truly being used for. Owain's heart sank. They were unlikely to be able to warn her, if she didn't, and if she didn't, she would have little reason not to do the repair.

Especially with as much as the Graspars would offer her. Missus Graspar was not one to let the field of profit lie fallow.

'Now get out of my sight and get to work.'

Weeks passed before Owain heard from Deri. When he did see him, he certainly wasn't expecting it to be in the garderobe. Owain nearly screamed, Deri had startled him so.

'Shhh!' Deri made a shushing gesture but his eyes were sparkling. 'We don't want to draw any more attention than we have to.'

'Why hello!' Owain drew close and punctuated his words with a fast, firm kiss. 'How did you get in here?'

Deri kicked the wooden bench next to him. The sewers. He'd come up through the sewers. Strange. He didn't smell like he came up through the sewers. Owain tried to take a surreptitious sniff, in case Deri was messing with him.

'Buttonhole.' Deri gestured to the ragged rose at his lapel. It had a few petals clinging to it still. 'There's a small posey of them hidden right below. Vimukti will need them. Oh. Can you go fetch Vimukti and bring her here? Grab the prosperity you decanted from the siphons while you're at it.'

'What?' Owain stood blinking.

'Chop-chop! We haven't much time. Me even less than you. I have a plan, but I need both of you.' Deri made a shooing motion with his hands.

Owain sighed and slipped off to find Vimukti. He returned quickly, with both her and the bottles of prosperity in tow. Deri was still leaning against the wall.

'Excellent! You're both here,' he said, claiming the bottles from Owain. 'Now, I have a plan. One that will work this time,' he forestalled Vimukti before she could speak, 'but I've barely enough time as it is, so listen first, all questions later, right? Right.'

Deri plucked a petal from his boutonnière, crushed it between his fingers, and tossed it down the garderobe. The scent of fresh roses filled the close space. Vimukti's eyes widened.

'Good.' Deri nodded. 'They work just like that. Glad you were paying attention, V. More on that in a moment. Owain.' He fixed the other young man with his gaze. 'I need you to get rid of the siphons for me. I'll tell you how. With my mystrer working so closely with the Graspars it's not safe to keep them up any longer. If yse spots them…' Deri shook his head.

'What do I do with them when they're down?' Owain asked.

'Vimukti can stash them in the sewers on one of her trips. I'll collect them and what they've managed to collect, and use it to further the plan.'

'I beg your pardon? One of my *what*?'

'V, I need your power,' Deri explained earnestly. 'I have a list of key people throughout the city that I need you to convince to trade me three minutes of their life in exchange for me providing nine minutes cover for their contract of indenture. And I need you to get them to convince everyone else at their factory or workhouse to sign on as well. Or at least as many as they can.' Deri pulled out a few rolls of parchment. 'If they agree, they just need to add a single drop of blood to this. Hard sell, I know, but I've only got access to so much ink of night.'

'You want me to sneak in and out through the sewers, don't you?' Vimukti asked flatly.

'Well, yeah. That's why I marked the routes for you and left you a cache of blooms. You'll always come out smelling like a rose!' Deri hit the hard sell. He needed her to do this. 'Listen, I know it's dangerous, but if I can pull this trick off, we won't just cripple the Graspars, we'll cripple the whole indenture system.'

Owain let out a low whistle. Deri didn't know when to quit. He felt a warmth kindle in his chest. And he wouldn't have it any other way, really.

'Fine,' Vimukti said, 'but only because it will hurt the bastards. And I want something in exchange.'

'What is it?' The demand put a slight crimp in Deri's good mood.

'You have to keep us posted as to your mystrer's progress in securing a replacement for the gallowsglass gear Junior broke. As soon as that machine is back up and running, our lives – well, our youths – are in danger.' Vimukti glowered. 'I'd ask you to sabotage the whole thing, but I know that's too dangerous a thing to ask.'

'Deal.' Deri grinned. Vimukti was on board! He had his prosperity. Owain was covering his tracks here at the workhouse. And if things went according to plan, soon he'd be in a position to strike a crippling blow to Maurlocke, the indenture system, and possibly come out of it a very rich man on the other side.

Now if only he could figure out how to get a laugh out of Maurlocke. Then he'd have everything he wanted *and* everything he needed. But he was no closer to figuring that one out.

'Why the long face?'

'What?' Deri looked up to see Vimukti and Owain staring at him.

'Something's bothering you,' Owain said gently. 'What is it?'

'Nothing much. I just need to find something impossible to trade for everything I ever wanted.' Deri tried to brush it off with a flippant, though honest, answer. 'Though I'm starting to think those trade goods don't exist.'

'Then offer a substitute,' Vimukti said, matter-of-factorily. 'What merchant wouldn't accept goods of equal or greater value?'

'It'll have to be greater,' Owain added drily. 'I've spent enough time with this one to know it'll have to be greater.'

That… that was an idea worth exploring. And from someone outside the Market, no less! Deri blinked, then smiled.

'Good advice. Thank you! Well, that's a bonus to today!' He grinned at the two across from him. 'Then I just need one last thing and I'll be off!'

'What is it?' Owain asked.

'Oh, not much. I just need you two to tell me the best way to go about convincing Silvestra Steele to help me.' Deri's eyes were distant, his mind running through possibilities.

'She isn't here today,' Vimukti said, 'so you won't be able to talk to her anyway.'

'Oh, that's fine. I know where she lives. I'm going to have to be unspeakably rude and call unannounced, but there's not much I can do about that.' Deri grimaced.

'How do you know where she lives?' Vimukti demanded.

'Let me guess. You saw it when we broke into Missus Graspar's office and you memorised the address.' Owain shook his head.

'You are, in fact, correct.' Deri grinned.

'Even so, if you're showing up unannounced you need to do something to make up for it. She appreciates machines and loves her sister. Use that.' Vimukti crossed her arms.

Deri winced. He was far from flush, at the moment. And even though he was collecting an influx of prosperity from the siphons today, there was no guarantee it would even be enough for his deal with Jack Trades, let alone provide extra.

'I'll see what I can do,' he said.

'Do more than see.' Vimukti would have nothing less.

'All right, all right!' Deri raised his hands in surrender. 'Sweet mother of coin, you make her sound downright dangerous.'

42

Deri sat, bemused, at the table as Silvestra Steele calmly prepared some tea. He watched in fascination as she worked the – to him – arcane and unknowable machinery of the mechanism on the strange device that heated the water in the teapot. So far as he could see, it involved no coal and no sorcerous heating elements.

'It stores excess kinetic energy from my other experiments and converts it into heat,' Silvestra explained, noting his curious gaze.

That hadn't really explained anything. Before Deri could ask for further explanation, a sharp whistle sounded the readiness of the hot water. Silvestra poured, pausing briefly to measure Deri with a glance and the sugar with a small spoon, before stirring in a touch of milk for Deri and some lemon for herself.

'Thank you,' Deri said, accepting the proffered cup.

'You are very welcome.' Silvestra raised her cup but didn't drink from it. Instead she sat serene behind the rising steam, peering through it at Deri like a Delphic Oracle through the fabled vision-inducing Parnassian vapours.

It was an uncomfortable sensation. Deri, however, was well used to such things. One doesn't grow up in the Untermarkt without developing a resistance to – a fondness for, even – strange and unusual sensations.

Deri sipped his tea. So far as he could tell, it was perfect, exactly the way he preferred it. His idea just might work after all. He held his cup up in a small salute. 'Thank you. It's just right.'

'Close enough,' Silvestra said, before finally taking a sip of her own tea. Her lips twitched, as if they wanted to stiffen in a frown, but the motion was present and gone before Deri could divine anything further.

There are moments when one knows that to act now could shift the entire basis of the future. Deri felt one, then and there, stepping from the shadow of that tiny facial movement. And, acting on some fey instinct heretofore unknown to him, he jumped at the chance.

'It must be hard, knowing that even though it's a good cup of tea, it could be better. Seeing the flaw, clear as crystal, but only when it's too late to fix.' Deri toyed with his own cup, watching Silvestra from the corner of his eye.

Silvestra went very still for a long moment, before she pointedly raised her cup to her lips and drank. 'It is not so bad, I suppose. Not enough lemon. That can be fixed. Though such things are always a case of diminishing returns. The flaw can be lessened, but never totally eliminated.' She took another sip and grimaced. 'That's what I get for putting on a brave face. No, you are correct. It's maddening.'

'I was given the impression that your particular talent only worked with machinery.' Deri nudged the conversation toward its ultimate destination. He was, after all, short on time.

'It always works on machines, but it has, at times, given me some insight into complex systems of a, well, less tangible nature. The less tangible, the less often it happens, thank goodness. I don't know what I would do if it worked on everything.' Silvestra's eyes narrowed. 'Though why I'm telling you this is beyond me.'

Deri smiled. He could have pretended to innocence, but there was a chance Silvestra might have seen through it, and that would ruin everything. So he went with a version of the truth: sympathy. After all, he at least knew what it was like to have a unique talent that sometimes spoke to him and ruined his day. Though that was hardly the bells' fault.

'I just have one of those faces,' Deri said.

'You also have one of those agendas,' Silvestra retorted. 'And I would appreciate it if you would, as they say, get to the point.'

'I'd like to borrow your talent.' No point to beat around the bush. 'I'm sure we can come to an arrangement that benefits both of us.'

'I doubt it. You have nothing I want.'

'Maybe. Maybe not. Would I have come here if I thought there wasn't anything I could offer you?' Deri smiled and leaned in closer. 'I at least have something your sister wants.'

Silvestra went very still once again. Deri tensed. Had he gone too far, too fast? But after a long moment Silvestra blinked and the tension went out of the room.

'That's hardly gentlemanly.' Silvestra looked at him sharply over her teacup. 'It's very bad form to use one's family against one.'

'Firstly,' Deri held up a finger, 'that is not what is happening here. I'm merely stating the fact that there are things you want, if only indirectly, even if you may not have thought of them yourself.

Secondly, gentlemen don't tend to survive very well, in either the Untermarkt or the topside workhouses. As you well know.'

'I can't argue with that,' Silvestra said with a trifle more heat than was precisely ladylike, 'but again, it's a rather ungentlemanly thing to say.'

'I've found that social niceties are less about being kind and more about reinforcing unfair systems of power.' Deri shrugged. 'Why make things easier for the parasites at the top, benefiting from a corrupt system? And before you answer, consider how closely you have, or have not, looked at the systems of power that run this city, this Empire, this system of wealth.' Now that was playing dirty. As soon as Deri framed things that way, Silvestra couldn't help but look at them that way, if only for a moment, and with her particular gift, well, he expected it would be hard to look away.

But he had one more knife to twist, one more thing he wanted to know, so even though he could already see the roseate bloom fading from Silvestra's cheeks, Deri casually uttered one more devastating sentence.

'How closely, in fact, did you look at what the machine you helped build was capable of? Especially if it was misused on, say, human subjects?'

Silvestra had gone white as a sheet. Deri watched her, closely, and sipped his tea. He could only imagine what she was seeing, which made it hard to judge how long to let her look before he interrupted the locomotive of her thoughts.

'I never considered—' She broke off, eyes lost in the distance. 'How could they—'

When she started shaking, Deri decided that that was probably the sign he was waiting for. She clearly had been used ruthlessly by the Graspars, if not to the same degree as the children in the workhouse had been. He clinked his empty teacup onto the saucer with a good deal more force than necessary.

'Oh, I'm sorry!' Deri's apologies were also far louder than necessary. Well, far louder than socially acceptable, anyway.

'That's all right,' Silvestra said, a faraway look still haunting her eyes. 'You've made your point. I'm prepared to entertain your offer.'

'I didn't—' Deri began to protest.

'Enough.' Silvestra cut him off with a sharp motion of her hand. 'You did. And you were justified, even if your means were – forceful.' She took a sip of tea with unsteady hands.

Deri waited for her to continue. He knew better than to push right now.

'You want the use of my talent,' Silvestra said when she had steadied a bit. 'I will tell you right now that I will not part with it. If you want to make use of it, it will have to be through me.'

'But—'

'Either trust me or go elsewhere. Those are my terms. I am willing to be bound in secrecy, so long as I can refuse if your request is something I would not personally approve of. Given your choice of tactics, however, I suspect you have more noble aims in mind, though you might pretend otherwise.'

Deri snapped his mouth shut and considered. He hadn't been entirely certain Silvestra was trustworthy, given the work she had done for the Graspars, but Owain and Vimukti seemed to think it worth the risk, and after seeing her reaction there he felt he had the woman's measure. She was a good person, at the core.

'I believe I can work with that,' Deri said carefully. 'I have some rather intricate strategies to test, and some variations on standard contract language I would like to have carefully tested. I think everything should be entirely acceptable.'

'Then let us get to it.' Silvestra cleared the table. 'I owe—' Her gaze went distant again before she focused in on him. 'I suppose I owe you that much, at least, for helping to open my eyes.'

She took another sip of tea and this time she didn't even grimace at the bitterness. Deri supposed it probably tasted sweet in comparison to the realisation she had just come to.

'Yes,' the lady artificer said, suddenly regaining the edge she had held when he arrived. 'Let us get to it. And we can discuss just what you are going to offer my sister – no strings attached – to pay for this consultation.'

Deri blinked. Someone else might have found the sudden shift to self – or at least familial – interest rather cold, but he was a creature of the Untermarkt.

He knew everything came with a price.

43

Deri moved through the Untermarkt, past the Street of Lingering Lights where women and men could buy stars to adorn their eyes or aurorae to mantle their shoulders in glory, past a stall of warped and warping mirrors, one of which vapoured forth a stream of bread-and-butterflies as he passed. Some of the butter landed in his hair as they flitted by.

It was robin's-egg blue and tasted of spring.

He winced at the sensory overload. His mind was still tender from his encounter with Silvestra's 'gift'. He blinked away the spectres of black lines, memories of the cracks and flaws in everything. It had been overwhelming. It had been informative.

It had showed him the potential failings in his plan.

A sick weight settled into the pit of his stomach. With Silvestra's help he'd managed to find two alternate fixes, though one… Deri pushed the thought away. He could figure out what to do about his budget gap – and what it might cost him to bridge it – later. First things first. He had some prosperity to deliver!

There was a secret way into Jack Trades' stall. Probably more than one. Deri flipped a shilling, heads to tails, the coin spinning in the air as he turned a certain corner in the Alley of Beasts. The next step he took landed him on the plush rugs carpeting a small antechamber to Jack Trades' main merchant stall.

Deri paced the small space nervously. He had no more time to spare. He'd used it all. These minutes he had were rare and precious, shaved off of his other duties for Maurlocke. If the merchant summoned him back before he was able to talk to Jack…

'Come on in,' Jack called through the curtain. 'I'm free now.'

Deri all but bolted through into the main space of Jack Trades' merchant stall. It was largely unchanged from the last time he had been here, but now there was a new frame hanging upon the wall. It enclosed no picture, but rather held a blank canvas. It as good as told the other merchants coming to this place for business that Jack had his eye on a potential heir.

They must be fuming. Deri couldn't help but grin at that. Jack was leaning against his heavy wooden desk, arms crossed. He quirked an eyebrow as Deri entered.

'I've the second item,' Deri said by way of explanation. He pulled a bottle from his pocket. He'd sweated every step of the way here, afraid Maurlocke would summon him and catch him with this much wealth on his person. That would not have ended well.

'Set it here.' Jack gestured to the desk. He moved around it and pulled out a set of fine scales.

Deri set the bottle down. Rich motes of green and gold seemed to dance on the interior. There was the occasional flicker of red, the exact shade of a gallowsglass gear. Deri tried not to think too hard about that. The gear had shattered and the machine was lost beyond repair without Silvestra, but even the idea of benefiting from the theoretical theft of life didn't sit well with him. It so easily could have been Owain in that machine.

Jack Trades set out three small weights, representing the exact amount of prosperity Deri owed him as part of their deal. Unstoppering the bottle, he poured motes of golden light like sand onto the scale. It balanced one of the three weights by itself. Shaking the bottle, Jack added most of the green light swirling in the bottle. The scales tilted back and forth. Jack added a touch more green light.

Deri held his breath. The scales balanced. The bottle still glowed with prosperity, though most of the light was red with only the barest touches of green and gold now.

'And so the second part of our three-part agreement is settled,' Jack said formally. Then he looked at Deri, a sharp smile in his eyes. 'Now where could you have gotten so much prosperity? No, no. You need not tell me now. Though I reserve the right to hear the story in full, should you succeed in becoming my heir.'

'I suppose that is reasonable enough,' Deri said, careful not to commit to anything.

'Do you have a plan for the final item?'

Ugh. Laughter from the lips of Merchant Maurlocke. Deri did not have a plan to acquire that, no. However, he did have another idea.

'I might,' he temporised, 'but there is another option that has recently presented itself that may serve as an appropriate substitute?'

Jack made a noncommittal noise. Deri risked a glance. The merchant's face was entirely neutral. Was that a hint of disapproval at the corner of his lips? Deri shoved the thought away. Now was not the time to second-guess himself.

'What would seeing the humiliation of the same individual

named in our original agreement – the same as was to provide the laughter – theoretically be worth? More or less than the laughter?' Deri asked, the lightness in his voice belying the tension in his frame.

Jack pursed his lips in thought. Deri could see the calculus in his eyes. The merchant was weighing several factors of probability, faster than Deri had ever seen. Though, to be fair, it was impossible to see anything in Merchant Maurlocke's eyes.

'It could well be equitable,' Jack Trades said at last. 'I have heard of the rare merchant besting your mystrer in a deal. 'Tis a commoner story than laughter from that cold gold tyrant. That said, I would possibly take even more delight in such a thing, which offsets the slight difference in rarity.' He looked at Deri. 'I take it you have something in mind?'

Deri opened his mouth to reply, but before he got the chance another voice sliced into the market stall from outside.

'Trades! Trades, where are you? The High Council of the Untermarkt has business with you. Come now, I haven't all day!'

Deri's heart nearly stopped at the sound. He knew that voice. Maurlocke? Here?

44

'I'm not waiting, mortal,' Maurlocke's voice preceded ym into the market stall.

'Sorry about this,' Jack said to Deri as he snapped his fingers. 'I'll turn you back as soon as I can.'

Deri was unable to reply because he found himself in the form of a decorative golden bell. His outrage rang out as a tinny jangle. Jack shot him a look and Deri stilled his clapper. Oh, this was weird. But at the same time, he felt entirely comfortable. The bells were going to ring themselves silly when he told them about this later.

Maurlocke swept in, disrupting any further thoughts Deri might have had about his temporary form. The merchant was dressed in even more finery than Deri was used to seeing ym in: robes all of cloth of gold with accents of darkest night threaded through for contrast. Around the merchant's neck was ys chain of office, which marked ym as one of the seven Merchant Councillors that oversaw the workings of the Untermarkt.

Was the merchant nervous? Deri did not often see this much of a show of power. Usually, Maurlocke would opt for understated elegance, the better to pretend everyone else was beneath ys notice. He froze as Maurlocke's gaze rested upon him.

Greetings, little one. Maurlocke spoke to him in the Language of Gold.

If Deri had still had blood, it would have frozen within his veins. His confusion must have glittered across his surface because he saw a slight smile tilt Maurlocke's lips.

Fear not. I shall not ask you to betray a trust. Unless there is something you want that would be fair recompense…?

Deri focused very hard on the idea of 'No.' He felt the shine around him. It was a surreal way to speak. Even the Language of Bells was more audible than visual. This was an entirely different experience. So much so that it almost entirely distracted him from the actual conversation Jack Trades was having with Maurlocke.

'…I have not yet named an heir, no,' Jack was saying.

Maurlocke looked highly sceptical. 'Technicalities. You clearly have someone in mind. The Council wishes to know who.'

'The Council may wish as it likes, but unless they plan to pay me in actual wishes, then they can sit with their curiosity. The candidate in question has not yet passed all the trials I have set. It is far from a done deal.' Jack shrugged.

Maurlocke sniffed. Then stiffened. The merchant's eyes darted about the stall.

'It would certainly be an admirable destiny,' yse said.

Jack didn't blink. Deri's alarm must have flared across his surface, because Maurlocke smiled. The merchant clearly thought yse knew something.

'I'm sure it would be, but if you are implying something, I'm sure I don't know what it might be,' Jack said easily.

Maurlocke stood silent, clearly considering ys next words. What they were, Deri could not follow. He was too busy concentrating to keep his emotions from blazing across his surface like an aurora. One thing, however, was clear.

Deri needed to move on his plan, and soon. Someone, sooner or later, would manage to uncover Jack Trades' intended heir. When that happened, Deri had best be free or ready to move immediately. If he wasn't… well, it didn't bear thinking about.

45

Deri tried to breathe normally but the butterflies in his stomach kept catching the air and throwing it back out before it had a chance to properly settle. It had nothing to do with the near-deserted streets swathed in shadow, nor the acrid, angry scent of the London Fog, rising from the Thames. No, it had to do with the other youth beside him and what this evening meant.

He glanced over at Owain and received a moon-bright smile in return. They were sneaking away again, flouting the contracts that bound them. It was dangerous, but Deri judged it well worth the risk. This would be the last time – for better or worse – he'd be able to sneak Owain out of the workhouse or himself out of the Untermarkt.

St. Cathbad's Grove was behind them, the rustle of its leaves on the wind. Rising hundreds of feet into the air, a living monument to the forest that shamed the mountain stone. The druids could still them, even in the harshest gale, but the sound was comforting, harmonious, almost like a never-ending hymn. Their destination was in front of the two, however.

St. Mariwen-le-Bow was a stone circle grown into a miniature cathedral, counterpoint to St. Cathbad's cathedral turned sacred grove. It was constructed at the same time, rebuilt after the Great Fire, but the druids no doubt wanted no distractions from their living masterpiece so near, and directed that the former church be rebuilt in the style of the megalithic circles of old. Sir Christopher Wren took that as a base and ran with it, of course. He was never one to leave a thought (or a design) unembellished.

Being a place of worship, the door was unlocked. Owain looked briefly confused as Deri led him up the steps and into the sacred space. There was an adorable look on his face and Deri's heart ached for the risk he was about to put them both in. Even if everything went well there was a chance… no. He wasn't thinking about that tonight. Tonight was about him, and Owain, and making the most of the time they had, whatever was coming.

'What are we doing here?' Owain asked, his voice hushed in the shadows and the silence.

'You remember how you were asking about my parents? And I told you about how the goblin midwife gave birth to me?' Deri kept moving, drawing Owain along in his wake.

'Yes.' Owain followed without hesitation.

'Well, that wasn't all she gave me.' Deri stopped in the centre of the circle, near to the altar.

'What do you mean?'

'You know I can hear bells,' Deri said, abruptly. 'I mean I can understand what they're saying. They speak to me, and I can hear the words in their ringing. It's the first thing I ever heard, actually.'

Owain knew. Even when he first found out he didn't question it as fact. With goblins beneath the streets and faery godparents in

352

attendance at many naming ceremonies across the city, it was hard to gainsay any blessing, howsoever odd. Deri continued.

'So, in talking of our parents, I thought perhaps you'd like to meet mine. I really need – want you to meet mine. At least, the closest thing I have. While we had the chance. Here, hold out your hand.'

'Is everything alright?' Owain asked. Something in Deri's words, in his manner, seemed off. Fluttery.

'It will be. Yes. It is. Here. Just hold out your hand.'

Owain did as he was asked and Deri took it, awkwardly tying a short bit of very thin rope about their clasped hands. He whispered a word in a strange tongue and a strange doubling took their senses.

'What's this?' Owain asked. His voice echoed in a bizarre blend. One part was the sound he was accustomed to, another was his voice but weirdly altered. The two spoke in unison, an odd harmony.

'A charm braided of twins' hair and the leaves of a single tree with two forks,' Deri said. His voice in Owain's ear was similarly strange. 'We're sharing one another's senses. You should be able to hear what I hear.'

'How remarkable!' Owain reached out and touched Deri's face with his hand. The sensation of touch and being touched was pleasantly disorientating. 'I hope you have another of these for later.'

Deri went absolutely beet red. 'Not here,' he whispered through clenched teeth. He looked upward.

'Owain, meet my mother.'

Hello Owain, Deri's beau, gently rang the Bell of Bow.

Owain gaped and put his free hand to his ear. Deri elbowed him. Owain suddenly recalled his manners.

'Hello! It's a pleasure to meet you, Missus... Bow.' Owain grabbed for the most sensical name he could.

His efforts were repaid in tinkling laughter ringing down from above. The voice of the Great Bell of Bow was a resounding tenor, sonorous and clear. It sounded rich and strange to Owain's curiously doubled ears, though whether that was hearing the words within the ring or an effect of the braided cord around his wrist he could not say.

Dear Danu! He'd just teased Deri about bedding him later! In front of what might as well be his truest mother in the world. The urge to shrivel up and expire on the spot suddenly became absolutely paramount in Owain's mind. He flushed deepest crimson.

Oh, he flushes prettily! Bring him close so we can see!

'My siblings, too.' Deri added, seeing Owain's confused look at the snatches of teasing he was able to pick out from the ringing. 'Pay them no mind. They mean well, or so I'm told.' Deri glared upward.

'A pleasure to meet you all,' Owain managed.

There were rounds of introductions, then, and hospitality. Bells required no food nor drink, of course, so there was none to offer. Rather, music and communication gave them sustenance. Owain foresaw a great deal of gossiping in the future. The bells couldn't seem to get enough of it. They were utterly fascinated by all the petty details of life in the workhouse, particularly the squabbles and the friendships (better still if those had been mended after cracking).

The best part of the visit, however, was the gossiping bells chatting to Owain about Deri. A wealth of childhood mishaps and mistakes forming an arpeggio of hilarity. Owain quite enjoyed the particular and deepening shades of red that coloured Deri's face throughout the evening.

Yet hear him speak in our tongue though, did chime the Smallest Bell of Bow.

'Your tongue?' Owain looked from the hanging bells to Deri.

Deri, for his part, was studiously examining his shoes. 'I don't think we need to do that,' he muttered, not looking toward Owain.

'Oh, now I have to hear it!' Owain grinned.

The bells chimed in, egging Deri on, until, at last, the lad threw up his hands.

'Fine! Alright!'

Poetry? I love it so, gently asked the Bell of Bow.

Deri rolled his eyes but made no other protest. Owain watched as Deri took a couple deep breaths, and then, forming his mouth into a perfect O, he began to ring.

He started with the higher tones, alternating notes, but every sound that came out of his mouth had the tone and timbre of a bell.

Listen there! He sounds like me! pealed the Bow Bell tuned to B.

Do I really sound like that? asked the Bow Bell tuned B-flat.

Owain, senses still linked to Deri's, twice over felt the resonance deep in his chest. The recitation was almost like music, hearing as he did both Deri's voice as the pealing of bells and his voice in words of poetry.

The verse was Spenserian, a popular choice as his *Faery Queene* had been gifted as part of the final ceremonies when High Queen Elizabeth, first of her name, finalised the treaty with Faery. Titania herself had walked the streets of London that day. Events like that tended to stick in the collective mind.

The bells loved it. Perhaps it had something to do with the nature of rhyme. It was like a secondary harmony. It was certainly an experience unlike Owain had ever had before; he had heard poetry recited but rarely, on occasional trips outside the workhouse.

Deri had a remarkable range. He hit notes both high and low, and though he could not quite match the basso profundo of the Great Bells, he came close. The various bells rang out in delight as he assigned their voices to the hero or a beloved side character. Owain noticed Deri didn't assign the voice of any bells present to the villain of the piece. That was made particularly clear when the merriment rang out as Deri even tuned his voice to – apparently – that of a rival bell choir from another church.

Owain accepted fairly quickly and easily that bells could have rivalries. After all, he could hear them speaking, and had spent quite some time gossiping with them. That they had personalities and emotions and even rivalries was no longer a shock. Instead, he looked at Deri with new eyes.

Living with Maurlocke meant Deri had a tendency to keep secrets, even when there was no real reason for it. If Owain was honest, he'd admit to himself that he enjoyed ferreting out these harmless little mysteries more than a bit. This, though... this was a big mystery.

The bells rang around them, joyous (somehow familial) peals. Owain sat back and watched and heard and felt. This was a new side of Deri, and he didn't want to miss any of it.

But eventually the evening came to an end, as it had to. There was only so much time they could steal. Owain and Deri set off back to their respective prisons, arm-in-arm.

'Thank you for that,' Deri said as they walked, the city around them slowly beginning to brighten with the advance of dawn. 'I think – just thank you.'

'What's haunting your mind? You've been odd all evening.' Owain looked at Deri quizzically.

Deri fidgeted and Owain felt a weight settle over them, brushing away some of the euphoria of the past night.

'What's wrong?' he asked quietly.

'I—' Deri chewed on his bottom lip. 'I just—' He blew out an explosive breath. 'Why is this so hard?'

'Out with it.' Owain felt ice down his spine.

'I – look. There are a lot of things that could go wrong over the next few days. I think I've fixed everything. I'm sure the plan will work. But you never know what might go wrong. These are... powerful people. I might have to do things I'm not proud of. Things that... things that you won't be happy about either.'

Deri wasn't looking at him.

That wouldn't do. Owain stopped and reached out, grabbing the man he loved by the chin and drawing him around to face him.

'I trust you,' he said. 'It's as simple as that. And you should trust me to know you. Especially after tonight. Is there anyone now who knows you better?'

'No,' Deri said softly. 'There isn't.'

He looked then like he was about to say something more, but the whistle of a passing policeman cut the dawning air and reminded both of them how little time they had to get back to where they were supposed to be.

They ran.

46

Deri paced the interior of Rhys' pawnshop. In spite of his recent flush of prosperity, even after paying Jack Trades' share, he felt underfunded for what was coming. Time to put his plan in motion. He was feeling the effects of spreading himself rather too thin, and the longer he waited the less chance he would have of success.

Rhys finally waved Deri forward and led the way up to his office. Inside, settled, Deri cut right to the chase.

'I need a forgery. The best you can manage, and I need it now.'

To his credit, Rhys didn't immediately laugh Deri out of the pawnshop. 'That will be a very expensive project,' he noted, instead. 'Though I know you wouldn't ask if you weren't prepared to pay. Why don't you tell me what it is, exactly, you need me to forge?' He waved a hand dismissively as Deri opened his mouth. 'Yes, I agree to the standard bindings of secrecy. Move it along, please.'

Deri reached into an inside pocket and pulled out a stained, much-folded piece of parchment. He unfolded it carefully and set it on Rhys' desk.

The pawnbroker – the forger – leaned forward to inspect it. A low whistle howled past his lips. 'This is your contract of indenture.'

'Yes,' Deri said. 'I want you to forge it.'

'A copy won't be easy, or cheap,' Rhys said, cautiously turning the paper over in his hands. 'I'll need ink of night, for one—'

Deri set a vial on the desk. The contents glimmered darkly. 'That won't be a problem.'

'You're sure that's enough?' Rhys glanced dubiously between the vial and the contract in his hand.

'More than enough. In fact, you won't need more than a few drops.'

'What? There's no way to copy this many words—'

'I don't want a copy,' Deri said, 'I want you to make the real contract, here, look like a forgery. One good enough to fool Maurlocke.'

'I'm sorry, what?' Rhys blinked.

'I need Maurlocke to think that the real contract is a forgery. I need ym to think that it's a forgery so good it almost fooled ym. I need you to add a few, almost imperceptible thickening of lines, and to change the indenture, there,' Deri pointed to the ornately ragged edge of the contract, 'just enough, just the slightest bit, that it won't line up perfectly with Maurlocke's half.'

Rhys thought about that. Deri forced himself to stand, still and patient, while the clock in the corner ticked through several minutes. Finally, the forger spoke.

'I can do that, yes. It won't be easy, tricking a master merchant of the Untermarkt into mistaking the work of ys own hand, but I can do it. I've all the materials I need, here. So the question comes down to price. What are you going to offer me for this piece of master-level forgery?'

Hoping it would be enough, Deri drew a handful of coins, black with age but glimmering with stored prosperity, and set them on the table. It was everything he had left after paying Jack Trades what he had owed.

Please let it be enough.

'I'm sorry.' Rhys shook his head. 'As tempting as that is, it's nowhere near enough.'

His stomach sank. Deri had expected this, but he'd had to try. He blinked back the sudden burning sensation in his eyes and settled his merchant face firmly in place.

Right. He had a plan.

Time for a bit of showmanship.

Deri pulled out another bottle, but this one he kept firmly in hand. 'I could pay with this, I suppose. The bottled destiny of a royal of the Empire.'

'But you're not going to, are you?' Rhys narrowed his eyes, shrewdly.

'I'm going to need it close to hand in case anything goes wrong with my plan. And, I've a mind to make your other profession a part of this deal as well.'

'I'm sorry?'

Deri stowed the bottle back in his pocket and looked away. Danu's tears but this was hard. Harder than he expected it to be.

'I want to pawn something to you, as payment for your services. I want as much grace period to buy the thing I'm pawning you back as I can haggle. If I don't, you can sell it on and we're square, but I want the chance to buy it back from you with merchandise of equal or greater value.'

He took a deep breath and ran his fingers lightly over his sternum a few times, like running a knife along the edge of a crack in a crystal goblet. Then, like forcing that self-same knife inside the crystal and turning it with a sharp *crack*, Deri pressed his nails through his chest and dug lightly into his own heart. With a hiss of pain and a sound like the shattering of a thousand mirrors, Deri gingerly pulled out a bit of his own heart. At least, that is how it appeared to Rhys, watching, whose eyes were not attuned to the ways of Faery as Deri's. Deri held the softly glowing bit of flesh in front of him for a thoughtful moment before wrapping it in silk and knotting it up with silver thread.

'True Love. That should more than cover your price, unless I am very much mistaken.'

'What? Why?' Rhys stared at the package. Of all the things he had been offered, in all his years as a pawnbroker, he had never expected to see such a thing.

'If I answer, will you guarantee the pawn terms I've requested?'

'Yes,' Rhys answered immediately, eyes afire with curiosity.

'Several reasons. Because it's the only thing other than the destiny that is valuable enough to secure your services. Because if Maurlocke thinks I've sold the destiny he won't try to cleverly compel me to give it to him. Because I'm going up against a master merchant of the Untermarkt and I'm afraid if I still have all my feelings, Maurlocke will be able to use O— them, against me. Because I believe that I can return here and buy it back before it's too late. And because if something goes wrong, I'm going to need the destiny as a fallback. This is the safest way to ensure I win my freedom and secure the future I want. Savvy?'

Rhys nodded. A question twitched at his lips, but he shook his head and cast it away unspoken.

'Then let's get started. You don't have much time. Let me draw up the contract, and then I'll get to work on your forgery.'

'I'll require a thief's candle as well.' Deri nodded. 'Thank you.'

'Don't thank me yet, young master Deri,' Rhys warned, 'This is going to cost you dear.'

'I know,' Deri whispered, too softly for Rhys to hear, even had the pawnbroker not already turned his attention to writing out the pawn agreement.

Owain hesitated before lighting the thief's candle. It wasn't much more than a stub, so the message inside couldn't be overlong. Bess had delivered it, but other than saying it was from Deri and to let her get back to her hunting, she hadn't said anything as to what the contents might be, nor even how Deri was doing.

So here he was, sitting on the floor of the attic hiding space, a lucifer in one hand and the candle in the other, afraid to light it. He didn't know why. He just was. Something about it seemed foreboding, somehow.

But it was from Deri. If he lit that wick he'd see Deri's face, hear Deri's voice. The need to see him soon outgrew the fear of what the message might contain.

Owain touched fire to the wick.

'Hey, boyo.' Deri grinned out at him from the heart of the flame. 'I don't have much time, and I wanted to make sure I said this while I still could.'

The image grew clearer. Deri was standing in a pawnshop? There didn't seem to be anyone else around. Maybe it had been after hours?

'We're almost set. I've got everything I need. It—' Deri's voice wobbled. 'Whew. Wow. This is hard. It was expensive, Owain. So expensive. It's taken everything I had, and then some, to set this shot up.' Deri crooked a grin, but it seemed tired. 'Come on, Deri, focus. You're burning daylight.' Literally.

'Owain.' Deri took a deep breath and stood up straighter. 'The other day I took you to see the bells of St. Mariwen-le-Bow? I was going to tell you something then, but we were late, and—'

The image of Deri paused again as he ran his fingers through his hair. 'Sorry. I should be better at this. I should have had time to make this better. But I don't. So I'm just going to come out and say it, tell you now what I really, really wanted to tell you then, with those stones rising around us.'

Owain's breath hung suspended, a moment of silence between hosannahs.

'I love you, Owain.' Deri's voice drifted across the room, salvation in five syllables. 'I love you more now than I can possibly bear, and I need you to know that whatever happens, it was my love for you that made me able to take this leap. I have to do this. For us. I can't wait five more years to be together. I can't wait five more days.'

Deri laughed. 'I'd say I can't wait five more minutes, but I'm afraid I'll have to. What I will say is that I will see you, and soon, and if I am half as good as I think I am, we'll be able to be together.' He cocked his head to one side. 'This is where you say that I'm not half as good as I think I am, but I'm not half bad, either.'

Owain laughed, though, curiously, there were tears streaming from his eyes. When had that happened?

'I have to go now,' Deri said, the candle flickering. 'I've got just one or two more pieces to put in place, and then I'm off to teach a certain merchant the true price of cheating us out of our lives together. Think of me, eh?' Deri's grin was suddenly full of rakish fire. 'I'm sorry I can't give you a bit o' something special to think of, right now, but I'm afraid I'm going to need all my wits about me, and I don't think Rhys would appreciate what I'd do to his establishment in the process. But hey, you've got your memories. You're a clever lad. I'm sure you'll figure something out.'

Deri's eyes flicked over to the side. 'I have to go. Rhys will be ready with my order soon. Owain, remember, no matter what happens, I love you.' Then Deri reached out and the message ended. Owain was left in the darkness, tears slowly drying on his cheeks, and a bright spark of something flaring in the depths of his heart.

'I love you, too,' he whispered.

47

That was it. He'd done it. Every piece was in place. Well, every piece that Deri could think of, after carefully checking his plans over with Silvestra Steele. The insight that woman had! The agreements he could forge if he had the loan of her gift for even a day!

Deri wrenched himself away from the daydream. He had more important things to do than lounge in the imagined spaces of easy solutions. He had a very real dream to usher into being, and it was going to take all his focus to do it.

He grinned suddenly. Even if it all went pear-shaped, it was going to be glorious. How many mortals can say they took a run at a master merchant of the Untermarkt and so much as shook the hem of ys robe? If Deri pulled this off, well, it'd shake more than Maurlocke's robe. It would rattle the foundation stones of London itself.

Well then, he'd best get to it. There were a few more messages to send, and he couldn't rely on the bells to send all of them. Deri grimaced. Relying on ink and paper was nerve-wracking, but it couldn't be helped. The most he could risk was a small charm to speed the thing on its way. Oh well.

If all went according to plan, he and Owain would be free in no time, with enough wealth at Deri's command to set them up for three lifetimes.

Owain found himself once again summoned to Missus Graspar's office. He had been expecting this. Why it had taken so long, however, he didn't quite understand. Everyone else had had their contracts amended days ago, even Vimukti. The Graspars had carefully closed the loophole that had allowed the strike. Owain's would be the last. There was probably some sort of poetry to that, but Owain wasn't really in the mood to appreciate it.

Garog set the new contract in front of him and Owain watched as the ink literally crawled off his old one onto the new. The sight was enough to make his blood run cold. Missus Graspar signed with a quick flourish and then Garog jammed a quill into Owain's hand.

'Sign,' he growled.

Owain didn't have much choice. He could fight them on it, try to stick to his old contract, but they'd eventually find some way to punish him, or make him sign the new one.

'Sign and you will be excluded from ever having anything to do with the new machinery Miss Steele has just installed,' Missus Graspar said sourly. 'It seems someone is willing to pay a great deal to have your contract amended in a particular way.'

Owain's heart began to beat, just a bit quicker. He signed.

'Merchant Maurlocke will be pleased,' Missus Graspar said as soon as the ink was set. 'Yse was most particular that you sign this precise contract.'

Owain's heart all but stopped in his chest.

The bells were ringing out a warning as Deri left the pawnbroker's.

The ink is dry! The words are writ! did ring and sing the Bells of Whit.

Deri began to run toward Covent Garden Market.

Auld Maurlocke calls, through market stalls! in chorus rang the Bells of Khalls.

A flare of pain swiftly followed the warning of the bells. Maurlocke was calling him home. Time to deliver the new wording to the inksmith. Time to condemn his friends to tighter bonds. Time, perhaps, to act.

Deri touched his pockets, ensuring he still had the vial of ink of night, that he still had the roll of paper, covered with words and words and crossed-out lines, one of the fruits of his bargain with Silvestra. The right words, hopefully, in the right order.

Pain flared again. Deri ran. As he ran, he rang out instructions to the bells. He might not get another chance, so he'd best prepare them now. They needed to ring at just the right time if his plan was going to work.

Deri waited as long as he dared before giving the signal, hiding in the shadow of Merchant Yahr'Kron's stall where sands of many colours shifted and coiled in pretty patterns that marked all kinds of time. He knew that thousands of contracts of indenture in the capital had been updated, but he had no way of knowing how many remained. Still, something, some inner voice, told him he dared wait no longer. So he gave the signal to the bells, which rang throughout the city and the Market, passing gossip from one to another until it reached the small bell made all of gold that now hung in Maurlocke's tent.

The little spy would deliver the gossip to the pavilion and the pavilion would make sure Maurlocke paid it heed. Before the echoes died down, Maurlocke would know that Deri had somehow tricked ym, that ys servant in fact held the bottled destiny of a member of the royal family, one that might, with a bit of luck, inherit the Throne of the Empire someday.

Before Maurlocke's furious will could reach out through the contract and compel him, Deri invoked the little deal he cooked up via Vimukti. Hours changed hands, obligations were diluted, and when the pain hit, Deri passed it along, through the newly worded contracts, to those who had agreed to share it. It made it more than bearable.

Maurlocke would expect him to come running. Deri instead sat down on the edge of the curb and turned his face to the sun. It was a cold day, but bright, and his face warmed. He'd have read a book, if his nerves would have allowed it. They didn't.

An hour passed, and then another. By the end of the third, Deri was considering making his way to the Untermarkt out of sheer boredom. Before he could decide whether or not to let Maurlocke stew on just what Deri's seeming immunity to pain meant, disaster struck.

Beware, my boy, of Maurlocke's joy! bewailed with woe the Bell of Bow! *His words profound have Owain bound!*

His masters cruel, the witch, the fool, delivered him to merchant's whim,
resounded then the Bell of Ren.

Deri's blood froze. He had to go. Now.

48

Deri forced himself to walk calmly into Maurlocke's tent though every fibre of his being cried out for him to storm inside with all the might and magic he could muster. No. He needed to present an unruffled front. It would give him a stronger bargaining position. Deri pushed his way inside. The cloth of the tent glimmered in the Language of Gold, announcing his presence to Maurlocke.

'Young master Deri, so glad you could join us,' Maurlocke drawled before turning around.

The trick was a lot less impressive now Deri could see the tent speaking. He was glad he wore no gold, or he might have snorted his derision in that language and given that small advantage away.

As it was, Deri barely registered Maurlocke's greeting. He was staring at Owain, mentally prodding the numb place where he vaguely remembered feelings once beating. It was an odd sensation. Deri kept his face impassive.

It wasn't easy. Even in the absence of love's urging, the sight of Owain was a thing to prompt pity, possibly even horror. He was bruised and bloodied and bound fast. Thick, dark lines circled his throat like a gorget. Deri couldn't tell if they were ink or blood, but he could see enough to know they held Owain fast. Even if the chains of bronze around his wrists and ankles could be broken, those lines would bind Owain to the Graspars' commands.

The Graspars themselves stood one to either side of Owain, each with a hand firmly clasped around the youth's upper arms. As if the other bindings weren't excessive enough, Junior leered when he caught Deri looking, and gave a suggestive wink.

Deri let it pass. The Graspars were far from the most dangerous thing in the tent. That dubious honour went to Maurlocke. Deri finally looked at the merchant and was rewarded with a thin smile.

'Merchant Maurlocke,' Deri acknowledged.

True to form, Maurlocke was decked out in fullest finery, every thread an expression of power. Many arms seemed to sprout from Maurlocke's shoulders, a pattern in the cloth, each hand clenched or grasping or cleaving tight to chains of gold and silver and ebon-black. Each detail of embroidery a statement to remind Deri that it was he, mere mortal that he was, who was bound to Maurlocke's will and service. The effect was more than unsettling.

It was also expected. Deri threaded a string of calm down his spine, drawing relaxation into his shoulders and ease into his stance. This was the game, and he had to play it to the hilt.

'Don't be shy. Come closer.' The sentence carried with it the weight of a command. Deri felt the tug of it deep in his solar plexus, the words given weight by the force of the contract that bound them.

Deri let the force slide outward, spinning it along the network of threads that he himself was now connected to through the agreements he had struck with indentured servants across London. Someone else would step closer, so he himself would not have to.

'I'm quite all right here, Merchant.' Deri put just a touch of nonchalance into his reply.

Maurlocke's eyes went sharp as Deri remained standing. Deri stretched inwardly, keeping himself from tensing. The opening salvo had been fired, and the weight of a master merchant's full regard was the answering volley. He was well and truly in for it now. This would be a fight to the death, financially speaking.

'Very well.' Maurlocke remained standing behind the desk.

Deri didn't reply to that. He stood, hands in pockets, spinning the silence out between them like fine silk thread. The silence lengthened. No one spoke.

Maurlocke would speak first. There wouldn't be any question of it. Time was money, and Maurlocke, a master merchant, would know to the second how much to afford this business before it began to eat away at potential profit.

Of course, with a possible seat upon the Throne of the Empire, that might be longer than Deri could physically hold out. Sweat began to bead above Deri's eyebrow. It was getting hotter. A glimmer of light teased at the corner of his eye. It was just a word in the Language of Gold, but it was enough. Maurlocke had instructed the tent to make things uncomfortable.

Well, that suited Deri just fine. He could take a little heat, but the Graspars... now, they were another story. Unused to the rigours of service, they'd be complaining long before Deri would, and as Maurlocke's guests – or business partners – the merchant would have to respond.

Sure enough, Junior shifted first. Then Missus Graspar coughed, awkwardly. They swapped a glance or three, but eventually Missus Graspar spoke.

'Well? Where is it?'

'Did you require something, madam?' Maurlocke looked to her, but the weight of ys attention still fell crushingly upon Deri.

'Where's the bloody bottle of destiny?' Missus Graspar demanded. 'We're here for business so let's get to it. I'm not one to stand about all day.'

'Ah yes, of course.' Maurlocke looked back to Deri. 'Hand it over.'

This was trickier. Deri felt the pull of his indenture like hot barbed wire tearing at his hands. But again, he cast the compulsion out along the net of obligations he'd carried into the tent with him and the power of it lessened. After all, no one else had the bottle to give, and impossible commands lost much of their bite.

'I don't think everything is in place for negotiations,' Deri replied, fighting to keep his manner cool and offhand. His thumbs prickled wildly.

'Negotiations? With whom?' Missus Graspar demanded. 'Force him to hand it over.'

'That doesn't appear to be an option right now,' Maurlocke replied calmly. 'Most interesting.'

'Then let us take a turn,' Junior suggested, pulling out a knife and raising it to Owain's face. 'Give us the bottle or your light o' love here gets it.'

'That would be a crime, Mister Graspar,' Deri replied, wrapping numbness around himself. 'And I don't think prison would agree with you terribly well.'

'Who's to know?' Junior toyed with the knife.

'Oh, I assure you the authorities will have more than enough evidence of any wrongdoing.' Deri sharpened his words like the blade of that knife. 'They may overlook mistreatment, beatings, and malnourishment, but mutilation and murder of a child? Well, that's sure to move them. Particularly when the papers get hold of it.'

'No one will believe the likes of you over us,' snapped Missus Graspar.

'Don't be dense,' Maurlocke cut in. 'He works for me. His word is almost as trusted as mine. Moreover, if he says they will believe him, you had best be certain he has some way to ensure that they do. He wouldn't be here otherwise.' Maurlocke flipped Deri a glance. 'I've taught him that well, at least.'

Deri smiled brightly at the Graspars. Junior growled. Missus Graspar tightened her grip on Owain.

'Very well,' she said. 'But five years is quite a long time to work at hard labour, particularly in a dangerous factory. Why subject your lover to that when you could so easily buy his freedom with that little bottle you have?'

'We can negotiate that, of course,' Deri replied, 'but as I said, not all parties are yet present.'

'Who are we waiting for?' Junior looked around the tent, as if to find someone lurking behind a table leg.

'I believe that would be me.' Jack Trades stood at the entrance to the tent, framed by falling waves of cloth of gold to either side.

'What are you doing here?' Maurlocke's face was impassive.

Too impassive. Deri had lived with the merchant for seventeen years. Breathed the same air, ate the same food, watched countless negotiations. Maurlocke had not been expecting Jack Trades. Good. Exactly as planned. Jack would keep Maurlocke off balance, and Deri would need every advantage he could wring from the situation if he and Owain were going to make it out successfully.

'I've a vested interest in this matter.' Jack Trades gestured toward Deri. 'This one thinks he has a shot at being my heir.'

'Ah. So we're going to talk terms, then.' Maurlocke resumed ys position behind the desk. 'Very well. Shall we begin?'

Before anyone could reply, the pavilion flaps swept open again and Dame Aurelia swept into the tent, eyes crackling and face like a storm cloud. The Graspars stiffened. Deri hid a grin.

Everyone was in place.

'Show us the bottle,' Garog Graspar rumbled, ignoring the sharp look his mother shot him.

'Let me ask Owain one question and I'll let you see it.' Deri turned to the workhouse owners.

'Very well,' Missus Graspar said, her eyes still flicking between him and the Knight of the Verge, 'but be quick about it.'

Deri stepped up to Owain. 'Are you alright?'

'Don't worry about me.' Owain smiled at Deri. 'I know you can handle the likes of these. Just do what you do.'

Deri nodded. He walked over to Maurlocke's desk and retrieved the bottled destiny from his most secure inner pocket. It clinked slightly too loudly for such a small bottle when he set it down on the wood. A thumbprint, bright and red, glimmered on the glass.

'What's that mark?' Junior Graspar asked suspiciously.

'It's a thief deterrent,' Deri answered. 'Any hand but mine that picks up that bottle will melt right off.'

The look on Junior's face was worth every scrap Deri'd had to pay to get that particular trick.

'Allow me to cut to the chase. We all know what that is worth.' Deri pointed to the bottle. 'Even given the difficulties that are associated with the sale of such an item, it is easily worth enough to buy out my contract and Owain's, buy me a merchant charter with the Untermarkt, and erase any ill will that may have arisen out of the various and sundry, ah, let's call them preliminaries, to this negotiation.'

'Well, that leaves these two out,' Jack Trades said cheerfully, gesturing toward the Graspars. 'Their whole operation isn't enough to get them a buy-in on something like this.'

'Not even if our operation, as you put it, has the capability to offer a certain select clientele eternal youth?' Missus Graspar snapped waspishly.

That garnered Missus Graspar the full attention of both Maurlocke and Jack Trades.

'She's not lying,' Jack Trades said, looking at her intently.

'No, she is not,' Maurlocke said slowly. 'Though how she has circumvented the Treaty on this matter is – call it a stroke of alchemechanical genius.'

'That's quite a feat. Must have a terribly high cost, though.'

'So, you agree that secret is worth enough to justify our presence?' Missus Graspar's tone was venomous.

'Not to mention we have this 'un!' Junior shook Owain.

Deri added that to the list. The price the Graspars would have to pay was getting high indeed.

'So we know what the Graspars are offering as their starting bid, and I have already had some rather pointed discussions with Dame Steele.' Deri turned to Jack Trades. 'You're offering the position as your heir after buying my freedom and his.' Deri jerked his head toward Owain. Then he turned to Maurlocke. 'What are you prepared to offer?'

'What if I'm not interested?'

'If you're not interested, why the summons?'

'The Graspars desired your presence for negotiations.'

'That doesn't mean you're not interested as well.'

'It doesn't necessarily mean I am, either. After all, by rights, what is in that bottle belongs to me, as per the contract of indenture you serve under.'

Maurlocke studiously avoided looking at the Knight of the Verge. Aurelia looked thunderous, but her hands were tied. Though everyone here was walking a fine line, the Treaty was ever-so-slightly on the side of the Untermarkt in this matter.

'Ah, but can it truly belong to you?' Deri drawled. 'Because if it did, I wouldn't be standing here, with the bottle, and you standing there, without. You've left a loophole in the contract, and I found it.'

'It rightly belongs to the Crown,' Aurelia ground out. 'None of you should have it!'

'But I do have it,' Deri pointed out, 'and both the Treaty, and the loopholes in my contract, make me the undisputed owner at this time.'

'Excuse me one moment, would you?' Maurlocke gestured and a curtain of glimmering fabric drew itself around the Graspars and Owain, hiding them from view and cutting off their senses from the rest of the pavilion with its magic. 'It seems I have some other business to attend to first.'

Deri smirked at Maurlocke. Normally, he wouldn't have bothered with that move, but the presence of Jack Trades just might make it a viable one. His gamble was rewarded. Maurlocke had some choice words in the Language of Gold about Deri's expression! My! It was a surprise the tent wasn't blushing ruby at language like that. Good. Got to keep the old merchant off balance.

Pressing the advantage, Deri turned to Jack Trades. 'You haven't had any trouble with loopholes in your contracts, have you? I hear that several had to be changed, quite recently, at great expense, to keep most of London's workhouses operational.'

'I heard that as well.' Jack Trades seemed more than happy to play along. 'No, I've had no trouble at all with mine, humble though they are.'

'We shall see about that!' Maurlocke plucked a contract – well, half a contract – from thin air and smoothed it flat upon the desk. It was as clean and pristine as the day it had been written. The edges along three sides were crisp and neat. The fourth, where the contract had been cut in two, flared with edges and curves, a unique pattern that could be matched only by its original mirror. The merchant extended a hand. 'Your half of the contract, if you please, Deri.'

The moment of truth had come. Deri's heart hammered in his chest. What if Maurlocke saw through Rhys' work? What if the forger had double-crossed him? What if, what if, what if? Deri pushed his way through the panicked thoughts to pull his half of the contract of indenture free from safekeeping on his person. He handed it to Maurlocke, still folded.

Maurlocke allowed a small moue of distaste to cross that perfect face. Deri's contract was far from pristine. It was structurally sound enough, of course. The magic bound into the ink saw to that. Normal wear and tear wouldn't have much effect. But where Maurlocke's half was white as the day it was writ, Deri's half had been coloured by seventeen years in his possession. It was stained with the odd bit of sweat and rouged with colour from the weakening dyes of Deri's secondhand finery.

The merchant rubbed the parchment between ys fingers, eyes of flint sharp and sparking. Deri knew Maurlocke would read every word – could do it in a single glance – and compare the script to the copy. Both halves of the original would have been in the merchant's own hand. The right paper, the right ink, even a perfect copy of an image, those all had to be right, but more than that, the two halves had to line up perfectly. Deri couldn't help but catch his breath as his heart started to hammer when Maurlocke set the two halves of the contract next to one another and carefully began to line them up.

They were an almost perfect match. Almost.

A cruel smile broke across Maurlocke's face like the dawn of a particularly malicious day. 'Well, I'll give you this much credit. The forgery is excellent. You might almost have fooled me, but it appears your friend Rhys isn't quite so skilled as he claims to be.'

'What do you mean?' Deri's voice chose that moment to crack, warbling between manly baritone and boyish soprano. There may have been a tinge of desperation to the words. 'That is a fully valid and completely binding contract of indenture! I swear it!'

'This?' Maurlocke laughed, the sound pealing golden throughout the pavilion. 'This binds no one.'

And the merchant casually tore the contract to shreds.

49

Maurlocke had torn up the contract.

No, Deri couldn't focus on that right now. Maurlocke was laughing. Deri's fingers fumbled through his pockets until he seized upon the old comb of ivory and horn. Quickly, he began to draw it through the air.

Maurlocke had torn up the contract.

No. Focus on the laughter pealing through the pavilion. Comb it from the air. Maurlocke's laughter gathered in electrum strands and Deri moved the comb back and forth in wide sweeping strokes, as far as his arms could reach. He had to gather up as much as he could before it faded, echoes and all. Maurlocke's laughter. Laughter! Deri'd never thought to live to hear such a thing.

Maurlocke had torn up the contract.

The threads of laughter tangled in the teeth of Deri's comb glittered and gleamed, the pale gold of moon wasps. It was enough. It had to be enough. Deri swore as he gingerly pulled the shining mass from the teeth of the old comb to drop it in a small silk bag.

The threads of Maurlocke's laughter were sharp as razors and just as thirsty for blood.

'What are you doing?' Maurlocke's voice positively crackled with outrage, snapping like a whip. 'How dare you! Give me that bag, now.'

'I don't have to.' Deri glanced at Maurlocke. 'You tore up the contract.' Then he tossed the bag to Jack Trades. 'Here you are, just as we agreed.' And, just to twist the knife in Maurlocke's vitals a bit: 'Maurlocke's laughter in exchange for making me your heir.'

'I own you! No one else. I will not surrender up that control, not for any price. I. Own. You.' Maurlocke's ever-smooth face actually creased, the smooth metal crumpling and twisting like paper. The pavilion's wall of cloth of gold billowed in a spectral wind and every gleaming auric surface nearby blazed with furious light. Aurelia's hands went involuntarily to her weapons. Jack Trades stood, looking entirely unruffled. Deri flinched back, physically. He couldn't help it. This was a side of the merchant he had never seen, primal and furious. Still, he plucked the strings of his courage and sang out an insouciant reply.

'No, you don't. You freed me when you tore up my contract.'

'That,' Maurlocke said, neatly snipping off the word with suddenly sharp teeth, 'was a forgery. Do not think you can fool me with such an obvious ploy.'

'That's why it was obvious,' Deri explained, 'so you'd focus on the forgery, not the real contract that was used to make it.'

'What?' Maurlocke went very still.

'The contract you tore up wasn't a forgery. I just paid to have it made to look like one. You tore up the real contract, and, as per the privileges outlined on your half of that agreement, in so doing, ended the contract. I'm free. My own man.' Deri couldn't resist savouring the words. He was not quite brave enough to flaunt his victory over Maurlocke in the merchant's face. Not yet.

Maurlocke's hands darted, serpent quick, and ys half of the contract of indenture that had bound Deri to ym was in ys hand. Deri could see the ink was already fading, the parchment beginning to flake and crumble. There had been a lot of magic bound up in that small thing, the conditions and obligations, the privileges and prerogatives. Complexity was always expensive, and the ties that had bound Deri to Maurlocke moreso than most.

'How?' Maurlocke stilled. 'No, I can guess.' The merchant reached up with both hands and smoothed ys face back to its default flawless span. 'The pawnbroker. You traded the princess's destiny to him in exchange for that.' Maurlocke's lip curled as the merchant looked at the shreds of Deri's contract littering ys desk.

'You what?' Aurelia bounced an incredulous glance between the merchant and ys former servant.

Deri didn't answer. He just reached into a pocket and pulled out a pawnbroker's chit. Rhys' seal was quite clearly visible.

Maurlocke sniffed deeply and the merchant's eyes of flint glittered sharply. 'It reeks of destiny and it's certainly valuable enough to be the real thing.' The merchant was clearly taking no chances, bringing all of ys senses to bear on the receipt marker in Deri's hand.

Deri pocketed the chit. It was so hot with the regard of so many intent and focused pairs of eyes it had nearly scorched his fingers. 'I am willing to entertain offers for my right to repurchase any and all relevant destiny from Rhys the pawnbroker.' Deri outlined the offer with utmost care and delivered it in as offhand a manner as he could manage.

'Rein in your heir,' Maurlocke snarled at Jack Trades, 'before I take it upon myself to provide him with some pointed education, gratis.'

'Technically, he's not my heir until the proper paperwork is finalised,' Jack replied mildly. 'But even if he were, I'd hardly be in a position to demand anything of him. An heir is not an indentured servant, not someone you can demand any and all goods from, with no repercussions save those outlined in a contract.' Jack allowed himself a small smile. 'Though that also requires one to be clever enough to realise that indentured servants are people, and quite capable of acquiring things of value for themselves.'

Maurlocke's eyes glittered, but the merchant made no reply to that. Deri devoutly wished he could bottle Maurlocke's humiliation as easily as he'd combed the merchant's laughter from the air. Not that he'd ever sell it. No. Maurlocke's humiliation was something he'd savour all his own. Nevermind the king's ransom it would command on open auction in the Untermarkt.

'You promised me to restore that destiny to the Crown, boy.' Aurelia ignored the sniping of the older merchants and focused all her attention on Deri.

'I promised you the chance to buy the destiny on behalf of the Crown,' Deri corrected. 'And as I don't see the former princess here, I have to assume you've failed to persuade the relevant parties to agree upon a suitable replacement.'

Aurelia's fist clenched and she took a deep breath. Deri was not unsympathetic. Hers was a difficult position and he was certainly not making it any easier.

'Making an enemy of the Crown would be a grave error,' the knight said carefully.

'Trust me.' Deri flashed her a smile. 'The last thing I want is to be in the Crown's ill graces. Well, second-to-last, perhaps.' He stole a furtive glance at Maurlocke. Then he flicked his gaze to Aurelia, to make sure the knight caught his meaning.

Aurelia's lips tightened, but Deri could see his meaning had taken root. If he was lucky enough (and his supply would definitely be exhausted by the end of this day!) he might make quite the profit off the afternoon's work. Speaking of which.

'Of course, that is not the only item I will be offering up today.' This time Deri allowed just a shade of smug to colour his words. Maurlocke's head whipped around and the merchant's eyes narrowed. Jack Trades was unreadable, but Deri thought the degree of unreadability implied he had managed to surprise both merchants with his latest move. 'I also offer up for auction a secret shame of Merchant Maurlocke.'

'What?' It was impossible to tell whether that expletive had leapt from Maurlocke's mouth, Jack Trades', or both.

'You haven't any such thing to offer!' Maurlocke sneered, but Deri could tell the merchant was wrong-footed. The potential was there, the value heavy in Deri's voice. His words rang true enough.

'If all assembled will agree to surrender their memory of this particular part of the negotiation in the event that they do not purchase said secret, I am happy to provide proof.'

'Done,' said Jack Trades immediately.

'And done,' Aurelia echoed almost as swiftly.

'Proceed, then,' Maurlocke said, words as slow and cold as a glacier.

Deri reached into yet another pocket and retrieved a carefully folded bit of paper. The edge of one side plainly bore the tell-tale scrim of a contract of indenture. He set it on the desk in front of Maurlocke and gestured for the merchant to read it.

'The theatrics are hardly necessary,' the merchant groused, but glanced at the contract nonetheless. 'This is a boilerplate contract, just a standard indenture,' yse said after the barest glance.

'Yes,' Deri said. 'You'd recognise it easily enough. After all, it's almost the same as the one you penned not all that long ago, to close the loophole I exploited to pull off the strike at the Graspars' factory.'

'You're admitting that now, are you?' It was uncharacteristic for gold to sour, but Maurlocke was making a valiant effort at it. Then the full impact of Deri's words hit and Maurlocke's eyes whipped back to the contract, brow furrowed in concentration.

'Almost?' prompted Aurelia.

'The copy I delivered on behalf of the Honoured Merchant may have undergone some edits en route.' Deri smiled brightly. 'I'm sure the good merchant would have eventually realised that I needed the ink of night for something other than producing a forgery of my contract. It doesn't take much to make small alterations, after all.'

Maurlocke had paled from gold to platinum, the contract in question held in nerveless fingers. The merchant was so shocked that yse didn't even object when Jack Trades reached out, overcome with curiosity, and snatched the contract to read it for himself.

'Oh. Oh my.' Jack's lips thinned. 'You have been bold.'

'What? What has the little miscreant done now?' Aurelia all but snapped.

'There's a clause in here that, properly invoked, allows Deri to act as representative for anyone working under a copy of this boilerplate contract.' Jack shot Deri a measuring look. 'And I rather doubt he'd be here if he hadn't gone to the trouble to invoke it. Am I correct?'

'You are,' Deri replied, smiling.

'But what does it mean?' Aurelia asked. 'Plain as you can be, please. I haven't any more patience for being talked around.' She tightened her grip on her weapons to emphasise the point.

'It means when Merchant Maurlocke tore up Deri's contract, yse in effect tore up every other contract of indenture that uses this particular phrasing. They're all invalid now. Deri turned his contract into a stand-in and freed,' Jack did some quick mental maths, 'probably several thousand indentured servants.'

'There will be economic chaos!' Maurlocke blurted out the words, finally coming out of ys reverie. 'Do you have any idea what you've done?'

'What you've done,' Deri pointed out. 'After all, everyone knows that the new contracts are your finest work, do they not? If they've failed so quickly...'

'How dare you?' Maurlocke drew ymself up to ys full height and positively blazed with fury.

'Threats won't accomplish anything,' Jack Trades broke in mildly. 'What's done is done, and it was quite truthfully done by your own hand. There's no getting around that. Every contract that was copied out or updated under that boilerplate text has been invalidated. The only thing left to do is negotiate for the right to control the story.'

'Yes,' Maurlocke said, all too suddenly calm, 'you're quite right about that.'

Deri's hackles rose in response. He knew that tone of voice and it turned his blood to ice. He'd been with Maurlocke long enough to know the signs. The merchant had some hidden advantage and was about to deploy it to full and devastating effect. The tent knew it as well. Smugness gleamed in every shining thread of gold. That, more than anything, froze Deri's heart in his chest.

'I am prepared to negotiate,' Maurlocke said, 'for the destiny you have hidden, the secret of the indenture's failure, and,' Maurlocke looked Deri straight in the eye, 'the buyout of your status as Jack Trades' heir and the reinstatement of your indenture to me. And believe me, boy, you'll find that price cheap indeed for what I have to bring to the table.'

50

The pavilion was silent, save for the faint susurration of the samite drapery of the walls: the pavilion's laughter. Jack Trades and Dame Aurelia looked on. Maurlocke stood gleaming behind ys desk, radiant with confidence.

Deri forced himself to stand nonchalantly, though the hands in his pockets were as much about feeling secure as they were appearing diffident. He shrugged. 'I'm obliged to hear your offer, at least,' he said.

The merchant stepped from behind the desk. Deri's hackles raised even further. He knew what this performative side of Maurlocke meant, what it portended. His life had never been in more danger than in this very moment.

Maurlocke raised one elegant hand and snapped ys fingers. The walls of the pavilion rustled and moved of their own accord, drawing back to reveal the Graspars once again, Owain still held firmly between them. Chains of brass still rattled at his wrists and livid marks encircled his neck like a gorget.

Deri almost opened his mouth to protest, but whatever

protestations he may have uttered died aborning on his lips. The markings on Owain's neck – they should have faded, vanished. They hadn't. That meant something had gone wrong. That Deri had done something wrong. But what? He'd seen Maurlocke's reaction. The merchant had been shaken to the core when Deri revealed how he'd not only won his freedom but that of everyone who had had their contract reforged to match the new wording.

Which meant that Owain's contract hadn't been rewritten to match the new boilerplate. His love – the word rang hollow in his mind. His friend? Deri brushed a mental finger across the tender part of his chest. Yes. His friend, still. Bittersweet, that.

Then Deri set the feeling aside. Lost love or no, he wouldn't abandon his friend like this. Not to these monstrosities.

'Yes,' Maurlocke teased the word out, drawing it like a serpent from its den, 'you realise your mistake, don't you? You should have realised that our honoured guests here understood just how precious and valuable a servant they had in young Owain, and carefully worked with me to reforge his contract accordingly. An expensive custom working, but one that, it seems, is already paying dividends.'

This had not been in Deri's plans. He flushed, anger and a touch of fear beating in his throat. He forced himself to breathe deeply, to keep his mind from tangling about itself as it span through possibility after possibility.

It was easier to calm himself than he thought it would be; than he thought it rightly *should* be. The fact bothered him, on some level, but that part of him was distant, remote. Like someone shouting from a locked room in another house. That was good. The initial panic of the unforeseen passed and his thoughts moved in orderly fashion, like ripples across a still pool.

First, he needed to undercut the merchant's position. And the means for that was, conveniently, all too close to hand. 'I'm sorry, Merchant Maurlocke, I must confess to being confused.'

'Confused?' The weight of Maurlocke's regard settled, chill and heavy, on Deri's shoulders.

'You said you were prepared to negotiate, but it is the Graspars who hold Owain's contract, is it not? Surely as it is their property under discussion, it is them I should be negotiating with.' Deri looked straight at the miserable excuses for humanity currently holding Owain's chains and forced his face into a mask of innocence. 'Human to human, as it were.'

Maurlocke shot Deri a look of pure poison. Deri ignored it. The merchant could try all yse wanted to mitigate the situation, but the words were out, the idea had taken root, and the Graspars had been reminded that Maurlocke was something other than human and therefore not to be trusted. Deri could see the calculus in their eyes as plain as day. The Graspars were not difficult to read.

Unfortunately, Maurlocke could read them just as easily and the merchant had centuries of experience in coaxing reluctant humans to see things ys way. 'I'll be negotiating on their behalf, of course.' Maurlocke didn't so much as glance at the Graspars but Deri could see the glimmers of the Language of Gold shining along the tent walls. The merchant smiled. 'I'll even waive my usual fee.'

Deri raised a few more objections but did not waste overmuch energy in the protest. One way or another, Maurlocke would represent the Graspars and their interests. His objections and sly insinuations were as much to play for time as to undermine the Graspars' confidence in their untrustworthy ally. Any friction between the two was a bonus.

The first thing he had to do was weaken Maurlocke's position. Right now, Maurlocke held Owain's freedom, and was asking an astronomical price for it. But there was someone else in this tent with access to nearly unlimited funds, and even more power, should she choose to invoke it. Deri turned to Aurelia.

'And what is the Crown prepared to offer to ensure that this goblin merchant does not come into possession of something that will allow ym to choose who becomes a member of the royal family, and possibly heir to the Throne of the Empire?'

Jack Trades looked on, a broad smile on his face. That smile only grew as Maurlocke went deathly still at Deri's words. Yse was definitely off balance, for all ys air of control. Maurlocke should have expected that move. It was a blatantly obvious one, but no less effective for that.

'These negotiations are bound by secrecy?' Aurelia looked to Deri for confirmation. When he nodded, she continued, 'Then I can quite happily say that the Crown can offer sanctions against the Graspars, as well as a criminal investigation based off the evidence you hold regarding their violation of certain Treaty precepts having to do with trading in life essential.' There was a slight pause. 'For all those who knowingly pursued the creation of this method. We can't have innocents like the workhouse children caught up in this, after all.'

Ah. So, the knight had likely realised just what her sister had unwittingly had a hand in creating.

'No need to be so delicate,' Deri said. 'You can say that they're sucking the lives out of little children to make fat old men a few years younger.'

Aurelia winced. Yes. She definitely realised what Silvestra had helped to create, and what that machine had been used for.

'Prove it, whelp,' Junior Graspar bellowed, drawing the majority of Deri's attention back to him.

'Oh, I can,' the so-called whelp replied, eyes glittering like ice. 'I promise all of you that.' He shot Maurlocke a look. 'Of course, I'm willing to trade that evidence, and, in fact, all memory of the offending machinery, in exchange for Owain's papers of indenture.'

'Don't toy with me, boy,' Maurlocke responded just a shade faster than Dame Aurelia.

'What game are you playing? We had an agreement.' The knight began to colour.

'Oh, did you now?' Maurlocke turned to the Graspars and immediately began twisting Aurelia's statement to ys advantage.

Deri shot Aurelia a quelling glance and then also turned his focus to the Graspars. 'If you want to walk out of here with your business intact, I suggest you listen to me.'

'You?' Missus Graspar looked like she'd rather eat arsenic. 'I think not, young man. I think you are vastly overestimating your leverage here.' And Missus Graspar spoke a single word, a word that hissed through the air like a serpent and struck at Owain. The livid marks on his neck suddenly flared and Owain screamed, once, before a sharp command from Missus Graspar forced him to suffer in silence. Well, as near to silence as he could manage. Small cries echoed disproportionately loudly in the silence that fell throughout the pavilion.

Aurelia's sword was half-drawn before a glance from Maurlocke froze her in her tracks. 'There will be no violence here,' the merchant said smugly. 'The enchantments on this pavilion won't permit it.'

'No violence?' Aurelia was red in the face. 'What do you call that?' She thrust a stiff finger toward Owain and the Graspars.

'That,' Maurlocke said, each word dropping from ys mouth with relish, 'is merely an exercise of an indenturer's prerogative.'

'Loopholes.' Aurelia looked fit to spit.

'Oh, come now, my lady,' Maurlocke chided, 'after all, it was a loophole that oh-so-recently set half the indentured of London free of their contracts.'

'Closer to four-fifths,' Deri corrected. When Maurlocke whipped around to gape at him, he continued, 'I convinced the scribe that you would be most displeased were she not to work to full capacity to exercise your will in this matter.'

Maurlocke maintained ys façade of calm but it was a visible effort. 'Well, at least you've done me a favour, there. I'll make a mint off those children when they're forced to return to the Untermarkt and sell themselves back into indenture just to survive.'

Deri blanched at that. Aurelia looked horrified. Jack Trades, for his part, looked entirely unsurprised.

'And this time,' Maurlocke promised, 'there will be no meddling. I'll be sure to draw up each individual contract myself. It'll eat into my profits, a bit, but I'm sure the massive spike in demand will more than make up for it.'

As if to punctuate the merchant's words, Missus Graspar snapped out a fresh outpouring of agony and Owain's muffled scream tore through the pavilion.

'That's not really as effective as you think it is,' Deri found himself saying. It had all fallen into place. There was no way he could allow Owain to continue to suffer, to be tortured, in front of him like this. There was only one way out of this that he could see, that Maurlocke wouldn't expect. That Maurlocke couldn't conceive of. He'd have to be quick. He'd have to be careful. He'd have to be perfectly positioned.

'And why is that?' Missus Graspar, ever demanding, demanded.

'It should be obvious.' Deri strolled provocatively towards Owain. 'You're not accomplishing anything because, for your torture of him to be effective, I'd need to feel something when you do it.'

'Are you saying you don't?' Missus Graspar sent Owain into convulsive agony again.

Deri stood right in front of him and refused to flinch. He couldn't, not if this was going to work. 'Nothing more than I'd feel for anyone else cruelly tortured for no point. You really have no business being in charge of anyone, let alone children and young people. You're monstrous.'

Missus Graspar stared at him in disbelief. Deri ignored her, keeping his attention focused on Maurlocke, just out of the corner of his eye. The danger, when it came, would come from there.

Deri was so focused on Maurlocke, he didn't see Garog move. The big man shifted, preparing to strike Deri. Aurelia, however, was ready. Before Garog could do more than shift his weight, she was standing beside Deri.

'I do believe the honourable merchant said there were wards against violence in this pavilion,' she said coolly. 'Although should you wish to test that theory, I am more than happy to oblige you myself.' The steely threat in her eyes and voice left no doubt which outcome she would prefer.

Not even Garog was that much of a fool. He subsided, glaring sulkily from beside his mother. She, for her part, pursed her lips and glared at Deri.

'So,' she asked, 'why, exactly, should we believe you that this,' she gestured to Owain in chains, 'leaves you so coldly unaffected? You've risked so much for him, before. Stealing into the workhouse at night, breaking into my office, outright theft, running through the dangerous streets of London with my son in pursuit. All of these things are catastrophically dangerous. And there was no clear benefit to you. No item of value he could have promised you. You must have feelings for him. You must trade us your right to buy back the princess's destiny.'

'I can't do that,' Deri said calmly.

'And why not?' Missus Graspar demanded.

'Because I didn't trade the princess's destiny for the forgery work on my contract of indenture,' Deri said. 'I traded Rhys my feelings for Owain.'

'There's no way such a pittance would have purchased you such an exquisite piece of work,' Maurlocke snapped. 'I couldn't get tuppence for a bottle of teenage hormones. They're disgustingly ubiquitous.'

'True,' Deri agreed, 'if that's all it was. But True Love? That's worth far more.'

51

Everyone was staring at him. Deri's heart began to pick up speed. Everyone was staring at him. Maurlocke's eyes of flint were calculating. Aurelia's face was blasted apart by shock. Owain… no. Deri couldn't look directly at Owain. As it was, he struggled to force the panic and guilt and broken shards of once-bright memories into the numb darkness deep inside so he could think. Because if he was going to get out of this with his freedom intact, and rescue Owain in the process, he needed to be able to think clearly. And he had to free Owain. Rhys might hold Deri's love, but his guilt was still buried in his guts up to the hilt. What good was freedom if you couldn't live with yourself because of the price you paid to obtain it?

'You can torture him, but it'll only be for your own amusement, and to arouse the ire of a Knight of the Verge.' Deri locked eyes with Missus Graspar and let the cold, numb emptiness that filled the space where his love for Owain used to be frost over his eyes. The older woman looked away first.

'Well done.' It was Maurlocke's voice, strangely soft. 'I would never have expected so ruthless a move from you, Deri.'

'Then I suspect you don't know me nearly so well as you think you do,' Deri replied crisply. 'Can we proceed with negotiations? Time is money, as they say Above.'

'Of course,' Maurlocke answered. 'Now that we know precisely what is on the table, I expect things will move more smoothly.'

Your expectations would be wrong, thought Deri. He turned, deliberately snubbing the merchant, and addressed the Graspars instead. 'So, what do you offer for the best chance at putting Junior there on the Throne of the Empire you will ever have?'

'What?' Aurelia all but exploded. 'You cannot be serious. It's in the best interests of everyone for that destiny to go back where it belongs; with the royal family.'

'I agree,' said Deri, 'but just because I agree with you on that particular fact being right and proper, doesn't mean I'm not also willing to entertain other offers. After all, how else are we to know what is a fair price for the Crown to offer me in order to secure its, well, security?'

'You are grown cold, little servant.' Maurlocke sounded on the verge of laughter once again. 'I am almost impressed.'

'You're already impressed,' Deri shot back, bluntly. 'I outmanoeuvred you, I surprised you, and I secured a place as Jack Trades' heir in the process.'

Maurlocke's eyes flashed, but the merchant did not deign to respond. Or, if yse was planning to, any such response was interrupted by Missus Graspar's offer.

'Eternal youth,' she said. 'We can offer you free and eternal youth, so long as our factory remains in operation and we hold right to it.'

Stunned silence fell. It was a strong opening offer. And it was one the Crown could not match. At least, not in kind.

Deri glanced at Maurlocke. The merchant could easily afford the magic it would take to grant Deri eternal youth, and of a variety that would not require the yearly sacrifice of another's vitality. Maurlocke, however, remained silent. So, the merchant was not quite prepared to obviously violate one of the core precepts of the Treaty between the Empire and Faery. Deri wasn't sure why, but that surprised him.

'You know the Crown can neither offer nor countenance any such thing as eternal life or youth,' Aurelia said stiffly. 'Titles of nobility, offers of patronage, even mercantile appointments, yes, but not that. The Crown respects the Treaty.' The knight eyed the Graspars, measuring them and finding them wanting on some basic moral level.

Missus Graspar sniffed. 'The Crown can afford excess piety. Those of us who have to make a living in this world cannot.' She turned to Deri. 'Well? Do you accept our offer?'

'I don't know,' Deri replied. 'I've not heard from all the interested parties, yet. Or are you simply subservient to their interests in this matter?' Deri shot a look at his former mystrer and could not resist the needling choice of words.

Maurlocke drew ymself up to ys full height. 'Hardly,' the merchant replied, dropping the ambient temperature in the pavilion by several degrees.

'Well, it's quite clear that it isn't you making the offer on Owain's freedom, and even if it were I think we've established that that is hardly the power move you thought it would be. So, are you bringing anything to the table or should we adjourn to Jack Trades' tent and leave you to go back to whatever business it is currently concerning you?' Deri pushed harder than he needed to. This was a chance at the deal of several lifetimes and Maurlocke knew it. The odds of the merchant backing down now – well, Garog Graspar had a better chance of pulling Excalibur from the Thames.

He was playing for time. Deri needed all the time he could scrape from these negotiations. The split to his focus, to keeping all the parties balanced while trying to find a way out that would secure Owain's freedom as well as keeping him from future retribution, well, it was not an easy needle to thread whilst it was lost in that haystack, was it?

'Very well,' Maurlocke said, 'if you insist we play, let us play, little one. I offer to make you my heir. I will train you in all the lore and secrets of the Untermarkt. Things known only to those who have sat upon the Merchant Council. I will support you throughout your time at the Market, unreservedly, to the point of voting for your ascension to a Merchant Council seat of your own, someday. Contingent on an equitable alliance being brokered between us, of course.'

Deri felt the floor drop out from under his feet. This was everything he'd ever wanted and more, being offered by the person he trusted least in the world. Part of him screamed to take the offer, take it immediately, and let the consequences go and hang! Another, admittedly smaller part, shouted at the top of its tiny, metaphorical lungs that this had to be a trap, that even if it were in good faith, that even if he could trust his own negotiating skills to secure him at least a part of this opportunity as it was presented, it wouldn't be worth it.

Deri was ignoring that tiny voice. His weight shifted, almost imperceptibly, in preparation for taking that fatal step that would carry him back into the sphere of Maurlocke's influence, perhaps this time forever.

Then the smaller of the two voices inside him took the broken-glass sword of his guilt, stabbed it into his vitals, and twisted. Even though Deri had tried not to look at Owain, in the pavilion that was all but impossible. Glimpses from the corner of his eye, golden-hued reflections on every surface of the gilt-edged walls of the pavilion (and Deri had no doubt that the spiteful thing was deliberately casting those images into his retinas to unsettle and unnerve him), all were there and the smaller voice inside him coated the blade of his guilt with them like poison.

With titanic effort, Deri stilled his muscles and forced a contemplative mask across his face. There was no doubt in his mind that Maurlocke would see he was tempted, would see the struggle not to simply leap at the offer and seize it.

Maurlocke wasn't the only one who could read Deri's temptation. In fact, the entire room and probably the bloody pavilion itself could as well. Jack Trades watched the proceedings with hooded eyes, thoughts veiled. Aurelia and the Graspars took matters more immediately, erupting into shouted protestations mingled with greater promises (many of which were of lesser reliability than their earlier offers).

Maurlocke allowed them to bicker. Of course yse did. Their desperation only enhanced the appearance of his offer's value. They were amateurs in this. Maurlocke was a professional, and one with centuries – possibly millennia – of experience. No. There was only one other voice in the tent that might have an answer to Maurlocke's gambit, and Deri wasn't certain that its owner was possessed of the necessary funds to challenge such an offer.

Then Jack Trades finally spoke. 'And you would simply give all this to the boy?'

'Give?' This time Maurlocke did bark out a laugh. 'Not hardly. In exchange for the bottled destiny of a royal of the Empire. A true merchant of the Untermarkt never gives anything away.' The merchant outright sneered at Jack Trades.

'Well, what do you want, Deri? What do you need?' Jack Trades looked to him. 'What is it your heart truly desires?'

And there it was, shining and perfect, sprung fully formed in Deri's mind: the solution to his predicament. Deri shot a look at Jack Trades, one the merchant deflected with an enigmatic smile. Of course. Jack Trades was a merchant of the Untermarkt, but he was also human, and young enough to remember a bit of what it was like not being bound to Faery ideas and ideals of commerce.

The hammering of his heart slowed. He knew what he was going to do, now. All that remained was to do it and do it in such a way that no one might stop him.

Deri put on a thoughtful face, and set his feet to fidget and pace, slowly circling the room. When he stood in front of Maurlocke, he shot an artful little glance toward the Graspars.

'Accept my offer and you'll have the chance to buy your own eternal youth someday, if you're clever enough,' the merchant breathed, just loudly enough for Deri and Deri alone to hear.

Deri tugged at his chin and crossed the pavilion to Jack Trades.

'I think you know that serving as my heir, rather than Maurlocke, will be the more rewarding experience.' Jack smiled at Deri but the merchant's eyes were on his rival. Deri would have paid a great deal to see Maurlocke's face just then.

Deri fidgeted and continued his path around the room to stand in front of Dame Aurelia.

'You know what I offer; what is riding on this. How vital it is to the Crown and the security of the Empire.' Aurelia looked stern, but then hit him with a crafty look. 'What good is youth or wealth if there is no Empire to sustain you? If the Empire falls, that factory will cease to operate, the Untermarkt will fade from beneath London, and then what will remain for you?'

Deri blinked. That was unexpected. Aurelia wasn't playing. She had seen right to the flaws in the other offers. If he didn't know better, he'd think she had also made a deal with Silvestra.

He turned to continue his circuit toward the Graspars, but he shot a troubled look over his shoulder back at Aurelia. He daren't look like he had made his final decision. He had to keep everyone off balance until he was ready.

Deri came to a stop in front of Owain, a Graspar standing to either side of their captive. He glanced from Garog to Missus Graspar. She pursed her lips at him.

'You know our offer,' she said coldly, 'but to show we're not averse to bargaining, we'll also offer Owain's contract. You can keep him or free him as you see fit. He's certainly not worth as much as the destiny in that bottle.'

Deri might have bristled at that, once, before he had traded the love from his heart for a chance at freedom. Now, he merely shrugged, glancing at Owain in an offhand matter.

Trust me, he rang out quietly in the Language of Bells.

Owain's eyes widened but the other boy didn't reply. Deri glanced at the other figures assembled in the pavilion and carefully reached into his jacket to pull out the bottle holding the destiny that once belonged to Princess Boudicca.

The silence that fell throughout the pavilion was sharp as a razor. The full focus of several powerful people was fixed on the small container in Deri's hands. That was good. It meant they weren't listening to the sounds ringing out from his lips.

'I know you won't thank me for this gift, but it is mine to give and I know you will accept it. If you didn't, you wouldn't be the person I fell in love with.'

Then Deri uncorked the bottle and held it up to Owain's lips. Owain, after only a moment's hesitation, breathed in the contents, his eyes never leaving Deri's.

And then the pavilion erupted into chaos.

52

Dame Aurelia drew her sword. Maurlocke shouted and lunged for Deri. The Graspars had drawn back in fear of what contents the bottle might have held. Jack Trades was the only one who held his ground. Maurlocke, in ys panic to stop Deri, smacked the bottle right out of his hand. It went spinning to the floor and smashed with a high-pitched retort.

For a long moment no one moved. Then, 'What have you done?' slipped from Maurlocke's lips, and the merchant was responsible for a second shattering as shards of silence exploded throughout the tent, everyone suddenly freed to talk at once.

Aurelia grabbed Deri by the shoulder and spun him around to face her. 'What have you done?'

'What? You said you wanted a replacement heir!' Deri said, a bit frantic. The point of Aurelia's sword was perilously close to his eye. 'Now you have one! And frankly you couldn't ask for better.'

'Oh no,' Missus Graspar shrieked, 'he is ours! The heir, you say? You cannot have him. We hold his contract. He is ours.' She smiled, suddenly. 'Though I suppose for the right price, yes, yes indeed you may have him back.' She practically cackled in delight.

She would have done well to pay more attention to her charge. For Owain was undergoing a transformation. Subtle, yes, but apparent to any who watched closely enough. In all the tent, however, it was only Jack Trades who marked it.

Owain held himself too tightly, too rigidly, as he simultaneously felt freer than he ever had before in his life, and also more bound by invisible ties. Chains of duty tightened around his soul, sinking deep as destiny drove its roots deep into the fertile soil of his being. Aggressive, thirsty things, the roots found the existing weft of Owain's original destiny and began to wind about it, pulling and carding it like wool, tearing it apart and spindling back together something new. Later, Deri would pluck the trailing filaments of excess destiny from Owain's shoulders and carefully bottle them up to keep them safe. But that would be later. At present Deri's attention was on rather more pressing matters, like the tip of the sword Aurelia was pressing to his throat.

'Answer that,' she demanded. 'I can't take protection of an heir to the throne if someone else owns him!'

'They don't, though,' Deri said, not daring to spare a glance at Owain. 'That contract is void. Or it will be in a few moments.'

'What?' Missus Graspar screeched and fumbled with the paper in question. 'What have you done? Cheated! I will not be cheated!'

'Oh, do be quiet,' Maurlocke snapped, body heavy with resignation. 'That contract is void because the person it applies to no longer exists.'

'But he's standing right here,' Garog Graspar objected, rattling the chains that held Owain.

'No,' Deri said quickly, focusing on Aurelia. 'The person bound by that contract is Owain Wynn. The person you're holding, illegally, in chains is Prince Owain of Saxe-Coburg and Gotha. Those are two very different people indeed.'

As Deri spoke, the ink-dark marks around Owain's neck were fading, and fast. With no indentee to bind, the power of the contract was broken. Missus Graspar called out command after command, invoked clause after clause, but each crashed and broke like a wave over the rock of Owain's new – and very different – identity.

Owain flexed his wrists, and the manacles holding them sprang open and fell to the ground. Garog, never the quickest on the uptake, reached out to grab Owain by the shoulder. Aurelia stopped him. Well, her weapon at his throat stopped him. Deri's shoulders dropped in relief.

'I will thank you both to step away from my charge,' Aurelia said coldly to the Graspars.

The duo backed away. Not even their greed was a match for the icy promise of violence in Aurelia's eyes. As soon as they were safely back, Aurelia placed a protective hand on Owain's shoulder. Owain, head still spinning with strange memories and the strange sensation of feeling somehow too large for his body, didn't notice, didn't object. His shoulders relaxed, though. Some part of him, at least, recognised Aurelia.

'We're going now,' the knight announced.

That, at last, reached through Owain's haze. 'Wait, what?' He looked about him. 'But—'

'No buts,' Aurelia said firmly. 'I have to get you back to the palace before anything else can go wrong.' Her tone was not one to brook argument. 'Though how I'm going to explain this…' she muttered to herself.

'I could—' Deri began.

'No!' Aurelia cut him off ruthlessly. 'You have done quite enough, thank you very much. I'm not letting you within hailing distance of any of my charges ever again.'

'You what?' Owain turned to look at her, outraged.

'He's too dangerous,' Aurelia said, not taking her eyes off Deri.

If she had, even for a moment, returned her attention to her new charge, she might have been able to forestall the outburst. As it was, she missed what few signs she might have been able to pick up on. Certain qualities beneficial to leadership but occasionally unpleasant to experience had already taken root in Owain, by virtue of his new destiny, and he, so new to them, hadn't the faintest idea of how to control them.

'I say who I see and do not see, not you,' Owain snapped, 'and I'll rip this destiny out of my soul and sell it to the highest bidder if you dare ever again threaten to stop me from seeing the man I love.'

Aurelia whirled on Owain. 'What? You what?'

Maurlocke laughed, a waspish tone, flat and dull, without the golden tones that usually graced the merchant's voice.

'I'll solve this one for you, Dame Steele, free of charge.' The merchant's eyes glittered maliciously at Deri before darting over to Owain. 'I think you'll find, Your Highness, that is rather a moot point.'

'And why is that?' Owain eyed Maurlocke disdainfully. It was a heady thing, being free for the first time in his life, and it was definitely going to his head. A small part of Owain noticed, but it couldn't shout loudly enough to make itself heard over the strident voice of the royal blood currently sweeping through every vein of Owain's body.

'Because young Deri here did not use the destiny that is even now knitting itself to the threads of your fate to acquire work of this quality, there's only one other thing that would serve.' Maurlocke flicked a scrap of Deri's former contract of indenture from the desk. 'He's already told us. It was his love for you. True Love, of course. Nothing less would have served.' The merchant's smile was a butcher's blade. 'Pity to lose such a pretty thing.'

Silence fell, the silence of springs wound so tightly there was no room for movement, no sound. At least, not until the explosive recoil. Deri stared at Owain, who studiously ignored him, keeping his eyes fixed instead on Maurlocke. Deri was quickly discovering that the loss of True Love in no way removed empathy, nor guilt. It did not sever all those ties that bind. Perhaps if he had been a master merchant and knew all the proper strands to cut when carving his love for Owain out of his own heart, he could have insulated himself against these feelings, but he wasn't, and he hadn't, and though the love was gone, something complex and tangled still remained. Something soft, that still cared for Owain and his feelings, persisted. It still hurt Deri to hurt him.

When Owain finally turned to look at Deri, Deri turned away before he could make eye contact. What he'd done had been necessary, he told himself. The plan would have worked no other way. He should have been able to look Owain in the eye, but he flinched. He had to force himself to breathe deep, find his strength, and lift his eyes as he pulled it up from within.

Owain was looking at him, eyes sharp. Deri had lived his whole life in the Untermarkt and had never before felt so measured and weighed, calculated and evaluated. It was deeply unsettling, and yet, at the same time, because it was Owain, he felt seen and known in an unsettlingly comforting way.

The turmoil inside Owain was unlike anything he'd ever felt before. There was hurt, betrayal, and pain, those things were familiar enough in his life, but there was a strange cast to them, almost a doubling, and there was rage, self-righteous fury, and a defensive dismissiveness that burned coldly. That last one came with a mask that settled over his features, diffident and sharply neutral.

But there was something else. That little voice inside, the one that had been struggling to make itself heard over the brass-brazen royal voice echoing through his veins, it was speaking, and it refused to not be heard. The voice that knew Deri, all the way down. The voice that knew Deri would have had a reason, and, more than a reason, that Deri would have a plan. Yes, something had clearly gone wrong. This was not the expected or desired outcome, but that didn't mean there wasn't still something—

'Is this true?' Owain demanded, watching Deri carefully.

'More or less,' Deri answered, meeting that gaze.

'You see, your Highness—' Maurlocke began to interject, oil-smooth.

'I've heard quite enough from you, thank you,' Owain cut the merchant off.

'It was the only way to free everyone,' Deri said, drawing Owain's attention back to him. 'Everyone who could be freed, that is.' Deri forced a sudden smile. 'I imagine Vimukti has her hands full up there.' Deri all but waggled his eyebrows at Owain.

'What else have you done?' Dame Aurelia looked to be on the verge of apoplexy. The day was not going at all to plan, and this was wearing on her very last nerve of steel.

Deri put on a puzzled face. 'You didn't think we'd go to all the trouble of negating that many contracts without a plan of

action, did you? I imagine London has ground to a halt by now.'
Deri flicked a look at Maurlocke. 'It's really very inefficient to
build an economic system that relies so heavily on exploitation.
What do you do when people decide they aren't going to take it
anymore?'

'Vimukti would certainly go for the jugular,' Owain mused,
'especially after talking with Miss Steele these past weeks.'

'What?' Aurelia looked startled.

'Not you, your sister,' Deri explained. 'The one with the talent
for seeing the weaknesses in things.'

'I thought that only worked on machines,' Missus Graspar
protested.

Aurelia had gone pale. 'It only works reliably on machines,' she
said, absently, 'but sometimes she gets the odd insight into… other
things.' She shook herself and grabbed Owain by the shoulder.
'We have to go. I must get you to safety, Your Highness.' She didn't
bother questioning the truth of Deri's words. Hard experience had
taught her never to question that they were true, only the extent to
which they were.

'You should go,' Deri agreed. 'Maybe you could even check in
with Vimukti on the way.'

'No!' Aurelia snapped.

Owain caught the look Deri tossed at him. Yes. There was a
plan. This hadn't been a part of it, but Deri was clearly already taking
advantage of the shifting circumstances. The old Owain would
have gone along with things quietly, but now, now he wasn't quite
ready to skip off so sharpish.

'We need to go, Your Highness,' Aurelia said, firmly.

'One more question,' Owain said, shrugging off Aurelia's hand

and taking a step closer to Deri. 'Was it worth it? Toying with my – our – feelings like this?'

Deri cocked his head to one side, considering. 'It might be, but I suppose it depends on precisely what you do next.' Deri smiled, sadly. 'Your Highness.'

Aurelia had swept Owain out of the pavilion and the Graspars had wandered out after them, looking slightly lost and more than a little fearful. After all, they were faced with the consequences of attempting to circumvent the Empire's Treaty with Faery, on top of being the owners of a suddenly workerless workhouse. Deri was left alone with Maurlocke and Jack Trades.

'Well,' Maurlocke drawled to Jack Trades, 'congratulations on being the first Jack Trades with an heir who is, categorically, not a merchant of the Untermarkt.'

The merchant's words did not have the desired effect. Jack Trades looked on, amused. 'Oh, I imagine Deri and I can work something out. He's already proven that he's skilled in trading intangibles. I'm sure we can come to a mutually beneficial deal.' He smiled lazily.

Maurlocke looked sour and turned to Deri. 'Well, was it worth it? Your little stunt? It won't truly change anything, you know. There are always more people willing to sell themselves – or their children – into indenture. There will be a supply to meet the demand.'

'True,' Deri answered, 'but I expect the demand will be decreasing, sharply, in the near future.'

'Oh?' Maurlocke would have sneered would it not have

decreased ys standing in this exchange. 'And what makes you think that?'

'I imagine the appearance of a long-lost member of the royal family, appearing to tell his tale of oppression at the hands of the workhouse owners, might put a damper on it.'

Maurlocke gawped at him.

'What? Just because I had to change my plans a little doesn't mean I can't adapt on the fly. Owain can hear the bells. They'll steer him right. For me.' Deri smiled.

'And he will listen, even after you've sold your love for gain?' Maurlocke switched tack. 'Seems unlikely.'

'Owain is an unlikely person. Plus, he's strong enough to tug at destiny's yoke and make some of the inescapable weight work for him. He's good at things like that. Making better out of bitter.' Deri straightened his clothing. 'Now, if you good merchants will excuse me, I think I'd like to go Above and see how things are falling out.'

'Of course.' Jack Trades smiled. 'We can discuss your status as my heir later… and how much it might be worth to you.'

'You think this is the end?' Maurlocke interrupted. 'Things do not end at the Untermarkt. This is a place where stories pass through. This is not the end of anything. Mark my words, this is not the end of our story—'

'Stories may not end. Mine certainly won't. But this chapter? The story of my being your servant? That is over. Over and done with. Shut the book.' Deri looked Merchant Maurlocke up and down. The merchant was staring at him, speechless. 'If you know what's good for you, you'll leave it that way. Closed.' He turned to Jack Trades. 'Shall we?' Deri nodded to the exit and slipped out of the pavilion.

It didn't even bother to snap its edges at him.

EPILOGUE

Deri huddled in one of the arches along London Bridge, St. Cathbad's gleaming in the distance. The faint voices of the bells drifted toward him over the water, but they were too faint for him to make out what they might be ringing about. Instead of straining to hear, he flipped to the next page of the newspaper in his hands. There was an article on the seizure of a workhouse, formerly under the ownership and control of the Graspar family. Deri smiled to see that. They were so destitute that they themselves were being bound in contracts of indenture to repay their debts.

Poetic.

'All has turned out well then, kit?'

Deri glanced up, blinking in the light. Bess was perched atop the arch he was huddled in, head upside-down over the edge to look at him. He smiled at her.

'Well enough, milady,' Deri replied. 'Thank you.'

He said it mostly to be polite and was bemused when the cat sniffed and said, 'You are most welcome,' in return.

The cat vanished and Deri blinked after the absence. Then he shrugged and returned to reading. There was plenty of interest in this edition.

As the paper was one of the more salacious of rags, there was also a small piece about a growing labour movement sweeping London. The fiery leader with a talent for rousing speeches was mentioned once or twice.

Vimukti had landed on her feet too. Good.

The society section was rather more interesting, but Deri had been saving it for last, partly to savour it, partly from fear of what he might read. It looked as if Owain was settling into his new life with the expected level of turmoil. Small chance Her Majesty was pleased to have such a firebrand advocating for the rights of the oppressed of the Empire; given that Dame Aurelia was always in the background of any picture featuring Prince Owain, well, let's just say that Deri was glad his path had not crossed hers since they had left Maurlocke's tent.

Pierrick was in the background, too. Owain's valet, one caption said. Deri supposed that was to the good.

'You could just ask, you know,' a voice, amused, broke Deri's reverie. 'No need to stalk me in that dreadful old rag.'

'This is The London Eye,' Deri protested, ruffling the pages at Owain before adding, belatedly, 'Your Highness.'

'Shh. I'm incognito.' Owain stepped into the alcove, sheltered from the misting drizzle.

'Dame Aurelia will skin you alive if she catches you,' Deri warned.

'Then we'll just make sure she doesn't catch us, won't we?' Owain countered with a smile. 'Besides, I believe I still owe you one more night on the town.'

'That debt was held by a different Owain,' he said. 'You are free and clear of it.' Deri held Owain's eye for a split second before lowering his gaze once more. 'Your Highness.'

'I believe it is to me to say what I do and do not owe.' Owain's voice was firm. Commanding, even.

It was strange. A nice strange, but strange.

Deri took a moment to examine his old friend. Owain was the same, and different. Not just the clothes, which were very fine, if understated (a terrible attempt at a disguise – that was something that hadn't changed). No, Owain carried himself with more surety, now. There was a clarity to the strength he radiated, the strength that had before been hidden beneath a head weighed down by the sorrows of the workhouse life. Deri snorted. He was getting maudlin. Too much time spent topside, no doubt.

'I'm sorry,' he said, cutting through the levity to the tension beneath. 'I wasn't quite clever enough to pull it all off without losing… something. I'd hoped that a guaranteed place as Jack Trades' heir might be enough to get my love back out of pawn from Rhys,' Deri shook his head, 'but I guess my valuations were off.'

Owain had slipped a flask out of an inner pocket and was holding it, open, to his lips. Deri resisted the urge to roll his eyes. The thing was ridiculously ornate, another dead giveaway that Owain was more than he appeared.

'I'd offer to help, but I don't think my allowance would be enough to cover it.' Owain cleared his throat. 'That is, even if you wanted those feelings back. I imagine you feel quite different, without them.'

'Not as different as you might think,' Deri said, hiding his discomfort under cover of reshuffling the newspaper in his hands. Why had he said that? It was true, but not anything that would do

415

any good. 'At least I know it's safe from Maurlocke. I made sure that I'd be the only one who could buy it back from out of pawn. Well, if I can do so within seven years, that is.'

'Now how did you manage that?' Owain cocked his head quizzically at Deri.

It was a new mannerism. Deri found it oddly unnerving for some reason. 'There's a standard clause that basically says only the person the item belongs to may claim it within three, seven, etcetera years.' Deri shrugged. 'Standard stuff.'

'Makes sense.' Owain twiddled the fingers of his free hand. 'Do you think you'll try to raise the required – I suppose you can't call it funds – price?'

'That depends on you,' Deri said. 'I mean, even if I did, we wouldn't be able to do anything about it. You're a prince. I'm an orphan. Worse, I'm a goblin-brat who talks to bells.' Deri laughed, suddenly, with just a tinge of hysteria. 'It's not where I expected to be, actually. I mean, I knew I'd always live a life between worlds, but I'm not living it between the worlds I expected. I'd planned on living between worlds with you, but now, well, that can't happen. Not that I wouldn't try. Or not that I wouldn't help you sell off your feelings as well. A matched set would bring an exponentially higher price. Not that you need anything, now.' Deri laughed again and shook his head. 'It's all up in the air now, in ways I don't understand. I used to think that life made sense, that it was a balance, and exchange, and interplay of stuff. Sorry. I know that doesn't make much sense.'

'Do you want it to?' Owain cocked his head again and held the flask out to Deri. When Deri didn't immediately take it, Owain waggled it at him. 'Trust me. It'll make you feel better.'

Deri laughed and accepted the flask. 'Why not? Can't hurt.' And he took a swig.

And immediately doubled over. His chest felt like it was on the verge of exploding. His heart hammered within the cage of his ribs, and he was suddenly light-headed. He wheezed out something between a laugh and a wail as Owain stood over him, watching with all appearances of clinical detachment.

'What – what was in that flask?' Deri asked, and as soon as he did, he knew. He knew because his heart was full again in a way it hadn't properly been since the day he'd made that fateful deal with Rhys. He didn't wait for Owain to answer, he just changed his question for another. 'How did you get your hands on that?'

'As you said,' Owain's voice quavered with repressed laughter, 'only someone who had an ownership stake in the merchandise could redeem it from pawn, and if I don't have such a claim on it, I don't know who does. It's not like True Love is yours alone, after all.'

'But the price—' Deri's head was still swimming, so he could be excused for not grasping the obvious.

'A royal favour alone wasn't quite enough,' Owain said ruefully. 'I had to throw in my patronage for Rhys' artistic career as well.' He paused. 'Thankfully, his work is exceptional. I can't imagine why it hasn't done better.'

'A mystery for another day,' Deri said. His mind was settling back into its regular orbit. 'I can think of more pressing concerns.'

'Oh?' Owain shot him an arch look. 'And what might those be?'

'First, this.' Deri leaned in and pressed his lips to Owain's. Their arms enwrapped one another, as if to draw each into the other, forever. Eventually, a primal need for such pesky little concerns as oxygen interposed itself between them and they parted (though only the scant iota of space necessary to draw breath).

'Careful,' Owain teased, 'Dame Aurelia will skin you alive if you're caught assaulting the royal person like that.'

'Cheeky.' Deri freed one finger long enough to press it into the side of Owain's face, underscoring his words (well, word). The high was already fading, though, punctured neatly by the reality of Owain's words. 'Aurelia is the least of our problems. And, I'm afraid, your new grandmother might have a great deal to say as well.'

'Less than you might think,' Owain said. 'She's very pragmatic. Most of her grandchildren have been married off to secure some advantage or other. You just have to find that advantage and we can present our case for her consideration. That's your job.'

'Oh? And what's yours?'

'Becoming her favourite,' Owain said, seriously, 'so that when you make your offer, she's inclined to accept it and overrule anyone else in the government who might object.'

'I'm going to have to become respectable, aren't I?' Deri's words savoured just a bit of rue.

'You do realise that the most respectable people in London are also the most treacherous, don't you?' Owain flicked the end of Deri's nose. 'You'll fit right in. I don't think we can manage to secure you a dukedom, but with your knowledge of the Untermarkt, and whatever resources I can muster, I'll wager we can cook something up. Maybe if we start you off with a political office of some kind. You've enough goodwill amongst the newly freed. That could be a lot of votes!'

'Me? In politics?' Deri gave a performative shudder.

'Oh, I think you'd do alright. After all, it takes a certain skewed view of reality, just like being a merchant.'

'Hey! I resent that remark!' Deri slapped Owain's chest, lightly.

At that moment, the wind shifted, carrying the voices of the Bells of St. Cathbad's cold and clear across the water. Deri cocked his head, listening, and his eyes went wide as he began to laugh. He began to twirl himself within Owain's arms, coming to rest nestled snugly in their embrace, before looking up with a smile.

'How does Lord Mayor of London sound?'

THE END

Biography

Trip is an author, a doctor of creative writing, and a researcher of all things pursuant to bargains, exchanges, and compacts of a faery nature. It is inadvisable to attempt to make a deal with him. He has been, in the past, a reluctant cowboy, a living Toy Soldier, and an itinerant marketing professional. Frequently writes as a ghost. Currently teaches as one half of Underhill Academy for SFF Writers. Dwells in London with one true love, two brilliant writers, and a host of furious fancies, whereof he (sometimes) is commander. Mostly harmless. www.tripgaley.com

Acknowledgements

I don't think any book is created without great cost, and this one is certainly no exception. Writers pour themselves into the act of creation, purchasing words and worlds with countless hours, vast quantities of mental and emotional energy, and, if they are lucky, indulgences from a variety of invaluable friends and colleagues. I am truly indebted to these people, for this book would not be what it is without them. To purchase relationships like these at the Goblin Market would beggar the world.

I owe the most to Robert Berg, my partner and love of my life, who has supported me in everything I do, particularly in relation to this book. His encouragement set us on this path, saw us move across an ocean to live in our dream city amongst friends who are family, and helped me hew to the vision that is now made manifest in your hands. Moreover, without his talent for quashing typos and spotting small errors, or his dramaturgical insight to narrative, I would be bereft. For these and more reasons than I can type, thank you.

(Look at that, babes! A Dedication *and* first billing in the

Acknowledgements! You can stop campaigning for recognition now!)

Dr. Tiffani Angus has worn many hats throughout the realisation of this book. She began as my PhD supervisor, became my guide to the world of UK SFF publishing, then a tireless advocate for me and my work, and now, I'm very proud to call her not only my friend but also my business partner at Underhill Academy for SFF Writers. The debts I owe are many and varied, and I truly cannot begin to thank her enough for everything she has done and continues to do.

(And I've passed my viva! No one can accuse me of saying nice things to get better marks now! I'm *Doctor* Galey!)

Chris McCartney joined me for a drink one warm afternoon in 2019 and has been providing me with insightful, pointed, and adroit feedback on my work ever since. We began meeting up for a pint every week to talk fantasy and writing and life, and eventually he became the first beta reader to send me feedback on *A Market of Dreams and Destiny*. We became friends, and then writing partners; this man has honestly and truly made me a better writer, and this book is better in every page because of him. I hope I offer half as much to him as he's given me.

(He's squirming as he reads this, you know. Possibly reconsidering our friendship. Too late, sucker! We're family now!)

Mark Small and Jack Shoulder never fail to provide support and encouragement and knowledge whenever I need. They're only ever as far away as my phone, and our group chat is rarely idle. Mark and his work in archives helped me formulate a key plot point which I won't spoil, and Jack and his knowledge of museums and Antinous inspired a vital scene. Plus, thanks to these two boys and their work as @museumbums, I never want for callipygian inspiration. My life and this book would be poorer without them. We're family.

(Alright, boys, let's talk commission! How much do I get if I mention your book *Museum Bums: A Cheeky Look at Butts in Art*, available now from Chronicle Books?)

Meg MacDonald is an iconic feature of the UK SFF convention scene, she exploded into my awareness before I even met her, and I am so thankful for both. She has been a friend, a beta reader, a partner in crime, and given me so much love, as well as advice and insight into various details of my book. I cannot thank her enough for everything she's done, and cannot wait until enough time passes that we are once again in each other's company enjoying a drink and a few salacious stories.

(No, I won't tell you my favourite story about Meg before meeting her. Not here, at least! But it's a good one, I promise. Not Pratchett good, but still.)

Nick Coveney and Patrick Ness have been fierce friends and supporters at different points throughout the process of this book coming into existence. Nick was kind enough to not only beta read the book, but to also write a wonderful letter of endorsement for my latest UK visa. Patrick has been nothing but kind and generous with his time and experience. I'm very lucky to know you both and I hope there are many more game nights and nice meals in the future!

(There should have been a *Hocus Pocus* reference in there, really, but witch, please! It's *this* diva's time to shine!)

Jim Casey has been a true and steadfast friend and supporter throughout the creation of this book. While we knew each other at university, we reconnected shortly after I began writing and grew closer than I'd ever expected we might. Thank you for loving the book enough to read the roughest of drafts in one sitting, for sharing your love and appreciation for my writing with your friends, and for our amazing video calls. I truly treasure every moment we have together, and hope that time only increases in the future.

(Look, I'll even forgive you for being taller than me! Which is huge. So you're getting both thanks *and* grace out of this deal!)

My editors, George Sandison, Davi Lancett, and Daniel Carpenter, were each instrumental in bringing this book into your hands and I can't thank them enough for their support, insight, and enthusiasm.

My agent, Max Edwards, has been a boundless fount of energy and gone above and beyond in representing me and my interests, and it is a privilege to work with him.

Fellow writers who have helped me along the way, honestly, thank you so much for paying it forward, for sharing your time and your experience, and your hard-won knowledge. David Slayton, Adam Sass, Shveta Thakrar, Max Gladstone, Amal El-Mohtar – I can't wait until we next meet in person and we can talk shop and swap war stories over good food and fancy drinks.

To everyone who read and offered feedback on my work, I owe you an unquantifiable debt for your thoughts and careful responses. In particular, I would like to thank the attendees of the 2019 Milford SF Writers Conference at Trigonos, Wales. Amongst those, I would especially like to thank Kari Sperring, Liz Williams, and Jacey Bedford, who have gone above and beyond in offering me thoughtful help and myriad opportunities. And I would be remiss not to also thank those beta readers who have not already been mentioned: Michael Krawec and Alfredo Carpineti. *A Market of Dreams and Destiny* would not be the novel it is now without your help.

To my fellow travellers on the academic roads this novel travelled for much of its journey, for all your solidarity, support, and sessions of mutual kvetching, thank you. Christopher Owen, Ginger Lee Thomason: you're brilliant stars. Your insights helped light my way.

To all those who helped me in myriad ways beyond those I have listed, thank you, thank you, thank you. Thank you, Jo Lindsay Walton for providing me with not only wonderful opportunities in the UK SFF community but also for writing me an incredibly moving and effective sponsorship letter to stay here in the UK. Thank you to Dr. Dafydd Wyn Evans for making sure my Welsh was correct. Your kindness has been a boon.

To my family – found and otherwise – who have offered support in so many ways throughout this process, I could not have done it without you.

To all of the above and those I cannot name for lack of space (but not lack of thanks), or because I have not met all of you yet (those who will offer blurbs and reviews and other priceless support for this book), I offer my most heartfelt gratitude. Many of you wore multiple hats, and I'm sorry I haven't more room to sing your praises. I wouldn't trade a single one of you away at the Goblin Market!

For more fantastic fiction, author events,
exclusive excerpts, competitions, limited editions and more

VISIT OUR WEBSITE
titanbooks.com

LIKE US ON FACEBOOK
facebook.com/titanbooks

FOLLOW US ON TWITTER AND INSTAGRAM
@TitanBooks

EMAIL US
readerfeedback@titanemail.com